OOK OF

ICE

BY
STEVE VANCE

AND OVER 70 OF
THE WORLD'S TOP
COMIC WRITERS AND
ARTISTS!

PARADOX PRESS
NEW YORK

DC COMICS

JENETTE KAHN
PRESIDENT & EDITOR-IN-CHIEF

PAUL LEVITZ
EXECUTIVE VICE PRESIDENT & PUBLISHER

ANDREW HELFER
GROUP EDITOR

JIM HIGGINS
ASSISTANT EDITOR

GEORG BREWER
DESIGN DIRECTOR

RICHARD BRUNING
VP-CREATIVE DIRECTOR

PATRICK CALDON
VP-FINANCE & OPERATIONS

DOROTHY CROUCH
VP-LICENSED PUBLISHING

TERRI CUNNINGHAM
VP-MANAGING EDITOR

JOEL EHRLICH
SENIOR VP-ADVERTISING & PROMOTIONS

LILLIAN LASERSON
VP & GENERAL COUNSEL

JIM LEE
EDITORIAL DIRECTOR-WILDSTORM

JOHN NEE
VP & GENERAL MANAGER-WILDSTORM

BOB WAYNE
VP-DIRECT SALES

See page 187 for individual copyright holders.

Front and back cover designed by Steve Vance.

Title page illustration by Alan Kupperberg.

Publication design by Brian Pearce and Dennis Yurcik.

Principal Letterers: Bob Lappan and Kurt Hathaway.

TABLE OF CONTENTS

CHAPTER ONE

SIN CITIES

Strictly speaking, a vice is nothing more (or less) than any immoral or evil habit or practice. Of course, exactly what constitutes an immoral habit depends on who's doing the defining, but throughout history, certain habits have unfailingly qualified for bona fide vice status. Our inquiries into the history and perpetuation of those habits account for the bulk of this book's contents. But before we go into a vice-by-vice consideration of them all, this volume begins by looking at some of the places where the practice of vices was not only profligate, but practically institutionalized.

While Sodom and Gomorrah may be the very first and most well known of the Sin Cities, they are by no means the only ones. Las Vegas, New York, Havana, and Amsterdam are just a few of the bright lights on the highway of vice, havens where people have put aside everyday moral restrictions to indulge in a purely hedonistic (if only temporary) lifestyle.

Unlike the archetypal Biblical vice-towns, most modern Sin Cities are eventually brought down by political, social, or economic forces, leaving Sodom and Gomorrah with the distinction of being the sole dens of sin personally destroyed by God himself. Modern Sin Cities tend to be destroyed by more pedestrian forces, like the United States military, Communist rebels, or the Walt Disney Corporation.

Village of the Damned

BIBLICAL SODOM WAS AN EVIL PLACE. ITS PEOPLE CUSTOMARILY ROBBED AND TORTURED STRANGERS.

YOU'RE NOT WELCOME HERE!

THEY PRAYED TO FALSE GODS, AND WORSHIPED MONEY ABOVE ALL.

THEIR LEADER WAS A CUNNING LAWYER NAMED LOT.

TRUE, HE IS A KILLER, BUT HE IS ALSO AN ORPHAN—AND THUS DESERVES MERCY!

ONE DAY LOT'S UNCLE ABRAHAM—THE PATRIARCH OF THE JEWISH PEOPLE—CAME TO SODOM TO RELAY A MESSAGE FROM GOD.

IF YOU DO NOT FORSAKE YOUR EVIL WAYS, YOU WILL BE DESTROYED!

SOAP

ABRAHAM MANAGED TO CONVINCE HIS NEPHEW HE WAS IN MORTAL DANGER.

I WILL LEAVE WITH YOU TOMORROW, UNCLE.

THE NEXT MORNING, AS THEY LEFT THE CITY, THE SKY ABOVE SODOM TURNED TO FIRE.

DON'T LOOK BACK!

LOT'S WIFE REFUSED TO LISTEN. SHE WAS TURNED INTO A PILLAR OF SALT.

LOT STILL REFUSED TO BELIEVE IN ABRAHAM'S GOD. HE TOOK HIS WICKED WAYS, HIS DAUGHTERS, AND HIS LAW PRACTICE TO ANOTHER CITY.

SODOM ITSELF REMAINED A BARREN, LIFELESS DESERT.

Slot Machines

PHENIX CITY

Girls! Girls! Girls!

BAR

How a small southern town became "The Wickedest City in America!"

This small Alabama town is located just across the Chattahoochee River from Columbus, Georgia.

CHATTAHOOCHEE RIVER

ALABAMA · GEORGIA

PHENIX CITY · COLUMBUS

In the mid-1800s, Columbus, Georgia became a major port for river commerce, attracting sharp operators in search of a fast buck.

CARE TO TRY YOUR LUCK, FRIEND?

Gamblers, swindlers, and prostitutes soon realized that they could elude local lawmen by simply crossing the river into Alabama.

Phenix City grew up right on the border of two Alabama counties. Thus, a lawbreaker could escape to a different jurisdiction by walking across the main street.

LEE COUNTY

RUSSELL COUNTY

Crime dominated the town. In **WORLD WAR I**, gangsters controlled local draft boards, and helped many evade duty...

...IN EXCHANGE FOR FUTURE COOPERATION.

4F

In 1916, 40 special deputies arrived to smash a bootlegging ring. The sheriff and other local officials were turned out of office.

PERHAPS THE TIME HAD COME FOR PHENIX CITY TO CLEAN UP ITS ACT.

But in 1918, the U.S. government unwittingly provided Phenix City with a mother lode of new customers by establishing an army base in Columbus.

FORT BENNING

FORT BENNING GREW TO BECOME THE LARGEST INFANTRY TRAINING BASE IN THE WORLD -- JUST ACROSS A SHORT BRIDGE FROM THE DELIGHTS OF "SIN CITY."

HUBBA, HUBBA!

OVER THE YEARS, COUNTLESS BORED AND LONELY SOLDIERS SPENT THEIR FREE TIME -- AND PAYCHECKS -- IN PHENIX CITY'S RED LIGHT DISTRICT.

THERE WERE GAMBLING DENS REPLETE WITH CROOKED SLOT MACHINES...

%*#@!!!

...MARKED CARDS...

BUSTED!

...LOADED DICE...

SNAKE EYES -- AGAIN?!?

YOU'LL GET 'EM NEXT TIME, SOLDIER.

...AND PLENTY OF ROT-GUT LIQUOR IN PHONY, EXPENSIVE-LOOKING BOTTLES.

-GACK-

ILLEGAL NARCOTICS WERE ALSO READILY AVAILABLE.

THE MEN ALSO LINED UP TO SAMPLE THE WARES AT MA BEECHIE'S, THE LOCAL BROTHEL.

NEXT!

THE ARMY WASN'T THRILLED WITH THE SITUATION. IN 1940, GEORGE PATTON WAS PLACED IN COMMAND OF AN ARMORED BRIGADE AT FT. BENNING.

I'D LIKE TO TAKE SOME TANKS OVER THERE AND CLEAN UP THAT @#%°!

SECRETARY OF WAR HENRY STIMSON CALLED PHENIX CITY...

THE WICKEDEST CITY IN AMERICA.

Phenix City

...BUT WITH WWII IMMINENT, BOTH MEN WERE TOO PREOCCUPIED WITH OTHER MATTERS TO TAKE DRASTIC ACTION.

SOLDIERS WEREN'T THE ONLY CLIENTELE. CUSTOMERS CAME FROM THROUGHOUT THE SOUTHEAST, AND A NETWORK OF ILLEGAL LOTTERIES GREW ACROSS SEVERAL STATES.

BAMA CLUB

NOT ALL 24,000 RESIDENTS WERE MORALLY BENT, BUT VICE HAD LONG BEEN THE STATUS QUO...

THINGS'VE ALWAYS BEEN THIS WAY 'ROUND HERE.

KA-CHING!

$ $ $

...AND IT WAS ALSO BRINGING IN AN ESTIMATED $100,000,000 A YEAR..

BESIDES, CHANGE SEEMED IMPOSSIBLE, SINCE GANGSTERS CONTROLLED TOWN OFFICIALS AND BRAZENLY RIGGED ELECTIONS.

POLLING PLACE

$10

$

STATE OFFICIALS, LEERY OF BAD PUBLICITY, IGNORED THE PROBLEMS.

IN *1951*, A FEW LOCALS BEGAN A REFORM GROUP, THE *RUSSELL BETTERMENT ASSOCIATION.* GANGSTERS RETALIATED, BEATING MEMBERS AS POLICE LOOKED ON...

HELL, LADY, THEY AIN'T DOING NO HARM -- JUST USING THEIR *HANDS* AND *FEET.*

...AND DYNAMITING THE HOME OF ONE *RBA* LEADER. MIRACULOUSLY, NO ONE WAS SERIOUSLY INJURED.

XA-BLOOIE!!!

THE OFFICE OF THE *RBA*'S LAWYER, ALBERT PATTERSON, WAS SET ON FIRE IN AN ATTEMPT TO DESTROY INCRIMINATING EVIDENCE THE GROUP HAD GATHERED.

ALBERT PATTERSON ATTORNEY AT LAW

PATTERSON, A FORMER STATE SENATOR, DECIDED TO FIGHT BACK BY RUNNING FOR STATE ATTORNEY GENERAL.

CLEAN UP PHENIX CITY!!! VOTE PATTERSON

HE WON THE ELECTION DESPITE MASSIVE VOTE FRAUD, BUT TOLD SUPPORTERS...

I HAVE ONLY ONE CHANCE OUT OF *100* OF BEING SWORN IN.

HE WAS RIGHT. THE NEXT NIGHT HE WAS MURDERED BY A DEPUTY SHERIFF.

THIS, AT LAST, GOT THE ATTENTION OF THE STATE GOVERNMENT.

BANG!

THE GOVERNOR DECLARED MARTIAL LAW. THE NATIONAL GUARD TOOK OVER AND SHUT DOWN THE VICE DENS.

GAMBLING HALL CLOSED!

DECLARED OFF-LIMITS BY THE ARMY, PHENIX CITY'S WICKED REIGN WAS FINALLY OVER.

CUBA BEFORE CASTRO WAS A PLACE WHERE MONEY COULD BUY YOU ANYTHING.

FOR HALF A CENTURY, IT WAS A PLAYGROUND FOR THE WEALTHIEST PEOPLE IN THE WORLD — AND HOME TO THE MOST CORRUPT GOVERNMENT IN MODERN HISTORY.

A U.S. PROTECTORATE IN THE EARLY 1900s, CUBA WAS JUST A QUICK BOAT RIDE FROM THE MAINLAND. ITS CAPITAL, HAVANA, QUICKLY BECAME A FAVORED DESTINATION OF THE RICH AND FAMOUS...

WHEN PROHIBITION WAS PASSED ON THE MAINLAND, CUBA'S ALLURE GREW.

IT WAS SMART OF US TO GIVE CUBA BACK TO THE CUBANS. THAT WAY, WE CAN STILL BUY BOOZE THERE!

UNDER PRESIDENT JULIO MACHADO, CUBA SOON EARNED A REPUTATION FOR ITS NIGHT LIFE...

THEY CALL HIM "SUPERMAN!"

I CAN SEE WHY!

...AND ITS WOMEN. ARRIVING BUSINESSMEN WERE SHOWN PHOTOS FROM WHICH TO CHOOSE THEIR COMPANIONS.

OR THEY COULD PATRONIZE CASA MARINA, WHICH SPECIALIZED IN PROVIDING THIRTEEN-YEAR-OLDS — BOYS AND GIRLS.

THEY PAID EXTRA FOR VIRGINS.

MANY AMERICANS MOVED THERE PERMANENTLY — AMONG THEM ERNEST HEMINGWAY.

THE DEPRESSION — AND BLATANT CORRUPTION — FORCED MACHADO OUT OF OFFICE IN 1933. HE FLEW INTO EXILE CARRYING FIVE REVOLVERS AND SEVERAL BAGS OF GOLD.

AN ARMY SERGEANT NAMED FULGENCIO BATISTA SEIZED POWER.

A KEY BATTLE IN THIS STRUGGLE TOOK PLACE AT THE HOTEL *NACIONAL*— THE SITE OF THE LARGEST CASINO IN THE WESTERN HEMISPHERE.

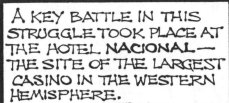

THE CASINO STAYED OPEN THROUGHOUT THE BATTLE, FOR THE BENEFIT OF TOURISTS.

AFTER BATISTA'S VICTORY, MOBSTER MEYER LANSKY FLEW DOWN TO HAVANA TO DISCUSS "BUSINESS." HE FOUND THE DICTATOR RECEPTIVE TO HIS OVERTURES.

LANSKY TOOK OVER THE *NACIONAL* AND CUBA'S RACETRACKS, CUTTING BATISTA IN FOR FIFTY PERCENT OF THE PROFITS.

THEN CAME W.W. II. GERMAN U-BOATS INVADED THE CARIBBEAN, AND THE TOURISTS STOPPED COMING.

THIS AIN'T NO WAY TO MAKE A LIVING!

IN 1944, BATISTA RELINQUISHED POWER AND RETIRED TO FLORIDA.

LANSKY MAINTAINED HIS INTERESTS IN CUBA. IN 1946, HE SUMMONED AMERICA'S MOST POWERFUL GANGSTERS TO THE *NACIONAL* FOR A CONFERENCE.

ENTERTAINMENT WAS PROVIDED BY FRANK SINATRA, WHO BROUGHT ALONG A SPECIAL GOLD CIGARETTE CASE FOR THE GUEST OF HONOR—LUCKY LUCIANO, WHO'D BEEN RECENTLY DEPORTED FROM THE U.S.

THE CONFERENCE AGENDA: WHAT TO DO ABOUT BUGSY SIEGEL, WHO'D BLOWN A FORTUNE OF THE MOB'S MONEY BUILDING THE FLAMINGO IN LAS VEGAS.

HE'S **GOT** TO BE HIT!

BUT LANSKY SAW THERE WAS MONEY IN SIEGEL'S IDEA OF SETTING UP HIGH-ROLLING CASINOS FOR HIGH-ROLLERS.

AND THIS SEEMS LIKE THE RIGHT PLACE TO DO IT!

IN BATISTA'S ABSENCE, THE GOVERNMENT HAD PROVED NOT ONLY CORRUPT BUT IRRESPONSIBLE. THE PEOPLE WANTED CHANGE. BATISTA RETURNED FROM FLORIDA AND SEIZED POWER AGAIN.

TO ROOT OUT GAMBLING, I APPOINT MY OLD FRIEND MEYER LANSKY AS MY PERSONAL ADVISOR.

FOR THE NEXT SEVEN YEARS, THE TWO RULED CUBA WITH NO CONCERN FOR ANYTHING BUT MAKING MONEY.

THEY PASSED NEW LAWS: AMERICAN TOURISTS NO LONGER NEEDED VISAS.

IMMIGRACIÓ

WELCOME

THEY CREATED A NEW AIRLINE TO HANDLE THE INFLUX OF TOURISTS.

THEY CREATED NEW BANKS, TO INSURE THE SMOOTH FLOW OF MONEY TO POLITICIANS.

THEY BUILT NEW CASINOS, AND LANSKY APPOINTED MOB BOSSES FROM ALL OVER THE U.S. TO RUN THEM.

THIS IS SAL FROM TAMPA. HE'S GONNA HANDLE THE TROPICANA.

CUBAN PROFESSIONALS FROM ALL WALKS OF LIFE — DOCTORS, TEACHERS, LAWYERS — GAVE UP THEIR JOBS FOR HIGHER-PAYING ONES IN THE CASINOS.

IN THAT TIME, AS GRAHAM GREENE WROTE, HAVANA WAS A PLACE WHERE EVERY VICE WAS PERMISSIBLE.

ONE WHO EXPLORED ITS LIMITS, ACCORDING TO SAL TRAFFICANTE, WAS THEN-SENATOR JOHN F. KENNEDY.

HE WAS WITH THREE GIRLS — AT THE SAME TIME!

CUBANS WHO SPOKE OUT AGAINST THE CORRUPTION RECEIVED ATTENTION FROM BATISTA'S INCREASINGLY BRUTAL SECRET POLICE.

IN THE HILLS OUTSIDE HAVANA, POCKETS OF RESISTANCE BEGAN TO FORM. AMONG THE LEADERS WAS A YOUNG LAWYER NAMED FIDEL CASTRO.

LANSKY IGNORED SIGNS OF THE COMING REVOLT, OPENING HIS OWN CASINO ON DECEMBER 10, 1958 — THE RIVIERA.

GRAND OPENING IN PERSON GINGER ROGERS

BUT ON NEW YEAR'S EVE, 1958, LANSKY WAS SURPRISED TO FIND OVER 200 NO-SHOWS ON THE SOLD-OUT MAIN FLOOR.

WHAT GIVES?

HAPPY '59!

BATISTA, HE DISCOVERED, HAD GIVEN UP THE BATTLE WITH THE REVOLUTIONARIES, AND RESIGNED, FLEEING WITH HIS FAMILY.

VIVA CASTRO   CUBA LIBRE   VIVA FIDEL   26 JULIO   LIBERTAD

LANSKY TRIED TO STAY ON AND NEGOTIATE WITH CASTRO BUT SOON REALIZED IT WAS USELESS.

I CRAPPED OUT!

THE PARTY WAS OVER.

13

IN 1829, A MEXICAN SCOUT TRAVELING THE SPANISH TRAIL FROM SANTA FE TO LOS ANGELES FOUND A SMALL OASIS IN THE DESERT AND CALLED IT "THE MEADOWS," OR--

Las Vegas

JAMES NYE, NEVADA'S FIRST GOVERNOR, OPPOSED THE GAMBLING RAMPANT IN THE THEN-WILD WEST.

OF ALL THE SEDUCTIVE VICES EXTANT, I REGARD THAT OF GAMBLING AS THE WORST.

MINERS AND FRONTIERSMEN IGNORED NYE'S BAN ON GAMBLING, AND FOLLOWING STATEHOOD IN 1864, IT WAS LEGALIZED OVER NYE'S VETO.

IN 1905, VEGAS BECAME A WATERING STOP ON THE NEWLY COMPLETED SALT LAKE CITY-LOS ANGELES RAIL ROUTE. A WILD FRONTIER TOWN BEGAN TO GROW.

AWARE OF ITS INEVITABILITY, PLANNERS SET ASIDE TWO CITY BLOCKS FOR GAMBLING AND PROSTITUTION.

Las Vegas

...AND BLOCK 16 IS FOR THE, UH, HOSPITALITY INDUSTRY.

MINING'S DECLINE IN THE LATE 1800S HAD LEFT NEVADA DEPENDENT ON GAMBLING FOR TAX REVENUES.

GOLD!

SILVER!

COPPER!

BUT MAJOR NEW STRIKES MEANT IT COULD BAN GAMBLING AGAIN IN 1909.

BUT BY THEN, GAMBLING WAS TOO ENTRENCHED. IT SIMPLY MOVED TO THE BACK ROOMS, AS OFFICIALS WERE BRIBED INTO SILENCE.

GOOD LUCK, CLEM.

THANKS, SHERIFF.

AND WITH NO LEGAL OVERSIGHT, CROOKED GAMES FLOURISHED.

DON'T THIS DING-BLASTED WHEEL EVER PAY OFF?

ALL THE TIME, SUCKER!

BUT AFTER AN EARLY BOOM, VEGAS LANGUISHED.

IN 1930, WORK ON NEARBY HOOVER DAM BEGAN, BRINGING IN 5000 MEN--WITH $500,000 OF WAGES TO SPEND EVERY MONTH.

LET'S GO TO TOWN!

VEGAS CASHED IN ON WORKERS--AND TOURISTS COMING TO GAWK AT THE CONSTRUCTION.

ARIZONA CLUB

AND MORE THAN 300 PROSTITUTES WORKED THE BROTHELS OF BLOCK 16.

MEANWHILE, THE LEGISLATURE, UNABLE TO STOP GAMBLING, LEGALIZED IT, OPTING TO GET A CUT OF THE REVENUES.

ALL IN FAVOR--

AYE!

THEY ALSO DROPPED THE WAITING PERIOD FOR A DIVORCE TO A THEN-UNHEARD-OF SIX WEEKS.

IN 1935, VEGAS TAPPED A NEW MARKET AS 5000 SHRINERS ATTENDED THE TOWN'S FIRST CONVENTION.

BUT BUSINESS SLOWED THE NEXT YEAR, AS THE DAM WAS FINISHED.

IN 1939, A NEW REFORM MAYOR CHASED GAMBLING OPERATORS OUT OF LOS ANGELES. MANY CAME TO VEGAS, INCLUDING EX-VICE SQUAD COMMANDER GUY MCAFEE.

HE BOUGHT THE PAIR-O-DICE CLUB OUTSIDE OF TOWN, AND DUBBED THE ROAD "THE STRIP," AFTER HOLLYWOOD'S SUNSET STRIP.

NIGHT CLUB

DINE DANCE

THE TOWN SOON BOOMED AGAIN AS WWII BROUGHT THE MILITARY TO VEGAS. THE POPULATION GREW TO 35,000.

BUT THE WAR WAS BAD FOR ONE INDUSTRY. UNDER PRESSURE FROM THE WAR DEPARTMENT, BLOCK 16'S BROTHELS WERE SHUT DOWN.

IN 1946, MOBSTER BUGSY SIEGEL SPENT $6 MILLION TO BUILD THE LAVISH FLAMINGO HOTEL AND CASINO ON THE STRIP.

IT'LL BE AN OASIS IN THE DESERT!

UNHAPPY WITH HIS EXTRAVAGANCE, BUGSY'S BACKERS BUMPED HIM OFF.

BUT THE MODERN GLITZ OF THE FLAMINGO POINTED THE WAY TO VEGAS'S FUTURE--AND THE MOB WANTED IN.

THE FIELD WAS WIDE OPEN, SINCE MANY LEGIT INVESTORS WERE RELUCTANT TO GET INVOLVED IN GAMBLING.

HOW ABOUT A VEGAS CASINO?

OUR SHAREHOLDERS WOULDN'T LIKE IT.

IN 1950, THE KEFAUVER INVESTIGATION SHOWED MOB INFLUENCE IN VEGAS GROWING--BUT THE NATIONWIDE CRACK-DOWN ON GANGSTERS ONLY SPED THE TREND.

I'M MOVIN' T' VEGAS--WHERE IT'S LEGAL!

LAS VEGAS Daily Gazette
GAMBLING DENS RAIDED!

IN 1949, THE LEGISLATURE AGAIN VOTED TO LEGALIZE PROSTITUTION--BUT THE GOVERNOR VETOED THE BILL--UNDER PRESSURE FROM CERTAIN HOTEL/CASINO OWNERS.

Nevada Legislature
LEGAL PROSTITUTION ACT
VETO

THE MOB KNEW SEX WAS PART OF VEGAS'S APPEAL, BUT THEY WANTED TO SET THE TERMS.

I DON'T WANT MY CUSTOMERS RUNNING OFF TO SOME WHOREHOUSE--I WANT 'EM TO STAY RIGHT HERE, NEAR THE TABLES!

EMPLOYEES PROVIDED GIRLS--FROM A MANAGEMENT-APPROVED LIST.

PRICES WERE STANDARDIZED (HIGH ROLLERS GOT GIRLS FOR FREE)--AND GUESTS NEVER LEFT THE PREMISES.

HOTEL/CASINO CONSTRUCTION WAS BOOMING--AS WAS THE DESERT. NEARBY NUCLEAR TESTS WERE TOUTED AS ANOTHER TOURIST ATTRACTION. TO HELP LURE THE CROWDS, CASINOS WENT AFTER BIG-NAME STARS.

FRANK SINATRA AND DEAN MARTIN WERE SOLD STOCK IN THE NEW DESERT INN.

LIBERACE GOT $50,000 A WEEK AT THE RIVIERA.

THE CASINOS WERE RAKING IN $50 MILLION A YEAR.

BUT BY 1955, THERE WERE 7 HUGE HOTEL/CASINOS ON THE STRIP, WITH MORE ON THE WAY--AND NOT ENOUGH CUSTOMERS TO GO AROUND. VEGAS HIT ANOTHER SLUMP.

SNAKE EYES!

MEANWHILE, THE NEW STATE GAMING COMMISSION TRIED TO COUNTER THE GROWING MOB PRESENCE WITH TIGHTER BACKGROUND CHECKS ON ALL CASINO OWNERS.

OH, WHAT A TANGLED WEB THEY WEAVE...

SLOWLY, BUSINESS PICKED UP AGAIN. GAMBLING PROFITS FOR 1963 WERE $375 MILLION.

VEGAS ALSO HOSTED 30,000 WEDDINGS--AND 10,000 DIVORCES.

EXISTING CASINOS EXPANDED, BUT FOR EIGHT YEARS, NO NEW ONES OPENED.

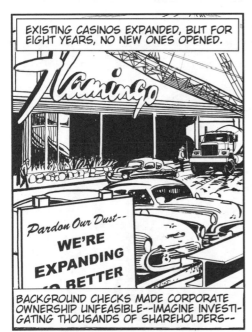

BACKGROUND CHECKS MADE CORPORATE OWNERSHIP UNFEASIBLE--IMAGINE INVESTIGATING THOUSANDS OF SHAREHOLDERS--

--AND HOW MANY INDIVIDUALS WERE BOTH RICH ENOUGH AND CLEAN ENOUGH TO OWN A CASINO?

SPEAKING OF CLEAN...IN 1966, NOTED NEAT FREAK HOWARD HUGHES ARRIVED.

HUGHES HAD JUST SOLD TWA FOR $500 MILLION. HE AND HIS MORMON ENTOURAGE MOVED IN TO THE TOP FLOOR OF THE DESERT INN. THEY BLACKED OUT THE WINDOWS AND INSTALLED A PRIVATE PHONE SYSTEM.

OWNER MOE DALITZ DIDN'T LIKE HAVING NON-GAMBLERS TAKING HIS BEST ROOMS-- SO HUGHES BOUGHT THE PLACE FOR $13.7 MILLION.

WRITE HIM A CHECK.

DALITZ, UNDER INVESTIGATION FOR HIS MOB TIES, WAS HAPPY TO SELL.

HUGHES SPENT $300 MILLION ON SEVERAL OTHER CASINOS. HE ALREADY OWNED VAST DESERT ACREAGE NEARBY, AND HE ENVISIONED BUILDING A HUGE AIRPORT FOR SUPERSONIC JETS.

HUGHES'S SPENDING SPREE ATTRACTED CORPORATE ATTENTION.

IF HUGHES IS IN ON IT, WE WANT IN ON IT!

GAMING COMMISSION RULES WERE CHANGED, AND BIG CORPORATIONS LIKE HILTON AND MGM BOUGHT IN TO THE VEGAS SCENE.

MANY THOUGHT THE MOB'S ERA HAD ENDED--

COUNTING ROOM

--UNTIL NEW INVESTIGATIONS IN THE '70S SHOWED MEYER LANSKY AND OTHERS WERE STILL SKIMMING MILLIONS FROM SEVERAL CASINOS.

WITH THE MOB BOSSES IN RETREAT, CHICAGO ENFORCER TONY "THE ANT" SPILOTRO TRIED TO TAKE OVER.

HE WAS LATER FOUND BURIED IN A MIDWESTERN CORN FIELD.

IT SEEMED THE MOB'S GRIP WAS FINALLY BROKEN. THEN VEGAS WAS HIT BY COMPETITION FROM NEWLY LEGALIZED GAMBLING IN ATLANTIC CITY AND A NATIONWIDE RECESSION.

CLOSED

BUT LAVISH NEW CASINOS HELPED VEGAS REBOUND.

DOUBLE DRAW
JACKPOT
DOUBLE DRAW

BY 1990, 20 MILLION VISITORS WERE SPENDING $10 BILLION A YEAR, HALF ON GAMBLING.

THE POPULATION HIT 750,000 MAKING VEGAS THE FASTEST-GROWING CITY IN THE U.S. BUT LEGAL GAMBLING WAS SPREADING...

HOTEL MANAGER

STATE LOTTERIES! INDIAN CASINOS! RIVERBOATS! WE'VE GOT TO DO SOMETHING!

VEGAS TRIED TO CHANGE ITS IMAGE TO APPEAL TO FAMILIES. IN THE MID-'90S, THE CITY TIED DISNEYWORLD FOR #1 TOURIST DESTINATION.

LAS VEGAS

VISIT LAS VEGAS

The FAMILY CITY

BUT THE STRATEGY BACKFIRED. KIDS CAN'T GAMBLE, AND PARENTS WITH KIDS IN TOW WERE SPENDING LESS TIME AT THE TABLES.

OOPS.

MEANWHILE, ASIA'S WOES MEANT FEWER FOREIGN HIGH ROLLERS.

NEW CASINOS ARE AIMING AT ADULTS-- BUT THE CITY SEEMS OVERBUILT AGAIN, WITH 9 OF THE WORLD'S 10 LARGEST HOTELS, 106,000 ROOMS--

--AND WE'RE MAKING MORE!

VEGAS CONTINUES TO STRUGGLE WITH THE ISSUE OF HOW TO BE AN ALLURING SIN CITY--WITHOUT BEING *TOO* SINFUL.

I'D SAY WE'VE GOT A BRIGHT FUTURE!

WANNA BET?

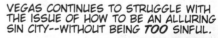

TODAY, TIMES SQUARE HAS BEEN SO SANITIZED YOU'D BE HARD PRESSED TO FIND A BLOWUP DOLL THAT WASN'T OF A DISNEY CHARACTER.

BUT IN ITS SLEAZY HEYDAY YOU COULD INDULGE EVERY VICE BY TAKING A SHORT WALK DOWN 42ND STREET, KNOWN THEN AS . . .

THE DEUCE

THE AREA SURROUNDING 42ND STREET AND BROADWAY OFFICIALLY BECAME TIMES SQUARE WHEN THE NEW YORK TIMES MOVED INTO THE NEWLY-BUILT TIMES TOWER IN 1906.

THEATERS AND DANCE HALLS SPRUNG UP THROUGHOUT THE AREA. BUT THE DEPRESSION AND THE DEMISE OF BURLESQUE KICK-STARTED A LONG, SLOW SLIDE INTO SLEAZINESS.

BY THE MID-'60S, THE AREA OF TIMES SQUARE ALONG 42ND STREET BETWEEN 6TH AND 8TH AVENUES HAD BECOME THE NATION'S CAPITAL FOR RETAIL SEX.

THERE WERE BOOKSTORES, MASSAGE PARLORS, AND PEEP SHOWS -- SHORT FILMS THAT COST A QUARTER FOR TWO MINUTES.

THE KING OF THE PEEP SHOWS WAS REPUTED MOBSTER MARTIN HODAS.

SHOW ME A MAN WHO DOESN'T ADMIRE A BEAUTIFUL WOMAN AND I'LL SHOW YOU A DEGENERATE.

HODAS CHURNED OUT FIFTY TO SEVENTY-FIVE OF THE TWELVE-MINUTE FILM LOOPS PER WEEK, PAYING HIS STARS $75.

IT'S NO STEPPING-STONE TO HOLLYWOOD.

IN 1973, HE WAS ACCUSED OF FIREBOMBING TWO COMPETITIVE "MASSAGE" PARLORS WHO TRIED TO LOWER THEIR PRICES.

THE AUTHORITIES CLAIMED HODAS WAS THE HEAD OF A MULTIMILLION-DOLLAR PORNOGRAPHY EMPIRE... BUT THEY WERE UNABLE TO CONVINCE A JURY.

THEY WERE MORE SUCCESSFUL ON THE NIGHT OF MARCH 21, 1968, WHEN POLICE CARRIED OUT A SIMULTANEOUS RAID ON TEN PORN STORES.

THEY CONFISCATED 34,000 PHOTOGRAPHS, 175 REELS OF FILM, AND OVER 400 BOOKS AND MAGAZINES IN THE OPERATION, WHICH REQUIRED SPLIT-SECOND TIMING FROM THIRTY-FIVE PLAINCLOTHES POLICEMEN...

...BECAUSE THE STORES THAT WERE BEING RAIDED WERE ALL HOOKED UP TO A SHARED EARLY WARNING ALARM SYSTEM.

MAYOR AFTER MAYOR TRIED TO CLEAN UP THE DEUCE. IN THE SUMMER OF 1971, MAYOR LINDSAY TOOK ON THE HOOKERS.

FOR ONE JULY DAY, THE SQUARE WAS COMPLETELY EMPTY OF PROSTITUTES.

A DAY LATER, THEY WERE BACK.

ANOTHER OF THE CITY'S SUCCESSES WAS THE BEAME ADMINISTRATION'S NUISANCE ABATEMENT LAW, WHICH ALLOWED THE CITY TO VIRTUALLY SHUT DOWN THE MASSAGE PARLOR INDUSTRY.

TIMES SQUARE'S BIGGEST PORN PALACE IS SHOW WORLD, AT THE CORNER OF 8TH AVENUE AND 42ND STREET.

ODDLY ENOUGH, THE OWNERS MANAGED TO OBTAIN A $65,000 LOAN FROM THE SMALL BUSINESS ASSOCIATION TO HELP BUILD SHOW WORLD.

IN 1977, MAYOR KOCH PROPOSED RELOCATING ALL SEX BUSINESSES TO CITY-OWNED PIERS ON THE HUDSON RIVER.

BY 1978 MORE THAN TWICE AS MANY STREET CRIMES WERE REPORTED ON THE BLOCK AS ON ANY OTHER IN THE CITY. THE CITY-PLANNING COMMISSION CONCLUDED:

WITH THE ADVENT OF HOME VCRS, THE BOTTOM DROPPED OUT OF THE SEX FILM INDUSTRY OVERNIGHT. MORE THAN TWO-THIRDS OF THE PORNOGRAPHIC MOVIE HOUSES FOLDED.

AS THE PROFIT MARGIN DISAPPEARED, SO DID THE MOB. SRI LANKANS AND ISRAELIS SOON BECAME THE OWNERS OF MANY OF THE PORN BUSINESSES ALONG 42ND STREET.

BY THE MID-'80S, THE TIMES SQUARE AREA WAS RIPE FOR REDEVELOPMENT. DETAILED PLANS WERE DRAWN UP, AGREED TO, AND ABANDONED SEVERAL TIMES.

FINALLY, IN 1996, CONSTRUCTION BEGAN. WALT DISNEY TOOK OVER THE OLD LYRIC THEATER, WARNER BROS. THE OLD TIMES TOWER.

ZONING CHANGES PROPOSED BY MAYOR GIULIANI SHUTTERED THE FEW REMAINING ADULT BUSINESSES ALONG THE DEUCE, INCLUDING SHOW WORLD.

BUT THE NEW TIMES SQUARE COMES WITH A PRICE TAG -- SKY-HIGH RENTS THAT HAVE DRIVEN NEIGHBORHOOD INSTITUTIONS, LIKE FRED HAKIM'S LUNCHEONETTE, OUT OF BUSINESS.

AS WRITER NIK COHN NOTED: "TIMES SQUARE HAS ALWAYS CHANGED, EVERY TWENTY YEARS. BUT THIS TIME, IT'S CHANGED TO A CORPORATE GENERIC AMERICAN CITY."

AS FAR AS THE REST OF THE WORLD IS CONCERNED, AMSTERDAM IS

RATED XXX

...AND NOT JUST BECAUSE THE TOWN'S OFFICIAL COAT OF ARMS IS EMBOSSED WITH THREE CROSSES.

IN THE 1960s ITS LIBERAL POLICIES ON SEX AND DRUGS MADE AMSTERDAM THE "FREE LOVE" CAPITAL OF THE WORLD. YOUNG PEOPLE GATHERED THERE BY THE THOUSANDS.

IT WAS ONLY NATURAL FOR JOHN AND YOKO TO STAGE THEIR SLEEP-IN FOR PEACE AT THE AMSTERDAM HILTON.

OFFICIALS ACTUALLY SUBSIDIZED NIGHTCLUBS LIKE THE PARADISO AND CONDONED DRUG USAGE THERE. THE RATIONALE: KEEP YOUNG PEOPLE OUT OF THE MORE DANGEROUS AREAS OF THE CITY.

PAMPHLETS WERE EVEN HANDED OUT IN THE CLUB DETAILING DRUG USE DO'S AND DON'TS.

TRIP ONLY WITH YOUR FRIENDS, DUDE.

EVEN TODAY IN THE CITY'S COFFEE BARS, SMALL AMOUNTS OF MARIJUANA AND HASHISH CAN BE LEGALLY SOLD.

HOW ABOUT A BROWNIE?

THE PEOPLE OF AMSTERDAM HAVE ALWAYS HAD A BUSINESSLIKE ATTITUDE TOWARDS SEX. WITNESS THE INFAMOUS RED-LIGHT DISTRICT WHERE PROSTITUTES DISPLAY THEM-SELVES FOR POTENTIAL CUSTOMERS.

THE CITY'S LATEST INVENTION? THE TIPPLEZONES, SPECIALLY CONSTRUCTED AREAS WHERE STREETWALKERS CAN LEGALLY OFFER THEIR WARES.

SEX IN AMSTERDAM TODAY REMAINS A HALF-BILLION DOLLAR BUSINESS. AND BUSINESS IS BOOMING.

CHAPTER TWO

ALCOHOL

O, that demon alcohol! It seems like it's been around forever, and like all the most alluring vices, won't ever go away. Not like we haven't tried to rid ourselves of it. But for all our efforts, alcohol and its destabilizing effects, are cherished like no other. It's the drink of kings! The breakfast of champions! And though some small number might argue whether alcohol actually TASTES good, once it gets down, it sure does FEEL good!

The consumption of fermented fluids has been practiced almost for as long as man himself has been around. A cask of crushed berries, left out in the sun too long and imbibed by a cave-dweller too thirsty to be put off by the unexpected bitterness of the drink, leads to a strange, not-unpleasant disorientation that just cries out to be reexperienced again and again. And so it has, across the sea of time. The acceptance or rejection of alcohol and its effects has been and remains in a constant state of flux depending on the political, religious, and social tempo of the times.

THE ANCIENT MESOPOTAMIANS LEARNED TO MAKE BEER FROM MALTED GRAIN OVER 9000 YEARS AGO. SINCE THEN PEOPLE HAVE TRIED FERMENTING JUST ABOUT EVERYTHING THAT GROWS TO MAKE ALCOHOL--

THE FIRST DRUG

THE EARLIEST VINEYARDS WERE GROWN IN THE CAUCASUS CIRCA 6000 TO 4000 B.C.

ALCOHOL WAS OFTEN CONSIDERED SACRED IN ANCIENT TIMES.

THE AZTECS GOT DRUNK AT MAJOR RELIGIOUS FESTIVALS, BUT PUNISHED SECULAR DRINKING WITH DEATH.

THE KING OF PERSIA AND HIS ADVISORS GOT DRUNK TO MAKE IMPORTANT DECISIONS-- THEN REVIEWED THEM SOBER. IF BOTH CONFERENCES AGREED, THE DECISION WAS ACTED UPON.

SOUNDS LIKE A GOOD IDEA, BUT -URP- LET US SLEEP ON IT.

WORSHIPPERS OF BACCHUS, THE GREEK GOD OF WINE, BELIEVED WINE COULD FREE THEM FROM THE RESTRAINTS OF FLESH.

BUT IT WORKS NO MATTER *WHAT* YOU BELIEVE!

JESUS REFERRED TO WINE AS HIS BLOOD, ESTABLISHING WINE AS A MAJOR CHRISTIAN SYMBOL OF DIVINE LIFE.

THE GREEKS WERE THE FIRST TO GROW GRAPES ON A COMMERCIAL SCALE. THEIR THICK, CONCENTRATED WINE WAS SOLD THROUGHOUT THE CLASSICAL WORLD.

AS IT IS TODAY, ALCOHOL WAS A PROBLEM IN THE ANCIENT WORLD. DRUNKENNESS WAS SO WIDESPREAD IN 1ST-CENTURY ROME THAT EMPEROR DIOMETIAN ORDERED HALF THE VINEYARDS DESTROYED.

THIS SIMPLY *HAS* TO STOP!

ATHENAEUS RECORDED A 3RD-CENTURY DRINKING CONTEST IN WHICH 41 CONTESTANTS DIED OF ALCOHOL POISONING.

THE WINNER, WHO TOOK HOME A GOLD TALENT AND MORE WINE, LIVED 4 MORE DAYS.

IN THE 6TH CENTURY, MOHAMMED FORBADE DRINKING BY HIS FOLLOWERS. MOST MOSLEMS STILL ABIDE BY THIS PROHIBITION.

MORMONS ALSO PROHIBIT THE USE OF ALCOHOL.

MEAD, MADE BY FERMENTING HONEY, WAS BREWED IN MUCH OF THE ANCIENT WORLD. AS SUGAR BECAME AVAILABLE, MEAD WAS USUALLY REPLACED BY BEER OR OTHER FERMENTED DRINKS.

MEAD IS GOOD...

...BUT BEER WOULD BE BETTER!

IN MEDIEVAL EUROPE EVERYONE WHO COULD AFFORD IT DRANK WINE OR ALE THROUGHOUT THE DAY. MOST OF THE MAJOR BATTLES OF THE PERIOD WERE FOUGHT DRUNK.

DRINKS MADE BY SIMPLE FERMENTATION CONTAINED LESS THAN 12% ALCOHOL. WITH DISTILLATION, FIRST MENTIONED BY 10TH-CENTURY ARABIAN ALCHEMIST ABUL KASIM, "ARDENT SPIRITS" BECAME POSSIBLE.

NOW, WHY -; HIC ;- DIDN'T I THINK OF THIS BEFORE?!

SOON AFTER EUROPEANS DISCOVERED DISTILLATION AROUND 1100, THE GAELS BEGAN MAKING A FIERY DRINK CALLED USQUEBAUGH, MEANING "WATER OF LIFE"-- NOW KNOWN AS WHISKEY.

MORE LIKE WATER OF DEATH IF Y'ASK ME!

NUMEROUS BRANDIES AND LIQUEURS SOON DEVELOPED AS WELL. MANY, SUCH AS BENEDICTINE, WERE ORIGINALLY MADE BY MONKS.

BUT MADE BY MONKS OR NOT, ALCOHOL CONTINUED TO BE A MIXED BLESSING.

THE ARRIVAL OF CHEAP DUTCH GIN IN BRITAIN CAUSED SOCIAL ILLS MUCH LIKE THE ADVENT OF CRACK COCAINE.

DRUNK FOR A PENNY DEAD DRUNK FOR 2 PENCE

THE 1736 GIN ACT RESTRICTING SALES CAUSED SEVERE RIOTS.

IN THE CENTURIES SINCE, ATTEMPTS AT PROHIBITION HAVE BEEN RARE IN EUROPE-- AND ALCOHOL REMAINS AN INTEGRAL PART OF THE CULTURE TODAY.

SINCE COLONIAL TIMES, ALCOHOL HAS BEEN POPULAR IN AMERICA -- PERHAPS TOO POPULAR. BUT ATTEMPTS TO REGULATE IT HAVE RESULTED IN...

THE BATTLE OF THE BOOZE

IN 1630, PETER STUYVESANT SAID OF NEW AMSTERDAM (LATER NEW YORK CITY) "ONE QUARTER...IS DEVOTED TO HOUSES FOR THE SALE OF BRANDY, TOBACCO, AND BEER."

BRONKS INN
WILLHELMS TAVERN
JOHAN'S TOBACCO

ALCOHOL WAS GENERALLY CONSIDERED BENEFICIAL. THE AVERAGE 18TH-CENTURY MAN DRANK ABOUT A GALLON OF HARD LIQUOR A MONTH.

TAMIN' A CONTINENT'S THIRSTY WORK!

IN 1735, THE BRITISH IMPOSED PROHIBITION ON GEORGIA -- BUT SMUGGLING FROM OTHER COLONIES WAS RAMPANT, AND AFTER EIGHT YEARS THE INEFFECTUAL BAN WAS REPEALED.

NO LAW CAN STOP MAN'S DESIRES!

BEFORE THE REVOLUTION, JOHN HANCOCK SMUGGLED ALCOHOL INTO BOSTON TO AVOID PAYING TAXES LEVIED BY BRITAIN.

BE VEWY, VEWY QUIET...

GEORGE WASHINGTON WAS SAID TO HAVE MAINTAINED HIS EQUANIMITY DURING THE WAR'S TRAVAILS BY DRINKING HEAVILY.

FIRST IN WAR, FIRST IN PEACE...

...FIRST TO THE PUB AT OPENING TIME.

IN THE LARGELY RURAL PIONEER U.S., THE MAIN MEETING PLACES WERE THE CHURCH AND THE TAVERN.

GOOD SERMON, REVEREND.

ALL THAT TALK OF HELLFIRE'S LEFT ME PARCHED!

MANY PREACHERS DRANK AS HEAVILY AS THEIR FLOCKS -- BUT A SPLIT WAS SOON TO EMERGE BETWEEN PREACHER AND PUBLICAN.

JOHN ADAMS OPPOSED DRINK--AND THE POLITICAL INFLUENCE OF TAVERN KEEPERS. OTHER POLITICIANS, INCLUDING WASHINGTON, FREQUENTLY REWARDED THEIR SUPPORTERS WITH LIQUOR.

ANOTHER ROUND, COURTESY O' OUR GRAND GENERAL!

IN 1777 CONGRESS CONSIDERED--AND REJECTED--PROHIBITION FOR THE NEW COUNTRY.

ALL IN FAVOR SAY AYE!

...IT'S UNANIMOUS, THEN!

THE NEW GOVERNMENT IMPOSED A LIQUOR TAX IN 1794, SPARKING AN UPRISING KNOWN AS THE WHISKEY REBELLION AMONG HOME-BREWING FARMERS. 15,000 TROOPS WERE CALLED OUT TO RESTORE ORDER.

PRESIDENT JAMES MADISON REGULARLY DOWNED A PINT OF WHISKEY BEFORE BREAKFAST--UNDERSTANDABLE, PERHAPS, SINCE THE BRITISH TORCHED THE CAPITAL DURING HIS TERM.

LOOKS LIKE A BAD DAY TO GIVE UP DRINKING!

IN THE EARLY 1800s, TEMPERANCE GROUPS BEGAN TO FORM, INSPIRED BY THE RESEARCH OF NOTED DOCTOR BENJAMIN RUSH. HIS STUDIES CATALOGUED LIQUOR'S DETRIMENTAL EFFECTS.

I'D SAY HE'S DEAD.

AND I'D SAY THE LIQUOR DID IT!

BY 1829 THERE WERE 1000 SUCH GROUPS IN THE COUNTRY--AND SOME BEGAN TO CALL FOR TOTAL PROHIBITION OF ALCOHOL.

REPENT!

TO: DRINK IS TO SIN!

BOOZE

NO DRINK!

SOME PREACHERS NOW CONCLUDED...

THE SALOON IS THE MOST FIENDISH, CORRUPT, HELL-SOAKED INSTITUTION THAT EVER CRAWLED OUT OF THE SLIME OF THE ETERNAL PIT!

PROHIBITIONISTS BLAMED LIQUOR FOR EVERY CONCEIVABLE MALADY--INCLUDING SPONTANEOUS COMBUSTION.

A PREVIEW OF HELLFIRE TO COME, PERHAPS?

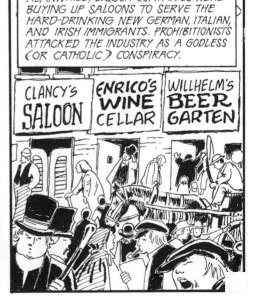

MEANWHILE, LIQUOR COMPANIES WERE BUYING UP SALOONS TO SERVE THE HARD-DRINKING NEW GERMAN, ITALIAN, AND IRISH IMMIGRANTS. PROHIBITIONISTS ATTACKED THE INDUSTRY AS A GODLESS (OR CATHOLIC) CONSPIRACY.

CLANCY'S SALOON

ENRICO'S WINE CELLAR

WILLHELM'S BEER GARTEN

IN THE 1840s THE PROHIBITIONISTS WERE GAINING MOMENTUM. MAINE BANNED ALCOHOL, AND SEVERAL OTHER STATES PREPARED TO FOLLOW ITS EXAMPLE.

WE DID IT IN MAINE!

WE'LL DO IT HERE!

DO IT HERE!

NO BOOZE!

BY 1850, PER CAPITA CONSUMPTION OF LIQUOR WAS DOWN TO TWO GALLONS PER YEAR.

THIS'LL DO ME.

A BROAD SOCIAL REFORM MOVEMENT HAD CREATED SOME STRANGE BEDFELLOWS, ALLYING CONSERVATIVE PROHIBITIONISTS WITH LIBERAL ABOLITIONISTS.

IMPROVE SOCIETY! BAN ALCOHOL!

IMPROVE SOCIETY! BAN SLAVERY!

NOW WITH THE CIVIL WAR LOOMING, THE SLAVERY ISSUE CAME TO DOMINATE, PUSHING PROHIBITION OFF THE NATIONAL AGENDA FOR DECADES. MAINE'S BAN WAS REPEALED.

IN 1873 A GROUP OF MIDWESTERN WOMEN REENERGIZED THE MOVEMENT BY HOLDING PRAYER VIGILS IN FRONT OF LOCAL SALOONS.

AND WE WON'T LEAVE UNTIL YOU STOP.

BOXING

AS THE COUNTRY'S MAKEUP CHANGED, BATTLE LINES WERE DRAWN BETWEEN "DRYS"-- RURAL, FARM-BASED NATIVE-BORN PROTESTANTS -- AND "WETS"--INDUSTRIAL-IZED, LARGELY CATHOLIC URBAN IMMIGRANTS.

IN THE SOUTH, DRYS SPREAD SCARE STORIES ABOUT "DRINK-CRAZED NEGROES"--THOUGH BLACKS GENERALLY DRANK LESS THAN WHITES.

DEFEND VIRTUE

OUTLAW DRINK!

THE WOMEN'S CHRISTIAN TEMPERANCE UNION WAS FORMED IN 1874. SENSING POTENTIAL DANGER FROM THE MOVEMENT, LIQUOR COMPANIES WORKED TO KEEP WOMEN FROM GETTING THE VOTE.

BUSIN

DISTILLERIES

THEY NEEDN'T WORRY THEIR LITTLE HEADS-- LET US MEN DECIDE!

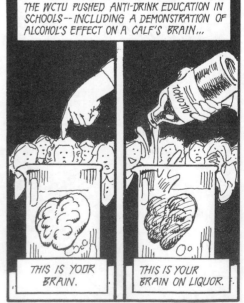

THE WCTU PUSHED ANTI-DRINK EDUCATION IN SCHOOLS--INCLUDING A DEMONSTRATION OF ALCOHOL'S EFFECT ON A CALF'S BRAIN...

ALCOHOL

THIS IS YOUR BRAIN.

THIS IS YOUR BRAIN ON LIQUOR.

IN 1893, THE ANTI-SALOON LEAGUE WAS FOUNDED. UNDER THE GUIDANCE OF WAYNE WHEELER, IT WOULD BECOME ONE OF THE NATION'S MOST POWERFUL POLITICAL FORCES.

THE ASL'S GRASSROOTS CAMPAIGN GOT LIQUOR BANNED IN MANY RURAL COUNTIES. POLITICIANS LEARNED THEY COULD WIN VOTES BY GOING ALONG WITH THE LEAGUE ON THIS HOT-BUTTON ISSUE.

HERE'S TO THE ASL!

VOTE FOR MORIARTY

EACH WEEK, THE ASL DISTRIBUTED ONE MILLION ANTI-DRINK PAMPHLETS ACROSS THE COUNTRY. AT ITS 1913 NATIONAL CONVENTION, THE LEAGUE CALLED FOR A CONSTITUTIONAL AMENDMENT OUTLAWING ALCOHOL.

DESPITE THE ASL, SALOONS WERE FLOURISHING, ESPECIALLY IN CITIES. THERE WAS ONE FOR EVERY 300 PEOPLE, AND MOST WERE OPEN 24 HOURS A DAY.

THINK I'LL CALL IT A NIGHT...

WHY NOT STAY ANOTHER FEW HOURS AND CALL IT A DAY!

INDUSTRIALISTS LIKE JOHN D. ROCKEFELLER, JR. SUPPORTED THE ASL. THEY WANTED SOBER WORKERS--AND SALOONS WERE POPULAR SPOTS FOR UNION ORGANIZING. HENRY FORD FIRED MEN FOR DRINKING EVEN OFF THE JOB.

WORKERS UNITE!

AS THE U.S. PREPARED TO ENTER THE WAR AGAINST GERMANY, JINGOISM FUELED THE GROWING PROHIBITION FERVOR--SINCE NEARLY ALL BREWERIES WERE OWNED BY GERMAN IMMIGRANTS.

VOGEL'S BREWERY

NO HUN BEER!

BREWERS ARE THE KAISERS TOOLS!

NO BEER

IN 1917 CONGRESS PASSED THE 18TH AMENDMENT BANNING THE SALE OF LIQUOR. BY EARLY 1919 IT WAS RATIFIED BY 2/3 OF THE STATES.

MY GOD!

U.S. GOES DRY!

THE VOLSTEAD ACT SETTING ENFORCEMENT AND PENALTIES WAS PASSED OVER PRES. WILSON'S VETO. THE ACT WAS LARGELY CRAFTED BY WAYNE WHEELER.

NATIONWIDE PROHIBITION BEGAN ON JANUARY 17, 1920 -- AND MANY THOUGHT THE BATTLE WAS OVER. AS ONE ENFORCEMENT OFFICIAL SAID:

THERE WILL NOT BE ANY VIOLATIONS TO SPEAK OF.

HOW WRONG CAN YOU BE?

FACTOID BOOKS

THOUGH TOO OUTLANDISH FOR THE MAINSTREAM TEMPERANCE MOVEMENT, SHE WAS A MIDWESTERN BAR OWNER'S WORST NIGHTMARE.

CARRY NATION SALOON SMASHER

CARRY AMELIA MOORE, DAUGHTER OF A PROSPEROUS PLANTATION OWNER, WAS BORN IN 1846 IN GERRARD COUNTY, KENTUCKY.

SICKLY AS A CHILD, SHE SPENT MUCH OF HER FORMATIVE YEARS READING THE BIBLE.

CARRY CAME FROM A FAMILY OF ECCENTRICS.

HER MOTHER CLAIMED TO BE QUEEN VICTORIA, WEARING PURPLE GOWNS AND REQUIRING FAMILY MEMBERS TO MAKE APPOINTMENTS TO SEE HER.

CARRY'S AUNT SOMETIMES CLAMBERED ONTO THE ROOF AND PRETENDED TO BE A WEATHERVANE.

AN OLDER COUSIN PREFERRED CRAWLING TO WALKING.

AS A YOUNG WOMAN, CARRY MARRIED A PHYSICIAN, DR. CHARLES GLOYD, AND SOON HAD A DAUGHTER, CHARLIEN,

UNFORTUNATELY, CHARLIEN WAS "AFFLICTED."

CARRY BELIEVED THAT CHARLIEN'S ILLNESS WAS A RESULT OF GLOYD'S DRINKING.

SHE TOOK CHARLIEN AND LEFT TO BECOME A SCHOOL TEACHER. GLOYD DIED SIX MONTHS LATER.

UNSUCCESSFUL AS A TEACHER, CARRY WED DAVID NATION, A MINISTER NINETEEN YEARS HER SENIOR.

SHE DEDICATED HERSELF TO LECTURING AGAINST THE EVILS OF TOBACCO AND LIQUOR.

IN 1890 DAVID BECAME PASTOR OF A CHURCH IN MEDICINE LODGE, KANSAS. EVER THE REFORMER, CARRY FREQUENTLY URGED HIM ON.

MORE FIRE, DAVID! MORE FIRE!

THE SALE OF ALCOHOL WAS ILLEGAL IN KANSAS, BUT TO CARRY'S DISMAY, THE LAW WAS NOT ENFORCED.

O LORD, USE ME TO SAVE KANSAS.

ACCORDING TO CARRY, THE VOICE OF GOD TOLD HER WHAT TO DO.

GO TO KIOWA. TAKE SOMETHING IN YOUR HANDS AND THROW AT THESE PLACES AND SMASH THEM.

ON JUNE 1, 1900, SHE LOADED HER BUGGY WITH BRICKS AND STONES AND DROVE TO DOBSON'S SALOON IN NEARBY KIOWA.

MEN, I HAVE COME TO SAVE YOU FROM A DRUNKARD'S GRAVE.

SINGING HYMNS ALL THE WHILE, CARRY SMASHED EVERY BOTTLE, MIRROR, AND WINDOW IN THE BAR.

GOD BE WITH YOU!

CARRY QUICKLY DESTROYED ANOTHER BAR DOWN THE STREET, BUT WAS ARRESTED WHILE DEMOLISHING A THIRD.

CARRY FELT THAT SINCE THE SALOONS WERE ILLEGAL SHE HAD THE RIGHT TO SMASH THEM. SHE WAS RELEASED AFTER THREE WEEKS IN JAIL.

AS A CONTEMPORARY IN MEDICINE LODGE NOTED...

WHATEVER SHE BELIEVES IN, SHE BELIEVES WITH HER WHOLE SOUL AND NOTHING EXCEPT SUPERIOR FORCE CAN STAY HER.

SEVERAL MONTHS LATER SHE STRUCK AGAIN AT THE ELEGANT HOTEL CAREY BAR IN WICHITA.

GLORY TO GOD!

CARRY CLEARED THE ESTABLISHMENT, SHATTERING MIRRORS AND OVERTURNING TABLES.

THE CHARGES WERE DROPPED, BUT HER TRIAL MADE HER A NATIONAL CELEBRITY.

ALL NATIONS WELCOME EXCEPT CARRY NATI

SHE CONTINUED WHAT SHE CALLED HER "HACHETATIONS", WRECKING MORE THAN 20 SALOONS IN THE NEXT YEAR.

GOOD DAY, YOU DONKEY-FACED BEDMATE OF SATAN.

YOU AIN'T NO PRIZE YOURSELF.

TO OFFSET HER MOUNTING LEGAL EXPENSES, CARRY BEGAN SELLING TINY PEWTER SOUVENIR HATCHETS.

SHE PUBLISHED A WEEKLY PAPER, SMASHER'S MAIL, WITH TIPS ON SALOON-BUSTING -- INSPIRING WOMEN ACROSS THE COUNTRY TO FOLLOW HER EXAMPLE.

THE FIGHT AGAINST LIQUOR WAS CONSUMING ALL OF CARRY'S TIME -- AND EXPOSING HER AND HER HUSBAND TO PUBLIC RIDICULE. WHEN SHE REFUSED TO GIVE IT UP, DAVID DIVORCED HER.

IN 1901 TEMPERANCE LEADERS CONVENED IN TOPEKA. THOUGH NOT INVITED, CARRY APPEARED -- TO MUCH ACCLAIM.

AFTERWARDS, SHE ORGANIZED SEVERAL HUNDRED DELEGATES INTO "GENERAL CARRY'S HOME DEFENDERS' ARMY."

CARRY NOTORIETY SPREAD, AND SHE WAS NOW MUCH IN DEMAND AS A LECTURER.

OH, I TELL YOU, LADIES, YOU NEVER KNOW WHAT JOY IT GIVES YOU TO START OUT TO SMASH A RUMSHOP.

LED BY CARRY, THE TOPEKA BRIGADE DESTROYED CASH REGISTERS, SLOT MACHINES, AND FIXTURES IN NUMEROUS SALOONS.

MANY WERE ARRESTED, INCLUDING CARRY.

FOLLOWING THE EXAMPLE OF THE TOPEKA BRIGADE, HOME DEFENDERS ALL OVER KANSAS DEMOLISHED BARS AND SALOONS.

CARRY JOINED WITH TEMPERANCE ORGANIZATIONS AND LOBBIED THE 1901 LEGISLATURE HARD, RESULTING IN THE FIRST SIGNIFICANT TEMPERANCE LAWS IN 15 YEARS.

IF YOU DON'T DO IT, THEN THE WOMEN OF THIS STATE WILL DO IT!

THIS WAS THE PEAK OF CARRY'S SUCCESS. THOUGH SHE CONTINUED HER CRUSADE, THE PUBLIC GRADUALLY LOST INTEREST IN HER. SHE DIED ALONE AND PENNILESS IN 1911.

CARRIE NATION 1846-1911 "SHE HATH DONE WHAT SHE COULD"

PRESIDENT HOOVER CALLED PROHIBITION A NOBLE EXPERIMENT. CONSIDERING THE CRIME, VIOLENCE, AND SOCIAL UPHEAVAL IT SPAWNED, IT MIGHT BETTER BE TERMED...

THE NOBLE DISASTER

ALCOHOL-RELATED DEATHS, ILLNESSES, AND MAYHEM DID DECLINE--AT FIRST.

THEY'LL BE BACK...IT'S ONLY A MATTER OF TIME...

TOO MANY PEOPLE STILL WANTED TO DRINK--AND THEY WEREN'T GOING TO LET THE LAW DETER THEM.

WITH MANY WILLING TO PAY A PREMIUM TO GET THE NOW-ILLEGAL LIQUOR, BOOTLEGGING QUICKLY BECAME A BILLION-DOLLAR-A-YEAR INDUSTRY.

GOOD TO SEE YOU GUYS. WE WERE RUNNIN' A LITTLE DRY...

THE LAW'S ENFORCEMENT MECHANISM ALMOST SEEMED DESIGNED TO FAIL-- THERE WERE ONLY 1550 FEDERAL AGENTS TO PATROL THE COUNTRY, AND JOBS WERE GIVEN BASED ON POLITICAL PATRONAGE, NOT MERIT.

GEE, THANKSH, UNCLE JOHN...

U.S. PROHIBITION BUREAU

MANY AGENTS SUPPLEMENTED THEIR MODEST PAY WITH LARGE BRIBES--IT WAS SAID THAT AN AGENT'S BADGE WAS A LICENSE TO PRINT MONEY.

...THANKS A LOT!

ISKEY   WH

OFFICIALS IN MANY LOCALES OPPOSED PROHIBITION, AND ENFORCED IT LOOSELY. OTHERS WERE HAPPY TO TAKE THE BOOTLEGGERS' MONEY AND LOOK THE OTHER WAY.

MAY NOT BE LEGAL--BUT IT SURE HITS THE SPOT!

KNOWING COMMITTED "DRY" VOTERS COULD SWING ELECTIONS, MANY CONGRESSMEN PAID LIP SERVICE TO THE BAN, BUT DRANK ANYWAY--AND A FEW WERE IN BUSINESS WITH LIQUOR GANGS.

IN WASHINGTON, THE SENATE BAR WAS SUPPLIED BY CUSTOMS SEIZURES, AND BOOTLEGGERS ROAMED THE CAPITAL FREELY, MAKING DELIVERIES TO LAWMAKERS FROM STOCK THEY STORED IN THE BASEMENT.

TO PROHIBITION!

WAYNE WHEELER AND THE ANTI-SALOON 'LEAGUE, PROBABLY THE NATION'S MOST POWERFUL LOBBY, WERE OBLIVIOUS TO LAWMAKERS' PERSONAL BEHAVIOR--

--AS LONG AS THEY CONTINUE TO VOTE DRY.

ALCOHOL FLOWED FROM NUMEROUS SOURCES. SMUGGLING FROM ABROAD WAS COMMON. JUST PRIOR TO THE NEW LAW, MANY LIQUOR COMPANIES HAD MOVED HUGE QUANTITIES OF SPIRITS TO THE BAHAMAS.

NOW ALL WE GOTTA DO IS SELL IT HERE AND SHIP IT BACK HOME!

WHISKEY

FLORIDA BOATMAN BILL McCOY DIDN'T DRINK, BUT DIDN'T THINK IT SHOULD BE ILLEGAL, EITHER--SO HE PUT THE LAST OF HIS CASH INTO A VESSEL FOR THE NASSAU RUN.

AN HONEST PROFIT FOR AN HONEST JOB!

SOLD

THE COAST GUARD COULD BOARD A U.S. BOAT ANYWHERE, SO McCOY AND OTHERS RE-REGISTERED UNDER FOREIGN FLAGS, MAKING THEM IMMUNE TO SEARCHES OUTSIDE U.S. TERRITORIAL WATERS.

IT'S AS GOOD A TIME AS ANY TO BE A BRIT, 'EY WOT?

McCOY COULD BUY LIQUOR LEGALLY IN NASSAU, THEN HEAD TOWARDS NEW YORK. GANGSTERS IN SPEEDBOATS WOULD MEET HIM JUST OUTSIDE U.S. WATERS TO BUY HIS CARGO.

McCOY INSPIRED A FLEET OF IMITATORS, AND A FLOATING MARKET, CALLED RUM ROW, FLOURISHED OFF THE ATLANTIC COAST--BUT IT WAS HIS QUALITY GOODS THAT CLAMORING CUSTOMERS DUBBED "THE REAL McCOY."

JUST ASK MY CUSTOMERS--IT'S WORTH THE TRIP!

HIS EXPLOITS WERE ROMANTICIZED BY A THIRSTY PUBLIC, TO THE FEDS' ANNOYANCE. THE COAST GUARD FINALLY WENT OUTSIDE U.S. WATERS TO NAB HIM.

THIS WASN'T IN THE PLAN!

AFTER EIGHT MONTHS IN JAIL, HE RETIRED TO FLORIDA, SET FOR LIFE.

MANY DISTILLERS HAD UNSOLD STOCK ON HAND AS PROHIBITION BEGAN, SO IT WAS SEALED IN BONDED WAREHOUSES BY THE FEDS. CINCINNATI LAWYER GEORGE REMUS SAW A BUYING OPPORTUNITY.

HE BOUGHT THE DISTILLERIES CHEAP-- THEN BRIBED OFFICIALS TO GET PERMITS TO TAKE LIQUOR OUT OF THE WAREHOUSES FOR MEDICINAL OR INDUSTRIAL USE.

MUST BE A LOT OF SICK FOLKS OUT THERE.

DISTILLERY

ACME SHIPPING

PERMIT

THE BOOZE WOULD THEN BE DECLARED "LOST" OR "STOLEN"--SO REMUS COULD SELL IT TO BOOTLEGGERS AND SPEAKEASIES AT A HUGE PROFIT. SOON, HE WAS MOVING MILLIONS OF GALLONS COAST TO COAST.

HE BOUGHT OFF LAWMEN FAR AND WIDE, INCLUDING TOP JUSTICE DEPARTMENT OFFICIALS. MOST OF CINCINNATI'S COPS WERE ON HIS PAYROLL, SOMETIMES ACTING AS GUARDS FOR HIS SHIPMENTS.

T'ANKS FER DA RIGHT-O-WAY, OSSIFER!

ANY TIME, LADDIE!

FINALLY NAILED BY A FEW INCORRUPTIBLE AGENTS, HE TRAVELED TO PRISON IN A PRIVATE RAIL CAR AND SPENT HIS BRIEF SENTENCE IN A PLUSH CELL.

PRISON AIN'T SO BAD--IF YOU'RE CONNECTED!

MEANWHILE, HIS WIFE AND A DOUBLY CROOKED FED PLUNDERED HIS BANK ACCOUNTS. UNHINGED, REMUS SHOT HER. IN A SPECTACULAR TRIAL, HE GOT OFF DUE TO TEMPORARY INSANITY--BUT HE NEVER RECOVERED HIS FORTUNE.

GOOD LIQUOR, LIKE REMUS'S AND McCOY'S, WAS WATERED DOWN BEFORE REACHING THE PUBLIC. OTHER 'LEGGERS MIXED THEIR OWN, OFTEN WITH POISONOUS WOOD ALCOHOL.

HOME STILL KITS WERE ALSO POPULAR, AND SOME WINERIES MADE BIG BUCKS SELLING GRAPE JUICE REPLETE WITH A "WARNING" DETAILING WHAT NOT TO DO, LEST IT FERMENT INTO ILLEGAL WINE.

THAT ONE'S GONE BAD -HIC!-

VINE-GLO GRAPE JUICE WARNING:

GIMME ANNUDER BOTTLE!

FANCY NIGHTCLUBS--A SHARP CONTRAST TO THE DINGY, MEN-ONLY SALOONS OF EARLIER DECADES--SPRANG UP, ESPECIALLY IN NEW YORK, LENDING ALLURING GLAMOUR TO THE LAW-BREAKING.

SWORDFISH!

RIGHT. C'MON IN.

THE ALCOHOL SERVED WAS OFTEN AS BAD AS IT WAS EXPENSIVE. THIS HELPED POPULARIZE COCKTAILS, WITH VARIOUS OTHER INGREDIENTS TO HIDE THE LIQUOR'S DREADFUL TASTE.

I THINK I'M GONNA BE SICK!

WHO CARES, WHEN YOU KNOW YOU'RE GONNA BE DRUNK!

WITH 100,000 SPEAKEASIES IN THE CITY, NEW YORK AUTHORITIES WERE TOO OVERWHELMED--AND OFTEN TOO CORRUPT--TO OFFER MORE THAN TOKEN RESISTANCE.

A DOUBLE STANDARD OF ENFORCEMENT EMERGED, OFTEN FOCUSING ON THOSE TOO POOR TO PAY PROTECTION WHILE IGNORING THE LARGE-SCALE ACTIVITIES OF THE RICH AND POWERFUL.

COPPERS!

STEP AWAY FROM THE HOOCH!

DENATURED ALCOHOL

IN THE SOUTH, BLACKS WERE FREQUENT TARGETS, WHILE MUCH OF WHITE SOCIETY CONTINUED DRINKING AS BEFORE.

IN SOME STATES, OFFENDERS DREW LIFE SENTENCES FOR HAVING A PINT OF WHISKEY--

XXX

--WHILE ELSEWHERE, GUN-WIELDING GANGS OF BOOTLEGGERS LED BY THE LIKES OF AL CAPONE BATTLED FOR CONTROL OF ENTIRE CITIES, UNCHECKED BY POLICE.

BY THE MID-'20S, THE PUBLIC WAS TIRING OF THE WHOLESALE CORRUPTION, VIOLENCE, AND HYPOCRISY OF PROHIBITION--

--NOT TO MENTION THE MOUNTING DEATH TOLL FROM POISONOUS HOOCH.

IN 1927, WHEN WAYNE WHEELER DIED, 75% OF THE PUBLIC WANTED THE LAW OVERTURNED--THOUGH WITH THE ECONOMY BOOMING, DRY REPUBLICANS CONTINUED TO WIN ELECTIONS.

A SOBER WORKER IS A MORE PROFITABLE WORKER!

1927

BUT THE CALAMITY OF THE STOCK MARKET CRASH OF '29 AND THE SUBSEQUENT GREAT DEPRESSION MADE DEMON RUM SEEM TRIVIAL BY COMPARISON.

I NEED A DRINK!

1929

THE GOVERNMENT NEEDED MONEY--AND BEGAN PONDERING THE TAX REVENUE LEGAL ALCOHOL WOULD GENERATE.

WHI$KEY

MANY INDUSTRIALISTS WHO HAD BACKED THE ASL, HOPING PROHIBITION WOULD GIVE THEM A MORE PRODUCTIVE WORK FORCE, NOW SOUGHT REPEAL TO LOWER THEIR OWN INCOME TAX BILLS.

WHI$KEY

MONEYBAGS INDUSTRIES

IN 1932, FRANKLIN ROOSEVELT'S DEMOCRATS SWEPT INTO POWER, AND PROHIBITION WAS REPEALED--

VOTE FDR

FDR

--BUT ITS 13-YEAR REIGN UNDERMINED AMERICAN SOCIETY IN WAYS THAT STILL ECHO IN TODAY'S DRUG WARS.

TWO FEDERAL AGENTS USED INGENUITY INSTEAD OF GUNS TO FOIL BOOTLEGGERS ACROSS THE COUNTRY. REPORTERS LOVED TO WRITE ABOUT THE COLORFUL EXPLOITS OF...

IZZY & MOE

IN 1920 PROHIBITION BEGAN. THE GOVERNMENT NEEDED ENFORCEMENT AGENTS--FAST.

$50 A WEEK?! THAT BEATS MY POSTAL CLERK SALARY.

BUT AT 5'5" AND 225 POUNDS, IZZY EINSTEIN WAS TOLD:

WHAT CAN I DO? YOU DON'T *LOOK* LIKE A DETECTIVE.

SO? I COULD FOOL PEOPLE BETTER!

A GOOD POINT. ILLEGAL SPEAKEASIES WERE WARY OF CUSTOMERS THEY DIDN'T KNOW PERSONALLY.

YA LOOK LIKE A COP--SCRAM!

IZZY GOT THE JOB--AND MADE GOOD USE OF HIS JOVIAL MANNER AND COMIC LOOKS.

HOW'S ABOUT A DRINK FOR A HARDWORKING PROHIBITION AGENT?

-HA HA! THAT'S A GOOD ONE! C'MON IN, PAL!

TO COLLECT EVIDENCE, IZZY HID A FUNNEL IN HIS VEST POCKET WITH A TUBE LEADING TO A SMALL BOTTLE IN THE LINING.

THANK GOODNESS FOR THE FUNNEL-- THIS HOOCH IS TERRIBLE!

IZZY AND MOE STRIKE AGAIN

IZZY SOON PERSUADED HIS FRIEND MOE SMITH TO JOIN HIM ON THE FORCE. AT 5'8" AND 250 POUNDS, MOE DIDN'T LOOK LIKE A DETECTIVE, EITHER.

NEWSPAPERS PLAYED UP THEIR EXPLOITS, AND THE ODD-LOOKING PAIR SOON BECAME KNOWN AROUND NEW YORK...

AND AGAIN

...SO THEY BEGAN DONNING DISGUISES.

THEY GOT JOBS AS GRAVEDIGGERS NEXT TO A SUSPECTED DISTILLERY...

LOOKS LIKE HOT WORK. CARE FOR A SNORT?

THANKS...

Grape Juice

...FOR THE EVIDENCE! YOU'RE UNDER ARREST!

DISGUISED AS A SOUTHERN COLONEL, IZZY STAKED OUT THE 1924 DEMO-CRATIC CONVENTION AT THE REQUEST OF ANTI-SALOON LEAGUE LEADER WAYNE WHEELER.

"WET" CANDIDATE AL SMITH WAS A LEADING CONTENDER, AND IZZY FOUND BOTTLES BY THE TRUCKLOAD--BUT NO EVIDENCE.

THEY'RE ALL EMPTY.

THE DUO PLAYED COUNTLESS ROLES-- FISHERMEN, PICKLE SALESMEN, FOOTBALL PLAYERS, MUSICIANS...

THEY EVEN DONNED BLACKFACE TO PULL A RAID IN HARLEM.

IZZY TIMED HOW LONG IT TOOK HIM TO FIND A DRINK IN VARIOUS CITIES. IN NEW ORLEANS, ONLY 35 SECONDS.

KNOW WHERE A FELLA CAN GET A DRINK?

RIGHT HERE!

AFTER SEARCHING FOR AN HOUR IN WASHINGTON, HE FINALLY GOT DETAILED DIRECTIONS FROM A UNWITTING COP.

TELL 'EM I SENT YOU.

THANKS!

IZZY AND MOE WERE THE FEDS' TOP TEAM OF AGENTS, ARRESTING OVER 4000 AND SEIZING $15 MILLION WORTH OF BOOZE.

POLICE

NY·589

BUT IN 1925 A SUPERIOR COMPLAINED TO IZZY:

YOU GET YOUR NAME IN THE PAPERS ALL THE TIME, WHEREAS MINE IS HARDLY EVER MENTIONED.

BECAUSE THEY WEREN'T "DIGNIFIED," THE PAIR WERE FIRED.

BOTH MEN BECAME SUCCESSFUL SALESMEN. IN 1932 IZZY WROTE A BOOK ABOUT HIS EXPLOITS, BUT BY THEN THE PUBLIC HAD LOST INTEREST-- IT SOLD 575 COPIES.

PROHIBITION AGENT #1

BY IZZY EINSTEIN

THOUGH MOST PEOPLE THINK OF MOONSHINE AS A RELIC OF A BYGONE AGE, ILLEGAL STILLS EXIST TODAY, COOKING UP GALLONS OF...

WHITE LIGHTNING

MOONSHINE IS MADE FROM A FERMENTED MASH OF CORN MEAL, GRAIN, AND SUGAR. WHEN COOKED, ITS ALCOHOL CONTENT BOILS OFF INTO A COIL, WHERE IT RECONDENSES -- AT **80-100** PROOF!!

BLOP GLOP BLOOP, BLOGGLE

EARLY SCOTTISH AND IRISH SETTLERS BROUGHT THEIR KNOWLEDGE OF DISTILLING TO THE SOUTH IN THE 1700s. IN FRONTIER AMERICA, A NEIGHBOR'S STILL WAS OFTEN THE ONLY SOURCE OF LIQUOR AVAILABLE.

HEY NEIGHBA

XXX

IN 1862, THE FEDERAL GOVERNMENT ESTABLISHED A **20¢-PER-GALLON** TAX ON WHISKEY. RATHER THAN PAY, MANY MOONSHINERS HID THEIR OPERATIONS FROM THE "REVENUERS."

MOONSHINERS FLOURISHED DURING PROHIBITION-- AND AFTER, AS MANY SOUTHERN COUNTIES STAYED DRY. BOOTLEGGERS SOUPED UP THEIR CARS TO OUTRUN THE COPS -- AND SPAWNED STOCK-CAR RACING!

LIQUOR TAXES ARE NOW **$25** A GALLON IN SOME STATES, GIVING UNTAXED MOONSHINE A PRICE EDGE. VIRGINIA IS THE LEADING PRODUCER, TURNING OUT HALF A MILLION GALLONS A YEAR!

MUCH IS SMUGGLED INTO CITIES AND SOLD CHEAPLY BY THE GLASS IN "NIP HOUSES", WHERE OTHER BLACK MARKET ITEMS LIKE GUNS AND DRUGS ARE ALSO AVAILABLE.

VIRGINIA COPS RECENTLY BUSTED THE LARGEST STILL THEY'D SEEN IN 20 YEARS, AND MOONSHINING HAS COST MISSISSIPPI ALONE NEARLY **$1 BILLION** IN LOST TAXES SINCE THE MID-'60s!

HAVEN'T YOU EVER WONDERED-- WHAT'S IN ALL THOSE BOTTLES?

WHAT CAN I GET YOU?

WHAT'VE YOU GOT?

LOTS OF DIFFERENT BEERS. DOMESTICS--THOSE ARE MOSTLY YOUR LIGHTER-COLORED BREWS. Y'KNOW, THEY START WITH BARLEY MALT--GRAIN THAT'S SPROUTED, THEN DRIED.

THEY COOK THE MALT WITH HOPS (THAT'S DRIED FLOWER BITS FROM A VINE IN THE HEMP FAMILY) FOR FLAVOR, THEN ADD YEAST.

LAGER YEAST STAYS AT THE BOTTOM OF THE POT--ALE YEAST FLOATS. THE BREW FERMENTS FOR DAYS OR WEEKS, AND THE STARCHES IN THE GRAIN TURN TO ALCOHOL.

BY USING DIFFERENT BLENDS OF GRAINS, YEASTS, HOPS, AND WATERS--PLUS MAYBE SOME CARAMEL OR SUGAR-- YOU GET DIFFERENT BEERS, LIKE STOUT OR PORTER.

GOT LOTSA WHISKIES, TOO. SCOTCH IS DISTILLED MOSTLY FROM BARLEY MALT HEATED OVER A PEAT FIRE FOR FLAVOR. IRISH IS SIMILAR, BUT WITHOUT THE PEAT SMOKE.

IN CANADA THEY USE WHEAT, CORN, AND RYE ALONG WITH THE BARLEY. THE BLEND OF INGREDIENTS--AND LOCAL WATER-- AFFECTS THE TASTE.

IN THE STATES WE MAKE BOURBON, MAINLY FROM CORN, STRAIGHT MALT (MAINLY BARLEY), STRAIGHT RYE, AND BLENDS. WHISKEY (OR WHISKY, AS THE SCOTS AND CANADIANS PREFER) IS USUALLY 40-50% ALCOHOL.

GIN IS DISTILLED FROM GRAINS LIKE WHISKEY, BUT THEN IT'S FLAVORED WITH JUNIPER BERRIES. ADD SOME TONIC WATER TO STAVE OFF MALARIA OR VERMOUTH FOR A MARTINI.

PEOPLE HAVE TRIED MAKING LIQUOR FROM JUST ABOUT EVERYTHING THAT GROWS. VODKA -- RUSSIAN FOR "LITTLE WATER" -- WAS ORIGINALLY MADE FROM POTATOES.

THESE DAYS THEY USUALLY SUBSTITUTE GRAIN. MOST VODKA HAS ALMOST NO FLAVOR OF ITS OWN, SO IT'S AN EASY MIXER.

RUM IS MADE FROM SUGAR CANE MOLASSES, SO IT COMES MAINLY FROM THE TROPICS WHERE THE CANE IS GROWN. I CAN MIX YOU A TASTY FROZEN DAIQUIRI.

TEQUILA AND MESCAL ARE DISTILLED FROM DIFFERENT AGAVE PLANTS FOUND IN MEXICO. TO LOOK AT THOSE PLANTS, WHO'D EVER THINK YOU'D GET A MARGARITA OUT OF 'EM?

AND OF COURSE WE'VE GOT A CELLARFUL OF WINES -- THAT WHOLE FERMENTED GRAPE JUICE THING, AND BRANDY DISTILLED FROM WINE. OR COGNAC, BRANDY MADE NEAR THE FRENCH TOWN OF COGNAC.

OR CHAMPAGNE WHICH IS FERMENTED A SECOND TIME TO ADD BUBBLES.

AND THEN THERE'S THE JAPANESE SAKE. SOME CALL IT RICE WINE, BUT IT'S BREWED LIKE BEER.

OR MAYBE YOU'D LIKE A DESSERT LIQUEUR -- A FRUIT- OR HERB-FLAVORED ALCOHOL, LIKE COINTREAU OR OUZO.

SO, THERE YOU HAVE IT. WHAT'LL IT BE?

UH... HOW ABOUT A COUPLE OF ASPIRINS?

MANY PEOPLE CAN DRINK MODERATELY WITHOUT PROBLEMS, BUT FOR SOME REASON -- PHYSICAL, PSYCHOLOGICAL, OR HEREDITARY -- OTHERS BECOME ADDICTED. ONE OF THE MOST EFFECTIVE REMEDIES IS A GROUP CALLED ALCOHOLICS ANONYMOUS, ALSO KNOWN AS...

FRIENDS OF BILL W.
TONIGHT, 7:30

A.A. MEMBERS DON'T GIVE THEIR FULL NAMES -- JUST FIRST NAMES AND LAST INITIALS. WILLIAM WILSON, KNOWN AS BILL W., WAS ONE OF ITS FOUNDERS.

MY NAME IS BILL W., AND I'M AN ALCOHOLIC.

HE HAD FOUND SOME RELIEF IN CERTAIN SPIRITUAL TEACHINGS, AND IN WORKING WITH OTHER ALCOHOLICS.

IN 1935, HE WAS INTRODUCED TO DR. ROBERT SMITH, A LONG-TIME DRINKER WHO WAS TRYING TO QUIT.

MY NAME IS DR. BOB, AND I'M AN ALCOHOLIC.

TALKING TO SOMEONE WHO'D FACED THE SAME PROBLEMS HE WAS CONFRONTING WAS A GREAT HELP TO DR. BOB, AND HE WAS ABLE TO STOP DRINKING.

TOGETHER, BILL W. AND DR. BOB BEGAN MEETING WITH OTHER ALCOHOLICS. THEY FOUND WORKING IN A GROUP NOT ONLY HELPED THE OTHERS GET SOBER, IT HELPED BILL AND BOB STAY SOBER.

THEY DEVELOPED THE "TWELVE STEPS" TO RECOVERY. THESE INCLUDED ADMITTING TO A PROBLEM, MAKING AN HONEST SELF-ASSESSMENT, ASKING GOD'S HELP, AND SPREADING THE WORD TO OTHER ALCOHOLICS.

1. We admit we were powerless over alcohol...

IN 1939, THEY PUBLISHED A BOOK EXPLAINING THE GROUP'S PHILOSOPHY OF MUTUAL SUPPORT. A.A. GREW RAPIDLY, AND SOON THERE WERE CHAPTERS ACROSS THE COUNTRY.

ANYONE WANTING TO STOP DRINKING CAN JOIN. THERE IS LITTLE BUREAUCRACY AND NO DUES -- EACH CHAPTER IS AUTONOMOUS AND SUPPORTED BY MEMBERS' CONTRIBUTIONS.

SUGAR

For Coffee and use of the hall

A.A. IS NONSECTARIAN, BUT SOME PEOPLE ARE PUT OFF BY ITS EMPHASIS ON GOD. OTHERS FEEL THE INSISTENCE ON ABSTENTION IS UNNECESSARILY RESTRICTIVE FOR SOME PEOPLE.

decision to turn our will over to the care of God

ACCORDING TO A.A., AN ALCOHOLIC CAN NEVER BE "CURED"-- "RECOVERY" IS AN ONGOING PROCESS REQUIRING CONSCIOUS EFFORT EVERY DAY.

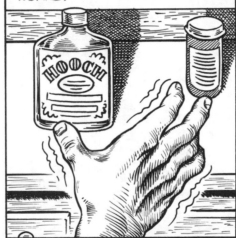

RECENT RESEARCH INDICATES THAT ADDICTIVE SUBSTANCES -- INCLUDING ALCOHOL, DRUGS, TOBACCO, CAFFEINE, EVEN SUGAR -- OPERATE SIMILARLY, BY OVER-STIMULATING THE BRAIN'S PLEASURE CIRCUITS.

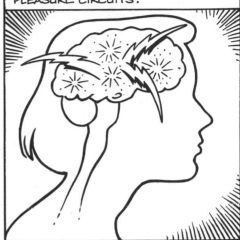

ADDICTIONS ARE OFTEN COMBINED -- FOR INSTANCE, ALCOHOLICS ARE MORE LIKELY TO BE SMOKERS, AND VICE VERSA.

NEW DRUGS SHOW GREAT PROMISE IN BLOCKING THE CRAVING ADDICTS FEEL. SOME IN A.A. OPPOSE TREATING ONE SUBSTANCE PROBLEM WITH ANOTHER SUBSTANCE; OTHERS SUPPORT "WHATEVER WORKS."

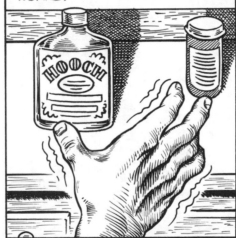

ADDICTION TO VARIOUS SUBSTANCES COSTS AMERICA ABOUT $240 BILLION A YEAR FOR HEALTH CARE, LOST PRODUCTIVITY, CRIME, AND EARLY DEATH. LIQUOR COMPANIES SPEND $1 BILLION A YEAR FOR ADVERTISING.

STILL, LITTLE TAX MONEY IS SPENT ON TREATMENT. BUT INSPIRED BY A.A., 12-STEP SUPPORT GROUPS HAVE SPRUNG UP FOR MANY OTHER PROBLEMS.

MY NAME IS BUD T., AND I'M A COCAINE ADDICT.

MY NAME IS SHIRLEY B., AND I HAVE AN EATING DISORDER.

MY NAME IS EDDIE R. AND I'M A COMPULSIVE GAMBLER.

THERE ARE NOW ABOUT 2 MILLION A.A. MEMBERS WORLDWIDE, AND COUNTLESS MEMBERS OF OTHER SUPPORT GROUPS -- ALL BECAUSE OF A MEETING YEARS AGO BETWEEN DR. BOB AND BILL W.

SO YOU WANT TO KNOW ABOUT ALCOHOL?

YES! YES I DO!

THE EFFECTS OF ALCOHOL VARY DEPENDING ON THE DOSAGE AND THE INDIVIDUAL. A SMALL AMOUNT CAN BE STIMULATING, AND CAN LOWER YOUR INHIBITIONS.

YOU'RE SHO BOO'IFUL--I WANNA BEAR YOUR CHIL'REN!

AFTER A FEW DRINKS, MOOD SWINGS AND EMOTIONAL OUTBURSTS ARE COMMON.

WATCH IT, BUB, OR I'LL CLOBBER YA!

nudge

ALCOHOL IS LINKED TO 40% OF VIOLENT CRIME.

AFTER THE INITIAL EUPHORIA, ALCOHOL ACTS AS A SEDATIVE. TOO MUCH CAN CAUSE UNCONSCIOUSNESS -- OR EVEN DEATH.

YOU WON'T FEEL THE FULL EFFECTS OF A DRINK FOR 30-60 MINUTES, SO IT'S EASY TO OVERDO BEFORE YOU KNOW IT.

LEAVING ALREADY? SAY, YOU REALLY SHOULDN'T BE DRIVING. EVEN A COUPLE OF DRINKS IMPAIRS YOUR COORDINATION --

DON' WORRY -- I'M JUSH FINE!

-- AND YOUR JUDGMENT.

VROOOOM! SKREEEEE KRASH! TINKLE TINKLE

DID I MENTION THAT 15,000 TO 20,000 PEOPLE A YEAR DIE IN ALCOHOL-RELATED CAR CRASHES?

IT TAKES YOUR LIVER TWO HOURS TO PROCESS EACH OUNCE YOU DRINK. TOO MUCH ALCOHOL LEAVES YOUR BODY CHEMISTRY OUT OF WHACK THE NEXT DAY--A HANGOVER, REPLETE WITH HEADACHE AND NAUSEA.

OOOOH...

LONG-TERM DRINKING CAN DAMAGE YOUR LIVER, HEART, BRAIN, AND OTHER IMPORTANT BODY PARTS. WHAT WITH STOMACH PROBLEMS AND DRINK'S EMPTY CALORIES, ALCOHOLICS OFTEN SUFFER FROM MALNUTRITION, TOO.

OOOOH...

ABOUT 100,000 AMERICANS DIE FROM ALCOHOL-RELATED CAUSES EACH YEAR, AND THE TYPICAL ALCOHOLIC DIES 10 TO 12 YEARS EARLY.

R.I.P.

AREN'T YOU GLAD YOU ASKED?

FACTOID BOOKS

44

CHAPTER THREE

DRUGS

The search for altered states of consciousness continues in this chapter, which makes us wonder what it is about drugs and booze that keeps mankind wanting more and more of it— or, more important, what it is about "normal" consciousness that makes mankind want less and less of that.

While naturally occurring consciousness-altering drugs have been with us since ancient times, the Industrial Age brought mankind undreamed-of levels of potency and variations on the basic organic versions. For every coca plant in nature there emerged a laboratory-refined cocaine. For every magic mushroom, an LSD. The motto "Better Living Through Chemistry," while intended to be a serious marketing slogan covering everything from polio vaccines to penicillin, was embraced by the counterculture with an irony-tinged emphasis on its mind-bending product line and the benefits to be had by ingesting them. Looking back, however, it seems that every age gets the drugs it deserves. The driving need for refuge from the ever-increasing pressures of life culminated in the early '90s emergence of crack, and then the new hallucinogens like Ecstasy. Unlike earlier synthetic drugs that came to be used recreationally, the major pharmaceutical firms have little to do with the latest crop; with the exception of a barrage of anti-depressants, today's drug manufacturers have become the darlings of Wall Street with their discoveries of remedies for maladies like sexual dysfunction, obesity, and the general effects of aging.

And for the 21st century, THOSE may be exactly the drugs we deserve.

THE STONED AGE

SOME BELIEVE THE DESIRE FOR INTOXICATION IS PART OF OUR NATURE. HUMANS PROBABLY FIRST STUMBLED ONTO IT BY WATCHING ANIMALS WHO'D EATEN VARIOUS PLANTS, FROM COCA LEAVES TO FERMENTED GRAPES.

THROUGHOUT HISTORY, PEOPLE OF NEARLY ALL CULTURES HAVE USED MANY SUBSTANCES TO COPE WITH LIFE'S TRIALS, OR JUST FOR FUN -- OFTEN TO THE DISMAY OF AUTHORITIES.

AS SOCIETY'S COMPLEXITY AND INDUSTRIALIZATION HAS GROWN, SO HAS CONCERN ABOUT SUBSTANCE ABUSE.

HMM... CAN'T HAVE PEOPLE GOING AROUND STONED ALL THE TIME.

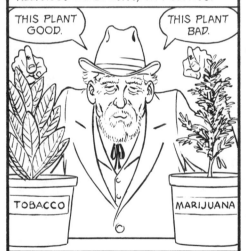

MANY SUBSTANCES HAVE BEEN BANNED -- BUT LEGAL DISTINCTIONS HAVE OFTEN BEEN ARBITRARY, BASED LARGELY ON CULTURAL AND RELIGIOUS TRADITIONS, OR POLITICS.

THIS PLANT GOOD.

THIS PLANT BAD.

TOBACCO

MARIJUANA

OUTLAWING DRUGS HAS CREATED A HUGELY PROFITABLE BLACK MARKET -- IRONICALLY SPAWNING MORE CRIME AS ADDICTS TURN TO THEFT OR PROSTITUTION TO SUPPORT THEIR HABITS AND DRUG GANGS BATTLE FOR TURF.

INCARCERATION HAS SOARED, AND THE PRISON INDUSTRY HAS BECOME A POWERFUL LOBBY OPPOSING DECRIMINALIZATION--

--JOINED BY TOBACCO AND LIQUOR COMPANIES WHO DON'T WANT COMPETITION.

THOUGH PROGRESS HAS BEEN MADE, MEDICAL TREATMENT FOR ADDICTION IS COSTLY AND OFTEN UNSUCCESSFUL. EDUCATION EFFORTS HAVE BEEN INCONSISTENT AND ARE OFTEN SEEN AS MERE PROPAGANDA.

HAHAHA HA HAH

teeheehee

DRUGS CAN KILL YOU.

THESE ADS KILL ME!

THE DRUG ISSUE IS COMPLEX -- MAKING IT ESPECIALLY INTRACTABLE IN AN ERA OF SOUND-BITE POLITICS.

JUST SAY NO.

I DIDN'T INHALE.

THE INCAS CALLED COCA THE "DIVINE LEAF OF IMMORTALITY" AND THOUGHT IT WAS A GIFT OF THE GODS. BUT TO ADDICTS, IT IS...

COCAINE: THE CURSE OF THE INCAS

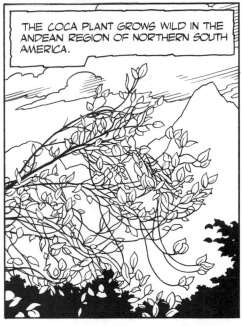

THE COCA PLANT GROWS WILD IN THE ANDEAN REGION OF NORTHERN SOUTH AMERICA.

PERHAPS 5000 YEARS AGO, NATIVES DISCOVERED THAT COCA LEAVES WERE A STIMULANT AND MOOD ELEVATOR.

IN 1510, AMERIGO VESPUCCI WROTE OF MEETING NATIVES WITH "CHEEKS BULGING WITH A CERTAIN GREEN HERB WHICH THEY CHEWED LIKE CATTLE, SO THAT THEY COULD HARDLY SPEAK."

WHAT WAS THAT YOU SAID?

AT FIRST, THE SPANIARDS TRIED TO SUPPRESS COCA USE, FEARING THAT IT WOULD SLOW THE NATIVES' CONVERSION TO CHRISTIANITY.

TEN LASHES!

THE SPANISH EASED UP WHEN THEY LEARNED THEY COULD PAY INDIANS IN COCA TO WORK THE GOLD AND SILVER MINES.

IT WAS CHEAP, AND THE COCA CHEWERS WORKED HARD.

THE COCA LEAF STILL PERVADES ANDEAN LIFE. EVEN TODAY, WHEN ANDEANS MEET ON THE TRAIL, THEY DON'T SHAKE HANDS, THEY TRADE LEAVES.

COCA LEAVES WERE EXPORTED TO EUROPE, BUT THE PRACTICE OF CHEWING THEM DIDN'T CATCH ON.

WHAT BEAUTIFUL GREEN TEETH YOU HAVE, SEÑOR!

HA HA HA HA HA HA HA HA HA HA

PURE COCAINE WAS EXTRACTED FROM COCA LEAVES IN THE MID-1800S. THIS NEW FORM WAS FAR MORE POTENT THAN THE CHEWED LEAF.

WOO HOO!

FIRST USED IN A WASH, IT WAS FOUND TO BE A GOOD TOPICAL ANESTHETIC FOR THE EYE -- WITH STRANGELY INVIGORATING PROPERTIES.

WHILE YOU'RE AT IT, DOC, HOWSABOUT WORKING ON THE OTHER EYE?

IN 1885, DR. WILLIAM HALSTEAD DISCOVERED THAT COCAINE COULD BE INJECTED DIRECTLY INTO A NERVE TO PRODUCE LOCAL ANESTHESIA.

UNFORTUNATELY, HALSTEAD AND HIS ASSISTANTS ALSO DISCOVERED THE DRUG'S ADDICTIVE POWER, BECOMING AMERICA'S FIRST COCAINE ADDICTS.

NONETHELESS, IT WAS GAINING A REPUTATION AS A WONDER DRUG.

AT THE TIME, MANY BELIEVED THAT MOST DISEASES WERE CAUSED BY "BRAIN EXHAUSTION." COCA TONICS WERE THOUGHT TO BE THE CURE.

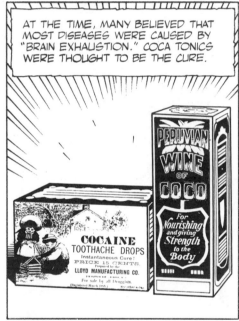

VIN MARIANI, A COCA WINE, WAS ENDORSED BY NUMEROUS HEADS OF STATE AND POPE LEO XIII.

IT'S REALLY GOOD!

ALEXANDER DUMAS CALLED IT "THE ELIXIR OF LIFE."

PROMINENT MEN SUCH AS SIGMUND FREUD, JULES VERNE, AND THOMAS EDISON ALL ADVOCATED THE USE OF COCA OR COCAINE.

YOU PERCEIVE AN INCREASE IN SELF-CONTROL AND POSSESS MORE VITALITY.

ROBERT LOUIS STEVENSON WROTE "DR. JEKYLL AND MR. HYDE" IN SIX DAYS AND NIGHTS OF COKE USE.

SOME SAY HE BASED THE CHARACTER'S MONSTROUS TRANSFORMATION ON THE EFFECTS OF THE DRUG.

PERHAPS THE MOST FAMOUS USER WAS ARTHUR CONAN DOYLE'S FICTIONAL DETECTIVE, SHERLOCK HOLMES.

I ABHOR THE DULL ROUTINE OF EXISTENCE.

IN 1886, GEORGIA DRUGGIST JOHN S. PEMBERTON CREATED A COCAINE-BASED "BRAIN TONIC." HE CALLED IT COCA-COLA.

COKE WAS ADVERTISED AS "THE DRINK THAT RELIEVES EXHAUSTION."

SOON, SOME CUSTOMERS WERE DRINKING 50 BOTTLES A DAY!

ONLY COCA-COLA GIVES ME THE ENERGY TO LUG AROUND ALL THESE EMPTIES!

DUE TO PUBLIC PRESSURE, COCAINE WAS FINALLY REMOVED FROM THE DRINK IN 1903-- AND REPLACED WITH CAFFEINE.

BESIDES THE USE IN TONICS, COCAINE BECAME A COMMON INGREDIENT IN CIG-ARETTES, CHEWING GUM, AND BEVERAGES.

AND THEY AL-WAYS COME BACK FOR MORE!

IN THE 1890S, COCAINE WAS POPULAR IN SOCIETY CIRCLES. SOME "SNUFF" WAS REALLY PURE COCAINE.

BUT THE REALITIES OF ADDICTION REACHED EVEN THE UPPER CRUST.

CHICAGO SOCIALITE ANNIE MEYERS TOOK A COCAINE-BASED PATENT POWDER TO RELIEVE A COLD.

AH! MY NOSE FEELS MUCH BETTER!

SOON, SHE WAS SNORTING COKE AROUND THE CLOCK.

A RECENT WIDOW, MEYERS WAS QUICKLY BROKE. SHE TURNED TO SHOPLIFTING AND FORGERY TO SUPPORT HER HABIT. SHE DANCED IN PUBLIC FOR SPARE CHANGE.

SHE EVEN PRIED OUT A GOLD TOOTH WITH SCISSORS AND HOCKED IT.

SHE WAS FINALLY ARRESTED TRYING TO BLOW A SAFE. BY THEN SHE HAD LOST MOST OF HER HAIR AND TEETH, AND PART OF HER JAW WAS ROTTED AWAY. SHE WEIGHED 80 LBS.

IN 1902, SHE PUBLISHED HER MEMOIRS, EIGHT YEARS IN COCAINE HELL.

THOUGH THE 1906 PURE FOOD AND DRUG ACT REMOVED COCAINE FROM MANY PRODUCTS, USE WAS STILL EPIDEMIC. AS MUCH COCAINE WAS SHIPPED TO THE U.S. IN 1906 AS IN 1976.

BY 1910, COCAINE'S IMAGE HAD CHANGED FROM GLAMOUR TO DEPRAVITY.

ADDICTS BECAME KNOWN AS "DOPE FIENDS."

I WISH HE'D STOP COMING BACK!

RACISM HELPED SHAPE PUBLIC OPINION OF THE DRUG. TESTIFYING TO CONGRESS IN 1914, DR. CHRISTOPHER KOCH SAID:

MOST OF THE ATTACKS UPON WHITE WOMEN OF THE SOUTH ARE THE DIRECT RESULT OF A COCAINE-CRAZED NEGRO BRAIN!

THE HARRISON NARCOTICS ACT SOON BANNED COCAINE.

POLICE DEPARTMENTS ADOPTED THE .38 SERVICE REVOLVER, BELIEVING THAT THE SMALLER .32 COULDN'T STOP A COCAINE-CRAZED BLACK MAN.

DON'T TAKE CHANCES, BOYS. I HEAR ONE OF 'EM TORE THE ARMS OFF A PATROLMAN.

DURING WORLD WAR I, BRITAIN BANNED COKE AMID RUMORS THAT GERMAN AGENTS WERE DEALING TO BRITISH TROOPS.

THE DRUG'S EVIL REPUTATION, COMBINED WITH HARSH LAWS, LED TO DIMINISHED USE FOR SEVERAL DECADES.

I'LL SHTICK T' TH' SHAFE SHTUFF!

COCAINE USE ROSE AGAIN AMID THE DRUG EXPERIMENTATION OF THE '60S.

THE COKE-DEALING HEROES OF 1969'S "EASY RIDER" HELPED PUT THE DRUG BACK ON THE CULTURAL MAP.

WITH ITS DANGERS LONG FORGOTTEN, COCAINE BECAME FASHIONABLE AGAIN.

CONFISCATIONS BY LAW-ENFORCEMENT ROSE 150% FROM 1967 TO 1970.

PEOPLE FLAUNTED THEIR DRUG USE. COCAINE PARAPHERNALIA BECAME A TRENDY ACCESSORY.

I DIG YOUR COKE SPOON!

COKE'S STIMULATING EFFECTS MADE IT POPULAR ON THE PARTY-ALL-NIGHT DISCO SCENE.

MANY BELIEVE THE U.S. AIDED DRUG LORDS IN RETURN FOR POLITICAL INFLUENCE IN LATIN AMERICA. TRUE OR NOT, OVER 50 TONS OF COCAINE POURED INTO AMERICA ANNUALLY.

IN THE LATE '80S, SOME STUDIES SHOWED THAT OVER 90% OF U.S. BILLS SHOWED TRACES OF THE DRUG.

BUT JUST AS IT HAD DECADES EARLIER, COKE'S GLAMOUR FADED AS ADDICTS BURNED OUT AND SMOKABLE CRACK COCAINE HIT THE STREETS.

CRACK QUICKLY DELIVERS A SHORTER, MORE INTENSE HIGH -- WITH A HEAVIER CRASH. IT'S EVEN MORE ADDICTIVE THAN POWDER COCAINE.

ONCE AGAIN, IMAGES OF COCAINE-CRAZED BLACKS APPEARED. MOST JAILED ON DRUG CHARGES ARE BLACK -- THOUGH BLACKS ARE ONLY 13% OF DRUG USERS.

NEWSTIME

INNER CITY CRACK PLAGUE!

RECENT STUDIES HAVE DEMONSTRATED COCAINE'S POWER. LAB MONKEYS PASS UP FOOD AND SEX TO GET MORE COKE.

HEAVY USE CAN CAUSE PARANOIA, PERSONALITY DISORDERS, EVEN FATAL CONVULSIONS.

ADDICTS OFTEN ENCOUNTER "COKE BUGS," THE SENSATION THAT INSECTS ARE CRAWLING BENEATH THE SKIN.

YAAAH! THEY'RE ALL OVER ME!!

ADDICTS HAVE BEEN KNOWN TO USE KNIVES -- AND EVEN BLOWTORCHES -- TO RID THEMSELVES OF THESE IMAGINED BUGS --

-- AND THEN IMMEDIATELY RETURN TO DOING MORE COKE.

NOW WHERE WAS I?

USE HAS SLOWED IN THE '90S AS A NEW GENERATION HAS LEARNED OF COKE'S HAZARDS.

BUT ITS ADDICTIVE POWER, PLUS THE $9 BILLION-A-YEAR TAKE OF U.S. TRAFFICKERS, SEEM TO ENSURE THAT THE CURSE OF THE INCAS WILL BE HERE A LONG TIME.

FACTOID BOOKS

HUMANITY HAS KNOWN THE POPPY AND ITS INTOXICATING EFFECTS FOR MILLENNIA, BUT ITS PRODUCTS—OPIUM, MORPHINE, AND HEROIN—CONTINUE TO BAFFLE SOCIETY.

THE POPPY'S STRANGE FRUIT

OPIUM IS A NARCOTIC MADE FROM THE SAP OF A TYPE OF POPPY. THE NAME COMES FROM A GREEK WORD FOR "PLANT JUICE."

THE ANCIENT GREEKS CONSIDERED OPIUM A CURE-ALL. THEY ALSO USED IT RECREATIONALLY IN CAKES AND CANDIES.

BECAUSE OF THE DROWSINESS OPIUM INDUCES, THE POPPY WAS ASSOCIATED WITH MORPHEUS, THE GOD OF DREAMS, AND THANATOS, THE GOD OF DEATH.

UNDER ALEXANDER THE GREAT, THE GREEKS SPREAD OPIUM TO PERSIA AND INDIA.

OPIUM BECAME POPULAR IN THE ISLAMIC WORLD, SINCE THE KORAN FORBADE ALCOHOL.

ARAB PHYSICIANS GAVE THE EARLIEST KNOWN DESCRIPTION OF OPIUM ADDICTION AROUND 1000 AD.

IN 1680, NOTED ENGLISH DOCTOR THOMAS SYDENHAM INTRODUCED A COMBINATION OF OPIUM AND SPICES IN WINE HE CALLED LAUDANUM.

AMONG THE REMEDIES WHICH IT HAS PLEASED ALMIGHTY GOD TO GIVE TO MAN TO RELIEVE HIS SUFFERINGS, NONE IS SO EFFICACIOUS AS OPIUM.

MORE LAUDANUM, DOCTOR—PLEASE!

BUT SYDENHAM ALSO FOUND THAT THE MIXTURE COULD BE ADDICTIVE.

IN 1805, FREDERICH SERTUENER ISOLATED OPIUM'S KEY COMPOUND. HE CALLED IT MORPHEUM, AFTER THE GOD MORPHEUS. HE WON THE NOBEL PRIZE FOR IT IN 1831.

ES IST POWERFUL SHTUFF!

MANY ARTISTS OF THE DAY SOUGHT INSPIRATION THROUGH OPIATES. SAMUEL TAYLOR COLERIDGE CLAIMED HE COMPOSED HIS MOST FAMOUS POEM IN AN OPIUM DREAM.

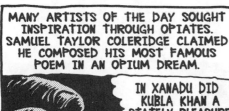

IN XANADU DID KUBLA KHAN A STATELY PLEASURE DOME DECREE...

IN 1840, NEW ENGLANDERS BROUGHT OVER 24,000 POUNDS OF OPIUM INTO THE U.S.

NOTING THE VOLUME OF THE TRADE, U.S. CUSTOMS ESTABLISHED AN IMPORT DUTY.

PRIOR TO ANESTHETICS, THE MOST COMMON SURGERY WAS AMPUTATION. STRONG MEN HELD THE PATIENT DOWN WHILE THE DOCTOR WORKED AS QUICKLY AS POSSIBLE.

THE HYPODERMIC SYRINGE, PERFECTED IN 1853, PROVED A MORE EFFECTIVE WAY TO ADMINISTER MORPHINE THAN ORAL USE.

AND, SINCE THE DRUG BYPASSES THE STOMACH, I BELIEVE THERE IS LITTLE RISK OF HABITUATION.

THE NEW OPIATES GAVE PHYSICIANS TIME TO WORK, MAKING MODERN SURGERY POSSIBLE.

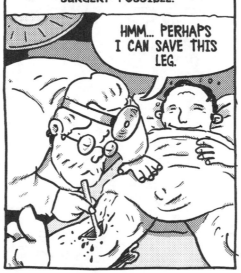

HMM... PERHAPS I CAN SAVE THIS LEG.

MORPHINE WAS WIDELY USED DURING THE CIVIL WAR, THE PRUSSIAN-AUSTRIAN WAR, AND THE FRANCO-PRUSSIAN WAR.

BUT ADDICTION OFTEN RESULTED -- A CONDITION KNOWN AS "SOLDIER'S DISEASE."

IN 1874, PHYSICIANS AT LONDON'S ST. MARY'S HOSPITAL CREATED A HIGHLY CONCENTRATED OPIATE APPROXIMATELY SIX TIMES STRONGER THAN MORPHINE.

MANUFACTURED BY THE BAYER COMPANY, THE NEW DRUG WAS NAMED HEROIN, DUE TO ITS "HEROIC" POWER TO RELIEVE PAIN.

BAYER HEROIN

BAYER HEROIN NATURE'S CURE-ALL

IT WAS SOLD OVER THE COUNTER AS A COUGH REMEDY. BAYER'S OTHER NEW WONDER DRUG, ASPIRIN, REQUIRED A PRESCRIPTION.

MORPHINE AND HEROIN WERE USED TO TREAT ALCOHOLISM. IT WAS EVEN BELIEVED THAT HEROIN COULD CURE MORPHINE ADDICTION.

OBSERVE, DOCTOR -- AFTER BEING TREATED WITH HEROIN, HIS CRAVING FOR MORPHINE HAS VANISHED!

CLEARLY, OPIATES WERE NOT WELL UNDERSTOOD AT THE TIME.

OPIATES ARE A DEPRESSANT, SLOWING BODY FUNCTIONS AND CAUSING DROWSINESS. THEY AFFECT THE BRAIN'S ENDORPHIN RECEPTORS, BLOCKING PAIN AND CAUSING A SENSE OF WELL-BEING.

HEROIN AT FIRST TRIGGERS A BRIEF EUPHORIC RUSH.

BUT THE USER'S TOLERANCE QUICKLY INCREASES, REQUIRING ESCALATING DOSES TO ACHIEVE THE SAME EFFECT.

IF USE IS STOPPED, WITHDRAWAL SYMPTOMS SOON BEGIN, INCLUDING NAUSEA, DIARRHEA, AND BODY PAINS.

TOO LARGE A DOSE CAN DEPRESS THE RESPIRATORY SYSTEM TO A FATAL EXTENT.

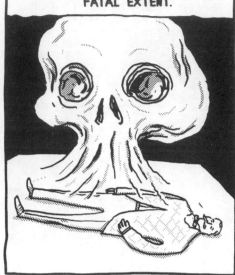

THE FIRST AMERICAN ANTI-DRUG LAW, ENACTED IN SAN FRANCISCO IN *1875*, OUTLAWED ONLY SMOKING OPIUM, SOMETHING PRACTICED MAINLY BY CHINESE IMMIGRANTS.

DEGENERATE (HIC) YELLA DEVILS!

IN THE *1890s*, TABLOIDS OWNED BY WILLIAM RANDOLPH HEARST RAN AN ANTI-DRUG CAMPAIGN THAT PLAYED UP THE FEAR OF THE "YELLOW PERIL."

MEANWHILE, OPIATES IN OTHER FORMS COULD BE PURCHASED IN ANY DRUGSTORE. SYRINGE KITS WERE EVEN ADVERTISED IN THE SEARS CATALOG.

MANY PATENT MEDICINES CONTAINED AS MUCH AS *50%* MORPHINE. LAUDANUM WAS CHEAPER THAN BEER OR WINE.

I NEEDED THAT!

BY *1900*, *75%* OF OPIATE ADDICTS WERE WOMEN. MOST BEGAN USING DRUGS FOR "FEMALE COMPLAINTS" —— OFTEN UNDER DOCTORS' ORDERS.

I TAKE IT EVERY DAY —— AND NO MORE CRAMPS!

THE LAW THAT MOST REDUCED ADDICTION WAS NOT A CRIMINAL STATUTE BUT THE *1906* PURE FOOD AND DRUG ACT. STRICT TESTING AND LABELING SOON TOOK MOST PATENT MEDICINES OFF THE MARKET.

WITH THE U.S. EMBROILED IN THE POLITICS OF THE OPIUM TRADE,* THE *1914* HARRISON NARCOTICS ACT SOUGHT TO REGULATE DRUG USE WITH STRICT TAX AND LICENSE REQUIREMENTS.

IT'S NOT A PROHIBITION, IT'S A TAX.

* SEE "THE OPIUM WARS"

THE LAW DID ALLOW A DOCTOR TO PRESCRIBE DRUGS "IN THE COURSE OF HIS PROFESSIONAL PRACTICE."

BUT AUTHORITIES SOON DECIDED THIS DIDN'T INCLUDE GIVING DRUGS TO MAINTAIN AN ADDICTION.

OVER THE NEXT 25 YEARS, AS MANY AS 25,000 PHYSICIANS WERE ARRESTED. 3,000 WENT TO PRISON AND THOUSANDS HAD THEIR LICENSES REVOKED.

DRUGS BECAME AN INCREASINGLY URBAN PROBLEM AS ADDICTS MOVED TO THE LARGER CITIES WHERE BLACK MARKETS EXISTED — BUT THESE SOURCES WERE EXPENSIVE AND UNRELIABLE.

THE HEALTH, BEHAVIOR, AND SOCIAL STATUS OF ADDICTS DECLINED QUICKLY AS MANY TURNED TO CRIME TO PAY FOR THEIR HABITS. THEY BEGAN TO FILL MENTAL ASYLUMS AND PRISONS.

AUTHORITIES BLAMED THE DETERIORATION OF ADDICTS ON INCREASED USE OF HEROIN OVER MORPHINE, THOUGH THERE'S LITTLE DIFFERENCE IN THE MEDICAL EFFECTS OF THE TWO.

SYMPTOMS OF HEROIN ADDICTION

IN *1924* ALL MANUFACTURE OF HEROIN WAS BANNED.

AGAIN, THE PAPERS RAN SCARE STORIES OF THE EFFECTS OF NARCOTICS ON RACIAL MINORITIES, AND THEIR HORRIBLE CRIMES AGAINST INNOCENT WHITES.

EXTRA! EXTRA! MORPHINE-MADDENED NEGRO SLAYS GOOD SAMARITAN!

NOT ONE OF THE STORIES USED TO PROMOTE THE EARLY DRUG LAWS CAN BE SUBSTANTIATED.

BY THE *1930*s, SOME BEGAN TO QUESTION THE DRACONIAN APPROACH. BERKELEY POLICE CHIEF AUGUST VOLLMER SAID:

VIGOROUS PROSECUTION OF ADDICTS AND PEDDLERS HAS PROVED NOT ONLY USELESS AND ENORMOUSLY EXPENSIVE BUT IS ALSO UNJUSTIFIABLY AND UNBELIEVABLY CRUEL!

HO HUM.

SOME COUNTRIES ALLOWED MEDICAL MAINTENANCE OR THE SUBSTITUTION OF THE LESS POTENT DRUG METHADONE. THIS REDUCED HABIT-SUPPORTING THEFT, AND MANY USERS WERE ABLE TO LEAD NORMAL LIVES — THOUGH THE ADDICTION REMAINED.

BUT MOST AMERICANS BELIEVED THEY NEEDED STRONG LAWS TO PROTECT THEM FROM DRUG-CRAZED MINORITIES. THE UNDERGROUND HEROIN TRADE GREW INCREASINGLY PROFITABLE.

IN THE '50s AND '60s, THE U.S. MARKET WAS DOMINATED BY CORSICAN GANGSTERS. TURKISH OPIUM WAS REFINED IN MARSEILLES, THEN SMUGGLED TO NEW YORK—

— AS SEEN IN THE FACT-BASED FILM "THE FRENCH CONNECTION."

IN VIETNAM, MANY WAR-WEARY SOLDIERS TRIED HEROIN. USAGE SOARED AT HOME AS G.I.s CAME BACK FROM OPIUM-RICH SOUTHEAST ASIA.

DURING THE WAR, U.S. INTELLIGENCE SUPPLIED WEAPONS TO ANTI-COMMUNIST WARLORDS — WHO ALSO CONTROLLED OPIUM PRODUCTION IN THE "GOLDEN TRIANGLE" OF LAOS, THAILAND, AND BURMA.

IN THE MID-'60s, THE CIA SET UP "AIR AMERICA" TO FLY OPIUM FROM BURMA AND LAOS. MUCH OF IT CAME TO THE U.S. VIA MARSEILLES.

THE NUMBER OF HEROIN USERS PEAKED AT ABOUT 750,000 IN THE LATE 1960s.

IN 1970, JANIS JOPLIN DIED OF AN OVERDOSE. HER DEATH AND OTHERS LIKE IT RAISED AWARENESS OF HEROIN'S DANGERS. WITH THE END OF THE WAR, USE WAS DECLINING.

IN THE 1980s, USERS ENCOUNTERED A NEW HAZARD — AIDS, SPREAD THROUGH SHARED NEEDLES.

BUT IN THE '90s, SOUTH AMERICAN COKE CARTELS BEGAN PUSHING HEROIN AS A NEW CASH CROP. "HEROIN CHIC" FLOURISHED BRIEFLY IN FASHION ADS AND FILMS LIKE "TRAINSPOTTING" AND "PULP FICTION."

GLOBAL HEROIN PRODUCTION HAS RISEN ABOUT 30% SINCE THE EARLY '90s. ABOUT HALF THE TOTAL IS CONSUMED IN THE U.S.

10% OF ADDICTS DIE EACH YEAR — BUT THE SUPPLY OF REPLACEMENTS CONTINUES UNABATED.

FOR OVER A CENTURY, THE OPIUM TRADE DRAINED THE WEALTH OF CHINA INTO THE COFFERS OF THE BRITISH EMPIRE. CHINA'S RESISTANCE TO THE DRUG FLOW LED TO...

THE OPIUM WARS

AFTER BEGINNING IN GREECE AND MESOPOTAMIA, THE CULTIVATION OF OPIUM POPPIES SPREAD INTO INDIA. ARAB TRADERS INTRODUCED OPIUM INTO CHINA IN THE 7TH CENTURY.

BUT OPIUM SMOKING DIDN'T CATCH ON IN THE FAR EAST UNTIL AFTER THE DISCOVERY OF AMERICA.

BY THE EARLY 1600s, THE USE OF PIPES TO SMOKE TOBACCO REACHED CHINA. SOON, PEOPLE BEGAN MIXING IN OPIUM.

REPORTS OF THE EVILS OF OPIUM GRADUALLY REACHED THE IMPERIAL PALACE.

...THE FEATURES OF THOSE WHO SMOKE OPIUM ARE SHRIVELED AND THEIR LIVES ARE SHORTENED...

IN 1729, EMPEROR YUNG CHEN BANNED ITS SALE OR USE.

IN 1750, THE BRITISH EAST INDIA COMPANY GAINED CONTROL OF BENGAL AND BIHAR AND WITH THEM THE HUGE OPIUM OUTPUT OF INDIA-- BUT WHAT TO DO WITH IT?

BRITAIN WAS THEN SPENDING VAST SUMS FOR CHINESE TEA. THE SOLUTION TO THIS TRADE IMBALANCE WAS OPIUM.

WE'LL SELL THE OPIUM TO THE CHINESE AND USE THE PROCEEDS TO BUY TEA TO SELL IN ENGLAND!

THE ONLY CATCH: SELLING OPIUM IN CHINA WAS ILLEGAL. SO THE BRITISH CONDUCTED THEIR DEALS OFFSHORE OR IN BRITISH-CONTROLLED ZONES, "LICENSING" CHINESE MER-CHANTS TO SELL THE 125 lb. CHESTS.

TRADE IN OPIUM GREW FROM 200 CHESTS IN 1729 TO 1,000 CHESTS IN 1767. IN 1796 THE EMPEROR ISSUED ANOTHER BAN ON THE IMPOR-TATION OF OPIUM AND THE EXPORT OF THE CHINESE SILVER USED TO BUY IT-- AGAIN TO NO AVAIL.

THE INCREASING USE OF THE DRUG DAMAGED CHINA BOTH SOCIALLY AND ECONOMICALLY. MEANWHILE, PORTS SUCH AS MACAO, WHERE GOVERNMENT CONTROL WAS WEAK, WERE BOOMING.

BY 1838, BRITISH SHIPS WERE BRINGING OVER 40,000 CHESTS OF OPIUM TO CHINA EACH YEAR. OPIUM ALONE REVERSED CHINA'S PREVIOUSLY FAVORABLE BALANCE OF TRADE.

THE EMPEROR WROTE QUEEN VICTORIA TO PROTEST BRITISH ACTIONS...

OPIUM IS VERY STRICTLY FORBIDDEN BY YOUR COUNTRY. THAT IS BECAUSE THE HARM CAUSED BY OPIUM IS CLEARLY UNDERSTOOD. LET US ASK: "WHERE IS YOUR CONSCIENCE?"

...HE RECEIVED NO REPLY.

FINALLY, THE EMPEROR APPOINTED A RADICAL PATRIOT NAMED LIN TSE-HSU TO THE POST OF IMPERIAL COMMISSIONER.

IN 1839, LIN TSE-HSU AND HIS IMPERIAL TROOPS ARRIVED IN CANTON, SEIZING AND DESTROYING OVER 20,000 CHESTS OF OPIUM.

OUTRAGED THAT CHINA SHOULD ATTEMPT TO ENFORCE ITS OWN LAWS, BRITISH MERCHANTS APPEALED TO THEIR GOVERNMENT. BRITISH WARSHIPS WERE DISPATCHED TO HONG KONG.

IN 1841, THE BRITISH FORCES EASILY TOOK THE WALLED CITY OF CANTON THANKS TO THEIR NAVAL ARTILLERY.

THE BRITISH SENT STILL MORE FIREPOWER. THE NEXT YEAR, THEY CAPTURED SEVERAL OTHER CITIES, INCLUDING SHANGHAI AND NANKING.

THE WAR WAS ENDED BY THE TREATY OF NANKING WHICH CEDED HONG KONG TO BRITAIN ALONG WITH AN INDEMNITY OF $21 MILLION. MORE PORTS WERE OPENED TO BRITISH TRADE WITH VERY LOW TARIFFS.

LIN TSE-HSU WAS OFFICIALLY DISGRACED FOR HIS ACTIONS IN CANTON AND SENT TO AN OBSCURE POST IN TURKESTAN.

HONG KONG, ONCE A QUIET FISHING VILLAGE, BECAME THE PRINCIPAL PORT FOR OPIUM.

FRANCE AND THE UNITED STATES SOON FORCED CHINA TO SIGN SIMILAR TRADE DEALS. MANY PROMINENT AMERICANS FOUND THE OPIUM TRADE QUITE LUCRATIVE.

BUT CHINA STILL RESISTED FOREIGN COMMERCE. IN 1856, CANTON POLICE SEIZED THE *ARROW*, A BRITISH-REGISTERED SHIP BEING USED BY CHINESE PIRATES.

BRITAIN, NOW JOINED BY FRANCE, AGAIN ATTACKED.

A NEW TREATY FORCED THE EMPEROR TO LEGALIZE OPIUM, BUT ALLOWED HIM TO TAX IT. BY 1858, 70,000 CHESTS OF OPIUM WERE BEING IMPORTED INTO CHINA EACH YEAR.

THE SAME TREATY REQUIRED CHINA TO PERMIT THE ENTRY OF CHRISTIAN MISSIONARIES.

SEEING NO WAY TO PROHIBIT OPIUM, THE CHINESE GOVERNMENT BEGAN PROMOTING DOMESTIC CULTIVATION, HOPING TO AT LEAST KEEP THE PROFITS INSIDE THE COUNTRY.

AFTER THE SPANISH-AMERICAN WAR THE U.S. INHERITED AN OPIUM PROBLEM OF ITS OWN IN THE NEWLY-ACQUIRED PHILIPPINES.

A COMMISSION OF INQUIRY SOON URGED THAT TREATIES BE DRAWN UP TO CONTROL THE DRUG TRADE. AMERICAN BUSINESS SAW THIS AS A POSSIBLE WAY TO END BRITISH COMMERCIAL DOMINANCE IN CHINA.

PRESIDENT THEODORE ROOSEVELT CALLED FOR AN INTERNATIONAL OPIUM CONFERENCE. CHINA SAW ITS CHANCE TO BE RID OF THE DRUG.

IN 1907, CHINA AND BRITAIN AGREED TO BEGIN PHASING OUT BOTH DOMESTIC CULTIVATION AND INDIAN IMPORTS.

BY 1917, CHINA WAS LARGELY FREE OF OPIUM, BUT THE LEGACY OF THE ERA REMAINS--

--THOUGH TODAY IT IS THE NATIONS OF THE WEST THAT ARE ON THE RECEIVING END.

CALLED **LA FÉE VERTE**, OR "THE GREEN FAIRIE", THIS POTENT EMERALD-GREEN LIQUEUR FASCINATED FRENCH CAFÉ SOCIETY AND MANY PROMINENT ARTISTS AND WRITERS FOR DECADES. IT WAS...

THE Age of ABSINTHE

DR. PIERRE ORDINAIRE, A FRENCH EXILE IN SWITZERLAND, FIRST DISTILLED ABSINTHE IN 1792 WHILE ATTEMPTING TO CREATE A TONIC.

THE BITTER LIQUEUR CONTAINED NUMEROUS HERBS OF SUPPOSED MEDICINAL VALUE...

EUREKA! HIC!

...AND AN ALCOHOL CONTENT OF NEARLY SEVENTY PERCENT.

PERHAPS THE MOST NOTABLE INGREDIENT WAS WORMWOOD--

--AN HERB USED TO TREAT WORMS AND OTHER INTESTINAL AILMENTS SINCE THE DAYS OF THE ANCIENT GREEKS.

IN 1797, ORDINAIRE'S HEIRS SOLD THE ABSINTHE RECIPE TO FRENCH DISTILLER HENRY-LOUIS PERNOD.

ABSINTHE REMAINED OBSCURE UNTIL THE 1840s, WHEN THE FRENCH SOLDIERS FIGHTING IN ALGERIA WERE ISSUED RATIONS OF THE DRINK TO PREVENT FEVERS.

WHEN THE TROOPS RETURNED HOME IN 1847, MANY HAD LEARNED TO LIKE ITS INTENSE BITTER FLAVOR.

WHEN SOLDIERS RETURNED FROM THE FRANCO-PRUSSIAN WAR IN 1871, ABSINTHE USE SPREAD RAPIDLY THROUGHOUT FRENCH SOCIETY.

I'LL HAVE WHAT THEY'RE HAVING...

THE DRINK'S UNUSUAL PREPARATION SEEMED TO ADD TO ITS EXOTIC ALLURE.

FIRST, THE ABSINTHE WAS POURED INTO A GLASS. A SPECIALLY PERFORATED SPOON WAS PLACED ON THE MOUTH OF THE GLASS AND SEVERAL SUGAR CUBES WERE PILED ON TOP.

COLD WATER WAS SLOWLY POURED OVER THE SUGAR. AS THE WATER DRIPPED INTO THE GLASS, THE ABSINTHE TURNED FIRST MILKY GREEN, THEN OPALESCENT.

FOR PARISIANS, THE LATE AFTERNOON ABSINTHE RITUAL GREW SO POPULAR THAT THE CUSTOMARY TIME BECAME KNOWN AS L'HEURE VERTE, OR "THE GREEN HOUR."

MANY ARTISTS, WRITERS, AND POETS TOOK TO THE DRINK, CLAIMING THAT THE NARCOTIC EFFECTS OF ABSINTHE PROVIDED UNIQUE INSPIRATION.

I'M FEELING INSPIRED...

...TO GET ANOTHER BOTTLE.

VERLAINE AND RIMBAUD BOTH WROTE ABOUT ABSINTHE'S SUPPOSED HALLUCINO-GENIC QUALITIES. VAN GOGH PAINTED MANY OF HIS FAVORITE ABSINTHE CAFÉS.

OSCAR WILDE ALSO HELPED TO POPULARIZE ABSINTHE.

AFTER THE FIRST GLASS YOU SEE THINGS AS YOU WISH THEY WERE. AFTER THE SECOND, YOU SEE THINGS AS THEY ARE NOT. FINALLY, YOU SEE THINGS AS THEY REALLY ARE...

...AND THAT IS THE MOST HORRIBLE THING IN THE WORLD.

NATURALLY, NEW ORLEANS WAS ALSO A STOP FOR ABSINTHE DEVOTEES.

SUCH NOTABLES AS ALEISTER CROWLEY, MARK TWAIN, WALT WHITMAN, AND WILLIAM HOWARD TAFT VISITED THE OLD ABSINTHE HOUSE IN THE FRENCH QUARTER.

BUT BY 1900, SOME CLAIMED THAT THUJONE, A TOXIN IN WORMWOOD, WAS CAUSING CONVULSIONS, MADNESS, AND VIOLENCE IN ABSINTHE DRINKERS-- THOUGH ALCOHOL WAS THE MORE LIKELY CULPRIT.

DEGENERACY
MURDER
MADNESS

BOTH THE WINE INDUSTRY AND PROHIBI-TIONISTS WERE QUICK TO BLAME FRANCE'S SOCIAL ILLS ON THE EMERALD DRINK.

ABSINTHE'S REPUTATION WASN'T HELPED BY THOSE USERS COMMITTING DRUNKEN OUTRAGES ON A DAILY BASIS.

YOU CALL THIS SERVICE? I'LL CUT YOU UP!

RIMBAUD SHOULD PUT MORE WATER IN IT.

ABSINTHE WAS OUTLAWED IN THE U.S. AND SWITZERLAND. SOON AFTER WORLD WAR I BEGAN, FEAR OF ITS EFFECTS ON TROOPS LED TO ITS BAN IN FRANCE.

CAN THESE WRETCHES DEFEAT THE HUN?

LESS POTENT REFORMULATIONS OF THE DRINK, THOUGH LEGAL, FAILED TO CAPTURE THE PUBLIC. AN AGE HAD COME TO AN END.

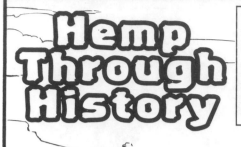

Hemp Through History

THE CANNABIS SATIVA AND CANNABIS INDICIA PLANTS ARE BETTER KNOWN AS HEMP OR MARIJUANA. WHEN SMOKED OR EATEN, THE LEAVES ARE A POWERFUL INTOXICANT.

MARIJUANA HAS BEEN KNOWN TO HUMANITY SINCE PREHISTORIC TIMES. THE PLANT FIBERS WERE USED TO MAKE FABRIC AND ROPE, THE SEEDS WERE EATEN, AND THE LEAVES AND FLOWERS WERE USED MEDICINALLY.

ANCIENT CHINESE DOCTORS RECOMMENDED HEMP FOR EVERYTHING FROM RHEUMATISM TO ABSENT-MINDEDNESS.

THE GREEK TRAVELER HERODOTUS DESCRIBED ITS USE IN FUNERAL RITES AMONG THE NOMADIC SCYTHIANS OF THE SIBERIAN STEPPES ABOUT 450 BC.

"IT SMOLDERS AND SENDS FORTH SUCH BILLOWS OF SMOKE THAT NO GREEK STEAMBATH COULD SURPASS IT," HE WROTE. "THE SCYTHIANS HOWL WITH PLEASURE."

HEMP'S INTOXICATING QUALITIES WERE ALSO NOTED BY THE ANCIENT GREEK PHYSICIAN GALEN WHO WROTE THAT ROMANS CONSUMED IT IN CAKES, CANDY, AND WINE TO "PROMOTE HILARITY AND ENJOYMENT."

THE CULTIVATION OF HEMP GRADUALLY SPREAD THROUGH MUCH OF EUROPE.

QUEEN ELIZABETH WAS SAID TO USE MARIJUANA TO RELIEVE MENSTRUAL CRAMPS. HER SUCCESSORS ORDERED COLONIAL AMERICAN FARMERS TO GROW HEMP TO SUPPLY RIGGING FOR THE BRITISH FLEET.

GEORGE WASHINGTON AND THOMAS JEFFERSON BOTH GREW HEMP--AND THE DECLARATION OF INDEPENDENCE WAS WRITTEN ON HEMP PAPER.

FOR REASONS UNKNOWN, WASHINGTON HAD HIS GARDENER REMOVE THE MALE PLANTS FROM THE HEMP CROP. WHICH, WHILE ADDING NOTHING TO IT'S ROPE-MAKING QUALITIES, WOULD MAKE THE DRUG MORE POTENT.

IN THE LATE 19TH CENTURY, HEMP WAS STILL COMMONLY USED IN MEDICINES AND ROPE, AND AS AN INTOXICANT.

MANY CANNABIS PREPARATIONS WERE AVAILABLE AT THE CORNER DRUGSTORE IN BOTH EUROPE AND NORTH AMERICA.

AT THE COLOMBIAN EXPOSITION OF 1894, THE TURKISH PAVILION GAVE OUT MAJOUN, A CANDY MADE WITH A CONCENTRATED HEMP EXTRACT CALLED HASHISH, TO ADVENTUROUS VISITORS.

BUT THIS CASUAL ACCEPTANCE OF MARIJUANA WOULD SOON END--AS WE SHALL SEE.

REEFER MADNESS

MARIJUANA: GROOVY TURN-ON, OR ASSASSIN OF YOUTH? THE PENDULUM OF PUBLIC OPINION CONTINUES TO SWING.

HEMP FIRST BECAME A PUBLIC ISSUE IN ENGLAND IN 1893 WHEN REPORTS FROM INDIA OF WILD BEHAVIOR LINKED TO MARIJUANA CAUSED THE BRITISH PARLIAMENT TO INVESTIGATE.

...THE WEIGHT OF EVIDENCE IS THAT THE MODERATE USE OF HEMP DRUGS IS NOT INJURIOUS...

IN THE EARLY 1900s, MARIJUANA CAME TO THE SOUTHWEST, BROUGHT BY MEXICAN LABORERS AS A CHEAP SUBSTITUTE FOR ALCOHOL. AT THE TIME, THERE WERE NO LAWS IN THE U.S. CONCERNING ITS USE.

THE HABIT SOON MOVED UP THE MISSISSIPPI RIVER TO OTHER PARTS OF THE COUNTRY. PROHIBITION IN 1919 ONLY HASTENED MARIJUANA'S SPREAD, MAKING IT PART OF THE JAZZ-AGE CULTURE.

A SECT OF MORMONS WHO MOVED TO MEXICO IN 1910 RETURNED SMOKING MARIJUANA. THE CHURCH SOON BANNED IT.

IN 1915, THE UTAH LEGISLATURE FOLLOWED SUIT, BECOMING THE FIRST STATE WITH AN ANTI-MARIJUANA STATUTE.

OTHER STATES DID LIKEWISE. THE GENERAL MOOD OF THE PROHIBITION ERA WAS PARTLY RESPONSIBLE—BUT OTHER FORCES WERE AT WORK.

ONE FACTOR WAS RACISM. IN THE WORDS OF A TEXAS LEGISLATOR SPEAKING IN FAVOR OF TEXAS' FIRST ANTI-MARIJUANA LAW:

ALL MEXICANS ARE CRAZY, AND THIS STUFF IS WHAT MAKES THEM CRAZY.

AS A MONTANA LEGISLATOR PUT IT:

GIVE ONE OF THESE MEXICAN BEET FIELD WORKERS A COUPLE OF PUFFS OF A MARIJUANA CIGARETTE AND HE THINKS HE IS IN THE BULL-RING AT BARCELONA!

OTHER STATES OUTLAWED MARIJUANA OUT OF FEAR THAT RECENT BANS ON OPIATES AND ALCOHOL WOULD DRIVE USERS TO THE WEED.

FORGET MORPHINE-- TRY SOME OF THIS "TEA".

IN 1932, TREASURY SECRETARY ANDREW MELLON APPOINTED HARRY J. ANSLINGER COMMISSIONER OF THE U.S. NARCOTICS BUREAU.

ANSLINGER SOON BECAME OBSESSED WITH "THE EVILS OF THE WEED."

HE LAUNCHED A HARD-HITTING MEDIA CAMPAIGN AGAINST MARIJUANA.

MARIHUANA
THE ASSASSIN OF YOUTH

IN A SERIES OF LURID EXPOSES, HE DESCRIBED CASES OF POT-CRAZED MURDERERS, UNSUSPECT- ING USERS DRIVEN TO SUICIDE, AND SCHOOL CHILDREN DRUGGED INTO SIN AND DEGRADATION--

--ALL ENTIRELY FICTITIOUS.

MOST NOTORIOUS WAS "REEFER MADNESS", RELEASED IN 1936. ORIGINALLY TITLED "TELL YOUR CHILDREN," THE FILM PAN- DERED TO AMERICA'S FEARS THAT MARI- JUANA WOULD TRANSFORM THEIR KIDS INTO MURDERERS AND DEGENERATES.

PUBLIC OPINION WAS TURNING AGAINST THE WEED. BY 1937, 46 STATES HAD BANNED THE DRUG, LARGELY DUE TO ANSLINGER'S EFFORTS.

MARIJUANA IS AN ADDICTIVE DRUG WHICH PRODUCES IN ITS USERS INSANITY, CRIMINALITY, AND DEATH.

UNABLE TO ACHIEVE FEDERAL PROHIBITION, ANSLINGER LOBBIED FOR A "TRANSFER TAX" ON MARIJUANA. NONPAYMENT WOULD CON- STITUTE A FEDERAL CRIME. IN HEARINGS, ANSLINGER CONTINUED HIS RANT.

YOU SMOKE THE WEED AND YOU'RE LIKELY TO KILL YOUR BROTHER.

IRONICALLY, THE ONLY VOICE RAISED AT THE HEARINGS IN DEFENSE OF MARIJUANA WAS THAT OF THE AMERICAN MEDICAL ASSOCIATION.

THE AMA KNOWS OF NO EVIDENCE THAT MARIJUANA IS A DANGEROUS DRUG.

DOCTOR, IF YOU CAN'T SAY SOMETHING GOOD, WHY DON'T YOU GO HOME?

IN 1937, CONGRESS PASSED BOTH THE TRANSFER TAX AND A LAW DECLARING MARIJUANA TO BE A NARCOTIC.

SINCE THIS IS YOUR FIRST OFFENSE, I CAN IMPOSE NO MORE THAN A TWENTY- YEAR SENTENCE.

ABOUT 250,000 AMERICANS BECAME CRIMINALS OVERNIGHT.

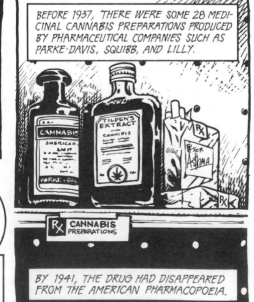

BEFORE 1937, THERE WERE SOME 28 MEDI- CINAL CANNABIS PREPARATIONS PRODUCED BY PHARMACEUTICAL COMPANIES SUCH AS PARKE-DAVIS, SQUIBB, AND LILLY.

Rx CANNABIS PREPARATIONS

BY 1941, THE DRUG HAD DISAPPEARED FROM THE AMERICAN PHARMACOPOEIA.

AT THE TIME THE NEW LAWS WENT INTO EFFECT, MORE THAN 10,000 ACRES OF HEMP WERE UNDER CULTIVATION. ANSLINGER BEGAN EFFORTS TO WIPE OUT THE PLANT.

BUT HEMP IS HARDY AND DIFFICULT TO ERADICATE. EVEN NOW, WILD HEMP IS NOT UNCOMMON IN MANY STATES.

WARNING
IT IS A FEDERAL OFFENSE TO PICK OR POSSESS HEMP!

DESPITE THE LAWS, POT SMOKING WAS COMMON IN '50s "ARTY" CIRCLES. BEAT POET ALLEN GINSBERG CHAMPIONED ITS USE.

POT IS FUN

BY THE EARLY '60s, REPORTS ON MIND-ALTERING DRUGS LIKE LSD CAUGHT THE PUBLIC'S INTEREST.

IN 1964, THE THELIN BROTHERS OPENED THE FIRST "HEAD SHOP"--SPECIALIZING IN DRUG-CULTURE PARAPHERNALIA--IN SAN FRANCISCO'S HAIGHT-ASHBURY DISTRICT.

SOON, HEAD SHOPS WERE OPENING ALL OVER THE COUNTRY.

GETTING HIGH BECAME AN INTEGRAL PART OF THE '60s HIPPIE SCENE.

EVERYBODY MUST GET STONED!

MARIJUANA WAS ALSO BEGINNING TO BE SEEN BY MANY AS AN APHRODISIAC. BY THE MID-SEVENTIES, A FIFTH OF AMERICANS HAD TRIED MARIJUANA.

DIG IT, MAN!

PUBLIC OPINION HAD SHIFTED. MARIJUANA WAS BECOMING COMMON EVEN IN SUBURBIA.

LAWS WERE LOOSENED. BETWEEN 1973 AND 1975, EIGHT STATES REDUCED MARIJUANA POSSESSION TO A MISDEMEANOR.

BUT IN THE '80s THE TIDE OF LAW AND PUBLIC OPINION TURNED AGAIN, MOST STATES RECRIMINALIZED MARIJUANA POSSESSION.

ONLY DOPES DO DOPE!
JUST SAY NO
JUST SAY NO
4 MORE YEARS

THE REAGAN ADMINISTRATION WENT TO NEW EXTREMES TO STOP ITS USE.

IN THE '90s, MARIJUANA HAS COME BACK AS BOTH A DRUG AND A FASHION STATEMENT. SOME SUPPORTERS CALL HEMP AN "ECO-FRIENDLY" SOURCE OF FIBER AND PAPER. OTHERS CLAIM VARIOUS MEDICAL BENEFITS.

JUDGING FROM THE PAST, THIS DEBATE WON'T END ANYTIME SOON.

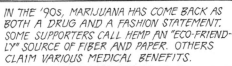

FACTOID BOOKS

PEYOTE, SACRED CACTUS of the SOUTHWEST

PEYOTE, OR MESCAL, IS A SMALL, BUTTON-SHAPED, BITTER-TASTING CACTUS FOUND ONLY NEAR THE RIO GRANDE. FOR OVER 3,000 YEARS, IT HAS BEEN USED IN NATIVE CEREMONIES TO INDUCE HALLUCINATORY VISIONS.

EARLY SPANISH EXPLORERS WITNESSED THE PEYOTE RITUALS. IN 1560, ONE WROTE: "THOSE WHO EAT OF IT SEE VISIONS EITHER FRIGHTFUL OR LAUGHABLE."

HORRIFIED BY ITS SEMI-MYSTICAL EFFECTS, THE SPANISH CALLED PEYOTE "RAIZ DIABOLICA" -- THE DIABOLICAL ROOT.

THEY TRIED STAMPING OUT PEYOTE BY TORTURING ITS USERS.

DESTROYING THE AZTEC TRADE ROUTES MADE PEYOTE AVAILABLE ONLY IN THE SMALL AREA WHERE IT GREW WILD.

AFTER THE CIVIL WAR, INCREASED CONTACT BETWEEN NATIVE PEOPLES IN MEXICO AND THE UNITED STATES BEGAN TO SPREAD PEYOTE USE NORTHWARD.

IN THE 1880s, JOHN WILSON, AN INDIAN LEADER IN THE GHOST DANCE MOVEMENT, LEARNED OF PEYOTE FROM A COMANCHE.

WILSON CLAIMED HE WAS SHOWN THE PROPER CEREMONIAL USE OF PEYOTE IN A VISION. HIS RITUALS SPREAD TO MORE THAN 50 TRIBES BY 1900.

IN OKLAHOMA IN 1907, THREE KICKAPOO INDIANS WERE ARRESTED AND FINED $25 FOR USING PEYOTE.

LAWS BANNING THE USE OF PEYOTE WERE ENACTED BY 11 SOUTHWESTERN STATES, BUT ITS USE STILL GREW.

IN 1918, MEMBERS OF MANY TRIBES MET IN OKLAHOMA TO CHARTER THE NATIVE AMERICAN CHURCH, AND ASSERT THEIR RIGHT TO USE PEYOTE.

BY THE EARLY 1920s, THERE WERE NEARLY 15,000 PEYOTISTS IN NORTH AMERICA.

BUT AS LATE AS THE 1950s, PEYOTE REMAINED UNKNOWN TO MOST NON-INDIANS, EXCEPT FOR A FEW PSYCHEDELICS RESEARCHERS SUCH AS ALDOUS HUXLEY.

IN 1960, COURTS OVERTURNED THE ARIZONA BAN, PROCLAIMING:

THE USE OF PEYOTE BY INDIANS IS CONSTITUTIONALLY PROTECTED.

OVER 250,000 PEOPLE — ABOUT HALF THE INDIAN POPULATION — NOW BELONG TO THE NATIVE AMERICAN CHURCH.

THE DRUG CULTURE OF THE '60s BROUGHT NEW ATTENTION TO PEYOTE AND ITS MOST POTENT DERIVATIVE, MESCALINE, SYN-THETIC MESCALINE BECAME MORE COMMON.

CHECK IT OUT — IT'S A TRIP!

ART KLEPS DISTRIBUTED PEYOTE ON THE STEPS OF THE JUSTICE DEPARTMENT BUILDING IN HONOR OF NIXON'S ELECTION.

DESPITE OR BECAUSE OF SUCH EFFORTS, PEYOTE WAS OUTLAWED FOR MOST AMERICANS UNDER THE FEDERAL DRUG ACTS OF 1968.

HOWEVER, RECENT DECISIONS HAVE CONTINUED TO ALLOW NATIVE AMERICAN USE, EVEN IN THE ARMED FORCES.

CAN'T SAY I APPROVE OF THIS, SOLDIER.

THAT'S RIGHT, SIR — YOU CAN'T!

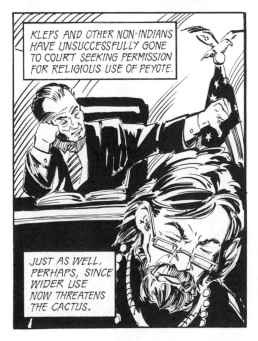

KLEPS AND OTHER NON-INDIANS HAVE UNSUCCESSFULLY GONE TO COURT SEEKING PERMISSION FOR RELIGIOUS USE OF PEYOTE.

JUST AS WELL, PERHAPS, SINCE WIDER USE NOW THREATENS THE CACTUS.

POSSIBLY THE SLOWEST-GROWING PLANT IN EXISTENCE, IT TAKES OVER THIRTEEN YEARS TO BLOOM FOR THE FIRST TIME.

ZZZZZZZZZZZZ

WHILE MOST NATIVE AMERICANS CUT ONLY THE TOP OF THE CACTUS, THE IGNORANT UPROOT THE WHOLE PLANT.

YOW!

PEYOTE HAS VANISHED FROM EASILY ACCESSIBLE AREAS. ONLY TIME WILL TELL IF IT CAN SURVIVE HUMAN INTEREST IN ITS PSYCHEDELIC POWERS.

FACTOID BOOKS
100% TRUE

IN THE SPRING OF 1943, A SWISS RESEARCH CHEMIST STUDYING ERGOT RYE-MOLD ALKALOIDS FOR SANDOZ, LTD. WAS ABOUT TO MAKE A DISCOVERY THAT WOULD CHANGE THE LIVES OF MILLIONS AND MAKE HIM--

WORKING ON DRUGS TO CONTROL POST-PARTUM BLEEDING AND CIRCULATORY DISORDERS, HOFFMAN SYNTHESIZED LYSERGIC ACID DIETHYLAMIDE (LSD) IN 1938, BUT IT PRODUCED LITTLE EFFECT ON ANIMALS.

BUT WHILE WORKING WITH IT AGAIN IN 1943, HE BECAME STRANGELY INEBRIATED. APPARENTLY HE HAD GOTTEN A SMALL AMOUNT OF LSD ON HIS SKIN.

THREE DAYS LATER HE TOOK THE DRUG INTENTIONALLY. THIS TIME THE EFFECTS WERE MUCH GREATER. HOFFMAN TRIED TO TAKE NOTES, BUT SOON COULDN'T WRITE.

5:00 PM: SLIGHT DIZZINESS, UNREST, DIFFICULTY IN CONCENTRATION, VISUAL DISTURBANCES, MARKED DESIRE TO LAUGH!

HOFFMAN AND HIS ASSISTANT THEN HEADED TOWARDS HOFFMAN'S HOUSE, ALBERT FELT LIKE HE WAS PEDALING FURIOUSLY, BUT NOT GETTING ANYWHERE.

BY THE TIME HE GOT HOME, EVERYTHING HAD BECOME TERRIFYING, BUT HOFFMAN KNEW HE HAD MADE AN AMAZING DISCOVERY.

NO OTHER SUBSTANCE COULD HAVE ANY EFFECT IN SUCH A TINY DOSAGE. LSD WAS OVER 5,000 TIMES STRONGER THAN EITHER MESCALINE OR PSILOCYBIN.

BY THE TIME A DOCTOR ARRIVED, HOFFMAN WAS EXPERIENCING AN INTENSE FEELING OF HAPPINESS ACCOMPANIED BY VIVID COLORS AND IMAGES.

HE SLEPT WELL THAT NIGHT AND WOKE UP THE NEXT DAY FEELING FINE.

FELLOW PROFESSOR ERNST ROTHLIN DOUBTED LSD COULD BE SO POWERFUL AND BELIEVED HIS WILL COULD SUPPRESS ITS EFFECTS. AFTER TAKING 1/4 OF HOFFMAN'S DOSE, ROTHLIN STOOD CORRECTED.

THE SOUNDS! EVERY SOUND WAS ACCOMPANIED BY A STREAM OF FANTASTIC IMAGES. IT WAS LIKE A KIND OF RAPTURE.

WHILE HOFFMAN OPPOSED RECREATIONAL USE OF LSD, HE CONTINUED HIS EXPERIMENTS, BELIEVING IN LSD'S SPIRITUAL AND THERAPEUTIC VALUE.

I REALIZED THAT WE HAVE THE CHOICE TO SEE THINGS IN DIFFERENT WAYS, THAT THERE IS NO SUCH THING AS AN OBJECTIVE REALITY.

FACTOID 100% TRUE BOOKS

A CONVENTIONAL PSYCHOLOGIST'S BELIEF IN THE CONSCIOUSNESS-EXPANDING BENEFITS OF LSD LED HIM TO BECOME FAMOUS AS...

TIMOTHY LEARY, PSYCHEDELIC GURU

TIM'S TEEN YEARS WERE MARKED BY A DRINKING SCANDAL AT WEST POINT AND HIS EXPULSION FROM THE UNIVERSITY OF ALABAMA FOR SLEEPING OVER AT THE GIRLS' DORMITORY.

OUT OF COLLEGE, TIM WAS DRAFTED, BUT WAS ALLOWED TO FINISH HIS DEGREE IN THE SERVICE. HE GOT MARRIED, AND LATER EARNED A DOCTORATE IN CLINICAL PSYCHOLOGY FROM THE UNIVERSITY OF CALIFORNIA.

BY THE MID-'50s, TIM WAS TEACHING AT BERKELEY AND WAS DIRECTOR OF PSYCHOLOGICAL RESEARCH AT THE KAISER FOUNDATION.

BUT HIS RESEARCH SHOWED THAT ABOUT A THIRD OF PSYCHOTHERAPY PATIENTS IMPROVED, A THIRD STAYED THE SAME, AND A THIRD GOT WORSE.

TIM CONCLUDED THAT PSYCHOTHERAPY WASN'T REALLY WORKING.

MEANWHILE, HIS OWN PERSONAL LIFE WAS FALLING APART. HIS WIFE, MARIANNE, SUFFERED FROM DEPRESSION, AND LEARY BEGAN AN AFFAIR.

HE WOKE UP ON HIS 35TH BIRTHDAY TO FIND THAT MARIANNE HAD COMMITTED SUICIDE.

IN A BLACK DEPRESSION, LEARY QUIT HIS JOB AND TRAVELED TO EUROPE.

IN SPAIN, TIM BECAME FEVERISH AND SANK INTO A PARALYSIS WHICH HE LATER DESCRIBED AS HIS FIRST BREAKDOWN-- AND BREAKTHROUGH.

AFTER HE RECOVERED, A COLLEAGUE, FRANK BARRON, TOLD LEARY HE'D HAD A RELIGIOUS EXPERIENCE AFTER EATING PSILOCYBIN MUSHROOMS IN MEXICO.

IRONICALLY, TIM WARNED HIM THAT SUCH BEHAVIOR ENDANGERED BARRON'S SCIENTIFIC CREDIBILITY.

VACATIONING IN CUERNAVACA IN 1960, TIM WAS GIVEN SOME PSILOCYBIN MUSHROOMS. REMEMBERING FRANK BARRON'S STORY, LEARY TRIED THEM.

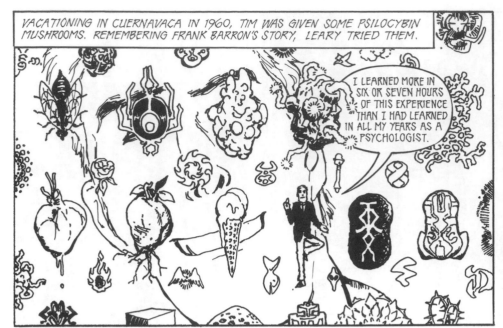

I LEARNED MORE IN SIX OR SEVEN HOURS OF THIS EXPERIENCE THAN I HAD LEARNED IN ALL MY YEARS AS A PSYCHOLOGIST.

TIM PERSUADED HARVARD TO LET HIM EXPERIMENT WITH PSILOCYBIN AND HE BEGAN WORKING WITH ASSISTANT PROFESSOR RICHARD ALPERT (LATER KNOWN AS THE SPIRITUALIST RAM DASS).

THE MORE TIME I SPENT WITH TIM, THE MORE I REALIZED HE HAD AN ABSOLUTELY EXTRAORDINARY INTELLECT.

ONE EXPERIMENT USED VOLUNTEER DIVINITY STUDENTS TO LEARN IF MYSTICAL VISIONS COULD BE INDUCED BY PSILOCYBIN.

I THINK I FEEL SOMETHING.

I...I SEE GOD. HE'S SO BEAUTIFUL.

IT WORKED.

TIM JOINED WITH ALDOUS HUXLEY AND ALLEN GINSBERG TO TURN ON PEOPLE SUCH AS WILLIAM BURROUGHS, JACK KEROUAC, AND THELONIUS MONK.

THOUGH HUXLEY BELIEVED ITS USE SHOULD BE RESTRICTED TO INTELLECTUALS, LEARY AND GINSBERG THOUGHT PSYCHEDELICS WERE GOOD FOR EVERYONE.

IN 1962 A BRITISH PHILOSOPHY STUDENT NAMED MICHAEL HOLLINGSHEAD APPEARED AT HARVARD WITH A JAR OF LSD.

HE TAUNTED LEARY, SAYING THAT COMPARED TO LSD, PSILOCYBIN WAS JUST "PRETTY COLORS." AGAIN, TIM TRIED IT.

IN LEARY'S WORDS, LSD "WAS SOMETHING DIFFERENT. IT WAS THE MOST SHATTERING EXPERIENCE OF MY LIFE."

LEARY BEGAN TO BELIEVE HE HAD FOUND THE KEY TO PSYCHOLOGICAL TRANSFORMATION.

BUT THE STUDENT EXPERIMENTS GENERATED TOO MUCH CONTROVERSY. BOTH THE NARCOTICS BUREAU AND THE CIA INQUIRED ABOUT LEARY'S RESEARCH.

IN 1963 LEARY AND ALPERT WERE ASKED TO LEAVE HARVARD.

DETERMINED TO CONTINUE, LEARY AND ALPERT MOVED TO A RAMBLING MANSION IN MILLBROOK, NEW YORK. IT BECAME A GATHERING PLACE FOR THE INTELLECTUAL AND HIP.

BUT IN THE MID-'60s, ANTI-DRUG SENTIMENT WAS ON THE RISE. G. GORDON LIDDY ACHIEVED NATIONAL ATTENTION WHEN HE LED A FRUITLESS RAID ON THE MILLBROOK HOUSE.

DEPRAVED INTELLECTUALS!

IN 1966, LIFE MAGAZINE ESTIMATED THAT OVER A MILLION PEOPLE HAD TAKEN LSD. ACID HORROR STORIES FILLED THE MEDIA, CAUSING THE SENATE TO INVESTIGATE LEARY AND OTHER LSD ADVOCATES.

WITH LITTLE EXPLANATION, LSD RESEARCH— CONSIDERED VALUABLE A FEW MONTHS BEFORE— WAS OUTLAWED.

TIM BECAME FRUSTRATED BY THE DISTORTIONS. HE CONSULTED MARSHALL McLUHAN TO LEARN TO USE THE MEDIA.

DREARY SENATE HEARINGS AND COURTROOMS ARE NOT THE PLATFORMS FOR YOUR MESSAGE. YOU MUST USE THE CORRECT TACTICS FOR AROUSING CONSUMER INTEREST.

TIM CAME UP WITH THE SLOGAN "TURN ON, TUNE IN, AND DROP OUT," MEANING "ACTIVATE YOUR NERVOUS SYSTEM, INTER-ACT HARMONIOUSLY WITH YOUR WORLD AND DETACH FROM UNCONSCIOUS COMMITMENTS."

HOWEVER, MOST OF THE PRESS TOOK THIS TO MEAN "GET STONED AND RUN AMOK." THE PHRASE HELPED GET LEARY ON RICHARD NIXON'S ENEMIES LIST.

TIMOTHY LEARY IS THE MOST DANGEROUS MAN IN AMERICA.

IN 1969 LEARY WAS ARRESTED FOR POSSESSION OF TWO JOINTS OF MARIJUANA. AND WAS SENTENCED TO TEN YEARS, REMAINING IMPRISONED WHILE AN APPEAL WAS SOUGHT.

LEARY WAS SENT TO A MINIMUM-SECURITY PRISON FROM WHICH HE ESCAPED, FLEEING TO SWITZERLAND TO MEET ALBERT HOFFMAN. LEARY WAS EXTRADITED TO THE U.S. IN 1972.

BUT ONCE NIXON WAS OUT OF OFFICE, TIM'S LEGAL PROBLEMS EASED. HE WAS FREED IN 1976.

DURING THE NEXT FIFTEEN YEARS, TIM LECTURED AT COLLEGES AND EVEN TRIED STAND-UP COMEDY AND ON-STAGE DEBATES WITH G. GORDON LIDDY.

LEARY BEGAN TO HYPE THE CONSCIOUSNESS-EXPANDING POTENTIAL OF COMPUTERS, WHICH HE BELIEVED WOULD BE THE LSD OF THE '90s.

IN 1995 TIM LEARNED HE HAD INOPERABLE PROSTATE CANCER. THE PROSPECT OF DEATH FASCINATED HIM.

THE TWO MINUTES BETWEEN BODY DEATH AND BRAIN DEATH... THAT'S THE TERRITORY.

TIM DIED ON MAY 13, 1996, AFTER ARRANGING FOR HIS CREMATED REMAINS TO BE LAUNCHED INTO SPACE.

TO SOME, LEARY WAS AN EXPLORER OF INNER SPACE AND A POLITICAL HERO. TO OTHERS, HE WAS A DRUG PUSHER RESPONSIBLE FOR A GENERATION OF FREAK-OUTS.

OF COURSE, AS HE HIMSELF WAS FOND OF SAYING...

YOU GET THE TIMOTHY LEARY YOU DESERVE.

AMERICA'S HIDDEN PLAGUE

PRESCRIPTION DRUGS CAUSE MORE HARM EACH YEAR THAN ALL OTHER DRUGS SAVE ALCOHOL AND TOBACCO, YET AMERICA ATTACHES LITTLE STIGMA TO PRESCRIPTION DRUG ABUSE...

UNTIL THE LAST FEW DECADES, OPIATES, BARBITURATES, AND AMPHETAMINES ACCOUNTED FOR MOST PRESCRIPTION DRUG ABUSE.

EACH DRUG INNOVATION SEEMS TO BRING WITH IT A NEW WAVE OF MISUSE.

FIRST SYNTHESIZED IN 1864, BARBITURATES WERE WIDELY OVERPRESCRIBED DURING THE FIRST HALF OF THIS CENTURY, WITH OVER ⅔ OF THE PRESCRIPTIONS GOING TO WOMEN.

PRESCRIPTION MOTHER'S LITTLE HELPER

BY 1969 OVER 400 TONS OF BARBITURATES AND 750 TONS OF OTHER TRANQUILIZERS WERE PRODUCED IN THE U.S.

MURK PHARMACEUTICALS

I HAVE ANOTHER LOAD OF SECONAL TO DELIVER. YOU GOT ANY "GO PILLS?"

KEEP ON TRUCKIN'

AMPHETAMINES WERE CREATED DURING WORLD WAR II BY A BRITISH SCIENTIST LOOKING FOR SYNTHETIC EPHEDRINE TO TREAT ASTHMA.

IT OPENS YOUR SINUSES AND MAKES YOU FEEL LIKE CLEANING YOUR GARAGE!

AFTER THEIR ABILITY TO RELIEVE FATIGUE WAS DISCOVERED, BENZEDRINE TABLETS AND AMPHETAMINE NASAL SPRAYS WERE INCLUDED IN SOLDIERS' KITS. WHEN THE WARS WERE OVER, THE HABIT OFTEN LINGERED.

GOTTA GET READY TO "HIT THE BEACH" AGAIN.

SAMPLES

PROLONGED AMPHETAMINE USE CAN CAUSE PARANOID DELUSIONS. ONCE PRESCRIBED FOR ASTHMA, DEPRESSION, AND OBESITY, LEGAL USE IS RARE NOW--

ANGELS OF METH

--BUT METHAMPHETAMINE, OR SPEED, IS WIDELY MADE IN UNDERGROUND LABS.

TWELVE OF THE TOP 20 MOST ABUSED CONTROLLED SUBSTANCES IN THE U.S. ARE PRESCRIPTION DRUGS.

METAL

TODAY, AFTER COCAINE, HEROIN, AND MARIJUANA, THE MOST COMMONLY ABUSED DRUGS ARE THE SEDATIVES XANAX, VALIUM, AND ATIVAN.

IN 1994 MORE THAN 69,000 EMERGENCY ROOM VISITS INVOLVED THE ABUSE OF BENZODIAZEPINES, TRANQUILIZERS SUCH AS VALIUM AND LIBRIUM.

MERGENCY

PRESCRIPTION DRUG OVERDOSES OUTNUMBER HEROIN OVERDOSES 6 TO 1.

PRESCRIPTION DRUG ADDICTS AND THEIR FAMILIES ARE OFTEN IN DENIAL BECAUSE THE DRUGS COME FROM HEALTH CARE PROFESSIONALS.

OH, THAT'S JUST MOM! HER MEDICINE MAKES HER A LITTLE GOOFY SOMETIMES.

SOMETIMES FAMILY MEMBERS ARE DIRECTLY INVOLVED IN PRESCRIPTION DRUG ABUSE.

GRANDDAD'S YELLING AGAIN, DEAR. CAN'T YOU GIVE HIM ONE OF THOSE PILLS?

IN 1993, OVER $25 BILLION IN PRESCRIPTION DRUGS WERE SOLD ON THE BLACK MARKET.

TWO FOR GRANDDAD AND TWO TO SELL AT BINGO.

THOUGH SOME ARE SMUGGLED FROM ABROAD, MOST PRESCRIPTION DRUGS COME FROM MEDICAL OFFICES AND PHARMACIES.

HOPE YOUR "LUMBAGO" GETS BETTER.

ONE TO 1.5% OF PHYSICIANS KNOWINGLY PRESCRIBE TO ABUSERS. ANOTHER 5% ARE SIMPLY NEGLIGENT.

THE STRENGTH AND PURITY OF PRESCRIPTION DRUGS PUTS THEM AT A PREMIUM ON THE BLACK MARKET.

A PILL COSTING $2 CAN RESELL FOR $100.

SOME USERS FAKE INJURIES TO GET PRESCRIPTIONS, OTHERS FORGE PRESCRIPTIONS ON STOLEN PADS.

IT HURTS SO MUCH, DOCTOR.

THERE, THERE.

ONE WOMAN CONNED OVER 60 SAN DIEGO DOCTORS AND PHARMACIES INTO GIVING HER CODEINE TABLETS.

DOCTORS CAUGHT WRITING ILLEGAL PRE-SCRIPTIONS RECEIVE TINY SENTENCES COMPARED TO PEOPLE SELLING "STREET" DRUGS.

OF THE $13 BILLION A YEAR SPENT FIGHTING DRUGS, ONLY 0.5% IS AIMED AT PRESCRIPTION DRUG ABUSE.

UNTIL WE FACE THE IMMENSE ROLE ALL DRUGS PLAY IN OUR SOCIETY, PRESCRIPTION DRUGS WILL REMAIN A HIDDEN PROBLEM IN AMERICA.

FACTOID 100% TRUE BOOKS

CAFFEINE FIENDS

ACCORDING TO LEGEND, AN ETHIOPIAN HERDSMAN'S GOATS BECAME STRANGELY FRISKY. HE SAMPLED THE BERRIES THEY'D BEEN EATING--AND DISCOVERED COFFEE.

IT WAS CAFFEINE, A STIMULANT IN THE BEANS, THAT MADE THE GOATS SO LIVELY. EVENTUALLY, THE BEANS WERE BREWED WITH WATER TO MAKE A DRINK.

A TYPICAL CUP CONTAINS 100 MILLIGRAMS OF CAFFEINE.

CAFFEINE CAN BE HABIT-FORMING (JUST ASK A REGULAR DRINKER BEFORE HE'S HAD HIS FIRST CUP).

WITHDRAWAL SYMPTOMS CAN INCLUDE HEADACHES AND MOOD SWINGS.

FROM THE BEGINNING, ATTEMPTS HAVE BEEN MADE TO REGULATE THE BREW.

SOME MUSLIM CLERICS CONSIDERED COFFEE AN INTOXICANT AND TRIED TO BAN IT--BUT SOON COFFEE WAS PART OF ARAB CULTURE.

AROUND 1600, AS COFFEE SPREAD TO EUROPE, PRIESTS CALLED UPON THE POPE TO DENOUNCE IT. AFTER SAMPLING IT, CLEMENT VIII SAID:

THIS SATAN'S DRINK IS SO DELICIOUS THAT IT WOULD BE A PITY TO LET THE HEATHENS HAVE EXCLUSIVE USE OF IT.

IN 1656, THE GRAND VIZIER OF THE OTTOMAN EMPIRE OUTLAWED COFFEE. VIOLATORS WERE PUT IN LEATHER SATCHELS AND THROWN IN THE BOSPORUS STRAIT.

NEXT TIME I'LL HAVE DECAF!

THE LAW DIDN'T LAST.

CHINESE TEA CAME TO ENGLAND ABOUT 1640. CHARLES II ORDERED COFFEE AND TEA HOUSES CLOSED IN 1675, BUT PUBLIC OUTCRY CAUSED AN IMMEDIATE REPEAL.

STIFF TEA TAXES WERE THEN IMPOSED, SO MANY BRITONS TURNED TO SMUGGLING.

KOLA NUTS, USED IN SOFT DRINKS, CONTAIN CAFFEINE NATURALLY-- BUT MANUFACTURERS ADD MORE.

THE AVERAGE U.S. KID NOW DRINKS OVER 64 GALLONS OF SODA PER YEAR. A TYPICAL 12 OZ. CAN HAS 50 MILLIGRAMS OF CAFFEINE.

WORLDWIDE, WE DRINK OVER 400 BILLION CUPS OF COFFEE EACH YEAR--

--MAKING IT SECOND ONLY TO OIL AS THE MOST VALUABLE COMMODITY IN GLOBAL TRADE.

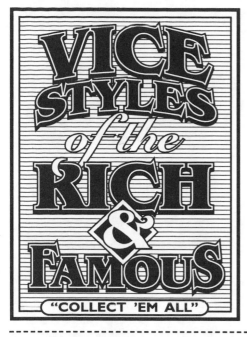

VICE STYLES of the RICH & FAMOUS

"COLLECT 'EM ALL"

CARY GRANT

SIGMUND FREUD

JUDY GARLAND

ADOLF HITLER

ALDOUS HUXLEY

LUGOSI & LORRE

ULYSSES GRANT

CLARE BOOTHE LUCE

VICE STYLES OF THE RICH AND FAMOUS
SIGMUND FREUD
(1856–1939)

FREUDIAN SNIFF: The father of psycho-analysis was an early proponent of cocaine, calling it a "magical drug," and recommending it for various physical and psychological ailments—including addiction to other drugs. Freud himself used it for many years; as a result, he suffered nasal sores and bleeding—which he treated with more cocaine. He later admitted his enthusiasm for the drug had been a great mistake. Freud delved deeply into the sexual symbolism in our everyday lives, but is also said to have admitted, "sometimes a cigar is just a cigar." In his case, it proved to be a death sentence—habitual cigar smoking led to his slow, painful demise from cancer of the jaw.

VICE STYLES OF THE RICH AND FAMOUS
CARY GRANT
(1904–1986)

CARYING ON: The legendary movie star was rarely taken seriously as an actor; many felt he was "just playing himself" onscreen. But the role was actually a difficult one; he began taking LSD under a psychiatrist's care in 1958 to help himself deal with the conflicts between his Hollywood persona of debonair Cary Grant and his natural-born identity of cockney Archibald Leach. Grant tripped more than 100 times, and claimed the drug helped him find peace of mind. He spent time with others intrigued by the drug, including Aldous Huxley, as well as with a young psychologist who was deeply impressed by the actor: "In a sense, Cary Grant got me into psychedelic experiences," Dr. Timothy Leary later said.

VICE STYLES OF THE RICH AND FAMOUS
ALDOUS HUXLEY
(1894–1963)

BRAVE NEW WORD: The British author moved to Los Angeles in 1947 and grew interested in mysticism. An early researcher into "psychedelics" (and partly responsible for coining the word), Huxley first took mescaline with psychologist Humphry Osmond in 1953 and was amazed at the drug's ability to elicit mystical experience. Huxley wrote about his experiments in *The Doors of Perception*, marking the real beginning of the psychedelic movement; he further explored the subject in *Heaven and Hell*. Huxley also participated in Timothy Leary's psilocybin experiments at Harvard in 1963. He was convinced of the value of drug-induced spiritual experiences. On his deathbed, Huxley requested that his wife inject him with LSD.

VICE STYLES OF THE RICH AND FAMOUS
ADOLF HITLER
(1889–1945)

HIGH HITLER: Hitler's own indoctrination in the twisted ideals of Aryan supremacy involved drugs. Dietrich Ekhart, a magician of the German occult Thule Society, gave Hitler a concoction made from peyote so the future führer could experience "Aryan racial memories." The Society believed that the ascended masters of Thule, a sort of icy Aryan Atlantis, could reveal their mystical secrets to the initiated. Hitler also wrote admiringly of cocaine. He wasn't the only high-level Nazi into drugs; after receiving morphine for a wound suffered in the failed Munich putsch of 1923, Hermann Goering remained addicted most of his life. He took Demerol to make it through the Nuremberg trials, then killed himself with a concealed poison capsule.

VICE STYLES OF THE RICH AND FAMOUS
JUDY GARLAND
(1922–1969)

THE END OF THE RAINBOW: MGM wanted to turn plump teenage vaudeville singer Frances Gumm into slender movie star Judy Garland. She was given amphetamines to curb her appetite; when those left her wired, she was given barbiturates to help her sleep; then more amphetamines to get her up for early-morning filming. She soon grew dependent on the pills, and alcohol as well. She tried detox hospitals, shock treatment, and hypnotism, but the pressures of work, weight, and her own insecurities caused repeated relapses. Still in her twenties, she began losing jobs; her finances became precarious. Though she made several brief, triumphant comebacks, the downward slide continued. She died of an overdose of sleeping pills.

VICE STYLES OF THE RICH AND FAMOUS
CLARE BOOTHE LUCE
(1903–1987)

LUCE TRIPS SINK YIP: At the 1972 Republican Convention, radical protester Abbie Hoffman encountered Luce—playwright, congresswoman, wife of Time-Life founder Henry Luce, and conservative G.O.P. icon. He tried to shake her by asking if she'd ever dropped acid, but it was the Yippie leader who was shaken as Clare calmly told him of her experiences with LSD, which both she and her husband had taken several times during a research project. She felt the drug had great promise, and wrote about her trips in her diaries, including one memorable note to herself to "capture green bug for future reference." She received the Presidential Medal of Freedom from Ronald "Just Say No" Reagan in 1983. Her diaries, detailing her drug use, were made public in 1997.

VICE STYLES OF THE RICH AND FAMOUS
ULYSSES GRANT
(1822–1885)

GRANT'S TOME: Ulysses Grant was a notorious drinker; during the Civil War, many urged President Abraham Lincoln to fire him. But Grant was the Union's most successful leader; Lincoln is said to have suggested, instead, that a large supply of whatever Grant was drinking be sent to all his other generals. While president, Grant smoked heavily—25 cigars a day. After leaving office, he lost all his money in a stock swindle; he also developed oral cancer. Broke and in pain, Grant began writing his memoirs to make money to leave his family. He used cocaine, morphine injections, and morphine-and-brandy cocktails to see him through; he finished the popular book shortly before his death.

VICE STYLES OF THE RICH AND FAMOUS
PETER LORRE (1904–1964)
BELA LUGOSI (1884–1956)

THE HUNGARIAN CONNECTION: Both men found success playing Hollywood heavies—and both met sad ends due to morphine addiction. Director Billy Wilder, a fellow European expatriate, roomed with Lorre in the '30s—and noted the ugly effects of his addiction even then. Due largely to his habit, Lorre's early roles in such classics as *M* and *Casablanca* gave way to parts in "B" horror films and a final appearance in a Jerry Lewis movie. Lugosi never matched his initial success as *Dracula*; substance abuse and too many bad career choices left him working with the notorious Ed Wood for $1000 per film. He checked himself into drug rehab in 1955; he died soon after getting out, during the filming of the infamously bad *Plan 9 From Outer Space*.

CHAPTER FOUR

TOBACCO

Tobacco has the distinction of being the most practiced, yet least cherished vice of them all. Almost everyone who smokes wishes they didn't. Smoking makes your breath smell bad. It stinks up your clothes. Non-smokers treat you like a pariah when you light up. And did we mention that it can (and probably will) eventually kill you?

More people are addicted to tobacco than to any other substance in history — and with good reason. Tobacco IS a miracle drug. What other drug can wake you up when you feel tired, or calm you down when you're tense? What other drug can do EITHER of those things depending on your need at the moment — and yet not dull or oversharpen your brain, or leave you with a hangover, or make you sick to your stomach, or even cause you to overdose? Besides, smoking makes you look glamorous (just like grown-ups and/or movie stars), and cigarettes and cigars give you something to do with your hands at parties. Sounds great, no? There are only two problems. One is a little ingredient called nicotine. That's the stuff that gets you hooked. Then there's the other stuff — the stuff that can (and probably will) eventually kill you.

Oddly enough, the potential for lung cancer, emphysema, heart attacks and a host of other life-terminating diseases isn't reason enough for most people to quit smoking. In some way, the addictive power of the smoke makes that understandable. More problematic is that knowing about those serious illnesses isn't enough to prevent people from starting to smoke. As we will see, the continuing success of tobacco is a testament to the effectiveness of American manufacturing knowhow, marketing, and sly legal maneuvering, all to benefit a product that can (and probably will) eventually kill you.

And that's what makes tobacco the most amazing and dangerous vice of them all..

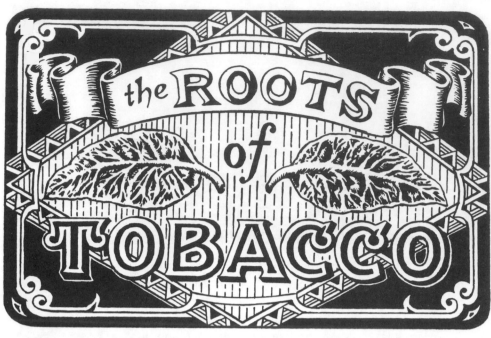

the ROOTS of TOBACCO

TOBACCO ORIGINALLY GREW WILD IN THE NEW WORLD.

NATIVES PRESUMABLY FIRST ENCOUNTERED ITS EFFECTS BY ACCIDENT WHILE USING IT AS FIRE FUEL.

THE PLANT TOOK ON AN IMPORTANT ROLE IN MAYAN RITUALS, AND IT WAS CULTIVATED BY PRIESTS.

AS TOBACCO SPREAD THROUGHOUT THE AMERICAS, IT WAS USED FOR RELIGIOUS, RECREATIONAL, AND MEDICINAL PURPOSES.

BESIDES BEING SMOKED IN PIPES AND IN ROLLED-UP LEAVES, IT WAS CHEWED, USED IN POULTICES, AND IN ENEMAS.

COLUMBUS WAS GIVEN TOBACCO BY NATIVES ON HIS FIRST DAY IN THE NEW WORLD.

NOT KNOWING WHAT TO DO WITH THE TOBACCO, COLUMBUS THREW IT AWAY.

SOON COLUMBUS'S MEN OBSERVED THE NATIVES' PRACTICES, WHICH THEY DESCRIBED AS "DRINKING SMOKE."

RODRIGO DE JEREZ BECAME THE FIRST EUROPEAN TO DEVELOP THE TOBACCO HABIT.

BUT WHEN RODRIGO RETURNED TO SPAIN, HIS NEIGHBORS WERE TERRIFIED TO SEE SMOKE POURING FROM HIS HEAD.

SURE THAT HE WAS IN LEAGUE WITH THE DEVIL, THE INQUISITION IMPRISONED HIM FOR SEVEN YEARS.

AS THE CONQUISTADORS EXPANDED SPAIN'S NEW WORLD EMPIRE, MORE OF THEM TOOK UP SMOKING.

THEY ALSO LEARNED OF ITS ADDICTIVE NATURE. A BISHOP REPORTED THAT ALTHOUGH HE CONDEMNED TOBACCO, THE MEN "FOUND IT IMPOSSIBLE TO GIVE IT UP."

RETURNING SEAMEN SPREAD TOBACCO TO EUROPE. BY THE EARLY 16TH CENTURY, CIGARS (FROM "SIK'AR", THE MAYAN WORD FOR SMOKING) WERE FASHIONABLE AMONG SPANISH GENTRY...

...AND THE POOR DEVELOPED A HABIT OF THEIR OWN — ROLLING THE REMAINS OF DISCARDED BUTTS IN PAPER TO MAKE MINI-CIGARS, OR "CIGARILLOS."

BY THE MID-1500s, TOBACCO WAS BEING GROWN ON A SMALL SCALE IN SEVERAL EUROPEAN COUNTRIES. IT WAS TOUTED AS A CURE FOR NUMEROUS AILMENTS, BOTH HUMAN--

--AND ANIMAL.

STICK IT IN -- 'TIS A REMEDIE MOST MARVELOUS.

IN 1566, JEAN NICOT, THE FRENCH AMBASSADOR TO PORTUGAL, SENT SNUFF TO CATHERINE DE MEDICI, WHO DUBBED IT "THE QUEEN'S HERB."

AAA-;CHOOO!-

NICOT ALSO LENT HIS NAME TO BOTH TOBACCO'S GENUS, NICOTIANA, AND ITS PRIMARY PSYCHOACTIVE COMPONENT, NICOTINE.

IN 1542, SHIPWRECKED PORTUGUESE SAILORS BECAME THE FIRST EUROPEANS-- AND THE FIRST SMOKERS--TO SET FOOT IN JAPAN.

MANY MORE FOLLOWED IN THE NEXT 50 YEARS, SPREADING THE HABIT.

THE RULING SHOGUNS TRIED TO STOP IT, BUT JAPANESE SMOKERS IGNORED INCREASINGLY SEVERE SANCTIONS--INCLUDING IMPRISONMENT AND PROPERTY CONFISCATION.

FINALLY IN 1625 THE RULERS BOWED TO THE INEVITABLE AND ALLOWED TOBACCO CULTIVATION.

AS THEY CONTINUED TO EXPLORE THE GLOBE, THE SPANISH AND PORTUGUESE PLANTED TOBACCO ALONG THE WAY--

--TO FEND OFF THE PANGS OF WITHDRAWAL ON FUTURE VOYAGES.

LOCALS, TOO, DISCOVERED THE ADDICTIVE NATURE OF THE PLANT.

FOLLOWING A CROP FAILURE ON THE ISLE OF NIAS OFF SUMATRA, NATIVES DESPERATELY GREETED THE NEXT SHIP:

WE DIE, SIR, IF WE HAVE NO TOBACCO!

BY 1600, PORTUGUESE TRADING POSTS COMPLETE WITH TOBACCO FARMS WERE IN PLACE ON ALL MAJOR SEA ROUTES.

TOBACCO HAD LITERALLY TAKEN ROOT AROUND THE WORLD.

FACTOID BOOKS

SEEDS of a NATION

A SINGLE BATCH OF TOBACCO SEEDS PLAYED A PIVOTAL ROLE IN THE GROWTH OF THE AMERICAN COLONIES--AND THE BIRTH OF THE UNITED STATES.

WHILE SPAIN AND PORTUGAL SPENT MUCH OF THE 16TH CENTURY EXPLOITING THE NATURAL RICHES OF THEIR NEW-WORLD POSSESSIONS--INCLUDING TOBACCO--

--ENGLAND WAS UNABLE TO ESTABLISH A SUCCESSFUL SETTLEMENT IN THE VAST AREA OF NORTH AMERICA.

ONE NOTABLE FAILURE WAS ROANOKE ISLAND, ESTABLISHED IN 1587 UNDER GOVERNOR JOHN WHITE. WHITE SOON WENT BACK TO ENGLAND FOR SUPPLIES--

--BUT BRITAIN'S ONGOING CLASH WITH SPAIN PREVENTED HIS RETURN UNTIL 1590. BY THEN, THE COLONY HAD VANISHED, LEAVING ONLY A MYSTERIOUS WORD CARVED ON A TREE.

WHITE DID BRING SOME TOBACCO SEEDS TO ENGLAND FOR THE COLONY'S SPONSOR, SIR WALTER RALEIGH, WHO EXPERIMENTED WITH THEIR CULTIVATION.

RALEIGH HAD BEEN INTRODUCED TO TOBACCO A FEW YEARS BEFORE BY THE MARINER SIR FRANCIS DRAKE. AS A FAVORITE OF QUEEN ELIZABETH, RALEIGH POPULARIZED SMOKING AMONG HER COURTIERS.

RALEIGH SOON FELL OUT OF ROYAL FAVOR--AS DID TOBACCO. IN 1604, KING JAMES I WROTE "A COUNTERBLASTE TO TOBACCO." HE CALLED IT...

LOATHSOME TO THE EYE, HATEFUL TO THE NOSE, HARMFUL TO THE BRAIN, DANGEROUS TO THE LUNGS...

...AND GENERALLY AKIN TO THE FIRES OF HELL.

NOT SURPRISINGLY, THIS CENSURE FAILED TO STEM THE PUBLIC USE OF TOBACCO.

HOWEVER, ENGLAND'S CLIMATE WAS ILL-SUITED TO PRODUCE BOUNTIFUL HARVESTS OF THE LEAF.

GROWING DEMAND CAUSED THE LIMITED SUPPLY OF TOBACCO TO SOAR IN PRICE.

TOBACCO WAS TRADED FOR SILVER, OUNCE FOR OUNCE, AND NOBLEMEN BANKRUPTED THEMSELVES IN PURSUIT OF THE HABIT.

EVEN THE VERY POOR BECAME ADDICTED, SPENDING FOOD MONEY TO BUY ANOTHER PIPEFUL.

MEANWHILE, IN JAMESTOWN, VIRGINIA- BRITAIN'S ONLY NEW-WORLD SETTLEMENT- CONDITIONS WERE DIRE.

OF 500 SETTLERS, ONLY 60 SURVIVED THE WINTER OF 1609-1610. MANY HAD TO RESORT TO CANNIBALISM.

IN 1612, THE TURNING POINT CAME. JOHN ROLFE (WHO LATER MARRIED POCAHONTAS) SOMEHOW MANAGED TO ACQUIRE SEEDS FROM TOBACCO GROWN IN SPANISH TERRITORY.

JAMESTOWN'S FIRST TOBACCO HARVEST WAS WELL RECEIVED IN ENGLAND.

SENSING THEY HAD FOUND THEIR ECONOMIC SALVATION, THE COLONISTS CONCENTRATED ON THE LABOR-INTENSIVE TASK OF CULTIVATING THE PLANTS...

...ALLOWING MUCH OF THE COMMUNITY, INCLUDING THE CHURCH AND THE STOCKADE, TO FALL APART.

WITH 700 TOBACCO SHOPS IN LONDON NEEDING PRODUCT, THE DECISION PAID OFF.

IN 1618, THE JAMESTOWN HARVEST YIELDED 20,000 POUNDS OF LEAF.

IN 1619, THE COLONISTS TOOK A MOMENTOUS STEP TO INCREASE PRODUCTION -- THEY BOUGHT THEIR FIRST SLAVES.

KING JAMES URGED THE COLONISTS TO SWITCH TO OTHER PRODUCTS -- BUT AS THE TAX ON TOBACCO BECAME THE CROWN'S LARGEST SOURCE OF REVENUE, HE DIDN'T FORCE THE ISSUE.

TEN YEARS LATER, THE COLONY'S TOBACCO HARVEST WAS 1.5 MILLION POUNDS.

TERRITORIAL EXPANSION SOON FOLLOWED. TOBACCO WAS HARD ON THE LAND, SO FARMERS PUSHED WESTWARD WHEN THEIR SOIL WAS EXHAUSTED.

MEANWHILE, INSPIRED BY VIRGINIA'S SUCCESS, TOBACCO WAS SOON BEING GROWN IN THE NEW COLONIES OF CONNECTICUT AND MARYLAND.

THE GROWING COLONIES NEEDED LABORERS, SO RECRUITERS IN ENGLAND TOLD TALES OF FABULOUS RICHES TO BE HAD IN THE NEW WORLD.

THOUSANDS ENTERED INTO INDENTURED SERVITUDE -- OFTEN MEANING YEARS OF VIRTUAL SLAVERY IN THE TOBACCO FIELDS-- IN EXCHANGE FOR PASSAGE TO THIS "LAND OF OPPORTUNITY."

TOBACCO WAS NOW LEGAL TENDER IN VIRGINIA AND MARYLAND-- AND COULD EVEN BE USED TO BUY A WIFE FROM AMONG THE WOMEN BEING SHIPPED OVER FROM ENGLAND.

TOBACCO CONSUMPTION IN ENGLAND CONTINUED TO INCREASE--SPURRED BY THE BELIEF THAT IT PROVIDED IMMUNITY TO THE GREAT PLAGUE OF 1665.

THE GROWING COLONIES IMPORTED MORE AND MORE SLAVES--MANY PURCHASED WITH TOBACCO.

COASTAL AFRICANS, INTRODUCED TO SMOKING BY THE PORTUGUESE, WOULD RAID INLAND TRIBES, THEN TRADE THEIR CAPTIVES TO SLAVERS IN EXCHANGE FOR THE LEAF.

OTHERS WERE SO ADDICTED THAT THEY TRADED AWAY THEIR LAND, PROVIDING THE BASIS FOR EUROPEAN COLONIZATION, PARTICULARLY IN SOUTH AFRICA.

AS ENGLISH SETTLERS SPREAD SOUTH, THE ESTABLISHED COLONIES, WORRIED ABOUT COMPETITION, TRIED TO KEEP THEM FROM GROWING TOBACCO.

THE 1663 CHARTER FOR THE NEW COLONY OF CAROLINA INCLUDED A BAN ON TOBACCO FARMING--BUT THE COLONISTS CONTINUED TO GROW IT AND SMUGGLE IT TO THE NORTH.

UNDER BRITISH LAW, THE COLONIES COULD SELL THEIR CROP ONLY TO ENGLAND, AND THE TRANSACTIONS WERE HEAVILY TAXED.

IN CAROLINA, JOHN CULPEPPER LED A TWO-YEAR REVOLT AGAINST THESE LAWS. THOUGH CULPEPPER'S REBELLION EVENTUALLY FAILED, IT FORESHADOWED EVENTS OF A CENTURY LATER.

THE COLONIES CONTINUED TO GROW RAPIDLY, AND PLANTERS' HOLDINGS EXPANDED WITH HUGE PLANTATIONS WORKED BY SLAVES REPLACING SMALL FAMILY FARMS.

MANY GROWERS BORROWED AGAINST FUTURE CROPS TO PAY FOR THEIR INCREASINGLY OPULENT LIFESTYLES.

IN THE MID-1700S, BRITISH BANKS INCREASED PRESSURE FOR REPAYMENT OF THESE DEBTS FOLLOWING FINANCIAL CRISES IN ENGLAND. AMONG THESE STRAPPED PLANTERS WAS GEORGE WASHINGTON...

IT IS BUT AN IRKSOME THING TO A FREE MIND TO BE ALWAYS HAMPERED BY DEBT

...AND THOMAS JEFFERSON. THEIR FINANCIAL WOES HELPED INCREASE THEIR HOSTILITY TO THE BRITISH.

PLANTERS WERE A SPECIES OF PROPERTY ANNEXED TO CERTAIN MERCANTILE HOUSES IN LONDON.

IN 1775, THE COLONIES HARVESTED 100 MILLION POUNDS OF TOBACCO. ALL OF IT--AS IS ALL U.S. TOBACCO TODAY--DESCENDED FROM THE SEEDS PLANTED BY JOHN ROLFE IN 1612.

SOON, THE COLONISTS WERE ARRANGING A LOAN FROM FRANCE TO HELP FINANCE A REVOLUTION--AND THE COLLATERAL WAS TOBACCO.

JAMES BUCHANAN "BUCK" DUKE TRANSFORMED THE TINY CIGARETTE BUSINESS INTO A GLOBAL INDUSTRY.

IN 1865 EX-REBEL OFFICER WASHINGTON DUKE RETURNED TO THE WAR-TORN REMAINS OF HIS NORTH CAROLINA FARM. HE SALVAGED WHAT HE COULD OF THE TOBACCO CROP.

WITH THE HELP OF HIS NINE-YEAR-OLD SON BUCK, WASH DUKE SOLD ENOUGH CHEWING TOBACCO TO SUPPORT HIS FAMILY -- BARELY.

GENUINE "BULL" DURHAM

IN NEARBY DURHAM, BULL DURHAM TOBACCO WAS FLOURISHING. THE ERA OF MASS-MARKETED BRAND NAMES WAS DAWNING, AND THE COMPANY'S TRADEMARK WAS BECOMING WELL KNOWN.

WITH BUCK TO HELP HIM, WASH DUKE LEFT FARMING AND WENT INTO THE TOBACCO PROCESSING BUSINESS HIMSELF, LAUNCHING THE DUKE OF DURHAM BRAND.

DUKE, SONS & Co.

THE DUKES WERE A MODEST SUCCESS, BUT BUCK SOON SAW AN OPPORTUNITY IN A NICHE MOST LARGER COMPANIES WERE IGNORING -- CIGARETTES.

CHEWING TOBACCO, CIGARS, AND PIPES ACCOUNTED FOR MOST OF THE MARKET. IN 1880 500 MILLION CIGARETTES WERE SOLD -- BY BULK, ONLY 3-5% OF THE CIGAR MARKET.

PTUI

LIKE CIGARS, CIGARETTES WERE ROLLED BY HAND -- BUT THEY SOLD FOR MUCH LESS (ABOUT 1¢ APIECE), SO THEY WEREN'T AS PROFITABLE. A GOOD WORKER ROLLED ABOUT 250 AN HOUR.

IN 1880 JAMES BONSACK PATENTED A MACHINE THAT COULD ROLL 10,000 AN HOUR. ALLEN AND GINTER, THEN THE LEADING CIGARETTE MAKER, PASSED ON THE DEVICE, FEARING THE MARKET WASN'T BIG ENOUGH.

BUCK DUKE GRABBED THE MACHINE. WITH IT, HE COULD CUT HIS PRICES IN HALF AND STILL MAKE A HUGE PROFIT-- IF HE COULD REALLY SELL THAT MANY CIGARETTES.

"THE FAMOUS DUKES"

DUKE of DURHAM CIGARETTES

SMOKING TOBACCO

10 for ~~10¢~~ 5¢

IN 1884 BUCK SET UP A FACTORY IN NEW YORK TO TAP THE GROWING URBAN MARKET FOR CIGARETTES.

DUKE SONS & Co.

HIS TIMING WAS GOOD. OVER THE NEXT 30 YEARS THE U.S. POPULATION NEARLY DOUBLED. CITIES FILLED WITH WAVES OF IMMIGRANTS.

THEY WERE TOO POOR FOR CIGARS, AND PIPES WERE TOO CUMBERSOME FOR FAST-PACED CITY LIFE, AND AS FOR CHEWING TOBACCO...

HOW DISGUSTING!

BUCK CREATED NEW BRANDS WITH CATCHY NAMES IN COLORFUL PACKAGES, ADDING TRADING CARDS AND COUPONS.

HIS SALESMEN GAVE GIFTS TO DEALERS WHO STOCKED HIS WARES.

BESIDES GIVING FREE CIGARETTES TO IMMIGRANTS AS THEY GOT OFF THE BOAT, DUKE SPENT 1/5 OF REVENUE ON PROMOTION.

BY 1885, SALES HAD TRIPLED.

BY 1889 DUKE WAS SELLING OVER 2 MILLION CIGARETTES A DAY-- $4 MILLION IN ANNUAL SALES.

COMPETING BRANDS

HE HAD 40% OF THE MARKET-- AND HE WANTED MORE.

FACING CUTTHROAT COMPETITION, THE OTHER TOP CIGARETTE MAKERS AGREED TO MERGE WITH DUKE. BUCK BECAME PRESIDENT OF THE RESULTING AMERICAN TOBACCO COMPANY.

ALL IN FAVOR OF ME--?

AYE!

BUCK NOW WENT AFTER SMALLER COMPANIES, UNDERCUTTING THEIR PRICES UNTIL THEY WENT UNDER OR SOLD OUT TO HIM.

OUT OF BUSINESS

TWO BIT TOBACCO

WITH A NEAR MONOPOLY, DUKE COULD NOW CUT AD COSTS AND DISTRIBUTORS' MARGINS AND PAY LESS TO FARMERS.

DAMN THAT DUKE!

AMERICAN TOBACCO CO.

DESPITE RECENT GROWTH, CIGARETTES WERE LESS THAN A THIRD OF THE MARKET--CHEW WAS STILL DOMINANT.

COMPETING CHEW

BUCK WENT AFTER IT THE SAME WAY HE HAD CIGARETTES.

SOON HE FORCED HIS MAJOR COMPETITORS, INCLUDING R.J. REYNOLDS, LORILLARD, AND LIGGETT & MYERS, TO SELL TO HIM.

ONE FOR ALL AND ALL FOR ME!

BY 1900 DUKE HAD 100,000 WORKERS AND SALES OF $125 MILLION. HE WAS ALSO SELLING A BILLION CIGARETTES A YEAR OUTSIDE THE U.S.-- BUT THAT WASN'T ENOUGH.

HE WENT AFTER THE VAST MARKET OF THE BRITISH EMPIRE. AFTER TENSE MANEUVERING, DUKE MERGED WITH THE HUGE IMPERIAL TOBACCO TO FORM BRITISH-AMERICAN TOBACCO.

IT WAS THE FIRST GLOBAL TRUST-- NATURALLY, DUKE WAS CHAIRMAN.

B.A.T. QUICKLY BUILT A HUGE FACTORY IN SHANGHAI TO SERVE THE ASIAN MARKET.

BACK IN THE STATES, HEALTH CRUSADERS WERE TARGETING CIGARETTES. MANY STATES WERE CURTAILING SALES. PROFIT MARGINS WERE BEING SQUEEZED.

BAN THE EVIL WEED

BAN THE EVIL!

SMOKING IS SATAN'S VICE!

IN 1902 THE SENATE FINANCE COMMITTEE REPEALED THE CIGARETTE TAX IMPOSED DURING THE RECENT SPANISH-AMERICAN WAR.

ARE BEST

SMOK

TAX REPEAL

(SEVERAL COMMITTEE MEMBERS HAPPENED TO HOLD TOBACCO STOCKS--THE CHAIRMAN OWNED OVER $1 MILLION WORTH.)

INSTEAD OF PASSING THE TAX CUT ON TO CUSTOMERS, DUKE POCKETED THE DIFFERENCE.

IN 1906 DUKE'S FRIENDS IN CONGRESS FOUGHT A BATTLE WHOSE CONSEQUENCES ARE STILL FELT TODAY--THEY PREVENTED TOBACCO FROM BEING COVERED BY THE PURE FOOD AND DRUG ACT.

PURE FOOD & DRUG ACT

MEANWHILE, DUKE TIGHTENED HIS GRIP ON THE U.S. MARKET. HE BOUGHT PACKAGING AND FLAVORING MANUFACTURERS...

UNITED CIGAR STORE

...AND SECRETLY ACQUIRED A CHAIN OF TOBACCO STORES TO PUSH HIS BRANDS.

TO EXPAND HIS CHAIN, DUKE ATTACKED COMPETITORS WITH PRICE WARS AND FREEBIES.

INDEPENDENT TOBACCONIST

SOMETIMES HE EVEN BOUGHT THEIR BUILDINGS AND KICKED THEM OUT.

DUKE'S TACTICS GREW MORE DEVIOUS. HE PAID OFF DISTRIBUTORS TO STOP CARRYING OTHER BRANDS. HE EMPLOYED SPIES IN RIVAL COMPANIES AND ENCOURAGED COMPETITORS' WORKERS TO STRIKE.

STRIKE!

UNFAIR

DUKE DROVE TOBACCO PRICES DOWN TO STARVATION LEVELS. FARMERS UNITED TO RESIST, SOMETIMES RESORTING TO EXTREME MEASURES.

DUKE FINALLY AGREED TO A SLIGHTLY HIGHER PRICE.

AMERICAN TOBACCO WARE

IN 1907 THE JUSTICE DEPARTMENT FILED ANTI-TRUST CHARGES AGAINST DUKE.

AMERICAN TOBACCO CO.

FOUR YEARS LATER THE SUPREME COURT ORDERED AMERICAN TOBACCO BROKEN UP.

THE REORGANIZED R.J. REYNOLDS, LIGGETT & MYERS, AND AMERICAN TOBACCO COMPANIES WOULD DOMINATE THE MARKET FOR DECADES TO COME.

CAMEL

CHESTERFIELD

LUCKY STRIKE

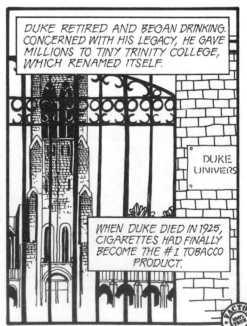

DUKE RETIRED AND BEGAN DRINKING. CONCERNED WITH HIS LEGACY, HE GAVE MILLIONS TO TINY TRINITY COLLEGE, WHICH RENAMED ITSELF.

DUKE UNIVERS

WHEN DUKE DIED IN 1925, CIGARETTES HAD FINALLY BECOME THE #1 TOBACCO PRODUCT.

FACTOID BOOKS

BY 1800, TOBACCO WAS USED AROUND THE GLOBE-- SMOKED IN PIPES AND CIGARS OR CHEWED-- BUT CIGARETTES WERE COMMON ONLY IN SPAIN AND PORTUGAL. WHAT SPREAD CIGARETTES? WAR!

GUNSMOKE

FRENCH AND ENGLISH SOLDIERS FIRST ENCOUNTERED CIGARETTES WHEN THEY CLASHED ON THE IBERIAN PENINSULA FROM 1808-14. MOST RETURNED TO THEIR OLD METHODS OF TOBACCO USE WHEN THEY GOT HOME.

SPANISH TRADERS HAD INTRODUCED CIGARETTES TO THE LEVANT, SO WHEN ENGLISH AND FRENCH SOLDIERS ARRIVED TO FIGHT THE RUSSIANS IN CRIMEA IN 1854, THEY FOUND TURKISH CIGARETTES.

FINE THING, THESE ORIENTAL SMOKES.

QUITE.

BACK HOME, MANY SOLDIERS ARRANGED TO KEEP GETTING THE STUFF AND CIGARETTES BECAME FASHIONABLE.

IT'S A LITTLE PAPER TUBE, DON'T YOU KNOW, FILLED WITH TURKISH TOBACCO.

PHILIP MORRIS TOBACCONIST

MANY SMOKERS TURNED TO CIGARETTES OUT OF NECESSITY DURING THE U.S. CIVIL WAR.

DADGUM PIPE! TOO MUCH TROUBLE!

BUT AGAIN, MOST WENT BACK TO THEIR OLD WAYS AFTER THE WAR.

BY WORLD WAR I, MECHANIZED MANUFACTURE MADE CIGARETTES PLENTIFUL. THE RED CROSS AND YMCA GAVE THEM TO U.S. SOLDIERS-- CREATING MANY NEW SMOKERS.

IT PASSES THE TIME.

GENERAL "BLACK JACK" PERSHING SAW SMOKING AS A MORALE BOOSTER.

YOU ASK ME WHAT WE NEED TO WIN THIS WAR. I ANSWER, TOBACCO AS MUCH AS BULLETS.

WITH CIGARETTES NOW CHEAP AND ABUNDANT AT HOME, RETURNING VETS CONTINUED TO SMOKE THEM. THEY SOON BECAME THE #1 TOBACCO PRODUCT.

IRONICALLY, THEY'VE KILLED MORE THAN THE WARS THAT HELPED POPULARIZE THEM.

FACTOID BOOKS 100% TRUE

SINCE TOBACCO WAS INTRODUCED TO THE WORLD, KINGS, TSARS, AND EMPERORS HAVE TRIED--AND FAILED--TO BAN IT. 100 YEARS AGO, A CRUSADING MID-WESTERN SCHOOLTEACHER MADE HER BID.

Lucy Gaston vs. The Coffin Nail

IN 1640, PERSIAN SHAH SEFI ORDERED MOLTEN LEAD POURED DOWN THE THROATS OF THOSE PRACTICING THE BLASPHEMOUS SMOKING HABIT.

TOBACCO USE WAS PUNISHABLE BY DEATH IN 17TH CENTURY RUSSIA AND CHINA TOO.

THOUGH EARLY BANS WERE LARGELY MADE ON MORAL OR FISCAL GROUNDS, HEALTH CONCERNS EXISTED, TOO.

IN 1761, AN ENGLISH DOCTOR PROVIDED EARLY MEDICAL EVIDENCE, NOTING NASAL CANCER AMONG SNUFF USERS.

BUT FEW WORRIED. BEING CHEAP, PLENTIFUL, AND ADDICTIVE, TOBACCO SPREAD. BY THE MID-1800S, MOST AMERICAN MEN USED IT IN SOME FORM.

SOME SMOKED IT IN PIPES, OTHERS CHEWED IT--BUT CIGARETTE USE WAS RARE.

LUCY PAGE GASTON WAS BORN IN 1860.

LIQUOR IS THE DEVIL'S BREW

STOP DEM RU

HER PARENTS WERE ACTIVE CRUSADERS AGAINST SLAVERY AND ALCOHOL. IN HER TEENS, SHE JOINED THE WOMEN'S CHRISTIAN TEMPERANCE UNION.

AS A TEACHER, SHE WATCHED STUDENTS WHO SNEAKED SMOKES. SHE CONCLUDED THAT A "COFFIN NAIL" HAD TWICE THE KICK AND 50 TIMES THE POISON OF A GLASS OF WHISKEY.

PASS THE SMOKE-- BUT KEEP AN EYE OUT FOR MISS LUCY!

GASTON OPPOSED ALL FORMS OF TOBACCO, BUT TARGETED THE NEW MACHINE-MADE (AND THEREFORE CHEAP) CIGARETTES BECAUSE OF THEIR POPULARITY WITH KIDS.

SHE BELIEVED SMOKING CAUSED "CIGARETTE FACE" AND LED TO A LIFE OF DRINK, CRIME, AND MISERY. SHE ORGANIZED YOUTH GROUPS, LEADING THEM IN A "CLEAN LIFE PLEDGE."

SHE PUBLISHED A TABLOID ATTACKING THE GROWING CIGARETTE INDUSTRY. IN 1899, SHE FORMED THE CHICAGO ANTI-CIGARETTE LEAGUE, SOON FOLLOWED BY A NATIONAL LEAGUE.

BAN THE COFFIN NAIL

CIGARETTES D SATAN'S TOOLS

ANTI-CIGARETTE LEAGUE

THREE STATES BANNED CIGARETTES, AND NATIONAL SALES FELL BY 1/3 FROM 1897 TO 1901 (HELPED BY A NEW CIGARETTE TAX AND AN ECONOMIC BOOM, MEANING MORE SMOKERS COULD AFFORD CIGARS).

EVENTUALLY, 11 STATES OUTLAWED CIGARETTES. WORRIED COMPANIES CIRCUMVENTED THE LAW BY GIVING AWAY CIGARETTES--WITH A 20-CENT BOOK OF MATCHES.

THEY'RE "FREE"-- IF YOU GET MY MEANING!

BUT THE BANS WERE LOOSELY ENFORCED. IN 1911, 11.7 BILLION CIGARETTES WERE SOLD--MORE THAN TWICE THE 1897 FIGURE. SMOKING GREW STILL MORE ON THE BATTLEFIELDS DURING WORLD WAR I.

Ahhh...THE PAUSE THAT REFRESHES!

CLAIMING A LINK BETWEEN CIGARETTES AND BOLSHEVISM, GASTON RAN FOR THE G.O.P. PRESIDENTIAL NOMINATION IN 1920.

STOP THE CIGA-RED MENACE

SHE RECEIVED FEW VOTES.

SAYING WINNER WARREN HARDING HAD A "CIGARETTE FACE," SHE PREDICTED HIS ADMINISTRATION WOULD BE SCANDAL-PLAGUED AND HE WOULD DIE BEFORE HIS TERM ENDED.

SHE WAS RIGHT.

BUT THE PUBLIC TIRED OF HER STRIDENCY, AND SHE WAS FORCED OUT OF TWO ANTI-SMOKING LEAGUES SHE HAD FOUNDED.

IN 1924, LEAVING A CHICAGO RALLY, SHE WAS HIT BY A STREETCAR.

THOUGH NOT BADLY HURT, SHE FAILED TO IMPROVE. DOCTORS FOUND SHE HAD THROAT CANCER--A DISEASE USUALLY LINKED TO SMOKING. SHE DIED A FEW MONTHS LATER.

AT HER SPARSELY ATTENDED FUNERAL, FOUR CHILDREN RECITED THE CLEAN LIFE PLEDGE.

THE FIGHT OVER CHILDHOOD SMOKING CONTINUES TO THIS DAY.

FACTOID 100% TRUE BOOKS

SMOKE and Mirrors

THE 1911 BREAKUP OF THE **TOBACCO TRUST** LEFT 50 MAJOR BRANDS COMPETING WITH LITTLE TO **DISTINGUISH** THEM-- EXCEPT THEIR **AD CAMPAIGNS.**

THE TOP SELLER, LIGGETT & MEYER'S **FATIMA,** WAS MADE WITH TURKISH TOBACCO, AS WERE THE **OTHER** LEADING BRANDS. IN 1912, L&M LAUNCHED **CHESTERFIELDS,** AN "ENGLISH-STYLE" SMOKE.

R.J. REYNOLDS NOW ENTERED THE CIGARETTE FIELD. THEY WANTED A NAME THAT WOULD HAVE "TURKISH" APPEAL-- THOUGH CONTAINING MOSTLY **AMERICAN** TOBACCO.

HMM... KISMET? NABOB? OR MAYBE SOME ARABIAN ANIMAL...

CAMELS **DIDN'T** TASTE LIKE TURKISH CIGARETTES-- AND PEOPLE **FLOCKED** TO THEM.

CAMEL
TURKISH & DOMESTIC BLEND

LIGGETT QUICKLY MOVED TO MAKE THEIR BLEND MORE LIKE **CAMELS**-- AND CHESTERFIELD SALES **IMPROVED.**

Chesterfield CIGARETTES

WHEN TURKEY JOINED THE GERMAN SIDE IN WORLD WAR I, ALL-TURKISH CIGARETTES BECAME "UNPATRIOTIC." CAMELS **SOARED,** CAPTURING 1/3 OF THE MARKET BY 1920.

GIMME AN AMERICAN SMOKE!

COMPETITOR AMERICAN BRANDS JUMPED ON THE AMERICAN BLEND **BAND-WAGON** IN 1917 WITH **LUCKY STRIKES**-- SUPPOSED TO TASTE BETTER BECAUSE "IT'S TOASTED!"

LUCKY STRIKE IT'S TOASTED
CIGARETTES

(AS WAS THE TOBACCO IN ALL **OTHER** BRANDS)

AMERICAN'S BEST ASSET WAS NOT LUCKY'S FLAVOR-- IT WAS SALES MANAGER **GEORGE WASHINGTON HILL,** SON OF THE COMPANY PRESIDENT AND **HUCKSTER SUPREME.**

GET OUT THERE AND SELL! SELL!

HILL, ALWAYS ONE FOR THE *BOLD* GESTURE, INITIATED *SKYWRITING* TO PUSH THE BRAND.

BUT CAMEL TOPPED HILL IN 1921 WITH A *NEW* SLOGAN CREATED WHEN A COMPANY AD MAN RAN OUT OF SMOKES ON THE *GOLF COURSE.*

I'D WALK A MILE FOR A CAMEL!

BY 1925, CAMELS HELD OVER 40% OF THE MARKET, THANKS TO AN *AD BLITZ* WITH THIS *UBIQUITOUS* SLOGAN.

I'd walk a mile for a— Camel

GEORGE HILL TOOK CONTROL OF AMERICAN IN 1925, AND PUSHED *HARD* WITH ADS MAKING PHONY *HEALTH* CLAIMS.

20,679 PHYSICIANS SAY LUCKIES ARE LESS IRRITATING!

DOCTORS WERE *PAID* FOR THEIR ENDORSEMENTS--IN *LUCKIES.*

IN 1926, #2 BRAND CHESTERFIELDS WENT AFTER THE PREVIOUSLY *TABOO* FEMALE MARKET.

Blow Some My way!

TEN CIGARETTE-SMOKING *WOMEN* IN THE 1929 EASTER PARADE MADE *HEADLINES* ACROSS THE COUNTRY.

DAILY INQUIRER
LADY SMOKERS IN "TORCH OF FREEDOM" MARCH

A *PUBLICITY STUNT* BY NOTED P.R. MAN EDWARD BERNAYS, HIRED BY HILL.

ANOTHER HILL AD SUGGESTED CIGARETTES AS A *DIET AID.* BY 1930 LUCKIES WERE THE *TOP SELLER.*

Reach for a Lucky instead of a Sweet!

REYNOLDS COUNTERED WITH ITS *OWN* HEALTH CLAIMS, SAYING CAMELS PROVIDED A "NATURAL" ENERGY BOOST AND AIDED *DIGESTION.*

"For Digestion's Sake Smoke Camels!"

ADS FEATURING *ATHLETES* SAID "SMOKE ALL YOU WANT" -- SINCE CAMELS "DON'T GET YOUR WIND".

BY 1937, CAMELS WERE AGAIN THE SALES *LEADER* (THOUGH A BLINDFOLD TEST SHOWED SMOKERS *COULDN'T* DISTINGUISH BETWEEN BRANDS).

HILL HIT BACK WITH A CAMPAIGN CLAIMING TOBACCO EXPERTS PREFERRED LUCKIES 2-1. THE STATISTICS WERE FICTION-- BUT THEY STILL HELPED LUCKIES RETAKE THE SALES LEAD BY THE EARLY 1940'S.

He's "SIZED UP" 21 Tobacco Crops!

RELATIVELY RARE A FEW DECADES EARLIER, CIGARETTES HAD NOW TAKEN AMERICA BY STORM. IN 1940, THE AVERAGE ADULT SMOKED SEVEN A DAY.

THE STORK CLUB

WORLD WAR II BROUGHT A NEW ADVERTISING ANGLE.

Camel

HOTEL ASTOR / ALL HOT / REVUE / CAFETERIA / BOND JEWELERS

CAMEL CAUSED A SENSATION WITH A HUGE BILLBOARD ON TIMES SQUARE FEATURING A U.S. SERVICEMAN THAT ACTUALLY BLEW SMOKE.

FOR YEARS, HILL'S ADVERTISERS HAD BEEN URGING HIM TO CHANGE LUCKY'S PACKAGE DESIGN, SAYING THE DARK GREEN PUT OFF BUYERS, ESPECIALLY WOMEN.

LUCKY STRIKE

LUCKY STRIKE THE TOASTED

CIGARETTES

CIGARETTES

HILL NOW GRABBED A PATRIOTIC EXCUSE TO SWITCH TO A WHITE PACK (BY FAMED DESIGNER RAYMOND LOEWY), CLAIMING GREEN INK WAS NEEDED FOR THE WAR EFFORT.

CHESTERFIELD, TOO, TRIED THE WARTIME APPEAL, BUT LUCKIES MAINTAINED THEIR LEAD EVEN AFTER HILL'S DEATH IN 1946-- FROM EMPHYSEMA.

Chesterfield Cigarettes

AFTER THE WAR, REYNOLDS TRIED THE HEALTH APPROACH AGAIN, TOUTING A SURVEY OF "ALL DOCTORS," HELPING CAMELS AGAIN TAKE THE SALES LEAD IN 1950.

More Doctors Smoke Camels Than Any Other Cigarette

THE PLETHORA OF CLAIMS FINALLY GOT THE ATTENTION OF THE FEDERAL TRADE COMMISSION. THEY FOUND ALL THE BRANDS' HEALTH CLAIMS TO BE FALSE.

BUT BY THEN, NEARLY HALF OF U.S. ADULTS SMOKED--THOUGH MANY WERE BEGINNING TO WORRY, AS REPORTS LINKING CIGARETTES TO LUNG CANCER BEGAN TO EMERGE.

STUDY LINKS SMOKING, LUNG CANCER

TO MUFFLE **CANCER** FEARS, COMPANIES PUSHED **FILTERED** CIGARETTES, WITH **MORE** EXTRAVAGANT DECLARATIONS.

EARLY **KENT** FILTERS USED ASBESTOS, *ITSELF A CARCINOGEN.*

IN 1952, LIGGETT CLAIMED THAT A SIX-MONTH **TEST** SHOWED CHESTERFIELD SMOKERS WERE NOT "**ADVERSELY AFFECTED**" BY THEIR BRAND.

SPOKESMAN ARTHUR GODFREY **HYPED** THE RESULTS ON HIS **RADIO SHOW.**

GODFREY WAS DIAGNOSED WITH **LUNG CANCER** IN 1959.

CELEBRITY **ENDORSEMENTS** WERE A POPULAR GIMMICK. MANY HAD **PERSONAL** EXPERIENCE WITH THEIR PRODUCT.

SPENCER TRACY (DIED OF LUNG CANCER AND HEART DISEASE, 1967).

JOHN WAYNE (HAD A CANCEROUS LUNG REMOVED IN 1963).

DESI ARNAZ (DIED OF **LUNG CANCER** IN 1986) AND LUCILLE BALL (DIED OF **HEART DISEASE** IN 1989).

RONALD REAGAN MAY NOT HAVE BEEN A HEAVY **SMOKER,** BUT YEARS LATER, AS PRESIDENT, HE WAS A HEAVYWEIGHT PROMOTER OF TOBACCO COMPANY **INTERESTS.**

THE MOST **ENDURING** CIGARETTE CAMPAIGN IS PHILLIP MORRIS'S "**MARLBORO COUNTRY,**" STARTED IN THE EARLY '60s TO REVIVE A FAILED "WOMEN'S BRAND."

WHILE THE ADS HAVE MADE THE BRAND THE WORLD'S **TOP SELLER,** AT LEAST **TWO** ACTORS WHO PORTRAYED "THE MARLBORO MAN" HAVE DIED OF **LUNG CANCER.**

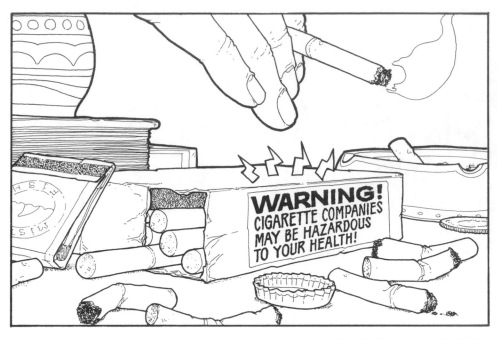

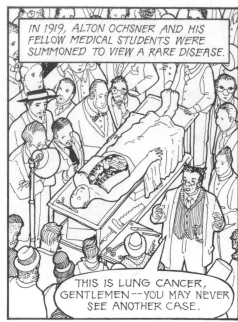

In 1919, Alton Ochsner and his fellow medical students were summoned to view a rare disease.

This is lung cancer, gentlemen—you may never see another case.

But in 1936, Ochsner suddenly began seeing more lung cancer patients. All had started smoking during World War I.

He and others began researching the disease.

Smoking surged during WWII. By 1952, when Reader's Digest ran an article on health findings, half of U.S. adults smoked—a record.

The next year, sales fell 3%.

CANCER by the CARTON

Worried, major companies formed the Tobacco Industry Research Committee to "study" the cancer issue.

We'll get to the bottom of this if it takes 100 years!

Or longer!

The T.I.R.C. avoided or cut off research that might show health risks and spent most of its budget on P.R.

What's the best way to deal with this problem?

More ads!

Some companies' own investigations showed the cancer connection. Needless to say, scientists remained silent and their results were not made public.

Sales of new filtered cigarettes grew as ads implied they were safer to smoke.

Filters mean we use less tobacco.

I feel healthier already!

THE FIRST COMPREHENSIVE FEDERAL STUDY, THE SURGEON GENERAL'S REPORT OF 1964, LINKED CIGARETTES TO LUNG CANCER AND HEART DISEASE.

EVIDENCE? WHAT EVIDENCE?

BUT TOBACCO FIRMS HAD POWERFUL ALLIES.

⅓ OF COMMITTEES IN THE HOUSE AND ¼ IN THE SENATE WERE CHAIRED BY TOBACCO STATE POLS. CONGRESS WAS SLOW TO ACT.

SMOKE FILLED ROOM

HEALTH CRISIS? WHAT HEALTH CRISIS?

?

THE AMERICAN MEDICAL ASSOCIATION WAS SILENT--NOT SURPRISING, SINCE THEY WANTED TOBACCO-STATE LEGISLATORS' HELP IN BATTLING MEDICARE.

STOP CREEPING SOCIALISM, EH, DOC?

I'LL SMOKE TO THAT!

MEDICAL CONVENTIO

WELCOME DOCTORS

FREE SAMPLE.

IN 1965, THE COMPANIES AGREED TO MILD WARNING LABELS ON PACKS (WHICH THEY COULD USE LATER TO SHIELD THEMSELVES FROM LAWSUITS).

YOU CAN'T SAY WE DIDN'T WARN YOU!

CIGARETTE ADVERTISING HAD TRIPLED IN THE '50s AND BY THE MID-60s ACCOUNTED FOR 10% OF TV AND RADIO AD REVENUES. THE BRAND WARS WERE INTENSE--AND EXPENSIVE.

SMOKE! SMOKE! SMOKE OUR CIGARETTES!

IN 1967, THE FCC ORDERED STATIONS TO GIVE TIME TO ANTI-SMOKING ADS AND BY 1970, THE SMOKING RATE HAD DROPPED TO 36%.

KOFF KOFF WHEEZE

IN 1971, THE MAKERS GRUDGINGLY ACCEPTED A BAN ON BROADCAST ADS--

SINCE IT ALSO ENDS THE ANTI-SMOKING ADS...

AND WITHOUT TV, NO NEW COMPETITORS CAN ENTER THE FIELD.

THE BAN SAVED THE COMPANIES MILLIONS--MUCH OF WHICH THEY POURED INTO PRINT ADS. MAGAZINE COVERAGE OF SMOKING'S PERILS VIRTUALLY VANISHED.

EDITOR

ARE YOU SUGGESTING MONEY COMPROMISED OUR EDITORIAL INTEGRITY?

THE COMPANIES FOUND NEW AVENUES FOR PROMOTION, BUYING PLACEMENT IN SPORTS ARENAS AND MOVIES.

CIGARETTES BECAME THE MOST HEAVILY ADVERTISED PRODUCT IN THE U.S.

SMOK

BUTTS

MAKERS NOW TOUTED NEW "LOW TAR" BRANDS TO SOOTHE PUBLIC FEARS--

--BUT MANY PEOPLE COMPENSATED BY SMOKING MORE AND INHALING DEEPER.

IN 1978, THE AVERAGE SMOKER WENT THROUGH 1½ PACKS A DAY-- UP NEARLY 50% FROM 25 YEARS EARLIER.

WE USE LESS TOBACCO--

--AND THEY BUY MORE!

PROFITS

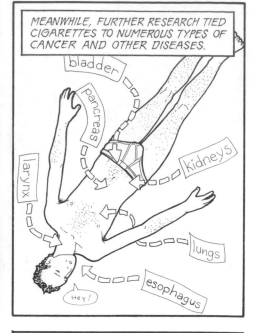

MEANWHILE, FURTHER RESEARCH TIED CIGARETTES TO NUMEROUS TYPES OF CANCER AND OTHER DISEASES.

bladder

pancreas

larynx

kidneys

lungs

esophagus

Hey!

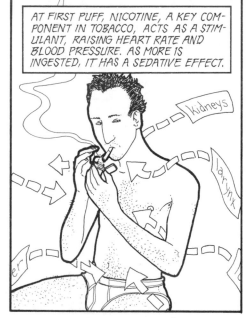

AT FIRST PUFF, NICOTINE, A KEY COMPONENT IN TOBACCO, ACTS AS A STIMULANT, RAISING HEART RATE AND BLOOD PRESSURE. AS MORE IS INGESTED, IT HAS A SEDATIVE EFFECT.

kidneys

larynx

THE EFFECTS WEAR OFF IN 30 TO 60 MINUTES-- LEAVING THE SMOKER CRAVING ANOTHER CIGARETTE.

THE SMOKE ALSO CONTAINS POISONOUS CARBON MONOXIDE, ALONG WITH DOZENS OF CARCINOGENIC COMPOUNDS.

THE MANUFACTURERS CONTINUED TO SAY THEY BELIEVED CIGARETTES WERE HARMLESS.

THE COMPANIES SPENT UNTOLD MILLIONS BECOMING ONE OF THE MOST POWERFUL LOBBIES IN WASHINGTON. THE FEDS BANNED CHEMICALS THAT CAUSED A HANDFUL OF CANCER DEATHS-- BUT CIGARETTES REMAINED UNREGULATED.

RED DYE #2 BANNED

IN THE LATE '70s, HEALTH SECRETARY JOE CALIFANO PROPOSED SWEEPING ANTI-SMOKING MEASURES--

PRIDE IN TOBACCO

--BUT PRES. JIMMY CARTER, NEEDING SOUTHERN SUPPORT, DIDN'T BACK HIM UP.

THE NEXT PRESIDENT, FORMER CIGARETTE PITCHMAN RONALD REAGAN, ASSURED TOBACCO FIRMS HIS CABINET MEMBERS WOULDN'T "WASTE THEIR TIME" ON TOBACCO REGULATION.

INVESTMENT WIZARD WARREN BUFFETT EXPLAINED CIGARETTES' BUSINESS APPEAL--

IT COSTS A PENNY TO MAKE. SELL IT FOR A DOLLAR. IT'S ADDICTIVE.

THE PERFECT PRODUCT.

THE MAKERS AND THEIR DEEP POCKETS HAVE TURNED ASIDE NUMEROUS LAW-SUITS--BUT RECENT CLAIMS BY STATES MAY FINALLY FORCE THEM TO PAY PART OF SMOKERS' $50 BILLION YEARLY MEDICAL TAB.

UH-OH...

BUT COMPANIES NOW INSIST HEALTH ISN'T THE ISSUE--

THIS IS ABOUT FREE CHOICE! DON'T LET BIG GOVERNMENT TELL YOU WHAT TO DO!

YEAH-- LET US TELL YOU WHAT TO DO!

FREE CHOICE? NICOTINE IS HIGHLY ADDICTIVE-- AND MAKERS CAREFULLY CONTROL THE DOSE.

ARE YOU NUTS?! THAT STUFF'LL KILL YOU!

PROPORTIONATELY, MORE HEROIN ADDICTS KICK THEIR HABIT THAN SMOKERS-- THOUGH 4 OUT OF 5 SMOKERS WANT TO STOP.

THE MAKERS KNOW THAT 9 OUT OF 10 SMOKERS ARE HOOKED AS TEENS-- BEFORE THEY UNDERSTAND THE DANGERS.

WITH 1100 CUSTOMERS DYING EVERY DAY, THE COMPANIES NEED MORE. THEY BOOST PROMOTIONS NEAR SCHOOLS AND DO YOUTH-ORIENTED ADS AND GIVEAWAYS.

LOOK-- I'M GIVING FREE AD SPACE TO A MEGABUCKS CORPORATION...

...AND I AGREED TO PAY 'EM A THOU-SAND BUCKS A YEAR FOR THE REST OF MY LIFE!

BY THE MID-'90s, U.S. SMOKERS WERE SPEND-ING $55 BILLION A YEAR ON THEIR HABITS.

CIGARETTES ARE THE #1 CAUSE OF PREVENTABLE DEATHS, KILLING OVER 400,000 AMERICANS A YEAR-- FAR MORE THAN AIDS, ALCOHOL, CAR WRECKS, FIRES, MURDER, SUICIDE, AND ILLEGAL DRUGS COMBINED.

I TOLD YOU I'D QUIT SOMEDAY.

R I P

AFTER WWII, G.I.s' AMERICAN SMOKES WERE BIG IN WAR-TORN EUROPE.

YOU GOT CIGARETTES, JOE?

BUT AS THE CONTINENT RECOVERED, LOCAL BRANDS REGAINED DOMINANCE.

AS U.S. SALES WEAKENED OVER HEALTH CONCERNS, PHILIP MORRIS AND R.J. REYNOLDS RESPONDED...

Sales for 19

...BY BUYING THEIR WAY INTO EUROPE AND OTHER MARKETS AROUND THE WORLD.

THE U.S. GAVE LOANS SO THIRD WORLD COUNTRIES COULD BUY AMERICAN TOBACCO. THE FIRMS THEMSELVES ALLEGEDLY PAID MILLIONS TO BRIBE LOCAL OFFICIALS.

CONGRATULATIONS! I'VE JUST RULED IN YOUR FAVOR!

CUSTOMS REGULATIONS

BUREAU OF IMPORTS

IN THE '80s THE REAGAN AND BUSH ADMINISTRATIONS LOOKED FOR WAYS TO COUNTER THE SOARING TRADE DEFICIT. AS V.P. DAN QUAYLE SAID:

TOBACCO EXPORTS SHOULD BE EXPANDED AGGRESSIVELY BECAUSE AMERICANS ARE SMOKING LESS.

BY 1982, PHILIP MORRIS WAS #1 IN EUROPE.

AFTER THE FALL OF COMMUNISM, THE COMPANIES SPENT BILLIONS TO MOVE INTO THE FORMER EASTERN BLOC.

Marlboro

IN VIETNAM, WHERE 73% OF MEN SMOKE, P.M. NOW MAKES CIGARETTES WITH THE STATE-RUN TOBACCO COMPANY -- BUT SMUGGLED MARLBOROS ARE MORE POPULAR.

NOW THE FIRMS ARE VYING FOR ENTRY INTO THE WORLD'S BIGGEST MARKET, CHINA-- WHERE A TYPICAL HOUSEHOLD SPENDS 15% OF ITS INCOME ON TOBACCO.

PHILIP MORRIS NOW HAS HALF THE U.S. MARKET-- AND SELLS NEARLY THREE TIMES AS MUCH OVERSEAS. THIS TRULY IS...

MARLBORO COUNTRY WORLD!

CHAPTER FIVE

SEX AND MORE SEX

First, we've got to point out: Sex is NOT a vice. It's a normal, healthy part of any marital relationship. Sure, different ethnic and religious groups place certain restrictions on the act, but sex between two consenting, married adults is normal, and, most people would agree, is good.

Those same people would agree that sex and commerce are mutually exclusive; sex, they insist, should be the outward manifestation of love — money should never figure into it. When it does, however, sex becomes a vice — and that's what this chapter is all about.

Prostitution has been around since the first man who couldn't get it unless he paid for it, did — which puts the moment of the first transaction somewhere slightly south of Adam and Eve. Since then, prostitution has infiltrated every empire of note — from the ancient Greeks right up to the present.

But Prostitution is only one facet of the vice known as Illicit Sex. The other, Pornography, is currently enjoying its greatest popularity ever, assisted, no doubt, by the proliferation of sexual diseases that gives the more traditional "contact vice" deadly potential.

PROSTITUTES OF THE GODS?

PROSTITUTION IS OFTEN CALLED "THE WORLD'S OLDEST PROFESSION," BUT THE PRIESTHOOD MAY BE OLDER... AND IN ANCIENT TIMES, THE TWO WERE OFTEN LINKED.

PROSTITUTES OFTEN SERVED IN THE TEMPLES... PERHAPS AN OUTGROWTH OF EARLY FERTILITY RITES... AND WERE AN IMPORTANT SOURCE OF INCOME.

ACCORDING TO GREEK HISTORIAN HERODOTUS, IN THE 5th CENTURY B.C., EACH BABYLONIAN WOMAN WAS REQUIRED TO PERFORM SUCH A SERVICE AT LEAST ONCE.

WORSHIPPERS OF ISHTAR, GODDESS OF SEX (AND TAVERNS), INCLUDED BOTH TEMPLE PROSTITUTES AND STREETWALKERS, WHO FREQUENTED THE ALEHOUSES.

SOME SCHOLARS BELIEVE THE EROTIC SCULPTURES ON MANY INDIAN TEMPLES WERE IN PART ADS FOR THE SACRED PROSTITUTES AWAITING WITHIN.

SOME TEMPLES HAD OVER 400 GIRLS.

ACCORDING TO MARCO POLO, TRAVELERS IN TIBET WERE ASKED TO TAKE THEIR PICK OF LOCAL GIRLS... IN EXCHANGE FOR THE PAYMENT OF A TOKEN.

A GIRL WHO ACCUMULATED MANY TOKENS WAS CONSIDERED BLESSED BY THE GODS, AND ONLY THEN FIT FOR MARRIAGE.

NOT ALL RELIGIONS BLESSED SEX. IN THE LATE ROMAN EMPIRE, CHASTITY MARKED A WOMAN NAMED LUCIA AS A MEMBER OF A BANNED SECT...

WHEN SHE REFUSED TO SERVE HER SENTENCE, SHE WAS EXECUTED. SHE IS NOW KNOWN AS ST. LUCIA, PATRON OF REFORMED PROSTITUTES.

IN THE 6TH CENTURY B.C., ADULTERY AND HOMOSEXUALITY WERE RAMPANT IN ATHENS. TO COUNTER THIS, SOLON, THE GREAT LAWGIVER, BEGAN...

THE GOLDEN AGE OF PROSTITUTION

ATHENIAN MEN NEEDED ANOTHER SEXUAL OUTLET, SOLON DECIDED, SO HE BOUGHT SOME SLAVE GIRLS AND SET UP A BROTHEL.

BETTER THEY SHOULD COME HERE THAN FOOL AROUND WITH A MARRIED WOMAN!

SOLON KEPT PRICES LOW, SO ANYONE COULD AFFORD IT. THE PLACE WAS A HIT, AND MORE BROTHELS SOON SPRANG UP.

I HEAR THE NEW PLACE DOWN THE BLOCK IS GOOD.

SOLON SPECIFIED COLORED ROBES FOR THE GIRLS, AND A UNIVERSAL SYMBOL--A PHALLUS--MARKED THE DOORWAYS TO THE BROTHELS.

SOME SAY PROSTITUTION WAS MORE PREVALENT--AND INFLUENTIAL-- IN GOLDEN-AGE ATHENS THAN IN ANY CITY SINCE.

IT'S WHAT MAKES LIFE HERE SUCH FUN!

THE BROTHELS PAID A TAX, AND TAX COLLECTING WAS FARMED OUT TO INDEPENDENT AGENTS, WHO TOOK A CUT--ANOTHER INCENTIVE FOR EXPANSION.

HERE'S TO MORE BROTHELS!

CERTAIN STREETWALKERS TURNED TO CLEVER ADVERTISING.

FOLLOW ME

WITH PLEASURE!

THERE WAS ALSO A HIGHER CLASS OF PROSTITUTES CALLED HETAIRAI, WHO WERE VALUED FOR THEIR MINDS AS WELL AS THEIR BODIES.

A DRACHMA FOR YOUR THOUGHTS.

AND 10 FOR THE REST OF ME.

THESE COURTESANS KEPT THEIR OWN HOMES, AND ARRANGED ASSIGNATIONS VIA MESSAGES WRITTEN ON TOMBSTONES IN THE LOCAL CEMETERY.

YAHOO!

THARGALIA MEET ME TONIGHT?

WHILE WIVES STAYED AT HOME AND WERE NOT ALLOWED TO MINGLE WITH OTHER MEN, THE HETAIRAI, TRAINED IN CONVERSATION, WERE WELCOME AT SOCIAL GATHERINGS.

PHRYNE, THE MOST FAMOUS COURTESAN OF HER TIME, WAS SO BEAUTIFUL THAT SHE POSED FOR STATUES OF APHRODITE, GODDESS OF SEXUAL LOVE.

I'M FINISHED-- YOU MAY GO.

÷ SOB! ÷

AT THE URGING OF JEALOUS WIVES, SHE WAS CHARGED WITH GODLESSNESS, A CAPITAL CRIME. IN HER DEFENSE, HER LAWYER RIPPED OFF HER CLOTHES BEFORE THE JUDGES.

HOLY APHRODITE!

ZEUS BE PRAISED!

SHE WAS ACQUITTED.

ASPASIA, PERICLES' LOVER, WAS PRAISED BY SOCRATES AND PLATO, AND HER HOME WAS A CULTURAL CENTER. MORE THAN ONE WAR WAS BLAMED ON HER BEHIND-THE-SCENES SCHEMING.

AND THAT'S FOR ASPASIA!

Sploot!

SOME HETAIRAI SERVED AN IMPORTANT RELIGIOUS ROLE AS WELL. CORINTH'S TEMPLE OF APHRODITE EMPLOYED OVER A THOUSAND GIRLS.

I SUDDENLY FEEL VERY PIOUS!

PERHAPS THE MOST POWERFUL OF ALL HETAIRAI WAS THAÏS, MISTRESS OF ALEXANDER THE GREAT.

AFTER HIS DEATH, SHE MARRIED PTOLEMY I, QUIT HER DAY JOB, AND BECAME QUEEN OF EGYPT.

FACTOID BOOKS

AFTER THE FALL OF DECADENT ROME, THE NEXT MILLENNIUM WAS MARKED BY THE GROWTH OF CHRISTIANITY, THE RISE OF CITIES... AND THE SPREAD OF PROSTITUTION.

HARLOTS AND HOLY MEN

THOUGH THE CHURCH TOOK A DIM VIEW OF SEX, ST. AUGUSTINE CONSIDERED PROSTITUTES A NECESSARY EVIL. THEIR REMOVAL WOULD...

...POLLUTE ALL THINGS WITH LUST.

ST. THOMAS AQUINAS FEARED WHAT MEN MIGHT DO WITHOUT WILLING WOMEN.

TAKE PROSTITUTES FROM THE WORLD AND YOU WILL FILL IT WITH SODOMY.

PERHAPS THIS EXPLAINS THE CHURCH-RUN BROTHEL IN AVIGNON, WHOSE GIRLS DIVIDED THEIR TIME BETWEEN PRAYER AND PAYING CUSTOMERS.

NOW I LAY ME DOWN TO WORK...

SIMILAR HOUSES FLOURISHED IN SEVERAL OTHER CITIES.

HARLOTS FLOCKED TO POTENTIAL CUSTOMERS, WHETHER MEN ON A PILGRIMAGE...

...OR THE CLERGY OF THE HOLY CITY OF ROME. THE PRICE OF SOME EXCLUSIVE ITALIAN COURTESANS EQUALED SEVERAL YEARS' WAGES FOR A COMMONER.

POPE JULIUS II, PATRON OF MICHELANGELO, ALSO ESTABLISHED A BORDELLO IN ROME IN THE EARLY 16TH CENTURY...

IF I BUILD IT, THEY WILL COME.

...JUST AS A CONTINENT-WIDE SYPHILIS EPIDEMIC SCARED AWAY MANY CUSTOMERS.

DIVINE RETRIBUTION, PERHAPS?

FACTOID BOOKS

MYSTERY JOHN

ONE SEVENTEENTH-CENTURY EVENING, TWO GENTLEMEN TRAVELING INCOGNITO ARRIVED AT A BAWDY HOUSE, SAID TO BE THE FINEST IN LONDON.

ONE MANAGED TO HAVE WORDS WITH THE GIRL WHO WAS TO SERVICE THE OTHER.

THE GIRL THEN WENT ABOUT HER BUSINESS AS USUAL...

...BUT AT THE FIRST OPPORTUNITY, PICKED THE POCKETS OF HER CUSTOMER.

LATER, THE MAN FOUND HIMSELF EMBARRASSED -- AND HIS FRIEND HAD VANISHED.

PERHAPS...YOU WOULD GIVE ME CREDIT TILL THE MORROW--?

NOT BLOODY LIKELY!

AS COLLATERAL, THE MAN OFFERED HIS RING -- WHICH THE DOUBTING WOMAN SENT TO BE APPRAISED.

GASP! 'TIS BUT ONE MAN COULD AFFORD THIS RING!

INDEED, THE VISITOR WAS KING CHARLES II, NOTORIOUS WOMANIZER. HIS FRIEND THE EARL OF ROCHESTER ARRANGED THE EVENING TO TEACH HIM A LESSON.

YOUR MAJESTY!

DID IT WORK? AS ONE WAG LATER SAID, "A KING IS SUPPOSED TO BE THE FATHER OF HIS PEOPLE -- AND CHARLES CERTAINLY WAS FATHER TO A GOOD MANY OF THEM."

HAPPY FATHER'S DAY, FROM ALL OF US! DAD.

LONELY, BORED, SCARED, AND FAR FROM HOME, SOLDIERS HAVE LONG BEEN EAGER CUSTOMERS FOR WOMEN KNOWN AS "CAMP FOLLOWERS" OR...

THE WHORES OF WAR

MANY WOMEN ACCOMPANIED ALEXANDER THE GREAT'S CAMPAIGNS. ONE, THAIS, APPARENTLY PERSUADED HIM TO LET HER TORCH THE CAPTURED CITY OF PERSEPOLIS.

NOW *THIS* IS FUN!

SHIPLOADS OF PROSTITUTES SAILED TO THE HOLY LAND TO PROVIDE COMFORT TO THE CRUSADERS.

THIS ANGERED RICHARD THE LIONHEARTED--AFTER ALL, THE MEN WERE SPENDING HIS MONEY.

IN THE 12TH CENTURY, THE HOLY ROMAN EMPEROR FREDERICK BARBAROSSA PUNISHED WHORES CAUGHT WITH HIS SOLDIERS BY CUTTING OFF THEIR NOSES.

MANY SUPPOSED JOAN OF ARC WAS A PROSTITUTE--WHY ELSE WOULD A WOMAN BE TRAVELLING WITH THE ARMY?

IN FACT, THE WOMEN PROVIDED MANY OTHER NECESSARY SERVICES, SUCH AS COOKING, CLEANING, AND TENDING THE WOUNDED.

FRENCH KING CHARLES VIII LED AN ARMY OF MULTINATIONAL MERCENARIES INTO ITALY IN THE 1490s, BUT WAS FORCED TO RETREAT WHEN MANY OF HIS MEN GREW ILL.

THE MEN--AND THEIR CAMP FOLLOWERS--RETURNED TO THEIR HOMES, TAKING THE NEW DISEASE WITH THEM. THUS BEGAN EUROPE'S FIRST SYPHILIS EPIDEMIC.

NAPOLEON DECLARED PROSTITUTES A NECESSITY.

WITHOUT THEM, MEN WOULD ATTACK RESPECTABLE WOMEN IN THE STREETS.

UNFORTUNATELY, THE MASS MOBILIZATION OF THE NAPOLEONIC WARS TOUCHED OFF A SECOND EPIDEMIC OF VENEREAL DISEASE.

THROUGH MUCH OF THE 19TH CENTURY, PROSTITUTES WERE BROUGHT ABOARD BRITISH NAVY SHIPS AS SOON AS THEY REACHED PORT.

YOO-HOO, SAILORS!

THANK GOD-- OUR SHIP'S COME IN!

IN 1814, HEARING OF MEN MASSING FOR THE BATTLE OF NEW ORLEANS, WHORES FLOCKED THERE. MANY STAYED ON AND THE CITY BECAME A DEN OF PROSTITUTION FOR OVER A CENTURY.

DURING THE CIVIL WAR, THE UNION ARMY TRIED TO REGULATE PROSTITUTES, GOING SO FAR AS TO BUILD A "CITY OF WHORES" NEAR A MAJOR DEPOT.

NEXT!

MARY'S HAPPY HOUSE

SOME SAY THE TERM "HOOKER" COMES FROM UNION GENERAL JOSEPH HOOKER'S FONDNESS FOR THE LADIES.

I'M ONE OF GENERAL JOEY'S GIRLS!

IN 1917, THE ARMY BANNED BROTHELS WITHIN FIVE MILES OF ITS U.S. BASES -- BUT MOBILE BROTHELS VISITED THE TROOPS NEAR THE FRONT LINES IN EUROPE.

SINCE WWII, PROSTITUTION HAS FLOURISHED NEAR U.S. BASES OVERSEAS, SEEMINGLY WITH THE PENTAGON'S TACIT ACCEPTANCE.

AS LONG AS MEN ARE SENT FAR FROM HOME TO DO DANGEROUS JOBS, VICE APPEARS SURE TO FOLLOW.

FACTOID BOOKS

DESPITE THE CONSERVATIVE MORAL TONE OF THE TIMES, PROSTITUTION FLOURISHED DURING THE 19TH AND EARLY 20TH CENTURIES. YOU MIGHT CALL THIS SURREPTITIOUS SEX TRADE...

The VICTORIANS' Secret

IN THE EARLY 1800s, THE GROWING ENGLISH MIDDLE CLASS WAS TRYING TO EMULATE THE (IMAGINED) WAYS OF EARLIER NOBILITY-- ESPECIALLY COURTLY (i.e., NON-PHYSICAL) LOVE.

VIRTUOUS LADIES WERE NOT SUPPOSED TO BE INTERESTED IN SEX, BUT WOULD SUFFER IT OCCASIONALLY FOR PURPOSES OF REPRODUCTION.

MEN, ALAS, WERE SLAVES TO THEIR BASER INSTINCTS --AND IF THEY COULD HAVE SEX WITH THEIR WIVES ONLY A FEW TIMES A YEAR...

...OTHER OUTLETS MIGHT PROVE NECESSARY.

BECAUSE THEY WERE RELIEVING THEIR WIVES OF THE "BURDEN" OF SEX BY TURNING TO PROSTITUTES, MANY MEN FELT...

I'M DOING MY WIFE A REAL FAVOR!

THE TRADE GREW TREMENDOUSLY. IN 1839 THERE WERE PERHAPS 50,000 PROSTITUTES AMONG LONDON'S 2 MILLION PEOPLE.

SO MANY WOMEN...SO LITTLE TIME.

PERHAPS SOME MEN DID FEEL A PANG OF GUILT-- MANY BROTHELS IN LONDON SPE- CIALIZED IN FLAGELLATION.

OOOH... TWICE MORE-- WITH GUSTO!

SOME BORDELLOS EVEN PROVIDED YOUNG GIRLS, DUE TO A MISTAKEN BELIEF THAT HAVING SEX WITH A VIRGIN WOULD CURE SYPHILIS.

WOULDN'T WANT MY WIFE TO CATCH IT, EH?

DUE TO IMMIGRATION PATTERNS, MEN OUTNUMBERED WOMEN IN MUCH OF 19TH-CENTURY AMERICA AND A SIMILAR DOUBLE STANDARD PREVAILED.

AMERICA! LAND OF OPPORTUNITY...

...AND WOMEN!

MEN OFTEN DIDN'T MARRY UNTIL THEIR 30s -- AND MOST WANTED A YOUNG VIRGINAL BRIDE. BUT UNTIL THEN...

SEE YOU AGAIN, HANDSOME?

NEXT WEDNESDAY, AS ALWAYS!

THE GOLD RUSH OF 1849 SWELLED SAN FRANCISCO'S POPULATION TO 25,000--MOSTLY MEN. 3,000 HOOKERS CAME FROM AROUND THE WORLD TO SERVE THE MARKET.

CITIES ACROSS THE NATION WERE SWARMING WITH "WORKING GIRLS." BY ONE ESTIMATE, HALF THE MEN IN NEW YORK VISITED ONE OF THE CITY'S 20,000 GIRLS THREE TIMES A WEEK.

SEND THE NEXT ONE UP, WILLYA?

NEW ORLEANS, WITH ITS BUSTLING PORT, BECAME A NOTORIOUS HAVEN FOR VICE IN THE 'TEENS -- ESPECIALLY A SECTION CALLED "THE SWAMP." WOULD-BE CUSTOMERS WERE OFTEN ROBBED AND BEATEN.

C'MON, BIG BOY -- GET READY FOR THE TIME OF YER LIFE!

FROM 1820 TO 1850, AT LEAST 800 MURDERS WERE COMMITTED IN THIS AREA OF HALF A DOZEN BLOCKS -- IN PART BECAUSE THE AUTHORITIES WERE AFRAID TO GO THERE.

CAN'T SAY I DIDN'T TELL YA SO!

PROSTITUTION AND OTHER CRIME EVENTUALLY SPREAD THROUGHOUT THE CITY, OUTRAGING THE LAW-ABIDING.

ELSEWHERE, LAWS AGAINST THE TRADE WERE HAVING LITTLE EFFECT, APART FROM ENCOURAGING POLICE CORRUPTION.

PENNY FOR YOUR THOUGHTS, OFFICER.

MAKE IT TUPPENCE AND WE'RE SQUARE.

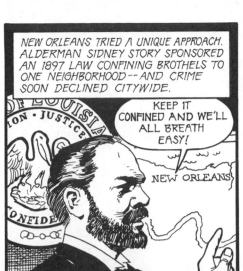

NEW ORLEANS TRIED A UNIQUE APPROACH. ALDERMAN SIDNEY STORY SPONSORED AN 1897 LAW CONFINING BROTHELS TO ONE NEIGHBORHOOD -- AND CRIME SOON DECLINED CITYWIDE.

KEEP IT CONFINED AND WE'LL ALL BREATH EASY!

NEW ORLEANS

THE 38-BLOCK AREA BECAME KNOWN, TO THE ALDERMAN'S DISMAY, AS "STORYVILLE." FROM ELEGANT MANSIONS--

--TO 25-CENT "CRIBS"; EVERY BUILDING IN THE NEIGHBORHOOD WAS DEVOTED TO VICE.

BROCHURES FOR VARIOUS BROTHELS WERE OFTEN GIVEN TO MEN AS THEY ARRIVED IN TOWN. THE BLUE BOOK, A COMPREHENSIVE GUIDE TO STORYVILLE, WAS PUBLISHED ANNUALLY.

"IF IT'S PRETTY WOMEN AND A GOOD TIME YOU ARE LOOKING FOR, MISS FISHER'S IS THE PLACE."

LET'S GO!

BLUE BOOK

WITH ABOUT 2000 GIRLS PLUS DOZENS OF SALOONS AND GAMBLING DENS, STORYVILLE PULLED IN $10-15 MILLION A YEAR.

BUT IN 1917 THE WAR DEPARTMENT ORDERED STORYVILLE CLOSED TO "PROTECT" A NEARBY MILITARY BASE.

CLOSED BY ORDER OF DEPT. OF WAR

ONCE AGAIN THE GIRLS SCATTERED ALL OVER TOWN--AS DID CRIME AND CORRUPTION.

AHH... THERE'S NO PLACE LIKE HOME...

BUT AS VICTORIAN ATTITUDES FADED DURING THE 20TH CENTURY, SO DID PROSTITUTION. IN 1950, 70% OF U.S. MEN HAD PAID FOR SEX; TODAY THE NUMBER IS ABOUT 10%.

GREAT GRAND-DAD PAID FOR THAT?

HOLLYWOOD'S RICH AND FAMOUS HAVE URGES, TOO -- AND TO SATISFY THEM, THEY HAVE LONG TURNED TO --

LEE FRANCIS, LEADING MADAM OF THE '20s AND '30s, ALWAYS MANAGED TO CLEAR OUT HER CUSTOMERS -- ESPECIALLY THE FAMOUS ONES -- BEFORE A RAID.

THEN SHE AND THE VICE SQUAD BOYS WOULD SIT DOWN TO CHAMPAGNE AND CAVIAR -- PART OF THEIR REWARD FOR TIPPING HER OFF IN ADVANCE.

LEE FINALLY DID TIME ON A MORALS CHARGE. ANN FORRESTER TOOK OVER THE TERRITORY -- QUITE SUCCESSFULLY, MAKING FIVE GRAND A WEEK.

ANN WAS CAUGHT BY REFORM MAYOR FLETCHER BOWRON'S CITYWIDE CLEANUP. HER TESTIMONY HELPED ROOT OUT MANY CORRUPT VICE COPS.

ONE OF HER GIRLS, MARIE MITCHELL, SWORE THAT ANN HAD LED HER INTO A LIFE OF SIN -- THOUGH SHE'D ACTUALLY BEEN A STREETWALKER WHEN FORRESTER RECRUITED HER.

WHEN ANN WENT TO JAIL IN 1940, MARIE CHANGED HER NAME TO BRENDA ALLEN AND WENT INTO BUSINESS FOR HERSELF. SOON, SHE HAD 114 GIRLS, RAKING IN $9000 A DAY.

PERHAPS HER GREATEST ASSET WAS A RUMORED BLACK BOX CONTAINING INFORMATION ON 250 "SPECIAL" CLIENTS -- STARS, MOBSTERS, AND POLITICIANS.

BRENDA MAINTAINED SEVERAL HOUSES. WHEN ONE WAS RAIDED, SHE JUST MOVED. SHE WAS ARRESTED 19 TIMES BUT SOMEHOW MANAGED TO STAY IN BUSINESS.

YOU AGAIN?

IN 1947, VICE SQUAD SERGEANT ELMER JACKSON WAS PARKED WITH HIS GIRLFRIEND WHEN A GUNMAN TRIED A HOLDUP.

GIMME YOUR DOUGH.

JACKSON KILLED THE MAN. AN INVESTIGATION EVENTUALLY REVEALED THE COP'S GIRLFRIEND WAS REALLY BRENDA ALLEN. IT SEEMED MAYOR BOWRON HADN'T NABBED ALL THE CROOKED COPS.

JACKSON WAS ALLEN'S PARTNER, AND OTHER VICE SQUADDERS WERE IN ON IT. THE CHIEF OF POLICE WAS FORCED TO RESIGN, AND ALLEN'S CAREER ENDED--

--BUT HER BLACK BOX NEVER SURFACED.

IN 1951, A NEW POLICE CHIEF QUICKLY CRACKED DOWN ON THE NEXT HOLLYWOOD MADAM, BARRIE BENSON.

BUT HER BUSINESS HAD BEEN OFF TO A FAST START. IN ONE BEDROOM, THE RAIDERS FOUND SIGNED PHOTOS OF NUMEROUS STARS.

I've never had better!

Barrie, you're an artist! Love.

TWO DECADES LATER, ELIZABETH ADAMS' SELECT STABLE OF JET-SETTING, HIGH-PRICED GIRLS EARNED HER THE NICKNAME "BEVERLY HILLS MADAM"-- AND $100,000 A MONTH.

SHE STAYED IN BUSINESS FOR 20 YEARS BY PROVIDING THE COPS WITH INFO HER GIRLS LEARNED DURING INTIMATE MOMENTS.

ADAMS WAS FINALLY REPLACED AS "MADAM TO THE STARS" BY A FORMER-PROTÉGÉ-TURNED-RIVAL--BY THE NAME OF HEIDI FLEISS.

THE REST, AS THEY SAY IS HERSTORY.

FACTOID BOOKS

XAVIERA HOLLANDER OPENED AMERICA'S EYES TO THE REAL LIFE OF A "WORKING GIRL" WHEN SHE WROTE

The Happy Hooker

BORN TO A WEALTHY DUTCH FAMILY IN INDONESIA, XAVIERA WAS BROUGHT UP IN A HOUSEHOLD WHERE SEX WAS PART OF EVERYDAY LIFE.

NITEY-NITE, LOVE!

SLEEP TIGHT, BABY.

SHE CAME TO NEW YORK IN 1967. WHEN HER THEN-FIANCÉ DUMPED HER, SHE THREW HERSELF INTO THE SINGLES SCENE.

Y'KNOW, BABE, I WOULD'A PAID FOR A TIME LIKE THAT!

SOON, XAVIERA WAS TAKING ON LUNCH-TIME "ASSIGNATIONS" TO SUPPLEMENT HER REGULAR INCOME.

WE'LL HAVE TO MAKE THIS A QUICKIE.

IN ONE WAY, XAVIERA WAS VERY DIFFERENT FROM HER "CO-WORKERS!"

I'M ONLY IN IT FOR THE MONEY.

ME, TOO.

I LOVE THE MONEY-- AND THE SEX.

SHE DECIDED SHE COULD HAVE MORE OF BOTH BY BECOMING A MADAME, AND BEFORE LONG WAS RUNNING THE MOST SUCCESSFUL HOUSE IN NEW YORK CITY.

IN 1972 THE KNAPP COMMISSION ON POLICE CORRUPTION ACCUSED HER OF MAKING PAYOFFS TO NEW YORK CITY COPS. XAVIERA WAS DEPORTED.

GOODBYE, MY LOVE!

I'LL NEVER FORGET YOU...

INTERNATIONAL DEPARTUR

ME NEITHER...

SHE RETURNED TO EUROPE, BECOMING A COLUMNIST FOR PENTHOUSE MAGAZINE.

not all prostitutes are uneducated. I myself can speak seven languages fluently, and always enjoy talking to my customers about their professional lives.

TODAY XAVIERA HAS LARGELY FADED FROM THE SPOTLIGHT, PERHAPS BECAUSE-- AS SHE ONCE SAID --

THERE'S NOTHING SADDER THAN AN AGING PROSTITUTE.

ITS STORY IS A STRANGE TANGLE OF CRIME, CORRUPTION, POLITICS, AND TAXES, BUT IT'S STILL GOING STRONG AFTER MORE THAN THIRTY YEARS...

MUSTANG RANCH

NEVADA'S FIRST LEGAL BROTHEL

IN THE MID-1950'S EX-GI JOE CONFORTE AND MADAM SALLY BURGESS WENT INTO COMPETITION WITH EACH OTHER TO PROVIDE ILLEGAL PROSTITUTION IN RURAL NEVADA.

HAVE A GOOD TIME HERE

HAVE A GOOD TIME HERE --FOR LESS!

FINDING MUCH IN COMMON, JOE AND SALLY MARRIED AND BECAME PARTNERS IN THE TRIANGLE RANCH.

TRIANGLE RANCH

THE RANCH WAS RUN OUT OF TRAILERS THAT SAT WHERE WASHOE, STOREY, AND LYON COUNTIES MEET.

IF THE SHERIFF OR D.A. OF ONE OF THE COUNTIES PLANNED TO CRACK DOWN, CONFORTE JUST WHEELED THE BROTHEL INTO ANOTHER JURISDICTION.

ENTERING WASHOE COUNTY

IN THE EARLY '60S, JOE SPENT A COUPLE OF YEARS IN PRISON FOR DODGING TAXES AND TRYING TO FRAME A WASHOE COUNTY D.A. IN 1967, HE AND SALLY TOOK OVER THE MUSTANG RANCH IN STOREY COUNTY.

A DISTRICT JUDGE ORDERED THE BROTHEL CLOSED AND DEMANDED THAT CONFORTE PAY $1000 A MONTH FOR FIVE MONTHS TO COVER THE COSTS OF EXTRA PATROLS TO ENFORCE THE ORDER.

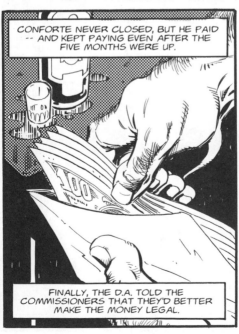

CONFORTE NEVER CLOSED, BUT HE PAID -- AND KEPT PAYING EVEN AFTER THE FIVE MONTHS WERE UP.

FINALLY, THE D.A. TOLD THE COMMISSIONERS THAT THEY'D BETTER MAKE THE MONEY LEGAL.

IN 1970, LAME-DUCK COMMISSIONERS PASSED THE ONLY BROTHEL-LICENSING ORDINANCE IN THE COUNTRY -- BENEFITING JOE, THEIR LARGEST TAXPAYER.

HELL, BOYS, WE'RE OUT OF HERE ANYWAY!

STOREY COUNTY COMMISSION

FEARING HARM TO THE CASINO INDUSTRY, THE NEVADA LEGISLATURE PROHIBITED PROSTITUTION IN COUNTIES WITH MORE THAN 200,000 RESIDENTS.

IF WE LET THIS SPREAD, LAS VEGAS WILL BE ASSOCIATED WITH SIN!

LAS VEGAS AND RENO WERE OFF LIMITS, BUT MOST COUNTIES WERE ABLE TO CHOOSE -- AND THAT'S HOW NEVADA GOT LEGALIZED PROSTITUTION.

THE SAGEBRUSH RANCH

THE GREEN LANTERN

SHERRI'S RANCH 2 MI

CHERRY PATCH RANCH

BUT JOE'S TROUBLES WEREN'T OVER. IN 1982, HE FOUND HIMSELF OWING 13 MILLION IN BACK TAXES. HE SPENT YEARS TRYING TO RESOLVE THE DISPUTE -- BUT FAILED.

IN 1990, THE IRS WAS COMING TO SEIZE THE RANCH. JOE GRABBED ALL THE CASH AND THE GIRLS' HEALTH CARDS -- WITHOUT WHICH THEY COULDN'T WORK -- AND SPLIT. THE GIRLS SCATTERED.

THE IRS WAS LEFT WITH A NON-FUNCTIONING ASSET -- AND COUNTY COMMISSIONER (AND EX-MUSTANG MANAGER) SHIRLEY COLLETTI TOLD THE TRUSTEE IT MIGHT TAKE MONTHS TO ISSUE A NEW BROTHEL LICENSE.

JUST FILL OUT THESE FORMS.

COUNTY CLERK

IN AN AMAZING COINCIDENCE, STOREY COUNTY INSPECTORS FOUND NUMEROUS FIRE CODE VIOLATIONS AT THE RANCH.

TSK, TSK -- SHOCKING LACK OF SAFETY MEASURES.

VIOLATION

AS WORD GOT OUT THAT THE U.S. NOW OWNED A BROTHEL, LATE-NIGHT COMEDIANS HAD A FIELD DAY.

-- SO I GUESS THAT MAKES GEORGE BUSH A PIMP!

HA HA HA HA HA!

THE GOVERNMENT WANTED OUT.

THE IRS SOLD THE RANCH FOR $1.5 MILLION TO MUSTANG PROPERTIES -- A CORPORATION REPRESENTED BY JOE'S LAWYER'S BROTHER. JOE AND HIS LAWYER WERE SOON INDICTED FOR FRAUD --

FEDERAL COURT HOUSE BUILDING

-- BUT JOE SKIPPED OUT.

THE RANCH IS PROSPERING -- EVEN SELLING T-SHIRTS, MUGS, AND PHONE CARDS BEARING ITS LOGO.

JOE CONFORTE IS A FUGITIVE OVERSEAS, BUT SOME SAY HE STILL OWNS PART OF THE BROTHEL HE MADE FAMOUS.

FACTOID BOOK

SINCE ANCIENT TIMES, WOMEN HAVE BEEN *ENSLAVED* AND *SOLD* INTO *PROSTITUTION* IN FOREIGN LANDS. TODAY, THIS BRUTAL *TRADE* IS GLOBAL -- AND GROWING.

SEX SLAVES

IT OFTEN STARTS WITH AN AD.

GRINDING *POVERTY* AND POLITICAL *TURMOIL* THROUGHOUT MUCH OF THE *WORLD* MAKES MANY WOMEN EASY PREY.

EARN UP TO $6000 A MONTH!

ATTRACTIVE, OUTGOING WOMEN WANTED!

DIFFERENT COVER STORIES ARE GIVEN TO THE WOMEN WHO *RESPOND*. THE RUSSIAN *MAFIA* HAS BEEN *QUICK* TO CATCH ON...

WE'RE *TRAINING* GIRLS TO COOK IN *RESTAURANTS* IN CHINA.

WITH THE *PROMISE* OF GOOD JOBS, THE GIRLS ARE SENT TO VARIOUS FOREIGN COUNTRIES, OFTEN WITH FORGED PAPERS.

ONCE THERE, THE TRUE NATURE OF THE "*JOB*" IS *REVEALED*.

THEIR PASSPORTS ARE TAKEN...

I'LL GIVE THIS *BACK* TO YOU -- FOR $15,000.

OF COURSE, *SAVING* SUCH A SUM IS IMPOSSIBLE.

YOUR RENT IS $800 A MONTH AND $500 FOR FOOD--

AND YOU OWE ME $5000 FOR YOUR *TRANSPORTATION*. I'LL TAKE IT OUT OF YOUR WAGES.

OFTEN, THE GIRLS ARE VIRTUAL *PRISONERS*. FIRES HAVE CLAIMED THE LIVES OF MANY.

AND EVEN IF THEY COULD GET OUT...

YOU DON'T SPEAK THE *LANGUAGE*. YOU'D BE *DEPORTED*-- THEN WE WOULD *FIND* YOU AND BRING YOU *BACK* HERE.

SOMETIMES AN *EXAMPLE* IS MADE OF THOSE WHO TRY TO *ESCAPE*.

WITHIN *EUROPE*, SEX TRAFFICKERS SMUGGLE HALF A *MILLION* WOMEN A YEAR, MOSTLY FROM THE *IMPOVERISHED* FORMER COMMUNIST EAST.

MANY OTHERS ARE SHIPPED TO THE *U.S.*, OFTEN VIA *MEXICO*. A RAID IN THE *WASHINGTON D.C.* SUBURBS REVEALED *RUSSIAN* WOMEN TURNING *TRICKS* IN A *MASSAGE PARLOR*.

THEY TOLD ME I WOULD BE AN *AU PAIR*...

...AND *I* A *WAITRESS!*

ISRAEL IS ANOTHER COMMON DESTINATION. LOCAL *PIMPS* BUY A GIRL FOR $500-$1000, BUT CAN MAKE AS MUCH AS $20,000 A *MONTH* OFF HER.

THE *GIRL*, OF COURSE, SEES VERY *LITTLE* OF THE *MONEY*.

IN THE *PACIFIC*, U.S. MILITARY BASES HAVE *LONG* BEEN A *POWERFUL* MAGNET FOR *PROSTITUTION*.

SHORE LEAVE! YEE-HAW!

LET'S GET SOME WOMEN!

PROSTITUTION HAS BEEN *RAMPANT* IN *OKINAWA* FOR *DECADES*. RECENTLY, *PROCURERS* HAVE BEGUN IMPORTING *FILIPINO* AND *THAI* GIRLS TO REPLACE THE MORE *EXPENSIVE* LOCALS.

...AND THESE *G.I.'S* DON'T *CARE!*

THE GIRLS ARE HIRED AS "*CULTURAL DANCERS*"-- BUT ARE OFTEN *FORCED* INTO *PROSTITUTION*. HERE, TOO, THEIR *PASSPORTS* ARE TAKEN AND THEY'RE KEPT IN *DEBT* TO THE BARS WHERE THEY *WORK*.

DURING THE *VIETNAM WAR*, PROSTITUTION IN *THAILAND* BOOMED. *BANGKOK* HAD AS MANY AS 70,000 GIRLS TO *SERVICE* SOLDIERS ON *LEAVE*.

AFTER THE WAR, LOCAL *BUSINESSMEN* SEARCHED FOR A NEW *SOURCE* OF *CUSTOMERS* TO REPLACE THE DEPARTING *SERVICEMEN* -- AND TURNED TO ORGANIZED "SEX TOURS."

THE PROMISE OF ILLICIT *SEX* DRAWS WEALTHY *VISITORS* FROM AROUND THE *WORLD* TO VARIOUS *ASIAN* DESTINATIONS.

EXOTIC ASIAN DELIGHTS

ABOUT *18,000* VIETNAMESE WOMEN NOW *WORK* AS *PROSTITUTES* IN *THAILAND.* MANY WERE *KIDNAPPED* AND *SMUGGLED* ACROSS THE *BORDER.*

ABOUT *10,000* WOMEN FROM THE FORMER *SOVIET* UNION, MOST FROM THE *UKRAINE,* NOW WORK IN *BANGKOK BROTHELS.*

CUSTOMERS WORRIED ABOUT *AIDS* HAVE DEMANDED EVER-*YOUNGER* GIRLS -- AND *BOYS.* CHILDREN ARE *KIDNAPPED* OR *BOUGHT* FROM THEIR *DESTITUTE PARENTS.*

SEX TOURISM IS *GROWING* IN *AFRICA,* TOO, AS COUNTRIES *DESPERATELY* SEEK FOREIGN *CURRENCY.*

SOME OPERATIONS NOW *ADVERTISE* ON THE *INTERNET.* DESCRIPTIONS INCLUDE HOTEL *PRICES,* TAXI FARES, AND THE *COSTS* OF *SPECIFIC SEX ACTS* ON THE LOCAL *MARKET.*

TRAVEL *Philippines*

COME EXPLORE THE PHILLIPINES WITH ME!

ACCORDING TO THE *U.N.,* GLOBAL SEX *SLAVERY* IS A *$7 BILLION-A-YEAR* BUSINESS -- NEARLY AS MUCH AS THE ILLEGAL INTERNATIONAL *TRADE* IN *DRUGS* OR *WEAPONS.*

THE SEX TRADE *STILL* RECEIVES RELATIVELY *LITTLE* ATTENTION FROM *LAW ENFORCEMENT.* IN THE LAST 25 YEARS, 30 MILLION WOMEN AND *CHILDREN* HAVE BEEN *ENSLAVED* -- AND THE NUMBER *GROWS* EVERY DAY.

EARN UP TO $6000 A MONTH

ATTRACTIVE OUTGOING WOMEN WANTED

FACTOID BOOKS

FOR CENTURIES, MUCH OF THE BUSINESS OF PROSTITUTION HAS BEEN CONTROLLED BY THE PROCURER OR BAWD, BETTER KNOWN TODAY AS...

THE PIMP

DON'T BE READIN' THIS STUPID COMIC BOOK, SWEET CHEEKS--GET OUT THERE AND MAKE US SOME MONEY.

FINDING NEW "TALENT"-- YOUNG VULNERABLE GIRLS--HAS ALWAYS BEEN A KEY ROLE FOR THE PIMP. ONLY HIS PATTER HAS CHANGED.

NEW IN TOWN? I'M IN THE ENTERTAINMENT INDUSTRY. WE'RE ALWAYS LOOKING FOR NEW FACES-- LET ME BUY YOU A DRINK.

CENTURIES AGO, POOR MOTHERS SOME-TIMES SOLD THEIR (OFTEN ILLEGITIMATE) DAUGHTERS TO PROCURERS OUT OF ECO-NOMIC NECESSITY.

MODELING, MOVIES, VIDEOS-- IT'S AN EXCITING LIFE. AND GOOD MONEY, TOO.

DUE TO FEAR OF DISEASE, CUSTOMERS-- AND THUS THE PIMP-- HAVE LONG PLACED A PREMIUM ON YOUNG GIRLS.

17? NO WAY! YOU'RE VERY MATURE FOR YOUR AGE.

SINCE THE INDUSTRIAL REVOLUTION, NAIVE YOUNG GIRLS HAVE STREAMED INTO URBAN CENTERS SEARCHING FOR JOB OPPORTUNITIES.

YOU'VE GOT GREAT CHEEKBONES. I'LL BET YOU'RE AN ACTRESS, RIGHT?

PIMPS ARE ADEPT AT SPOTTING INSE-CURE RUNAWAYS. GIRLS ARE RECRUITED FROM POOR AREAS WITH OFFERS OF FRIENDSHIP, ADVENTURE, AND EASY MONEY.

JUST COME WITH ME-- I'LL INTRODUCE YOU TO THE RIGHT PEOPLE.

PIMPS PREY ON GIRLS WHO CAN'T DEFEND THEMSELVES. WHILE SOME OLDER WOMEN WORK ALONE, UP TO 90% OF JUVENILE PROSTITUTES ARE CONTROLLED BY A PIMP.

WE'RE NOT GOING TO BE MAKING ANY MUSIC VIDEOS TODAY.

THE PIMP OFTEN MOVES HIS GIRLS FROM CITY TO CITY, PREVENTING THEM FROM MAKING FRIENDS.

HE BECOMES THE ONE CONSTANT IN THE ISOLATED GIRLS' DISORIENTING LIVES.

THE GIRLS MUST TURN OVER THEIR EARNINGS TO THE PIMP, KEEPING THEM ECONOMICALLY DEPENDENT ON HIM.

HERE--GET YOURSELF SOMETHIN' TO EAT.

BECAUSE OF THIS PSYCHOLOGICAL MANIPULATION, THE GIRLS COME TO ACCEPT AND RELY ON THE PIMP.

OH, YOU'LL GET USED TO HIM, HONEY.

AS PROSTITUTION HAS SHIFTED FROM BROTHELS TO THE STREETS, THE DANGERS FACED BY THE GIRLS HAVE INCREASED. THEY LOOK TO THE PIMP FOR PROTECTION.

YOU DON'T TREAT MY GIRLS LIKE THAT!

PIMPS ARE TERRITORIAL AND ARE ALWAYS ON THE LOOKOUT FOR RIVALS TRYING TO POACH THEIR GIRLS. PROSTITUTES FROM DIFFERENT "FAMILIES" ARE DISCOURAGED FROM MINGLING.

YOU STAY AWAY FROM WILLIE AND HIS SKANKY HOS.

MOST PROSTITUTES WORKING FOR PIMPS MUST MEET A QUOTA BEFORE THEY CAN LEAVE THE STREET EACH DAY.

PROSTITUTES WHO FAIL TO MEET THEIR QUOTA ARE OFTEN THREATENED, BEATEN, OR EVEN TORTURED.

BECAUSE OF THE WAY THEY OPERATE, PIMPS ARE DIFFICULT TARGETS FOR COPS. THE GIRLS ARE MUCH MORE FREQUENT TARGETS FOR ARREST--

--AND THE PIMP WILL USUALLY BAIL THEM OUT.

YOUR "FRIEND" SENT ME TO GET YOU OUT OF HERE.

DURING THE SUMMER, PIMPS OFTEN MOVE THEIR GIRLS TO TOURIST DESTINATIONS. SOMETIMES THEY "LOAN" THE GIRLS TO ASSOCIATES IN OTHER CITIES.

YOU GO WITH BIRD DOG. HE'S GONNA TAKE CARE OF YOU FOR A WHILE.

HONOLULU IS A MAJOR STOP. MANY FREE-SPENDING JAPANESE TOURISTS VISIT THERE AND IT'S A TRANSIT POINT FOR SHIPPING GIRLS TO THE FAR EAST.

WITH THE EMPHASIS ON YOUTH, THE WORKING LIFE SPAN OF A PROSTITUTE IS BRIEF -- SO THE PIMP IS ALWAYS ON THE LOOKOUT...

HEY, BABY--NEW IN TOWN?

IN THE SLEAZY WORLD OF NEW YORK PROSTITUTION, SYDNEY BIDDLE BARROWS' BLUE-BLOODED LINEAGE AND HIGH-CLASS OPERATION MADE HER UNIQUE. HER PILGRIM ANCESTRY EARNED HER THE TABLOID NICKNAME...

MAYFLOWER MADAM

SYDNEY GREW UP IN A WORLD OF DEBUTANTE BALLS AND BOARDING SCHOOLS-- BUT FAMILY MONEY WAS RUNNING LOW.

SHE WORKED HER WAY THROUGH COLLEGE, THEN ENTERED THE FASHION INDUSTRY. BUT AFTER A FEW PROMISING YEARS, SHE FOUND HERSELF OUT OF A JOB--AND BROKE.

SHE FOUND WORK ANSWERING PHONES AT AN ESCORT SERVICE--A THINLY-VEILED, POORLY-MANAGED CALL GIRL RING. SYDNEY SOON DECIDED SHE COULD DO IT BETTER--AND MORE PROFITABLY.

IN 1979, SYDNEY SET UP HER OWN WELL-ORGANIZED SERVICE, INSISTING ON INTELLIGENT, LADYLIKE GIRLS AND CATERING TO ONLY CAREFULLY SCREENED, WELL-TO-DO "GENTLEMEN."

FOR FIVE YEARS, HER GIRLS SERVICED THOUSANDS OF HAPPY EXECUTIVES, DIPLOMATS, AND THE LIKE--UNTIL A DISPUTE WITH HER LANDLORD ATTRACTED POLICE ATTENTION.

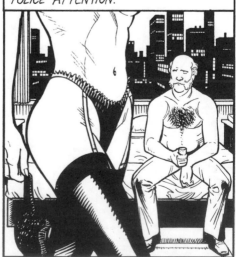

SYDNEY WAS BUSTED--AND THE CASE MADE THE FRONT PAGES FOR MONTHS. BUT SYDNEY HAD BEEN CAREFUL AND THE D.A. HAD LITTLE EVIDENCE. SHE GOT OFF WITH A $5,000 FINE.

NEW YORK POST
MAYFLOWER MADAM FREED

DESPITE NEWS REPORTS, SYDNEY DIDN'T GET RICH, BUT SHE'S SINCE BECOME A BEST-SELLING AUTHOR AND NOW TEACHES SEMINARS, PASSING ALONG HER TIPS ON HOW TO PLEASE A MAN.

AND I SHOULD KNOW!

FROM STONE-AGE CARVINGS TO TODAY'S DESKTOP PUBLISHING, EACH NEW FORM OF HUMAN COMMUNICATION HAS BEEN ONE MORE STEP IN...

THE EVOLUTION OF PORN

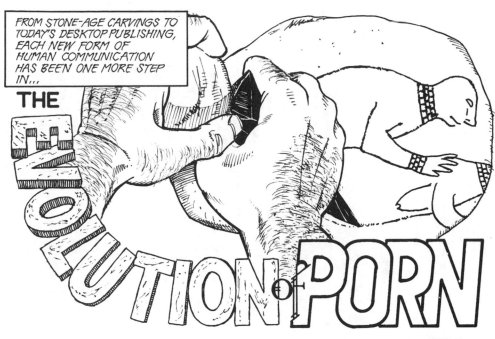

EIGHTEENTH-CENTURY SCHOLARS HAD LITTLE DIRECT KNOWLEDGE OF CLASSICAL GREECE AND ROME. THE ANCIENT CIVILIZATIONS WERE SEEN AS LIVING IN A HIGH-MINDED, VIRTUOUS GOLDEN AGE--

GOOD LORD!

--UNTIL THE EXCAVATION OF POMPEII.

AS THEY UNCOVERED EROTICA IN THE WELL-PRESERVED ROMAN CITY BURIED BY A FIRST-CENTURY VOLCANIC ERUPTION, THEY CONCLUDED...

-HARUMPH- THIS BUILDING MUST HAVE BEEN A BROTHEL!

BUT, AS MANY SIMILAR DISCOVERIES APPEARED --

ANOTHER BROTHEL?

AND ANOTHER?

--THEY FINALLY REALIZED THAT SEXUAL IMAGERY HAD BEEN A COMMON PART OF EVERYDAY LIFE IN ANCIENT TIMES.

THE POMPEII EXCAVATIONS BECAME A POPULAR TOURIST DESTINATION AS THOSE "IN THE KNOW" WERE ALLOWED TO VIEW THE SHOCKING FINDS, NOW KEPT IN A SECRET MUSEUM.

RIGHT THIS WAY, SIGNORI.

THE WORD PORNOGRAPHY COMES FROM THE GREEK TERM FOR WRITING ABOUT PROSTITUTION. AS FURTHER ARCHAEOLOGICAL SURVEYS WOULD REVEAL, THE GREEKS DID MORE THAN WRITE ABOUT IT.

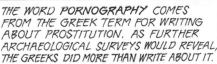

IN FACT, AS EUROPEANS LATER LEARNED, EROTICISM EXISTED IN CULTURES AROUND THE WORLD IN VIRTUALLY ALL FORMS OF EXPRESSION -- FROM JAPANESE WOODBLOCK PRINTS TO PRE-COLUMBIAN POTTERY.

Except for some salacious tales by Boccaccio & Chaucer, erotic content was restricted largely to stories and songs passed by word of mouth in church-dominated medieval Europe.

KEEP IT CLEAN, BROTHER BENEDICT!

WITH THE RENAISSANCE CAME A RENEWED OPENNESS TOWARDS DISPLAY OF THE HUMAN BODY.

AM I GLAD I WASN'T BORN A FEW HUNDRED YEARS EARLIER!

SOME WERE CONSIDERED A BIT TOO OPEN. PIETRO ARETINO, A MEMBER OF POPE CLEMENT VII'S COURT, WROTE A BAWDY SERIES OF SONNETS ACCOMPANIED BY ENGRAVINGS KNOWN AS "ARETINO'S POSTURES."

Hmmmm... WHAT RHYMES WITH "LUCK"?

THE EXPLICIT IMAGES WERE BANNED, BUT THEY—AND MANY IMITATIONS— WERE AVIDLY SOUGHT FOR CENTURIES TO COME.

AUTHENTIC ARETINO, SIR-- AS YOU CAN SEE!

THE PRINTING PRESS SPED THE SPREAD OF PORN. PERHAPS INSPIRED BY THE POMPEII DISCOVERIES, EROTIC BOOKS, PRINTS, AND EVEN PLAYING CARDS BECAME POPULAR IN THE MID-1700s.

NOW THIS IS A HOT HAND!

FANNY HILL, JOHN CLELAND'S NOVEL ABOUT THE LIFE OF A PROSTITUTE, WAS WILDLY POPULAR WHEN PUBLISHED IN 1748, BUT WAS WIDELY SUPPRESSED FOR THE NEXT 200 YEARS.

FANNY HILL BY JOHN CLELAND

A FEW DECADES LATER, THE MARQUIS DE SADE WAS JAILED FOR (AMONG OTHER THINGS) WRITING TWO LURIDLY SEXUAL BOOKS.

BUT THEY ALWAYS SAY "WRITE WHAT YOU KNOW!"

DESPITE ATTEMPTS TO SQUELCH IT, PORNOGRAPHY FLOURISHED AS PRINTING TECHNIQUES BECAME BETTER AND CHEAPER.

fine books

IN 1834 A SINGLE LONDON STREET CONTAINED 57 PORN SHOPS.

MY SECRET LIFE, PUBLISHED IN 1890, PAINTED A VIVID (AND APPARENTLY AUTOBIOGRAPHICAL) PICTURE OF VICTORIAN-ERA DEBAUCHERY.

"...PICKED UP HALF A DOZEN VIRGINS IN THE STREET..."

IN 1878 *THE NATIONAL POLICE GAZETTE* BEGAN PUBLISHING ENGRAVINGS TO ACCOMPANY ITS SPICY TALES OF PROSTITUTES AND CHORUS GIRLS, MAKING IT A FIXTURE IN BARBER SHOPS ACROSS AMERICA.

THE NEWLY INVENTED STILL AND MOVIE CAMERAS WERE SOON FOCUSED ON SEXUAL SUBJECTS. EADWEARD MUYBRIDGE SHOT NUDES IN MOTION IN THE LATE 1800s.

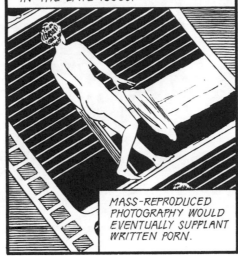

MASS-REPRODUCED PHOTOGRAPHY WOULD EVENTUALLY SUPPLANT WRITTEN PORN.

PHOTOGRAPHIC "FRENCH POSTCARDS", FEATURING ACTRESSES AND BATHING BEAUTIES, MADE THEIR WAY TO ENGLAND AND THE U.S. AROUND THE TURN OF THE CENTURY.

PSSt

BY THE 1920s, "STAG FILMS" WERE CIRCULATING UNDERGROUND, AND STORIES PERSIST ABOUT HOLLYWOOD STUDIOS BLACKMAILED OVER ILL-CONSIDERED PERFORMANCES BY THEIR STARS.

ISN'T THAT...?!

IT SURE IS!

"GIRLIE" MAGAZINES PROSPERED IN THE '30s. AS COLOR PRINTING IMPROVED, GLOSSY HARD-CORE SEX MAGS FOLLOWED IN THE '60s.

PRIVATE

PLAYBOY

PEP

JUNE 25¢ STORIES

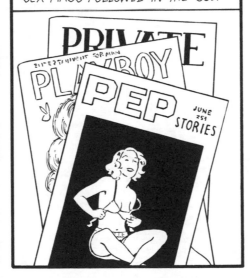

AS LEGAL BARRIERS FELL IN THE '70s, PORN FILMS PLAYED IN THEATERS --

WHAT IF THE NEIGHBORS SEE US?

NOW PLAYING

DEEP THROAT RATED X

--BUT IT WAS THE INVENTION OF THE VCR AND CAMCORDER THAT REVOLUTIONIZED THE INDUSTRY.

WITH PEOPLE ABLE TO WATCH IN THE PRIVACY OF THEIR HOMES, COUNTLESS THOUSANDS OF PORNO VIDEOS HAVE BEEN RELEASED. AMERICANS RENT OVER 600 MILLION A YEAR.

HOME GROWN PORN presents

tHORNY in the ROSEBUSHES

PLAY

NOW THE PERSONAL COMPUTER AND THE INTERNET HAVE COMBINED TO MAKE PORN ACCESSIBLE GLOBALLY. SEX SITES RAKE IN MILLIONS WHILE MOST MAINSTREAM SITES HAVE YET TO TURN A PROFIT.

KLIK KLIK KLIK KLIK

IT'S IMPOSSIBLE TO PREDICT THE FUTURE OF COMMUNICATION TECHNOLOGY, BUT WHATEVER FORM IT TAKES, THERE WILL PROBABLY BE PORN TO MATCH.

FACTOID BOOKS 100% TRUE

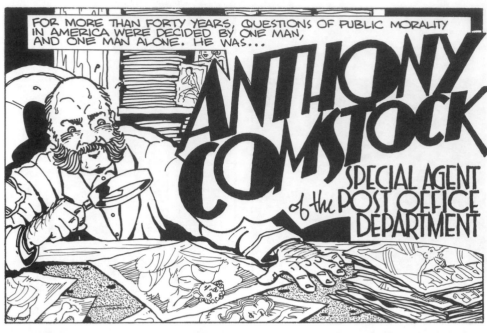

FOR MORE THAN FORTY YEARS, QUESTIONS OF PUBLIC MORALITY IN AMERICA WERE DECIDED BY ONE MAN, AND ONE MAN ALONE. HE WAS...

ANTHONY COMSTOCK
SPECIAL AGENT of the POST OFFICE DEPARTMENT

BORN OF PURITAN STOCK IN CONNECTICUT IN 1844, ANTHONY COMSTOCK WAS A TROUBLED BOY.

HIS MOTHER'S DEATH WHEN HE WAS TEN SENSITIZED HIM TO WHAT HE SAW AS the WORLD'S EVILS.

HE RAILED AGAINST ALCOHOL. WHILE STILL IN HIS TEENS, HE BROKE INTO A SALOON AND EMPTIED the KEGS.

BUT HIS GREATEST ANGER WAS DIRECTED AT WHAT HE CALLED **"FILTH."**

WHILE WORKING AS A DRY GOODS CLERK IN NEW YORK, COMSTOCK NOTICED COWORKER'S PASSING AROUND A PORNOGRAPHIC BOOK.

HE WAS SO ENRAGED THAT HE FOUND the DEALER WHO HAD SOLD IT AND DEMANDED HIS ARREST.

THOUGH HE FAILED INITIALLY, COMSTOCK CONTINUED HIS EFFORTS FOR FOUR YEARS, EVENTUALLY GAINING the ARREST OF SEVEN DEALERS.

the PUBLISHER, AN IRISH-AMERICAN NAMED WILLIAM HAINES, COMMITTED SUICIDE.

WEALTHY MEMBERS OF the YOUNG MEN'S CHRISTIAN ASSOCIATION NOTED COMSTOCK'S DETERMINATION.

WHEN HE SOUGHT MONEY TO FORM the NEW YORK SOCIETY FOR the SUPPRESSION OF VICE, THEY WERE HAPPY TO HELP.

COMSTOCK CONTINUED LOCAL EFFORTS AGAINST PORNOGRAPHY, BUT HE ALREADY HAD BIGGER PLANS. IN 1872, HE TRAVELED TO WASHINGTON TO LOBBY FOR A NEW ANTI-OBSCENITY LAW.

HE SET UP AN EXHIBIT IN the VICE-PRESIDENT'S OFFICE THAT WAS SOON DUBBED "the CHAMBER OF HORRORS."

IN 1873, PRESIDENT GRANT SIGNED WHAT WAS ALREADY UNOFFICIALLY CALLED "the COMSTOCK LAW."

"AN ACT FOR the SUPPRESSION OF, TRADE IN, AND CIRCULATION OF OBSCENE LITERATURE AND ARTICLES OF IMMORAL USE." HMPH!

THE NEW LAW HAD A SECRET CLAUSE THAT GREATLY IN-CREASED ITS EFFECTIVENESS.

THE COMMITTEE ON APPROPRI-ATIONS SET ASIDE $3,425 FOR A "SPECIAL AGENT" WITH the UNDERSTANDING THAT COMSTOCK WOULD GET the JOB.

ANTHONY WAS GIVEN A BADGE AND A FREE HAND. HE HAD NO DIRECT BOSS. THE INTER-PRETATION OF the 'COMSTOCK LAW' WAS ENTIRELY UP TO HIM.

COMSTOCK WAS EMPOWERED TO INSPECT ANY MAIL THAT HE BE-LIEVED MIGHT BE OBSCENE OR WHICH MIGHT CONTAIN INFORMA-TION ABOUT CONTRACEPTION OR ABORTION.

U.S. MAIL

IN the FIRST SIX MONTHS, COMSTOCK SEIZED 194,000 PICTURES, 14,200 STEREOPTICON PLATES, 134,000 POUNDS OF BOOKS, AND 60,300 "ARTICLES MADE OF RUBBER FOR IMMORAL PURPOSES"

AS HIS POWER INCREASED, HE PUBLICLY ATTACKED WRITERS, ARTISTS, ADVERTISERS, PUB-LISHERS, FEMINISTS, AND ANY-ONE ELSE HE BELIEVED WAS **PROMOTING LUST.**

EDITOR

HE ATTACKED the PLAY, "MRS. WAR-REN'S PROFESSION" BECAUSE IT DEALT WITH PROSTITUTION, AND DENOUNCED ITS AUTHOR, GEORGE BERNARD SHAW, AS "AN IRISH SMUT PEDDLER."

HEATE

THEATRE BY

LOSED

WARREN'S PROFESSION

REBUKING WHAT HE SAW AS NARROW-MINDEDNESS, SHAW COINED THE WORD 'COMSTOCKERY,' A TERM STILL IN USE TODAY.

COMSTOCKERY IS THE WORLD'S STANDING JOKE AT the EXPENSE OF the UNITED STATES.

OTHER WORKS TARGETED BY COM-STOCK INCLUDED WALT WHITMAN'S *LEAVES OF GRASS*, VOLTAIRE'S *CANDIDE* AND DANIEL DEFOE'S *MOLL FLANDERS.*

LEAVES OF GRASS

IN HIS 1883 BOOK, *TRAPS FOR the YOUNG*, COMSTOCK DESCRIBED A LURID AMERICA WHERE "HALF DIME" NOVELS, OBSCENE PAINT-INGS, SCULPTURE AND EVEN POSTCARDS WERE WAITING TO DE-BAUCH UNPROTECTED YOUTH.

LIKE MANY OF HIS TIME, COMSTOCK WARNED OF THE HORRIBLE CONSEQUENCES OF MASTURBATION.

FATHERS and MOTHERS—LOOK INTO YOUR CHILD'S FACE, AND WHEN YOU SEE the VIGOR OF YOUTH FAILING, the CHEEK GROWING PALE, the EYE LUSTERLESS AND SUNKEN, IN MANY CASES IT WILL BE FOUND TO COME FROM—

SECRET... ...PRACTICES!

HE CONTINUALLY HARASSED BIRTH CONTROL ADVOCATE MARGARET SANGER, WHO WAS INDICTED FOR MAILING FAMILY-PLANNING PAMPHLETS,

IF YOU OPEN the DOOR TO ANYTHING, the FILTH WILL POUR IN.

HER CASE WAS DISMISSED AFTER COMSTOCK'S DEATH.

SO PERVASIVE WAS COMSTOCK'S INFLUENCE THAT the WORD "PREGNANT" DISAPPEARED FROM BOOKS OF THE PERIOD.

IN SOME CASES, HE WAS ABLE TO PERSUADE PUBLISHERS NOT TO PRINT CERTAIN WORKS OR TO RECALL ALL COPIES AND DESTROY the PLATES.

ONE PROMOTER TURNED the TABLES ON COMSTOCK. HE HIRED A GROUP OF BOYS TO OGLE A PRINT OF the PAINTING "SEPTEMBER MORN" — THEN TOLD COMSTOCK OF THIS "SHOCKING" SCENE.

ART GAL

The RESULTING NOTORIETY HELPED SELL MILLIONS OF REPRODUCTIONS OF the IMAGE!

COMSTOCK ROUTINELY IGNORED OTHER LAWS WHILE ENFORCING HIS OWN, FREQUENTLY RESORTING TO FRAUD AND ENTRAPMENT.

YOU'RE UNDER ARREST!

HE OFTEN ANSWERED ADVERTISEMENTS UNDER FALSE NAMES AND WORE DISGUISES TO GAIN ACCESS TO SUSPICIOUS ITEMS.

ANN LOHMAN, A NEW YORK MIDWIFE WHOM COMSTOCK PROSECUTED FOR TEACHING ABOUT BIRTH CONTROL AND ABORTION, KILLED HERSELF RATHER THAN GO TO JAIL.

A BLOODY END TO A BLOODY LIFE.

IN ALL, SIXTEEN PEOPLE KILLED THEMSELVES IN RESPONSE TO COMSTOCK'S ATTACKS.

IN 1913, COMSTOCK WROTE THAT HE HAD "CONVICTED" ENOUGH PEOPLE TO FILL A PASSENGER TRAIN OF SIXTY-ONE COACHES, WITH SIXTY OF the COACHES CONTAINING SIXTY PEOPLE EACH."

ABORTIONISTS PANDERERS SMUT PEDDLERS

IN 1915, PRESIDENT WOODROW WILSON APPOINTED COMSTOCK TO REPRESENT the UNITED STATES AT the INTERNATIONAL PURITY CONGRESS IN SAN FRANCISCO.

ANTHONY COMSTOCK
1844–1915

IN MEMORY OF A FEARLESS WITNESS

WHILE THERE, HE CONTRACTED A FATAL CASE OF PNEUMONIA.

BUT FOR DECADES AFTER HIS DEATH, AMERICAN FILMS, BOOKS, PLAYS, MAGAZINES AND PAINTINGS WOULD BEAR the MARK OF COMSTOCK'S LIFELONG PASSION.

IF I COULD BUT LIVE WITHOUT SIN, I SHOULD BE the HAPPIEST SOUL LIVING. BUT SIN, THAT FOE, IS EVER LURKING, STEALING HAPPINESS FROM ME.

FACTOID BOOKS

EXOTIC DANCING DATES BACK AT LEAST TO THE SCANTILY CLAD *AULETRIDES* OF ANCIENT GREECE. IN VARIOUS FORMS, IT PROMISES AT LEAST A GLIMPSE OF...

LIVE NUDE GIRLS!

THE RISQUÉ, HIGH-KICKING CANCAN DEBUTED IN PARIS IN THE 1830S. IT REMAINED POPULAR FOR THE REST OF THE CENTURY AT CABARETS SUCH AS THE MOULIN ROUGE.

IN 1868 THE FIRST BURLESQUE SHOW CAME TO THE U.S., FEATURING CRUDE COMEDIANS AND A BEVY OF BEAUTIFUL CHORUS GIRLS. A NATIONAL CIRCUIT OF BURLESQUE THEATRES EMERGED TO SHOWCASE THEM.

TO-DAY LYDIA TH BRITISH

IN 1893, BELLY DANCERS PERFORMED AT CHICAGO'S WORLD FAIR. A SCANDALOUS STORY SPREAD ABOUT ONE, NAMED LITTLE EGYPT, WHO REMOVED HER CLOTHES AS SHE DANCED.

TRUE OR NOT, SEVERAL WOMEN LATER CLAIMED TO BE LITTLE EGYPT, AND THE "STRIPTEASE" WAS GRADUALLY INCORPORATED INTO BURLESQUE SHOWS, MAKING STARS OF THE LIKES OF GYPSY ROSE LEE.

Boom Bom! Ba Boom!

THOUGH NUDITY WAS MORE IMPLIED THAN DISPLAYED, THE SHOWS WERE OFTEN RAIDED. IN 1937 ALL OF NEW YORK'S BURLESQUE HOUSES WERE CLOSED.

OVER THE NEXT FEW DECADES, THE CIRCUIT DISAPPEARED.

IN 1964, A PUBLICIST FOR A SAN FRANCISCO BAR PERSUADED WAITRESS CAROL DODA TO WEAR A TOPLESS BATHING SUIT, CREATING A SENSATION. THE BAR WAS BUSTED--BUT WON IN COURT.

AS LAWS CHANGED, STRIP CLUBS OPENED ACROSS THE COUNTRY, CREATING A NEW "CIRCUIT."

TOTAL NUDITY IS COMMON, AND "NAME" PORN STARS NOW FIND MORE LUCRATIVE THAN FILMS.

FACTOID BOOKS

master of the pornoverse

REUBEN STURMAN WAS A HARD-NOSED BUSINESSMAN WHO BUILT A HARDCORE GLOBAL EMPIRE.

HE WAS BORN IN 1924 IN CLEVELAND. A NATURAL SALESMAN, HE BECAME A WHOLESALER OF CANDY AND TOBACCO THERE IN THE LATE '40s.

BY THE EARLY '50s. HE FOUND A SPECIALTY--COMIC BOOKS. HE TRAVELED THE MIDWEST, SELLING THEM FROM THE TRUNK OF HIS CAR.

COVERS OF UNSOLD COMICS WERE RETURNED TO THE PUBLISHERS FOR CREDIT. THE COVERLESS BOOKS WERE SUPPOSED TO BE DESTROYED, BUT STURMAN INSTEAD BAGGED THREE TOGETHER TO SELL FOR 10¢.

KIDS AND STORE OWNERS LOVED THE DEAL, AND STURMAN WOULD REMEMBER THIS SUCCESSFUL REPACKAGING.

HE SOON BECAME A MAGAZINE WHOLESALER, BUILDING A VAST DISTRIBUTION NETWORK.

IN 1964 ONE OF STURMAN'S MANAGERS SUGGESTED HE STOCK A NEW LINE OF RACY PAPERBACKS. THE FIRST, "SEX LIFE OF A COP," WAS A SALES SENSATION.

THEN THE FBI RAIDED HIS MAIN WAREHOUSE. HE WAS CHARGED WITH DISTRIBUTING OBSCENE MATERIAL.

FACING 15 YEARS IN JAIL, STURMAN FOUGHT THE CASE TO THE SUPREME COURT, WHICH RULED:

THIS BOOK IS PROTECTED BY THE FIRST AMENDMENT.

FOLLOWING HIS COURT VICTORY, STURMAN SAW A GREAT BUSINESS OPPORTUNITY. HE WENT TO EUROPE AND BOUGHT LOTS OF HARDCORE PORN, RECENTLY LEGALIZED THERE.

SINCE FEW U.S. STORES WOULD CARRY SUCH MATERIAL, HE OPENED A STRING OF HIS OWN OUTLETS-- THUS CREATING THE ADULT BOOKSTORE.

IF YOU'RE BOLD ENOUGH YOU'RE OLD ENOUGH!!!

ADULTS ONLY!

MAKE THE WORD "SEX" BIGGER.

HE BEGAN PUBLISHING HIS OWN MATERIAL, REPACKAGING OLD STUFF WITH NEW COVERS UNTIL IT SOLD.

HMM... MAYBE THIS'LL DO IT.

BY 1970 HE WAS PERHAPS THE BIGGEST DISTRIBUTOR OF PORN MAGS.

THE RECENT DEVELOPMENT OF SUPER 8 FILM HELPED FUEL A BOOM IN PORNO MOVIE PRODUCTION. STURMAN SAW ANOTHER OPPORTUNITY.

$$$!

HE CREATED THE PEEPSHOW BOOTH, A SMALL ROOM WHERE A CUSTOMER COULD WATCH SUPER 8 PORNO LOOPS IN PRIVATE.

AS LONG AS THEY KEEP PUTTING IN QUARTERS, THEY CAN KEEP WATCHING.

PEEP SHOW BOOTH

FROSTED WINDOW

MIRROR

COIN SLOT

DOOR

STOOL

PROJECTOR

25¢

MIRROR

HE INSTALLED THEM FOR FREE IN ADULT BOOKSTORES COAST TO COAST-- AND TOOK 50% OF THE PROCEEDS.

25¢

HE EVENTUALLY RAKED IN AS MUCH AS $2 BILLION, LARGELY IN CASH.

HE ALSO LAUNCHED A HIGHLY SUCCESSFUL MAIL-ORDER SEX TOY COMPANY CALLED DOC JOHNSON, WITH FACTORIES IN ASIA.

MARITAL AIDS
-VIBRATORS!
FRENCH TICKLERS!
NOW IN THE PRIVACY OF YOUR OWN HOME!
SEND FOR OUR CATALOG TODAY!
COUPON

IN THE MID-'70s, STURMAN SPOTTED HIS FUTURE-- THE VCR.

SALE

NEW BETAMAX!!!!

SEX ON TV. WHAT A DEAL!

FORMING COMPANIES IN THE U.S. AND EUROPE, HE QUICKLY BECAME ADULT VIDEO'S DOMINANT DISTRIBUTOR.

STURMAN HATED PAYING TAXES-- WITH THE FEDS STILL PRESSING OBSCENITY RAPS, HE CONSIDERED IT FUNDING THE ENEMY.

4TH BANK OF ZURICH

USING FAKE NAMES AND DUMMY CORPORATIONS, HE STASHED HIS LOOT IN SWITZERLAND AND THE CAYMAN ISLANDS.

THE IRS BEGAN TRYING TO UNTANGLE THE COMPLEX WEB OF STURMAN'S BUSINESSES -- A PROCESS THAT WOULD TAKE YEARS.

FINALLY IN 1985 ATTORNEY GENERAL ED MEESE INDICTED STURMAN, WHOM THE JUSTICE DEPARTMENT CALLED...

THE NUMBER 1 DISTRIBUTOR OF HARDCORE PORNOGRAPHY.

STURMAN MOCKED HIS TRIAL AND APPEARED WEARING A FAKE NOSE AND GLASSES.

BUT HIS ASSOCIATES CAVED AND HE WAS SENTENCED TO PRISON FOR TAX EVASION. MOST OF HIS ASSETS WERE SEIZED.

STURMAN APPEALED, BUT HIS EMPIRE WAS CRUMBLING. MANY OF HIS STORES STOPPED MAKING THEIR REGULAR PAYMENTS TO HIM.

HE FOUGHT BACK--HARD.

IN 1992 A BOMB INTENDED FOR A NON-PAYING STORE EXPLODED PREMATURELY, KILLING A STURMAN "ASSOCIATE." THREE SURVIVORS TURNED STATE'S EVIDENCE.

FINALLY STURMAN MADE A DEAL WITH THE FEDS AND IN JUNE OF 1992 BEGAN SERVING A 10-YEAR TERM IN BORON, CALIFORNIA.

6 MONTHS LATER, HE ESCAPED.

RECAPTURED 8 WEEKS LATER, STURMAN WAS SENT TO A FEDERAL PRISON IN KENTUCKY.

WITH STURMAN BEHIND BARS, RIVALRY AND RETRIBUTION SWEPT THE PORN INDUSTRY.

THE DOC JOHNSON PLANT MYSTERIOUSLY BURNED DOWN, AND A CAYMAN BANK WAS BOMBED.

FINALLY PEACE WAS RESTORED AS NEW PORN POWERS GAINED CONTROL. BUT PERHAPS NONE WILL EVER BE AS DOMINANT AS REUBEN STURMAN -- WHO DIED IN PRISON IN 1997.

FACTOID BOOKS 100% TRUE

JOHN HOLMES WAS THE BIGGEST OF ALL TIME -- THE ELVIS PRESLEY OF THE ADULT MOVIE INDUSTRY...THE ONE, THE ONLY

KING OF PORN

HOW DID THE SON OF A BIBLE-THUMPING BAPTIST GET INTO PORNOGRAPHY?

MY BOY HAD PERFECT ATTENDANCE AT SUNDAY SCHOOL.

HE WAS JUST DOING WHAT CAME NATURALLY. HOLMES FIRST DID IT AT TWELVE, WITH A FRIEND OF HIS MOTHER'S.

OH MY, AREN'T YOU EQUIPPED.

CENSORED

AT SIXTEEN, HE LEFT HOME TO JOIN THE ARMY, SERVING THREE YEARS.

TENT-HUT!

UH... AT EASE, SON.

CENSORED

COMING HOME, HE WORKED AS AN AMBULANCE DRIVER, WHERE HE MET A NURSE NAMED SHARON GEBENINI. THE TWO WERE MARRIED IN 1965.

BUT IT WASN'T LONG BEFORE HOLMES TOLD SHARON HE'D DECIDED TO START TRADING ON HIS NATURAL ASSETS.

I WANT TO GO INTO THE PORN BUSINESS, BABE. I THINK I COULD BE REALLY BIG.

DARLIN', YOU ALREADY ARE BIG.

MOVIE

CENSORED

HOLMES WAS REALLY BIG -- FOUR INCHES IN DIAMETER, AND OVER THIRTEEN INCHES LONG WHEN FULLY ERECT.

MAMA MIA! AT'SA ONE SPICY SALAMI!

IN 1970, HE DID THE FIRST FILM IN THE SERIES THAT WOULD MAKE HIM A STAR.

WHO ARE YOU?

JOHNNY WADD, DOLLFACE. PRIVATE DICK.

CENSORED

AT THE HEIGHT OF HIS FAME, HOLMES WAS JET-SETTING ACROSS THE GLOBE TO FILM PREMIERES, PARTIES...

OH! -- TEE-HEE -- THE BUBBLES TICKLE MY NOSE!

I'VE GOT SOMETHING THAT COULD TICKLE YOU ELSEWHERE, MA'AM.

...AND SERVING AS A HIGH-PRICED GIGOLO TO THE VERY WEALTHY.

~GASP~ "TICKLE" AWAY, STUDLY!

HE MADE OVER **2,200** PORN MOVIES. BUT THERE WAS A DARK SIDE TO HOLMES' FAST-PACED LIFESTYLE.

~TOOT-TOOT~ **WOW!** WHAT A **RUSH!**

AS HIS DRUG USE ESCALATED, HOLMES BECAME DIFFICULT TO DEAL WITH ON SETS. HIS WORK SUFFERED...

GET YOUR ACT **TOGETHER,** JOHNNY!

YEAH, YEAH...

~GRUMBLE, MUTTER~

CENSORED

...AND THEN DRIED UP ALMOST COMPLETELY. HOLMES WAS REDUCED TO SERVING AS A DELIVERY BOY FOR A GANG OF DRUG DEALERS IN HOLLYWOOD.

THANKS, KID! HERE'S FI' DOLLAHS EXTRA -- CATCH A **SHAVE,** HAH?

IN 1981, HOLMES WAS BUSTED BY THE POLICE. A DRUG DEALER NAMED **EDDIE NASH** BAILED HIM OUT.

THANKS, MR. NASH.

CALL ME **EDDIE.**

NASH, WHO HAD INTERESTS IN SEVERAL ADULT BUSINESSES, LOVED HAVING HOLMES AROUND AND SHOWING HIM OFF TO HIS GUESTS.

THIS HERE IS THE **HUGELY...** "TALENTED" JOHNNY **WADD.**

NASH KEPT A LOT OF MONEY -- AND DRUGS -- IN HIS HOUSE, SOMETHING HOLMES SOON BECAME AWARE OF.

HOLMES HAPPENED TO MENTION IT TO THE PEOPLE HE WAS RUNNING DRUGS FOR.

HE JUST LEAVES IT ALL LYING AROUND.

ON JUNE 28TH, 1981, THE **WONDERLAND CREW** ROBBED NASH AND HIS BODYGUARD OF THEIR CACHE OF DRUGS AND OVER $100,000.

ON THE FLOOR, **MOTHER-@#$%ERS!**

GRAB THE **CASH** AND LET'S **SPLIT!**

SUSPECTING HOLMES WAS INVOLVED, NASH CALLED HIM OVER TO HIS HOUSE.

TELL ME WHO *DID* IT, OR I'LL BLOW YOUR *BRAINS* OUT.

ON JULY 2ND, THE WONDERLAND GANG WAS BRUTALLY MURDERED.

ACCORDING TO THE COPS, HOLMES TOLD THEM NASH WAS RESPONSIBLE. BUT HE NEVER TESTIFIED TO IT IN COURT.

I DON'T KNOW *WHO* DID IT.

HE SPENT CLOSE TO A YEAR IN JAIL ON CONTEMPT CHARGES, THEN WENT BACK TO MAKING MOVIES. BUT HIS HEART WASN'T IN IT ANYMORE...

I JUST CAN'T GET EXCITED ABOUT THIS.

I CAN TELL.

CENSORED

THE HOME VIDEO MARKET FOR PORN WAS JUST BEGINNING TO BOOM. HOLMES WAS BITTER ABOUT NOT RECEIVING ANY RESIDUALS IN WHAT WAS CLEARLY GOING TO BE A MULTIMILLION-DOLLAR INDUSTRY.

I WAS THE *PILLAR* OF THIS LOUSY BIZ, AND I'M GETTING *DICK*. IT AIN'T RIGHT.

SOMETHING GOOD DID COME OUT OF HIS RETURN TO FILMS -- HE MET AND MARRIED AN ACTRESS NAMED *LAURIE ROSE*...

BUT SOMEWHERE ALONG THE WAY, HOLMES HAD CONTRACTED THE *AIDS* VIRUS. HE DIED ON MARCH 13TH, 1988.

~SOB~

THE MOVIE *"BOOGIE NIGHTS"* WAS IN LARGE PART A FICTIONAL RETELLING OF HOLMES' STORY.

AND YOU CAN STILL, IF YOU DESIRE, BUY A JOHN HOLMES *"PENIS PUMP."*

the original
John Holmes
PERSONAL PUMP

IT'S NOT STRETCHING THE POINT TO SAY THE HOLMES LEGACY LIVES ON...AND ON...AND ON...

THOUGH HE CAME FROM A RIGID MIDWEST METHODIST BACKGROUND, HUGH M. HEFNER LED A TRANSFORMATION IN AMERICAN VALUES THAT MADE HIM A --

SEXUAL REVOLUTIONARY

WHEN HE WAS A CHILD, HUGH'S PARENTS HAD SOME PRETTY STRANGE IDEAS ABOUT SHOWING AFFECTION.

DON'T! KISSING TRANSMITS GERMS.

PERHAPS THAT'S WHY HE DEVELOPED AN ACTIVE FANTASY LIFE, WRITING AND DRAWING HIS OWN COMIC BOOKS AND SPENDING A LOT OF TIME AT THE MOVIES.

-SNFF- THAT'S THE WAY LOVE OUGHT TO BE.

IN COLLEGE HE EDITED THE SCHOOL HUMOR MAGAZINE WHERE HE INSTITUTED A NEW FEATURE:
CO-ED OF THE MONTH.

HOLD THAT POSE, "MISS FEBRUARY!"

BUT AFTER GRADUATION, HEF FELT IT WAS TIME TO GROW UP. HE GOT MARRIED AND HAD A DAUGHTER AND A SON. IT DIDN'T TAKE HIM LONG TO REALIZE...

I'M MISERABLE.

IN 1953 HE STARTED PLAYBOY WITH $8000 OF HIS OWN MONEY. AMAZINGLY, THE MAGAZINE WAS A SMASH FROM THE START.

HAVING MARILYN MONROE NUDE IN THE FIRST ISSUE DIDN'T HURT.

IN THE REPRESSIVE, CONFORMIST FIFTIES, THE MAGAZINE STRUCK A CHORD WITH AFFLUENT, WELL-EDUCATED MEN ACROSS THE COUNTRY. ITS MESSAGE:

WELL, WHATAYA KNOW! SEX IS OKAY!

THE CENTERFOLDS REPRESENTED THE GIRL NEXT DOOR..THEY WERE NICE GIRLS WHO ALSO LIKED SEX.

HMM...
I WONDER...

BUT PLAYBOY WAS MORE THAN JUST A MAGAZINE -- IT WAS A WHOLE LIFESTYLE. AND HEF DECIDED TO MAKE A TASTE OF IT AVAILABLE TO HIS READERS BY OPENING THE PLAYBOY CLUB.

IN ITS FIRST YEAR, 90,000 MEN BECAME MEMBERS.

BUT THE REAL PARTY WAS DOWN THE STREET IN HEF'S PRIVATE CHICAGO MANSION. IT WAS THE ULTIMATE ADOLESCENT BOYS' FANTASY HOUSE.

BUFFET TABLE

STEREO SYSTEM

UNDERGROUND POOL

AFTER THE PARTIES, PEPPED ON DEXEDRINE, HEF WOULD STAY UP ALL NIGHT WORKING. NO DETAIL ESCAPED HIS NOTICE.

THE AIRBRUSH SHOULD FIX IT.

HE GAVE WRITERS, INCLUDING ALEX HALEY, RON KOVIC, WILLIAM F. BUCKLEY, AND SUPREME COURT JUSTICE WILLIAM O. DOUGLAS A FORUM TO EXPRESS THEIR OPINIONS. CIRCULATION HIT 7,000,000.

I BUY IT FOR THE ARTICLES!

WHATEVAH...

HEF'S OWN CIRCULATION SKYROCKETED TOO. BY HIS OWN ESTIMATE, HE SLEPT WITH CLOSE TO 1000 WOMEN.

BY 1971 HIS EMPIRE INCLUDED 23 PLAYBOY CLUBS, RESORTS, HOTELS, CASINOS, A MODELING AGENCY, A FILM AND TV PRODUCTION COMPANY, AND THE WORLD'S MOST FAMOUS PRIVATE JET -- THE BIG BUNNY.

BUT TIMES WERE CHANGING. THE FEMINIST MOVEMENT, THE ASCENDANCY OF CONSERVATIVE VALUES, MARKED THE END OF HIGH TIMES AT PLAYBOY.

PLAYBOY CLUB

WOMEN ARE NOT BUNNIES

PLAYBOY IS PORNOGRAPHY

HEFNER DEMEANING TO WOMEN

IN 1985, HEF HAD A STROKE AND TURNED PLAYBOY OVER TO HIS DAUGHTER CHRISTIE. NOW HAPPILY MARRIED, HE'S CONTENT TO SPEND HIS DAYS WITH HIS CHILDREN WATCHING HIS FAVORITE OLD MOVIES.

THIS IS THE WAY LOVE OUGHT TO BE.

FACTOID BOOKS 100% TRUE

HE'S AN UNLIKELY CHAMPION OF FREEDOM... BUT THERE ARE THOSE WHO SAY LARRY FLYNT BELONGS IN THE GREAT PANTHEON OF AMERICAN HEROES.

PATRIOT OF PORN

LARRY FLYNT WAS BORN IN 1942 IN RURAL KENTUCKY. AT THE AGE OF 7 HE HAD HIS FIRST SEXUAL EXPERIENCE.

WHO, ME?

AT NINE HE HAD A SIMILAR ENCOUNTER WITH A CHICKEN.

I THINK I LIKE GIRLS BETTER.

IN 1958 FLYNT LIED ABOUT HIS AGE AND JOINED THE ARMY.

HE GOT BOOTED FROM THE SERVICE FOR HIS LACK OF EDUCATION.

NEXT UP: THE NAVY. WHILE SERVING ABOARD THE U.S.S. ENTERPRISE, HE MET PRESIDENT KENNEDY--BY STEPPING ON HIS FOOT.

≥YOWCH!≤

AYE, AYE, SIR!

AFTER LEAVING THE SERVICE, FLYNT GOT INTO THE BAR BUSINESS IN DAYTON OHIO BY OPENING THE HUSTLER CLUB.

ONLY THE TRULY SUAVE APPLY!

BY 1973 HE HAD EIGHT HUSTLER CLUBS ACROSS OHIO, CATERING TO THE TRAVELING BUSINESSMAN.

SHAKE IT, BABY, SHAKE IT!

IN 1974, FLYNT DECIDED TO PUT OUT A NATIONAL MEN'S MAGAZINE. HE STUDIED THE COMPETITION...

THESE GIRLS NEED TO SPREAD THEIR LEGS A LITTLE WIDER.

...AND IN 1974 BROUGHT OUT THE FIRST ISSUE OF HUSTLER. MAGAZINE WHOLESALERS ACROSS THE COUNTRY WERE AFRAID TO CARRY IT.

THE COPS'LL SHUT ME DOWN!

FLYNT BOUGHT SOME "HARDCORE" PORN MAGAZINES. THEN HE WENT TO THE POLICE.

MY MAGAZINE IS MUCH TAMER THAN THESE.

THE COPS AGREED NOT TO GIVE THE DISTRIBUTORS A HARD TIME.

HUSTLER MADE FLYNT A MILLIONAIRE. BUT IN 1976, HE WENT ON TRIAL IN CINCINNATI ON CHARGES OF PANDERING, OBSCENITY, AND ORGANIZED CRIME.

IF MY MAGAZINE IS OBSCENE, WHAT ABOUT THESE?

INADMISSIBLE EVIDENCE!

FLYNT WAS CONVICTED ON ALL COUNTS. AT HIS SENTENCING, HE ASKED FOR PERMISSION TO ADDRESS THE COURT.

YOU HAVEN'T MADE AN INTELLIGENT DECISION DURING THE COURSE OF THIS TRIAL!

FLYNT WAS RELEASED ON BAIL TO FACE OTHER OBSCENITY CHARGES IN GEORGIA. DURING A LUNCH RECESS...

HE'S BEEN SHOT!

THE SHOOTING PARALYZED HIM BELOW THE WAIST (HE REMAINED SEXUALLY "FUNCTIONAL") AND LEFT FLYNT IN CONSTANT, AGONIZING PAIN.

THE LAWSUITS AGAINST HIM CONTINUED, AND HE SOON LANDED JAIL.

EVENTUALLY RELEASED, FLYNT'S FINEST HOUR CAME WHEN HUSTLER PUBLISHED A PARODY OF A LIQUOR AD, LAMPOONING JERRY FALWELL.

FALWELL SUED FOR DEFAMATION OF CHARACTER--AND WON.

HORRIFIED BY THE DECISION, GROUPS INCLUDING THE NEW YORK TIMES, THE ACLU, THE AUTHOR'S LEAGUE, ETC., STOOD AT FLYNT'S SIDE DURING HIS APPEAL BEFORE THE SUPREME COURT.

WHERE WERE YOU GUYS WHEN I REALLY NEEDED YOU?

ON FEBRUARY 24, 1998, THE VERDICT CAME THROUGH:

FLYNT CONVICTION OVERTURNED

TODAY FLYNT RULES OVER A PUBLISHING EMPIRE THAT INCLUDES OVER A DOZEN MAGAZINES, AS WELL AS A HUSTLER ONLINE WEBSITE.

the SULTAN of SLEAZE

BLOW ME

FOR THE LAST THIRTY YEARS, AL GOLDSTEIN HAS BEEN THE LOUDEST, MOST OBNOXIOUS MAN IN THE PORNOGRAPHY BUSINESS...AND PROUD OF IT.

AS A YOUNG BOY GROWING UP IN A HASIDIC NEIGHBORHOOD IN WILLIAMSBURG, BROOKLYN, AL WAS OBSESSED BY SEX.

I MUST BE SOME KIND OF FREAK.

HE SOON FOUND OUT HE WASN'T THE ONLY ONE.

ARTHUR MILLER...ALFRED KINSEY...D.H. LAWRENCE...ALL PERVS LIKE ME!

TROPIC OF CANCER

KAMA SUTRA

KINSEY REPORT

LADY CHATTERLY'S LOVER

AL FIRST HAD SEX WHEN HE WAS SIXTEEN. HE WAS OVERWHELMED BY THE INTENSITY OF HIS FEELINGS.

I THINK I SAW GOD.

IN THE EARLY SIXTIES, AL WORKED AS A FREELANCE PHOTOGRAPHER. HE WENT TO PAKISTAN WITH JACKIE KENNEDY.

UGH!

ACCUSED OF BEING AN AMERICAN SPY, HE SPENT A COUPLE OF WEEKS IN PRISON.

CAN I AT LEAST GET SOME READING MATERIAL IN HERE?

IN 1968 HE STARTED SCREW MAGAZINE.

I'M FOR FREE LOVE AND ALL--

--BUT THAT'S GROSS!

FROM THE VERY FIRST ISSUE, GOLDSTEIN WAS DEFIANTLY HARDCORE.

HE PUBLISHED CARTOONS LAMPOONING THEN NYC MAYOR JOHN LINDSAY'S SEX HABITS.

AND THAT'S PUTTING IT MILDLY!

AL GOLDSTEIN PUBLISHER

FORTY-EIGHT HOURS LATER, GOLDSTEIN WAS IN HANDCUFFS.

ALL TOLD, GOLDSTEIN WAS ARRESTED NINETEEN TIMES FOR VIOLATING STATE OBSCENITY LAWS.

IN 1976, THE FEDS DECIDED TO GO AFTER HIM. BUT THEY WANTED A TRIAL SOMEPLACE OTHER THAN NEW YORK CITY - SOMEPLACE GOLDSTEIN'S HUMOR WOULD BE CLEARLY OFFENSIVE TO "COMMUNITY STANDARDS."

SCREW · SUBSCRIBE TO SCREW · SCREW

THEY TOOK OUT SUBSCRIPTIONS TO SCREW TO BE MAILED TO WICHITA, KANSAS.

DEAR GOD, MARTHA...IS THAT WHAT I THINK IT IS?

the Smiths

SCREW

LAND O'GOSHEN!

TO RAISE MONEY FOR HIS DEFENSE, GOLDSTEIN JACKED UP HIS AD RATES. CUSTOMERS--MANY OF THEM "WORKING GIRLS"--WERE NOT HAPPY.

YOU'RE CUTTING INTO MY PROFIT MARGIN, AL!

THE TRIAL WAS DELAYED SEVERAL TIMES, FIRST FOR A CHANGE OF VENUE TO KANSAS CITY, THEN BY GOLDSTEIN'S CLAIM HE NEEDED SURGERY FOR SLEEP APNEA.

IT'S MY NOSE--IF I FALL ASLEEP, I COULD DIE!

IN DECEMBER 1977, GOLDSTEIN WAS SEIZED BY FEDERAL MARSHALS IN MANHATTAN, AND RETURNED TO KANSAS TO STAND TRIAL.

HE PLED GUILTY AND PAID A $30,000 FINE.

GOLDSTEIN BEGAN HOSTING HIS OWN XXX-RATED CABLE TALK SHOW, MIDNIGHT BLUE. HE OFTEN STARTED HIS INTERVIEWS WITH FEMALE GUESTS BY PERFORMING ORAL SEX ON THEM.

MIDNIGHT BLUE

IT'S JUST A FORMALITY...

IN 1993, TO THE CHAGRIN OF MANY, HE BECAME A MEMBER OF WASHINGTON D.C.'S PRESTIGIOUS NATIONAL PRESS CLUB.

WIENERS IN JACKETS-- YOU KNEW I WAS COMING!

GOLDSTEIN ALSO HOLDS AN HONORARY DOCTORATE FROM THE INSTITUTE FOR THE ADVANCED STUDY OF SEXUALITY.

STUDY HARD, AND YOU TOO CAN GET A-HEAD!

IN 1997, AL RECEIVED THE ULTIMATE TRIBUTE--HE WAS THE SUBJECT OF A DOCUMENTARY CALLED "SCREWED." HIS FIRST WORDS IN THE MOVIE?

DEATH BEFORE MARRIAGE

ARE THERE ANY WOMEN HERE WAITING TO BE PENETRATED?

HOPING TO OBTAIN WILLING SEX PARTNERS OR ENHANCE PERFORMANCE, PEOPLE HAVE LONG EXPERIMENTED WITH MANY BIZARRE POTIONS AND CONCOCTIONS KNOWN AS...

aphrodisiacs

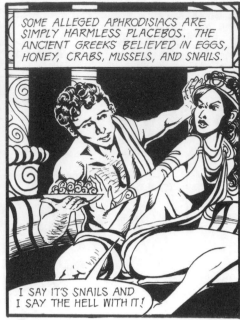

SOME ALLEGED APHRODISIACS ARE SIMPLY HARMLESS PLACEBOS. THE ANCIENT GREEKS BELIEVED IN EGGS, HONEY, CRABS, MUSSELS, AND SNAILS.

I SAY IT'S SNAILS AND I SAY THE HELL WITH IT!

IN CHINA, MIXTURES OF VARIOUS HERBS WERE THOUGHT TO BE STIMULATING.

WON'T YOU COME TO BED, DEAR?

IN A MINUTE -- NOW, HAND ME THE MILKWORT.

HERBS COMBINED WITH LIVER EXTRACT FROM A WHITE DOG KILLED DURING THE FULL MOON WERE SAID TO ENLARGE THE PENIS.

WINE MADE WITH DOG OR GOAT MEAT WAS ALSO CONSIDERED A SEX AID.

HERE, FIDO! GOOD BOY!

IN THE MIDDLE AGES IT WAS THOUGHT THAT A WOMAN COULD ENTICE HER HUSBAND BY SERVING HIM A FISH THAT HAD BEEN WRAPPED IN AFTERBIRTH WHILE STILL ALIVE.

THIS TASTES... DIFFERENT.

SOME "APHRODISIACS" ARE DANGEROUS. THE MARQUIS DE SADE WAS JAILED FOR POISONING SEVERAL WOMEN WITH SPANISH FLY, MADE FROM GROUND-UP BEETLES.

HMM... NOT THE EFFECT I HAD IN MIND!

ILLEGAL AND POTENTIALLY DEADLY KNOCKOUT DRUGS HAVE BEEN IMPLICATED IN NUMEROUS RECENT DATE RAPE CASES.

YOU'RE A REAL KNOCKOUT, DOLL--LEMME GET YOU A DRINK!

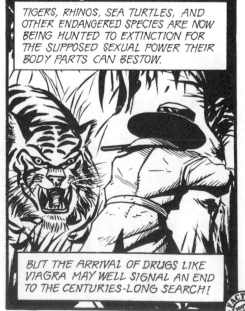

TIGERS, RHINOS, SEA TURTLES, AND OTHER ENDANGERED SPECIES ARE NOW BEING HUNTED TO EXTINCTION FOR THE SUPPOSED SEXUAL POWER THEIR BODY PARTS CAN BESTOW.

BUT THE ARRIVAL OF DRUGS LIKE VIAGRA MAY WELL SIGNAL AN END TO THE CENTURIES-LONG SEARCH!

CHAPTER SIX

GAMBLING

Nobody wants to be poor. It is better to have money than not to have money. The flip side of the traditional work ethic is the "get rich quick" scheme — and nowhere is the promise of spontaneous riches greater than when one is gambling. From lotteries to casino games, luck, chance and fate (and on rare occasions, a pinch of skill) are all the ingredients necessary to become a winner in the gambling arena. As one state lottery advertising campaign reminds us, "all you need is a dollar and a dream." A dollar is something all of us have...but not all of us have to lose.

But the promise of quick riches makes fools of us all. Who cares about the astronomical odds against ever scoring — "you've got to be in it to win it!" Who cares that our life savings are rapidly diminishing? Think of the bucket of bills at the end of the rainbow! Dreaming about what you'll do with all that money is FUN — and the tension, the anticipation, that edge-of-your-seat feeling you get as the dice are rolling is so EXCITING!

The biggest problem with gambling — and the reason it is a vice — is that, like all the other vices in this book, people just don't know when to stop. Too much of anything can be bad — but nothing's worse than losing a life's savings to a roll of the dice.

BASIC instinct

IT MAY NOT BE ONE OF THE SEVEN DEADLY SINS. BUT GAMBLING IS JUST ABOUT THE OLDEST VICE--A TRUE...

ACCORDING TO ONE LEGEND, EVE ATE THE APPLE BECAUSE SHE HAD A WAGER GOING WITH THE SNAKE.

BET YOU CAN'T GUESS THE NUMBER OF SEEDS IN THAT APPLE.

BET I CAN.

UNFORTUNATELY, SHE SWALLOWED ONE OF THE SEEDS, AND LOST THE BET.

IS SOMEBODY EATING DOWN THERE?

ULP!

SIN AND GAMBLING HAVE BEEN LINKED IN PEOPLE'S MINDS EVER SINCE. IN ANCIENT ISRAEL, THE JEW WHO WON MONEY AT GAMBLING FROM ANOTHER JEW WAS A THIEF.

IF THE LOSER WAS A GENTILE, NO PROBLEM.

THE ROMANS WERE SOME OF HISTORY'S MOST NOTORIOUS GAMBLERS, OFTEN COMBINING IT WITH AS MANY OTHER VICES AS THEY COULD MANAGE.

SOME HISTORIANS PUT GAMBLING RIGHT AT THE TOP OF THE LIST OF REASONS FOR THE EMPIRE'S FALL.

BARBARIANS AT THE GATE, CAESAR!

NOT NOW, I'M BUSY!

DURING THE CRUSADES, RICHARD THE LION-HEARTED FORBADE GAMBLING AMONG HIS TROOPS...EXCEPTING, OF COURSE, HIS KNIGHTS AND NOBLEMEN.

DO AS WE SAY, NOT AS WE DO!

OFFICIALLY, ORGANIZED RELIGION IN MEDIEVAL EUROPE TOOK A HARD LINE ON GAMBLING, PRONOUNCING IT A WASTE OF TIME AND ENERGY...

GAMBLING?!

...THOUGH IN PRIVATE, INDIVIDUAL MEMBERS OF THE CLERGY WERE A BIT MORE FLEXIBLE.

YOU SHOULD HAVE INVITED US, TOO!

DISGUSTED BY THE OLD WORLD'S VICES, THE PILGRIMS LEFT EUROPE TO BUILD A NEW KIND OF SOCIETY...

...ONLY TO DISCOVER SIMILAR HABITS AMONG THE NEW WORLD'S NATIVES...

THE WIDE-OPEN, ANYTHING-GOES NATURE OF THE AMERICAN FRONTIER SPURRED A RASH OF GAMBLING UNSEEN SINCE THE GLORY DAYS OF THE ROMAN EMPIRE.

FORTUNES WERE WON AND LOST ACROSS THE COUNTRY; IN THE MINING TOWNS OF DENVER AND SAN FRANCISCO, THE LOGGING CAMPS OF THE NORTHWEST, AND ON THE GREAT MISSISSIPPI RIVERBOATS.

AND WHEREVER THERE WAS GAMBLING, THERE WERE CHEATERS. NEVER BEFORE IN HISTORY HAD CON MEN BEEN SO WELL-EQUIPPED.

MARKED DECK OF CARDS

LOADED DICE

KNUCKLE DUSTER

IN RESPONSE, ANTI-GAMBLING FORCES RAISED THEIR VOICES LOUDER.

JOURNALIST HORACE GREELEY OF THE NEW YORK TRIBUNE HELPED FORM THE NEW ASSOCIATION FOR THE SUPPRESSION OF GAMBLING.

THE WILD WEST WAS EVENTUALLY TAMED--BUT GAMBLING CONTINUED UNABATED IN BIG-CITY CASINOS AND OVERSEAS.

THE CREME DE LA CREME OF NINETEENTH-CENTURY GAMBLING HALLS WAS MONTE CARLO, BUILT IN 1868 ALONG THE FRENCH RIVIERA.

ONE OF THE CASINO'S MAIN INVESTORS WAS POPE LEO VIII.

BUT LET'S JUST KEEP THAT BETWEEN US, OKAY?

BACK IN THE U.S., ORGANIZED CRIME WAS MUSCLING IN ON THE GAMBLING JOINTS.

IN CHICAGO, THEY BUILT THEIR CASINOS LIKE FORTRESSES TO PROTECT AGAINST POLICE RAIDS.

THEY ALSO GRABBED A PIECE OF THE BETTING ACTION ON SPORTING EVENTS, RIGGING THE 1919 WORLD SERIES...

SAY IT AIN'T SO, JOE!

...AND HORSE RACING. MOSES "MOE" ANNENBERG HAD A MONOPOLY ON THE NATIONAL WIRE SERVICE THAT PROVIDED RACE RESULTS TO BOOKIES.

M. ANNENBERG

YOU WANT TO KNOW WHO WON, YOU GOT TO COME TO ME!

AND OF COURSE, THERE WAS VEGAS.

WELCOME TO PARADISE!

WHILE THE GOVERNMENT TRIED TO CRACK DOWN ON THE MOB, IT WASN'T UNTIL HOWARD HUGHES SHOWED UP IN LAS VEGAS IN THE MID-SIXTIES THAT THEIR CONTROL BEGAN TO WANE.

I WANT TO BUY YOUR CASINO, SIR.

HUGHES SPENT MILLIONS ON LAS VEGAS PROPERTIES. THE TOWN'S PUBLIC IMAGE CHANGED OVERNIGHT.

WE'RE GOING TO DISNEY— ≥MFF≤

--LAS VEGAS!

GAMBLING'S IMAGE CHANGED TOO. IT WAS NO LONGER A SIN--IT WAS BIG BUSINESS FOR EVERYONE--

BINGO tonight

--FROM HIGH-ROLLERS TO SENIOR CITIZENS.

OPPOSITION TO GAMBLING STILL EXISTS, BUT SUPPORTERS ARE SCARCER THAN EVER.

GAMBLING CORRUPTS!

WITH UNTOLD RICHES POISED TO BE THE ANSWERS TO GAMBLERS' PRAYERS, GAMBLING OPPONENTS ARE OFTEN PREACHING TO EMPTY PEWS.

IS TODAY'S GAMBLING BOOM EVER GOING TO SLOW DOWN?

WITH STATE-SANCTIONED LOTTERIES AND OFF-TRACK BETTING PARLORS, INTERNET LOOPHOLE VIRTUAL CASINOS, AND ALMOST DAILY ADDITIONS TO THE ROSTER OF FEDERAL-REGULATION EXEMPT INDIAN NATION CASINOS, THE ODDS ARE AGAINST IT...

THE 14TH-CENTURY MONK ST. BERNARD OF SIENA DENOUNCED THEM AS...

THE DEVIL'S INVENTION

...AND PLAYING CARDS CERTAINLY HAVE BEEN ASSOCIATED WITH THEIR FAIR SHARE OF TROUBLE OVER THE CENTURIES.

THE FIRST CARDS APPEARED IN 12TH-CENTURY CHINA DESIGNED AS AMUSEMENTS FOR THE CONCUBINES OF EMPEROR SEUN-HO'S COURT.

THEY ENTERTAIN US... WHILE WE WAIT!

THESE "CARDS" WERE SIMPLY STICKS-- SHORTENED, WIDENED, WITH IMAGES PAINTED ON THEM.

GYPSIES FIRST BROUGHT PAPER CARDS TO EUROPE IN THE FORM OF THE TAROT.

I'VE GOT BAD NEWS...

THESE EARLY DECKS WERE OVERSIZED AND CONTAINED AS MANY AS SEVENTY-EIGHT CARDS.

AS CARDS -- AND THE GAMING THAT WENT WITH THEM -- SPREAD, THEY DREW THE IRE OF THE CHURCH.

IN 1397, FRENCH AUTHORITIES ISSUED AN EDICT...

NO CARD PLAYING DURING THE WORK WEEK!

IRONIC, THEN, THAT IT WAS FRENCH PRINTERS WHO WERE RESPONSIBLE FOR MASS-PRODUCING AND STANDARDIZING THE FIFTY-TWO CARD, FOUR-SUITED DECK.

THE SUITS REPRESENTED THE DIFFERENT CLASSES OF FRENCH SOCIETY:

SWORDS FOR KNIGHTS -- WHICH BECAME SPADES, DERIVED FROM THE SPANISH WORD FOR KNIGHT, "ESPADS."

HEARTS FOR THE CHURCH -- THE "HEART" OF FRENCH SOCIETY.

DIAMONDS FOR MERCHANTS.

CLUBS FOR PEASANTS, WHOSE SYMBOL WAS THREE BLADES OF GRASS.

PLAYING CARDS SOON SPREAD TO THE NEW WORLD -- WITH ONLY AN OCCASIONAL SETBACK.

SUPERSTITIOUS SAILORS ON COLUMBUS'S SHIPS BLAMED CARDS FOR FOUL WEATHER AND TOSSED THEM OVERBOARD.

BUT ONCE THEY REACHED DRY LAND SAFELY, THE SAILORS MADE NEW ONES.

AS THE NEW WORLD WAS SETTLED, SOME AREAS BECAME LESS TOLERANT OF GAMBLING THAN OTHERS.

IN NEW ENGLAND, A SECOND OFFENSE OF CARD PLAYING EARNED YOU A PUBLIC WHIPPING.

BY THE LATE EIGHTEENTH CENTURY, THE COLONIES WERE IMPORTING THOUSANDS OF DECKS PER YEAR.

CARDS WERE AMONG THE ITEMS TAXED BY THE INFAMOUS STAMP ACT OF 1765.

...THERE SHALL BE A TAX UPON EVERY PACK OF PLAYING CARDS--

THIS MEANS WAR!

THE TAX HIT HOME FOR VIRGINIA PLANTER GEORGE WASHINGTON FOR WHOM CARDS WERE A FAVORED PASTIME...

FOR CARDS AND COUNTRY...

at home all day, playing cards Jan 18 at home all day, cards

...THOUGH HE LATER TRIED TO TAKE A HIGHER MORAL GROUND.

ALL OFFICERS AND SOLDIERS ARE POSITIVELY FORBIDDEN PLAYING AT CARDS.

THAT PARTICULAR BATTLE WAS ONE HE WOULD NOT WIN.

DURING THE CIVIL WAR THE BLACK MARKET WAS THE ONLY WAY FOR REBEL SOLDIERS TO OBTAIN PLAYING CARDS.

BY HOOK OR BY CROOK, WE GOTTA HAVE 'EM!

CARDS

CARD PLAYING BECAME AN EPIDEMIC AMONG NATIVE AMERICANS WHO OFTEN MADE THEIR OWN CARDS, SOMETIMES FROM UNUSUAL MATERIALS...

IT-- IT'S MADE OUTTA HUMAN SKIN!

DIFFERENT CARD GAMES HAVE WAXED AND WANED IN POPULARITY OVER THE CENTURIES.

THE MOST POPULAR CARD GAME IN SIXTEENTH-CENTURY ENGLAND WAS A THREE-CARD-HAND ANCESTOR OF POKER CALLED BRAG--

I HAVE AN EXTRAORDINARY HAND!

--NAMED FOR OBVIOUS REASONS.

IN THE 1800s, FARO WAS THE GAME OF CHOICE ON THE GREAT MISSISSIPPI RIVERBOAT CASINOS.

YOU LEAD AND WE'LL FOLLOW!

THE GAME WAS FAST-PACED AND EXCITING -- SO MUCH SO THAT GAMES OFTEN WERE CONTINUED ONSHORE.

IN FARO, PLAYERS BET AGAINST THE HOUSE ON THE ORDER CERTAIN CARDS WOULD BE DRAWN FROM THE DEALER'S BOX.

THE NAME IS FRENCH, ARISING FROM THE FACT THAT KINGS IN SOME DECKS RESEMBLED...

LE PHARAON!

FARO WAS A MAJOR SOURCE OF FUNDS BEHIND THE MOST BIZARRE CRIMINAL CONSPIRACY OF THE NINETEENTH CENTURY...

...THE CLAN OF THE MYSTIC CONFEDERACY.

LED BY JOHN MURRELL, THE CLAN PLANNED SIMULTANEOUS UPRISINGS IN SEVERAL SOUTHERN CITIES.

WE'LL BUILD AN UNDERWORLD EMPIRE!

TENNESSEE PASSED A LAW OUTLAWING FARO, ATTEMPTING TO CUT OFF THEIR FUNDS.

ON JULY 4, 1835, THE CLAN ATTACKED.

GAMBLING HALL

THINGS DID NOT GO AS THEY HAD PLANNED.

IN EARLY NINETEENTH-CENTURY NEW ORLEANS, FRENCHMEN GAMBLING AT "POQUE" MIXED WITH YANKEE SAILORS PLAYING A PERSIAN GAME CALLED "AS NAS"...

FOUR OF A KIND! C'EST MAGNIFIQUE!

...AND THUS WAS BORN THE MODERN GAME OF POKER.

THE NEW GAME SOON BECAME A FAVORITE OUT IN THE WILD, WILD WEST.

WILD BILL HICKOK MET HIS DEATH HOLDING TWO PAIR-- ACES AND EIGHTS.

THAT'S A DEAD MAN'S HAND!

TODAY POKER IS THE MOST POPULAR CARD GAME IN THE WORLD. GAMBLING EXPERTS CONSIDER IT THE TRUE NATIONAL PASTIME.

PROFESSIONALS AND SERIOUS AMATEURS ALIKE COMPETE EACH YEAR IN A WORLD SERIES OF POKER HELD IN LAS VEGAS.

WORLD SERIES OF POKER

ARE YOU BLUFFING?

SHADDUP AND PLAY!

RUMMY IN ITS VARIOUS FORMS IS A DISTANT SECOND IN POPULARITY TO POKER.

GIN RUMMY IS A FAVORITE AMONG PROFESSIONAL GAMBLERS BECAUSE THERE'S ONLY ONE PERSON TO CHEAT... YOUR OPPONENT.

HE'S HOLDING TWO KINGS.

BRIDGE IS DESCENDED FROM THE ENGLISH GAME WHIST.

AMERICAN MILLIONAIRE HAROLD VANDERBILT REVISED THE RULES AND CREATED CONTRACT BRIDGE, STILL THE GAME OF CHOICE AMONG THE ULTRA-RICH.

THE GAMES MAY HAVE CHANGED OVER THE YEARS, BUT THE DECK ITSELF HAS REMAINED EXACTLY THE SAME, WITH A FEW MINOR EXCEPTIONS...

SOVIET CARDS WILL NOW INCLUDE A SUIT FEATURING THE WORKERS!

WAY TO GO, JOE.

IN THE 1930s, CARD MAKERS IN AMERICA AND ENGLAND JOINED FORCES TO CREATE A FIFTH SUIT.

WE'LL CALL IT EAGLES!

WE'LL CALL IT CROWNS!

THE NEW DECK NEVER CAUGHT ON.

TODAY PLAYING CARDS ARE MORE POPULAR THAN EVER. THE U.S. PLAYING CARD COMPANY IN CINCINNATI HAS OVER 1,000 EMPLOYEES WORKING TWENTY-FOUR HOURS A DAY.

THIS BABY CAN CRANK OUT 12,000 DECKS IN AN HOUR!

DEVIL'S INVENTION OR NO, IT SEEMS CLEAR THAT PLAYING CARDS ARE HERE TO STAY.

THE WINNING TICKET

Now Leaving
MASSACHUSETTS
Lotto Jackpot:
$15 million

Welcome to
NEW YORK
Lotto Jackpot:
$21 million

FROM THEIR VERY BEGINNING, LOTTERIES HAVE BEEN THE MOST SOCIALLY "ACCEPTABLE" FORM OF GAMBLING. IN AMERICA TODAY IT'S NOT UNUSUAL FOR PEOPLE TO DRIVE HOURS FOR A CHANCE TO PLAY.

...AND TODAY'S WINNING NUMBER IN THE CALIFORNIA LOTTERY IS...

THE WORD "LOTTERY" IS DERIVED FROM THE TEUTONIC "LOT"--STONES, STICKS, OR WOOD CHIPS THAT ARE EITHER CAST ON THE GROUND SO THEIR POSITIONING CAN BE INTERPRETED...

WHAT DOES IT MEAN, MOSES?

YAHWEH SAYS YOU GET THE DEAD SEA.

SUCKER!

...OR DRAWN TO MAKE A SELECTION.

WHEW!

WHEW!

ULP!

THE ROMAN EMPEROR AUGUSTUS FIRST THOUGHT OF SELLING LOTS, IN THE FORM OF NUMBERED TICKETS, AND AWARDING PART OF THE PROCEEDS AS PRIZES...

THE REST GOES FOR ADMINISTRATIVE EXPENSES.

LOTTERY PROCEEDS

LOTTERY

LATER EMPERORS EMBELLISHED HIS IDEA, BESTOWING VILLAS, SLAVES, GOLD, AND THE OCCASIONAL BOOBY PRIZE--AN OSTRICH, OR A DEAD DOG.

SICK PUPPIES, AIN'T WE?

IN 1776 THE CONTINENTAL CONGRESS RAN A LOTTERY TO HELP PAY FOR THE REVOLUTIONARY WAR. MUCH OF THE MONEY DISAPPEARED INTO THE HANDS OF LOTTERY OFFICIALS.

GENTLEMEN, I GIVE YOU THE WINNING TICKET!

RRRIPP!

TO HELP PAY HIS DEBTS, THOMAS JEFFERSON PUT UP HIS OWN BELONGINGS IN A LOTTERY. SALES WERE SO SLOW THAT IT WAS CANCELLED.

I CAN'T WIN IF YOU DON'T PLAY!

IN THE EARLY EIGHTEEN-HUNDREDS, LOTTERIES WERE USED TO FINANCE PUBLIC WORKS. THEY HELPED BUILD IVY LEAGUE COLLEGES LIKE HARVARD, YALE, AND DARTMOUTH.

THREE CHEERS FOR THE COMMON MAN!

BY THE MID-1800s, SWINDLERS HAD JOINED THE GAME. JAMES MONROE PATTEE MADE MILLIONS FROM HIS WYOMING STATE LOTTERY, GUARANTEEING OVER 70,000 PRIZEWINNERS A MONTH...

...BUT WHILE TICKETS COST A DOLLAR...

...MOST PRIZES WERE WORTH ONLY FIFTY CENTS.

THE GREAT LOUISIANA REAL ESTATE LOTTERY PROMISED TO AWARD SOME OF NEW ORLEANS' MOST VALUABLE BUILDINGS AS PRIZES. THOUSANDS OF TICKETS WERE SOLD.

SOME DAY, MY FRIENDS, ALL THIS CAN BE YOURS!

THE DAY OF THE DRAWING, PROMOTERS DISAPPEARED.

ONE OF THE MOST CORRUPT ORGANIZATIONS IN AMERICAN HISTORY WAS THE LOUISIANA STATE LOTTERY COMPANY, NICKNAMED "THE SERPENT."

ESTABLISHED IN 1869, THE COMPANY PAID $40,000 A YEAR TO CHARITY FOR ITS LICENSE. BY 1889 IT WAS OPERATING NATIONWIDE WITH ANNUAL PROFITS OF $13 MILLION.

THE LOTTERY OCTOPUS

THE LOTTERY COMPANY HIRED CONFEDERATE HEROES JUBAL EARLY AND G.T. BEAUREGARD TO FRONT FOR IT.

The LOUISIANA STATE LOTTERY COMPANY

THE SOUTH WILL RISE AGAIN!

ESPECIALLY IF THEY FIND OUT HOW THEY'RE GETTING SWINDLED.

THE COMPANY BRIBED LEGISLATORS STATE-WIDE. ONE THEY COULDN'T BUY WAS J.M. McCANN--NOT THAT THEY EVER GAVE UP TRYING.

PACKAGE FOR YOU, SIR.

COMPLIMENTS OF THE LOUISIANA STATE LOTTERY

OVER SEVENTY PERCENT OF THE LOTTERY'S TICKETS WERE SOLD BY MAIL. AT ITS HEIGHT, LOTTERY MAIL PROVIDED HALF THE WORK OF THE NEW ORLEANS POST OFFICE.

THE COMPANY'S CHARTER WAS FINALLY REPEALED IN 1895. THE SERPENT GAVE LOTTERIES SUCH A BAD NAME THEY WERE VIRTUALLY OUTLAWED IN THE U.S. FOR HALF A CENTURY.

GENTLEMEN, WE HAVE RID OUR NOBLE STATE OF AN INSIDIOUS MONSTER!

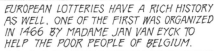

EUROPEAN LOTTERIES HAVE A RICH HISTORY AS WELL. ONE OF THE FIRST WAS ORGANIZED IN 1466 BY MADAME JAN VAN EYCK TO HELP THE POOR PEOPLE OF BELGIUM.

LEGENDARY LOVER AND GAMBLER GIOVANNI CASANOVA RAN A LOTTERY FOR KING LOUIS XV THAT RAISED MONEY TO FOUND THE FRENCH MILITARY SCHOOL L'ECOLE MILITAIRE.

MADAME, HOW CAN I CONVINCE YOU TO BUY A TICKET?

KING LOUIS XVI STARTED THE FRENCH NATIONAL LOTTERY IN 1776.

PERHAPS WE COULD RAFFLE OFF SOME DESSERTS, MY DEAR.

YOU MEAN-- LET THEM EAT CAKE?

THE IRISH SWEEPSTAKES IS THE MOST POPULAR LOTTERY IN THE WORLD. STARTED IN 1930 TO BENEFIT HOSPITALS, TICKETS WERE SUPPOSED TO BE SOLD ONLY IN IRELAND.

COULD YOU SEND THIS ...UH...PARCEL... TO ME BROTHER IN NEW YORK, FATHER?

IN 1948, U.S. OFFICIALS BOARDED THE OCEAN LINER AMERICA...

WHAT HAVE WE HERE?

TWO MILLION TICKETS WERE SEIZED.

IN TODAY'S CASH-STARVED RUSSIAN ECONOMY, MORE THAN HALF OF THE POPULATION PLAYS SOME FORM OF LOTTERY.

AND TODAY'S WINNING NUMBER IS

MOST OF THE GAMES ARE CROOKED.

THE GOVERNMENT IS NOW TOYING WITH THE IDEA OF A NATIONAL LOTTERY.

WE CAN RUN A LOTTERY JUST AS WELL AS THE MAFIA.

TODAY IN AMERICA THIRTY-EIGHT STATES HOLD LOTTERIES. THE ODDS OF WINNING ARE TERRIBLE...

YOU'VE GOT A BETTER CHANCE OF GETTING STRUCK BY LIGHTNING.

...FAR LESS OF THE MONEY WAGERED GOES TO PRIZE WINNERS...

LOTTERIES RETURN FIFTY CENTS OF EVERY DOLLAR BET TO THE WINNERS.

CASINOS GIVE BACK ABOUT EIGHTY.

...BUT PEOPLE STILL LOVE TO PLAY. FLORIDA RESIDENTS SPENT OVER THIRTEEN MILLION DOLLARS FOR TICKETS ON THE FIRST DAY THEIR STATE LOTTERY OPENED FOR BUSINESS.

THERE'S A LINE!

WINNING DOESN'T NECESSARILY SOLVE ALL YOUR PROBLEMS, THOUGH. TAKE JOSE CABALLERO. HE WON THE CALIFORNIA LOTTERY IN 1985.

TWO MILLION DOLLARS!

AN ILLEGAL ALIEN, HE WAS PROMPTLY DEPORTED TO MEXICO.

THANKS FOR PLAYING.

SINCE HE WAS A FOREIGN RESIDENT, THE IRS ALSO SEIZED THIRTY PERCENT OF HIS WINNINGS, AS OPPOSED TO THE USUAL TWENTY.

FIFTY-FIVE-YEAR-OLD WIDOW EUNICE BAYLOR ALSO HAD A NASTY RUN-IN WITH THE IRS. THEY TOOK $61,000 OUT OF THE $100,000 SHE'D WON.

THAT'S HIGHWAY ROBBERY!

WHEN SHE WENT TO COMPLAIN, SHE WAS TOLD BY ONE AGENT:

IF YOU DON'T WANT TO PAY TAXES, MOVE TO A FOREIGN COUNTRY.

BUT DON'T EVER COME BACK TO THE U.S., OR WE'LL GET YOU.

DESPITE EVIDENCE THAT THEY ENCOURAGE GAMBLING, LOTTERIES SEEM TO BE GROWING.

I'D LIKE TO EXCHANGE THESE FOR A POWERBALL TICKET.

AT LEAST THE LOTTERY IS A GOOD DEAL FOR THE GOVERNMENT, WHICH COLLECTS TAXES ON BOTH THE TICKETS SOLD AND WINNINGS PAID OUT.

I GET YOU COMING AND GOING!

152

ANCIENT CULTURES USED THEM TO INTERPRET DREAMS AND PREDICT THE FUTURE...

RULERS FROM ROME TO LONDON WAGERED UNIMAGINABLE FORTUNES ON A SINGLE ROLL...

...AND TODAY, THEY REMAIN THE MOST POPULAR GAMING IMPLEMENTS IN THE WORLD.

TUMBLIN' VICE!

ACCORDING TO PLATO, THE FIRST DICE WERE CREATED BY A DEMON NAMED THEUTH.

THEY ARE SIMPLICITY ITSELF, MASTER.

IT'S THE SIMPLE THINGS THAT WORK BEST.

HISTORICAL EVIDENCE, HOWEVER, SUGGESTS NATIVE AMERICAN ORIGINS.

ROLL THEM BONES!

THE ANCIENT GREEKS BELIEVED THE GODS ROLLED DICE TO DIVIDE THE UNIVERSE. ZEUS WON DOMINATION OVER THE EARTH, HADES THE UNDERWORLD, AND POSEIDON THE OCEANS.

BEST TWO OUT OF THREE?

SOME OF HISTORY'S MOST FANATICAL DICE PLAYERS WERE THE ROMAN EMPERORS. CLAUDIUS HAD HIS CHARIOT FITTED WITH SHOCK ABSORBERS TO ELIMINATE ANY MOTION SO HE COULD PLAY DICE WHILE TRAVELING.

MY DREAM MACHINE!

NOWHERE WERE "DICE" AND "VICE" SO LINKED AS IN IMPERIAL ROME...

THEIR HABITUAL USE CAUSED THEM TO BE EVENTUALLY BANNED, SAVE FOR DURING A SINGLE TWO-WEEK FESTIVAL.

SATURNALIA SPECIAL ON PIN

THEIR REPUTATION WAS FURTHER TARNISHED WHEN ROMAN SOLDIERS GAMBLED FOR CHRIST'S RAGS AS HE HUNG ON THE CROSS.

WHY DO I FEEL GUILTY ABOUT THIS?

Kingpin of America's betting parlors during the Roaring Twenties, Arnold Rothstein deserves the title...

THE GODFATHER OF GAMBLING

The son of Orthodox Jewish parents, he was supposed to follow in his father's dress goods business. But Rothstein had a passion for gambling.

ARNIE, WHERE YOU GOING WITH MR. BUBER'S TUXEDO?

I GOTTA SEE A MAN ABOUT A HORSE.

His first big money win came in 1909, in a game of pool that lasted thirty-two hours straight.

$4000 SMACKERS.

By 1910 he was running a string of gambling operations from the Lower East Side all the way up to Broadway.

Rothstein also owned a midtown gym called the Park View Athletic Club.

A LITTLE TO THE LEFT, DOLL-FACE.

THIS IS SOME SETUP YOU GOT HERE, ARNIE.

In 1919, the heavily favored Chicago White Sox lost the World Series to the Cincinnati Reds. American League Commissioner Ban Johnson accused Rothstein of fixing the games.

I'VE NEVER BEEN INVOLVED WITH A CROOKED DEAL IN MY LIFE!

The rumors persisted, though: Rothstein was a racketeer, a drug runner, a loan shark, a tutor to future mob bosses Meyer Lansky and Lucky Luciano.

RESULTS

BUT NOTHING WAS EVER PROVED.

CLICK!

He continued to make headlines as a gambler. In a single game of poker against Nick "the Greek" Dandolos, Rothstein won $605,000.

Ah, IT'S JUST CHUMP CHANGE.

AND YOU'RE THE CHUMP.

HE WON $800,000 ON A HORSE RACE-- AND A COOL HALF-MILLION ON THE FIRST DEMPSEY-TUNNEY FIGHT.

KNOCK 'IM OUT-- IT'LL MAKE ME RICHER!

ON SEPTEMBER 9TH, 1928, DURING A NIGHT OF GAMBLING, ROTHSTEIN PLACED THE LARGEST RECORDED WAGER IN A HIGH-CARD CUT GAME. HIS OPPONENT, NATE RAYMOND, CUT FIRST AND GOT A KING. ROTHSTEIN GOT A TEN.

HE LOST $40,000.

BY THE END OF THE EVENING, ROTHSTEIN HAD LOST CLOSE TO $320,000. WHETHER HE THOUGHT HIS OPPONENTS WERE CHEATING, OR HE JUST DIDN'T HAVE THE MONEY, HE LEFT WITHOUT PAYING.

WHAT ABOUT MY MONEY?

THE NAME ROTHSTEIN SHOULD BE GOOD FOR SOMETHING.

TWO MONTHS LATER, HE STILL HADN'T PAID UP...

ON NOVEMBER 4TH, HE WAS SUMMONED TO A MEETING AT THE PARK CENTRAL HOTEL...

THINK ABOUT THIS NEXT TIME YOU WELCH ON A BET!

BLAM! BLAM!

TRUE TO THE UNDERWORLD CODE, ROTHSTEIN REFUSED TO IDENTIFY THE SHOOTER.

I AIN'T GOT NOTHING TO SAY.

HE DIED TWO DAYS LATER, ON ELECTION DAY--JUST WHEN THE BET HE'D PLACED ON HOOVER'S VICTORY WOULD HAVE WON HIM $600,000, MORE THAN ENOUGH TO PAY OFF HIS LOSSES.

TWO MORE DAYS! YOU COULDN'T HAVE WAITED TWO MORE DAYS FOR HIM TO PAY?!

MOST OF ROTHSTEIN'S MONEY HAD BEEN OUT ON HIGH-INTEREST LOANS. HE KEPT A LIST OF THE DEBTORS IN A NOTEBOOK.

THIS AIN'T IN ENGLISH.

THE LIST WAS WRITTEN IN A CODE ONLY HE KNEW.

NEEDLESS TO SAY, FEW OF THE PEOPLE HE'D LOANED MONEY TO VOLUNTEERED TO PAY BACK THE ESTATE.

SHAME ABOUT ROTHSTEIN, AIN'T IT?

ROTHSTEIN'S REPUTATION LIVED ON, EVEN AFTER HIS DEATH. HE WAS THE INSPIRA- TION FOR MEYER WOLFSHEIM IN *THE GREAT GATSBY* AND NATHAN DETROIT IN THE MUSICAL *GUYS AND DOLLS*.

I NEVER KNEW ARNIE COULD SING!

FACTOID BOOKS

History-Making Bets

WE'D NEED A WHOLE NEW BOOK TO LIST ALL OF THEM, BUT HERE'S JUST A SAMPLING OF...

START WITH CLEOPATRA. BEST REMEMBERED FOR HER BEAUTY, SHE HAD A BIT OF THE GAMBLER IN HER TOO.

SHE TOLD HER LOVER, MARC ANTONY...

I'LL BET I CAN DRINK TEN MILLION SESTERIA*'S WORTH OF WINE AT ONE SITTING.

I ACCEPT!

*ABOUT $500,000.

SHE DROPPED TWO HUGE PEARLS INTO A GLASS AND DRANK THEM DOWN.

BEAUTY AND BRAINS... WOTTA GAL!

THE BOWEN SALOON IN SANTA FE, NEW MEXICO WAS THE SCENE OF THE WILDEST BET IN THE HISTORY OF THE WILD, WILD WEST.

I'LL RAISE YOU ANOTHER $100,000.

LET'S SEE THE CASH!

THE GAMBLER WROTE SOMETHING DOWN ON A PIECE OF PAPER, THEN TURNED TO THE GOVERNOR OF NEW MEXICO, WHO HAPPENED TO BE IN ATTENDANCE.

SIGN THIS PAPER OR I'LL KILL YOU.

=ULP!=

THE GOVERNOR SIGNED.

I RAISE YOU THE TERRITORY OF NEW MEXICO.

THE OTHER GAMBLERS FOLDED.

ONE OF AMERICA'S MOST FAMOUS GAMBLERS WAS JOHN W. "BET-A-MILLION" GATES. HE'D BET ON ALMOST ANYTHING --AND NOT JUST PENNY-ANTE STUFF.

I WANT TO BET ENOUGH TO HURT THE OTHER FELLOW IF HE LOSES, AND ENOUGH TO HURT ME IF I LOSE.

DINING WITH CHICAGO MILLIONAIRE JOHN DRAKE, GATES SUGGESTED THEY DUNK PIECES OF BREAD INTO THEIR COFFEE, THEN SEE WHOSE BREAD ATTRACTED MORE FLIES.

$1000 A FLY!

YOU'RE ON!

GATES HAD SPIKED HIS COFFEE WITH SUGAR, AND WON.

THEN THERE WERE *THE SONS OF HOPE*, A GROUP OF EARLY 1900'S AMERICAN MILLIONAIRES. A SINGLE CHIP IN THEIR GAMES WAS OFTEN WORTH $10,000.

DURING ONE OF THEIR GAMES, A PLAYER HAD JUST MADE A $300,000 RAISE WHEN HE HAD A COUGHING FIT, ACCIDENTALLY EXPOSING HIS HOLE CARD.

HE'S GOT KINGS!

I FOLD!

EXASPERATED, THE PLAYER DECLARED:

I SHOULD HAVE BOUGHT THE SMITH BROTHERS COUGH DROP FACTORY LAST WEEK. THIS WOULD HAVE PAID FOR IT!

MORE MONEY IS BET ON THE SUPER-BOWL THAN ANY OTHER SPORTING EVENT. IN 1989, BOB STUPAK PUT DOWN $1,050,000 ON THE BENGALS/49ERS GAME. HE HAD THE BENGALS AND 7 POINTS.

THE 49ERS WON BY 4 POINTS. STUPAK MADE A COOL $1 MILLION.

AND ELECTION BETTING GETS MORE ACTION THAN ANY GAME OR SPORTING EVENT.

THE BIGGEST ELECTION-DAY BET? ONE RACETRACK OWNER LOST $1.2 MILLION ON THE 1960 NIXON/KENNEDY RACE.

TED KENNEDY BET $25,000 ON THAT SAME ELECTION-- TAKING HIS BROTHER, NATURALLY.

HISTORY'S GREATEST LUCKY STREAK? HOW ABOUT THE ONE ENJOYED BY ACTOR SEAN CONNERY, FAMOUS FOR PLAYING SUPERSPY (AND SUPER GAMBLER) JAMES BOND.

NUMBER 17-- SIGNOR CONNERY WINS!

HE BET ON THE NUMBER 17, WHICH CAME UP THREE TIMES IN A ROW...

LET IT RIDE.

...THEN CASHED OUT TO THE TUNE OF $30,000.

HEY, IT HAPPENS ALL THE TIME IN THE MOVIES...AND EVERYONE KNOWS TRUTH CAN BE STRANGER THAN FICTION!

FACTOID BOOKS

WITH POLITICIANS JUMPING ON THE CASINO BANDWAGON...

...AND PEOPLE WAITING IN LINE FOR HOURS TO BUY LOTTERY TICKETS...

...IT'S HARD TO REMEMBER THAT THERE WAS A TIME WHEN GAMBLING WAS ACTUALLY CONDEMNED BY SOCIETY, OR WHEN GAMBLING MEN WERE OUTNUMBERED BY...

THE ANTI-GAMBLERS

IN MEDIEVAL EUROPE, BUSINESSMEN AND RELIGIOUS LEADERS ZEALOUSLY WATCHED OVER THEIR SERVANTS...

KNAVES! CARD PLAYING IS FORBIDDEN ON MY ESTATE!

THEY FELT GAMBLING BELITTLED THE WORTH OF AN HONEST DAY'S LABOR.

ACQUIRE WEALTH WITHOUT WORK?

SINFUL!

THEY WERE, OF COURSE, ABOVE SUCH RULES.

IN 1593, A CARD GAME CALLED BASSETTE SWEPT THROUGH EUROPEAN GAMBLING HALLS, DECIMATING THE FORTUNES OF THE NOBILITY.

IT'S ALL YOURS NOW!

EDICTS OUTLAWING THE GAME WERE ISSUED... UNLESS THE PLAYER WAS OF NOBLE BIRTH.

IN OTHER WORDS, ONLY THE RICH SHOULD GET RICHER.

THIS THEME WAS PICKED UP BY NEW YORK CITY'S SOCIETY FOR THE PREVENTION OF PAUPERISM.

IN 1818, THE SOCIETY APPOINTED NINE STANDING COMMITTEES TO DETERMINE THE EXTENT OF GAMBLING.

THEIR RECOMMENDATIONS HELPED ESTABLISH THE FIRST SAVINGS BANKS.

LET'S PUT YOUR MONEY TO WORK.

FOR ME.

SAVINGS BANK

IN THE DEEP SOUTH, ANTI-GAMBLERS HAD MORE SPIRITUAL CONCERNS. NEW ORLEANS PREACHERS WARNED THEIR WANDERING FLOCK THAT THEY WOULD SOON BE CONSUMED BY HELLFIRE.

IN 1811, EARTHQUAKES SHOOK THE CITY. EVEN THE MOST ARDENT GAMBLERS HAD TO SIT UP AND TAKE NOTICE.

LET ME FINISH THIS HAND, PLEASE LORD.

BRRRooooMM

OUT WEST, PREACHERS WERE A LITTLE MORE TOLERANT, OFTEN USING THE GAMBLER'S OWN LANGUAGE TO SPREAD THE WORD OF THE LORD...

...THE ACE THAT REMINDS US OF ONE GOD, THE DEUCE OF THE FATHER AND THE SON...

AMEN, BROTHER!

DR. CHARLES CALDWELL OF KENTUCKY'S TRANSYLVANIA UNIVERSITY ATTACKED GAMBLING FOR THE PHYSICAL CHANGES HE BELIEVED IT CAUSED.

GAMBLING ELEVATES MAN'S "ANIMAL ORGANS" OVER HIS "MORAL AND REFLECTIVE ONES"!

BY BEING CONSTANTLY AND INTENSELY EXERCISED, THE CEREBRAL ORGANS CONCERNED IN GAMBLING ATTAIN A SIZE AND DEGREE OF VIGOR.

NORMAL

moral animal

GAMBLER

moral animal

CALDWELL'S SOLUTION?

CLAY CAP

GAMBLERS MUST WEAR CLAY CAPS TO COOL THEIR BRAINS, AND CONSUME A DIET OF MY OWN DEVISING.

CALDWELL'S BIZARRE BELIEFS WERE MATCHED BY THOSE OF AUSTRALIAN JED McCADE.

A PROSPECTOR DURING AUSTRALIA'S GOLD RUSH OF THE 1850'S, McCADE DEVELOPED A BLIND HATRED OF GAMBLING AFTER SEEING MANY OF HIS FRIENDS LOSE THEIR FORTUNES.

...NO-GOOD DOUBLE-DEALING #$☆✦☆✦ GAMBLERS

HE PUT UP AN ESTABLISHMENT DESIGNED TO PREVENT ANYONE FROM EVER WANTING TO GAMBLE AGAIN.

MUSEUM OF DEATH?

MUSEUM OF DEATH

MCCADE'S "MUSEUM" HELD THE MOST GRAPHIC EXAMPLES HE COULD FIND OF MEN LITERALLY DONE IN BY GAMBLING.

THIS IS THE HAND OF JOHN SINGEST, STRICKEN WITH PALSY WHILE PLAYING THREE-CARD MONTE.

MCCADE CLAIMED EVERY PACK OF PLAYING CARDS IN AUSTRALIA WAS CONTAMINATED BY INFECTIOUS BACILLI.

SEE?

REFORMED GAMBLER JONATHAN GREEN STARTED THE NEW YORK ASSOCIATION FOR THE SUPPRESSION OF GAMBLING TO MAKE THE GENERAL PUBLIC AWARE OF THE GAMBLER'S TRUE NATURE.

THEY ARE THIEVES, CHEATERS, AND WORSE!

IN 1847, GREEN FOUND A WAY TO GET HIS MESSAGE TO ALL AMERICANS.

I HAVE PUBLISHED A BOOK.

THE SECRET BAND OF BROTHERS

GREEN WROTE OF A HIDDEN SOCIETY OF GAMBLERS, VAST IN NUMBERS AND INFLUENCE. HE CLAIMED THE "BAND" MARKED EVERY DECK OF PLAYING CARDS SOLD IN AMERICA SO THEIR MEMBERS COULD CHEAT.

YOU'RE BLUFFING, PARTNER!

GREEN, AS A FORMER MEMBER OF THE "BROTHERHOOD," SET UP DEMONSTRATIONS TO PROVE HIS CLAIM.

THREE OF SPADES.

RIGHT AGAIN!

LATER IT WAS DISCOVERED THAT GREEN HAD USED MIRRORS TO HELP HIM READ THE CARDS.

GREEN'S "SECRET BAND" MAY HAVE BEEN PURE FICTION, BUT SOON ENOUGH, A REAL SECRET BROTHERHOOD -- THE MAFIA -- BEGAN MUSCLING IN ON GAMBLING ACTION ACROSS THE COUNTRY.

TONY CORNERO RAN THE S.S. REX, A HUGE GAMBLING SHIP CATERING TO THE HOLLYWOOD ELITE THAT OPERATED JUST OFF THE CALIFORNIA SHORE.

YOU'LL SEE WE GOT A REAL FIRST-CLASS OPERATION HERE.

THE GOVERNMENT -- IN THE PERSON OF EARL WARREN, THEN ATTORNEY GENERAL OF CALIFORNIA (LATER GOVERNOR, THEN CHIEF JUSTICE OF THE SUPREME COURT) -- TOOK QUICK ACTION.

GIVE IT UP, CORNERO, YOU'RE SURROUNDED!

CORNERO CLAIMED HIS SHIP OPERATED OUTSIDE CALIFORNIA'S LEGAL JURISDICTION. WARREN DIDN'T ARGUE THAT POINT.

BUT WHAT ABOUT THE SHIPS YOUR CUSTOMERS USE TO GET TO THE REX?

CORNERO HAD FORGOTTEN TO GET LICENSES FOR HIS "WATER TAXIS."

THE REX WAS CLOSED DOWN.

SENATOR ESTES KEFAUVER'S HEARINGS ON ORGANIZED CRIME WERE TRIGGERED BY THE OPERATIONS OF THE LAST CHANCE SALOON, LOCATED RIGHT ON THE KANSAS/MISSOURI BORDER.

A WALL INSIDE THE SALOON RAN RIGHT ALONG THE BORDER. WHEN COPS FROM ONE STATE RAIDED THE PLACE...

THIS IS THE KANSAS STATE POLICE! PREPARE TO BE RAIDED!

to Missouri

THE GAMBLERS SIMPLY MOVED TO THE OTHER SIDE OF THE BUILDING.

to Missouri

COPS FROM BOTH STATES NEVER SEEMED TO ARRIVE AT THE SAME TIME -- A POINT KEFAUVER ZEROED IN ON DURING HIS INVESTIGATION.

to Kansas

THIS IS THE MISSOURI STATE POLICE! PREPARE TO BE RAIDED!

JOHN SCARNE WASN'T TECHNICALLY AN ANTI-GAMBLER -- HE WAS THE WORLD'S FOREMOST GAMING EXPERT -- BUT HE WAS RESPONSIBLE FOR PUTTING MORE CROOKED GAMBLERS OUT OF BUSINESS THAN ANY POLITICIAN.

AT FIFTEEN, HE EXPOSED HIS FIRST CROOKED CARD GAME.

THAT DECK IS FIXED!

DURING WORLD WAR II, THE ARMY HIRED SCARN TO SHOW THE TROOPS HOW TO DETECT CHEATERS.

HE RECEIVED A SPECIAL COMMENDATION FOR SAVING SERVICEMEN MILLIONS OF DOLLARS.

GAMBLERS ANONYMOUS, FOUNDED IN 1957, FOCUSES ON HELPING COMPULSIVE GAMBLERS KICK THEIR HABIT.

HI. MY NAME IS ANDY AND I'M A GAMBLER.

STATISTICS SHOW THE GAMBLER'S MAIN VICTIM IS OFTEN HIS FAMILY.

PROFILE OF ILLINOIS GAMBLERS ANONYMOUS CHAPTER

- 26% Divorced or Separated
- 34% lost/Quit their Job.
- 44% Stole from work to pay debts.
- 21% filed for Bankruptcy
- 16% Attempted Suicide.

BUT IN A WORLD THAT NO LONGER SEEMS TO REGARD GAMBLING AS A VICE, GROUPS LIKE GAMBLERS ANONYMOUS FACE A DIFFICULT TASK.

THIS NEW LOTTERY WILL BRING IN NEEDED TAX REVENUE FOR OUR CHILDREN!

TOM GREY -- AN EX-VIETNAM VET TURNED MINISTER -- CALLS SUCH CLAIMS A SHAM. THE "RIVERBOAT RAMBO" SAYS:

STATES THAT HAVE LOTTERIES SPEND LESS ON EDUCATION THAN STATES WITHOUT LOTTERIES.

THERE IS EVIDENCE THAT RELENTLESS SHILLING OF LOTTERY GAMES AND LEGALIZED CASINO GAMBLING CREATES MORE PROBLEM GAMBLERS.

SEVENTY-FOUR PERCENT MORE IN NEW YORK STATE SINCE 1986.

AND A HARVARD MEDICAL SCHOOL STUDY SHOWS A SHARP INCREASE IN TEENAGERS WITH GAMBLING PROBLEMS.

WHY AREN'T MORE PEOPLE SPEAKING OUT AGAINST THE EVER-GROWING GAMBLING INDUSTRY?

POWERBALL WINNER HIT JACKPOT

$1,000,000 Million

US GAMBLING $500 BILLION SPENT

HORSE RACING COMES TO THE INTERNET

YOU FIGURE IT OUT.

THE LURE IS EXCITEMENT. BOOZE. WOMEN. HORSES. NUMBERS.

IF YOU'VE GOT THE MONEY, THE BIG CITY'S GOT THE ACTION.

Bright Lights Big Bucks

TAKE NUMBERS. EVEN THOUGH IT COSTS A DOLLAR OR LESS TO PLAY...

...IT PUTS BILLIONS INTO THE POCKETS OF ORGANIZED CRIME EACH YEAR.

THE GAMES STARTED IN LONDON, WHERE PEOPLE TOO POOR TO BUY A LOTTERY TICKET COULD PURCHASE AN INSURANCE "POLICY" THAT A CERTAIN NUMBER WOULD COME UP.

WHEN LOTTERIES CAME TO AMERICA, SO DID POLICY.

CROOKED POLICY OPERATOR ALBERT ADAMS ADVERTISED HIS WINNING NUMBERS WOULD BE BASED ON NUMBERS DRAWN IN THE KENTUCKY LOTTERY.

AS SOON AS THEY ANNOUNCE THE NUMBERS, YOU'LL KNOW IF YOU'VE WON!

IN FACT, ADAMS MADE UP HIS OWN NUMBERS— USUALLY TO ASSURE WINNERS WERE FEW,

BETTER LUCK NEXT TIME!

ADAMS WAS BEYOND THE REACH OF THE LAW...

BECAUSE HE'D BOUGHT THEM ALL OFF.

IN 1892, THE REVEREND CHARLES PARKHURST SPOKE OUT:

THESE DENS OF VICE MUST BE ELIMINATED!

ADAMS WAS SENT TO SING-SING FOR EIGHTEEN MONTHS. ON HIS RELEASE, DEPRESSED AND IN POOR HEALTH, HE SHOT HIMSELF.

THE POLICY SHOPS WERE EXTINCT BY 1914.

POLICY OPERATORS BEGAN GETTING THEIR NUMBERS FROM A DIFFERENT SOURCE.

WE'LL TAKE THE FINAL THREE DIGITS OF THE NUMBER ANNOUNCED BY THE NEW YORK STOCK EXCHANGE CLEARING HOUSE.

THE NEW GAME, "NUMBERS," WAS BIG BUSINESS UP IN HARLEM.

IT WAS RUN OUT OF NEWSSTANDS AND MAGAZINE SHOPS BY LOCAL GANGSTERS LIKE MADAM ST. CLAIR.

WHEN PROHIBITION ENDED, DUTCH SCHULTZ AND OTHER FORMER BOOTLEGGING MOB BOSSES MOVED IN ON THE NUMBERS GAME.

I'M TAKING OVER THIS RACKET!

SCHULTZ KILLED ANYONE WHO STOOD IN HIS WAY.

IS HE GONE?

TWENTY MILLION PEOPLE PLAY THE NUMBERS TODAY.

THE GAME IS RUN USING THREE DIFFERENT SETS OF RUNNERS; ONE TO SEND OUT THE NUMBERS BOOKS...

ONE TO COLLECT THE MONEY...

AND ONE TO RETURN WITH THE SLIPS.

THE POLICE NEED TO FIND THE MONEY AND THE SLIPS IN THE SAME PLACE TO MAKE AN ARREST-- AN ALMOST IMPOSSIBLE TASK.

THEN THERE'S HORSE RACING...

...THE SPORT OF KINGS.

THE FIRST RACES WERE HELD IN THE ANCIENT MIDDLE EAST.

TRIBES DEPRIVED THEIR FASTEST HORSES OF WATER, PUT THEM IN CLEAR SIGHT OF AN OASIS, AND LET THEM GO.

ONE SUCH RACE TURNED UGLY WHEN, SEEING THEIR HORSE WAS LOSING, ONE TRIBE THREW ROCKS TO SPUR HIM ON!

FIGHTING BROKE OUT, LEADING TO A CENTURY-LONG WAR.

CITY STREETS WERE OFTEN USED FOR HORSE RACES IN COLONIAL AMERICA.

NOT EVERYONE LOVED THE IDEA.

EARLY RACES USED THE AUCTION BETTING SYSTEM. THE RIGHT TO BET ON EACH HORSE WAS SOLD OFF, WITH THE WINNER COLLECTING ALL THE PROCEEDS.

MORE AND MORE GROUPS OF PEOPLE PLACED BETS WITH THE AUCTIONEER, WHO EVOLVED INTO...

BELMONT RESULTS

...THE BOOKIE.

THE BOOKIE MADE HIS MONEY BY TAKING BETS FROM GAMBLERS WHO WEREN'T AT THE TRACK

THIS WAS, OF COURSE, ILLEGAL.

THE INVENTION OF WIRE SERVICES ENABLED BOOKIES TO GET RACING RESULTS FROM ACROSS THE COUNTRY INSTANTANEOUSLY.

BELMONT | HIALEH

SANTA ANITA | SARA

THAT MEANT MORE RACES TO BET ON, MORE MONEY FOR THE BOOKIE...

...AND MORE MONEY FOR MOE ANNENBERG. 15,000 BOOKIES NATIONWIDE USED HIS WIRE SERVICE. MOE MADE SO MUCH MONEY...

I CAN'T KEEP TRACK OF IT ALL !!!

166

MOE WAS FINALLY INDICTED FOR TAX EVASION...

BUT THE BOOKIE BUSINESS KEPT BOOMING. EVEN OTB COULDN'T PUT A DENT IN IT.

THEY GIVE ME CREDIT...

..AND BETTER ODDS!

AND THOUGH BOOKMAKING WAS ILLEGAL, THE GAMBLER COULD RIGHTFULLY ASK...

WHAT'S THE DIFFERENCE BETWEEN BETTING OFF-TRACK WITH THE GOVERNMENT, OR WITH HIM?

CHURCH LEADERS HAD ONE ANSWER...

It is not gambling but the abuse of gambling that is an immoral act.

B-75!

...ALTHOUGH AT TIMES THEIR ACTIONS SPOKE LOUDER THAN THEIR WORDS.

ESPECIALLY SINCE MOST OF THE GAMBLING AT SO-CALLED "CHARITABLE" STREET FAIRS...

...WAS AS ABUSIVE (READ: CROOKED) AS GAMBLING COULD GET.

BIG-CITY GAMBLERS ARE ADVISED TO LEAVE OFF THINKING ABOUT MORALITY AND RECALL NICK THE GREEK'S WORDS:

"THE GREATEST PLEASURE IN MY LIFE IS GAMBLING AND WINNING."

"THE NEXT GREATEST PLEASURE IS GAMBLING AND LOSING."

WELCOME, MY FRIEND, TO THE CASINO, OR AS WE LIKE TO THINK OF IT--

THE DREAM FACTORY

5¢ JACKPOTS 5¢

MY, WHAT A HANDSOME GROUP YOU ARE. SUCH A TYPICAL, RED-BLOODED AMERICAN FAMILY.

YOU GOT THE COMPLIMENTARY AIRLINE TICKETS WE SENT--? GOOD, GOOD,...

BUT WHERE ARE MY MANNERS...? I'M SURE YOU WANT TO GET YOUR KIDS STARTED ON *THEIR* PART OF THIS ADVENTURE...

HE DON'T CARE ABOUT THE KIDDIES, BUB. THEY JUST WANT TO GET ANY DISTRACTIONS OUT OF THE WAY.

NOW THEN,... HERE'S OUR LITTLE CASINO.

PRETTY BRIGHT IN HERE, EH? THEY LIKE TO KEEP YOU DISORIENTED ── NO SENSE OF NIGHT OR DAY.

WHAT--? OH, THOSE COINS... YES, THEY DO MAKE A LOT OF NOISE COMING DOWN THE CHUTE...

THAT'S 'CAUSE THE TRAYS ARE HOLLOW-- AND THE NOISE MAKES *YOU* WANNA TRY TOO!

ACTUALLY, WE JUST WANT THE SOUND OF RICHES BEING WON TO BE HEARD OVER THE ANNOUNCEMENTS.

ANOTHER JACKPOT!

THIS LADY'S BEEN HERE TWO DAYS STRAIGHT. ONE MORE JACKPOT AND SHE'LL JUST ABOUT BREAK EVEN.

BUT HERE'S WHAT YOU *REALLY* CAME TO DO.

HOWZABOUT IT, BUDDY? YOU WANNA ROLL?

BUFFALO HERDS ONCE ROAMED THE GREAT PLAINS. THEIR SEASONAL MIGRATIONS FORMED THE BASIS OF THE NATIVE AMERICAN ECONOMY...

...TILL THE WHITE MAN HUNTED THEM TO THE POINT OF EXTINCTION.

THE NEW BUFFALO

SOME THREE HUNDRED YEARS LATER, NATIVE AMERICANS HAVE FINALLY FOUND A REPLACEMENT.

DESPITE COURT DECISIONS AFFIRMING THEM AS "INDEPENDENT AND SOVEREIGN NATIONS," RESERVATION LIVING HAS FOR CENTURIES MEANT POVERTY AND STARVATION FOR NATIVE AMERICANS.

CONNECTICUT'S PEQUOT INDIANS FARED WORSE THAN MOST: THREE HUNDRED YEARS AGO, VIRTUALLY THE ENTIRE TRIBE WAS MASSACRED, AND THE FEW REMAINING SURVIVORS WERE INDENTURED ALONGSIDE AFRICAN SLAVES.

BY 1970, ONLY TWO ELDERLY HALF-SISTERS LIVED ON THE TRIBE'S 216-ACRE RESERVATION. CONNECTICUT LAWMAKERS APPROACHED THEM ABOUT BUYING THE RESERVATION AND TURNING IT INTO PARKLAND.

THE SISTERS REFUSED. INSPIRED, THE TRIBE SUCCESSFULLY SUED CONNECTICUT IN 1976 FOR THE RETURN OF 2,000 OTHER ACRES TAKEN FROM THEM OVER THE CENTURIES.

NEW YORK'S MOHAWK TRIBE HAD PREVI-OUSLY TAKEN ADVANTAGE OF THEIR STATUS AS "AN INDEPENDENT AND SOVEREIGN NATION"--NOT SUBJECT TO STATE GAMBLING LAWS--TO BUILD A STATE-OF-THE-ART BINGO HALL ON THEIR RESERVATION.

THE PEQUOT NOW DID THE SAME, OFFERING JACKPOTS FAR BEYOND THOSE ALLOWED BY STATE LAW.

IN 1988, RONALD REAGAN SIGNED THE INDIAN GAMING REGULATORY ACT INTO LAW.

LET THE GAMES BEGIN!

THIS ALLOWED TRIBES, SUBJECT TO NEGOTIATION WITH SURROUNDING STATES, TO OPEN CASINOS ON RESERVATION LAND.

IN 1993, THE PEQUOT OPENED FOXWOODS CASINO, GUARANTEEING CONNECTICUT A MINIMUM OF $100 MILLION PER YEAR IN TAX REVENUE.

TODAY FOXWOODS IS THE MOST POPULAR--AND PROFITABLE--CASINO IN THE WESTERN WORLD, CLEARING CLOSE TO $2 MILLION A DAY.

GAMBLERS BRAVE HOURS-LONG TRAFFIC TIE-UPS JUST TO UNLOAD THEIR MONEY THERE.

THE MONEY ENABLES THE TRIBE TO GUARANTEE EACH OF ITS MEMBERS (THERE ARE ABOUT 350 OF THEM) EMPLOYMENT, FREE EDUCATION THROUGH GRADUATE SCHOOL, FREE HEALTHCARE, AND FREE DAY CARE.

PLUS YEARLY BONUSES!

WHILE MEMBERS OF SOME TRIBES (PROMINENT AMONG THEM THE NAVAJO, THE COUNTRY'S SECOND-LARGEST TRIBE) STILL OPPOSE THE CASINOS...

WE DON'T LIKE THE NEGATIVE ELEMENTS GAMBLING MIGHT BRING IN.

...NONE CAN DENY THEY'VE GIVEN NATIVE AMERICANS THE MONEY--AND THE POLITICAL CLOUT--TO ADDRESS THEIR PROBLEMS AT HOME AND IN WASHINGTON.

LOBBYISTS? WE'RE JUST BUSINESSMEN, LOOKING OUT FOR OUR INTERESTS.

NATIVE AMERICANS ARE ALREADY PLANNING FOR THE NEXT BIG WAVE IN GAMBLING...

COME CHECK OUT OUR WEB SITE!

...INTERNET BETTING.

GAMING

TODAY, CLOSE TO A THIRD OF THE COUNTRY'S 557 TRIBES ALLOW GAMBLING ON THEIR LANDS. THEY'D ALL AGREE WITH THE WORDS OF FOXWOODS C.E.O. G. MICHAEL BROWN...

GAMING WILL TAKE NATIVE AMERICAN TRIBES INTO THE 21ST CENTURY!

FACTOID 100% TRUE BOOKS

WELCOME TO VIRTUAL VEGA$

...WHERE AMERICANS BET ALMOST $600 MILLION LAST YEAR.

WE'RE TALKING ABOUT THE INTERNET, OF COURSE, WHICH HAS THE POTENTIAL TO REVOLUTIONIZE EVERY FORM OF GAMBLING THERE IS.

IMAGINE--AN ENTIRE CASINO RIGHT IN THIS LITTLE BOX.

IF I CAN JUST FIGURE OUT HOW TO PROGRAM THAT HORSE RACE...

HOW DOES IT WORK? SET UP YOUR BUSINESS (AND YOUR COMPUTERS) SOMEPLACE WHERE GAMBLING IS LEGAL, LIKE ANTIGUA...

MIGHT AS WELL BE COMFORTABLE.

BETTORS SET UP A CYBER-CASH ACCOUNT WITH A CREDIT CARD, THEN DIAL IN. THEY CAN WAGER ON SPORTING EVENTS, CASINO GAMES, BINGO...

IDAHO'S COEUR D'ALENE TRIBE IS PLANNING A WEEKLY NATIONAL LOTTERY!

THE SURGE IN ON-LINE GAMBLING HAS CAUGHT THE GOVERNMENT'S EYE. IN MARCH 1998, THE FEDERAL GOVERNMENT DECIDED TO GO AFTER SIX ON-LINE GAMBLING COMPANIES...

YOU CAN'T HIDE ON-LINE AND YOU CAN'T HIDE OFFSHORE.

THE SIX WERE CHARGED WITH VIOLATING THE WIRE COMMUNICATIONS ACT, A LAW THAT SAYS YOU CAN'T USE THE PHONES LINES TO PLACE BETS...

AND THESE INTERNET GAMBLERS USE THE PHONE LINES!

THE COUNTRIES WHERE THE COMPANIES HAVE SET UP SHOP RESENT U.S. INTERFERENCE.

THE INTERNET BELONGS TO ANTIGUA AS MUCH AS TO THE UNITED STATES!

TO STOP ON-LINE GAMBLING DEAD IN ITS TRACKS, THE GOVERNMENT MIGHT NEED TO TAKE MORE DECISIVE MEASURES...

FBI-- YOU'RE UNDER ARREST!

...KEEPING IN MIND A LITTLE EXPERIMENT CALLED PROHIBITION.... THE LAST TIME THEY TRIED TO LEGISLATE A VICE OUT OF EXISTENCE.

CHAPTER SEVEN

THE DEVIL'S PLAYGROUND

Usually, adults are the targets of vice. In many vice-friendly cultures there are restrictions against indulgences by minors. In this country, kids can't buy tobacco, alcohol or lottery tickets. They can't enter the floors of casinos (at least, not till recently), gamble at racetracks, and they can't engage in sanctioned sex (i.e., marriage.) Basically, it is assumed that kids are too young and impressionable to make the reasoned judgments necessary before indulging in vice. When they reach "legal" age, they can be welcomed into the adults-only den of sins... but until then, keep it clean and pure.

That's the public relations line, anyway. The truth is a lot different. Sure, Joe Camel was sent packing, and even beer commercials have restrictions of one sort or another, but in reality, American youth are groomed to indulge in vices from a very early age, starting with the sort of "training vices" contained in this chapter. From sugar-infused candies, which provide quick rushes not unlike adult amphetamines, to gambling-friendly distractions like pinball machines and trading cards, these fondly remembered elements of childhood are more than merely parts of "growing up" — they set the stage for a lifetime of indulgences in VICE.

SOCIETY HAS LONG HAD MIXED FEELINGS ABOUT MANY KIDS' PASTIMES. SOME SEE THEM AS INNOCENT DIVERSIONS -- HARMLESS FUN AND GAMES. OTHERS VIEW THEM AS...

BREEDING GROUNDS OF VICE!

PARENTS TRY TO KEEP THEIR CHILDREN FROM BEING CORRUPTED BY THE "WRONG ELEMENT" -- BUT KIDS SEEM TO BE DRAWN BY THE LURE OF THE FORBIDDEN.

BILLIARDS, OR POOL, HAS LONG HAD UNSAVORY CONNOTATIONS, THOUGH WHEN IT BEGAN, CENTURIES AGO, ONLY THE RICH COULD AFFORD IT. GEORGE WASHINGTON IS SAID TO HAVE BEEN A SKILLED PLAYER.

IN THE 19th CENTURY, DOMESTIC PRODUCTION MADE TABLES MORE AFFORDABLE IN THE U.S., AND THEY BEGAN APPEARING IN HOTELS, COFFEE HOUSES, AND GAMBLING DENS--

-- KNOWN IN THOSE DAYS AS "POOL PARLORS," BECAUSE OF THE BETTING POOLS THEY OPERATED. IT WAS HERE THAT POCKET BILLIARDS BECAME KNOWN AS POOL.

THE POOL ROOM WAS A MALE DOMAIN, FULL OF SMOKING, DRINKING, FIGHTING, AND LEWD TALK, AND NO PLACE FOR A BOY -- AT LEAST ACCORDING TO WIVES AND MOTHERS, WHO NEVER VENTURED THERE.

CHEE!

NOT SURPRISINGLY, WAGERING ON THE GAME WAS COMMON -- AS WAS CROOKED PLAY, OR "DIRTY POOL," WITH NAÏVE YOUNG PLAYERS THE EASIEST VICTIMS.

THAT'S A BUCK YOU OWE ME.

IN MANY TOWNS, CRUSADERS FOUGHT THE GAME.

SAVE OUR CHILDREN FROM POOL!

EVEN TODAY, AS THE GAME FIGHTS FOR RESPECTABILITY, SOME AREAS STILL FORBID MINORS TO PLAY -- OR BAN POOL HALLS ALTOGETHER.

TRAVELING CARNIVALS HAVE BEEN AROUND FOR CENTURIES. THANKS TO PUBLIC TRANSIT, AMUSEMENT PARKS SPROUTED ACROSS AMERICA IN THE LATE 1800s. GAMES FOR THE GULLIBLE WERE A COMMON FEATURE EVEN THEN.

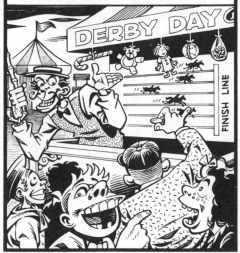

FROM SIMULATED HORSE RACES TO MARKSMANSHIP GAMES, IT ALMOST ALWAYS COSTS MORE TO PLAY LONG ENOUGH TO "WIN" THAN THE PRIZE IS WORTH.

AFTER ONLY 12 TRIES -- WE HAVE A WINNAH!

STEP RIGHT UP! TRY YOUR LUCK! TEST YOUR SKILL!

CHANCE? SKILL? SOUNDS LIKE SOME CASINOS WE KNOW -- AND OF COURSE THE ODDS ARE RIGGED TO FAVOR THE HOUSE.

WHEN THE GREAT DEPRESSION STRUCK, THREE QUARTERS OF U.S. AMUSEMENT PARKS WENT BROKE, ALONG WITH MANY CARNIVALS -- BUT OTHER PASTIMES PICKED UP THE SLACK.

DURING PROHIBITION, MANY SPEAKEASIES ADDED COIN-OPERATED SLOT MACHINES AND MECHANICAL GAMES TO ENTERTAIN CUSTOMERS.

WITH AN ARMY OF THE UNEMPLOYED NOW LOOKING FOR CHEAP AMUSEMENTS, THE GAMES FLOURISHED IN PENNY ARCADES -- STOREFRONTS DEVOTED ENTIRELY TO THESE DIVERSIONS.

NEW MACHINES DEVELOPED QUICKLY. ONE TYPE WAS BASED ON A 100-YEAR-OLD ENGLISH GAME CALLED BAGATELLE. IT INVOLVED ROLLING A MARBLE ON AN INCLINED BOARD STUDDED WITH NAILS OR PINS.

ONE OF THE MOST SUCCESSFUL OF THESE NEW "PINBALL" GAMES WAS CALLED BALLYHOO, WHICH SWEPT THE NATION IN 1932. THE DEVICES SHOWED UP EVERYWHERE FROM BARBERSHOPS TO BUS DEPOTS.

POINTS WERE SCORED DEPENDING ON WHICH OF VARIOUS HOLES THE BALLS LANDED IN. IN THESE EARLY GAMES, THE PLAYER HAD NO WAY TO CONTROL THE PATH OF THE BALL OTHER THAN BY NUDGING THE MACHINE.

SOON A NEW LURE WAS ADDED TO SOME PINBALL GAMES -- PAYOUTS, SIMILAR TO THOSE OF SLOT MACHINES.

MANY PINBALL MACHINES HAD NO PAYOFF, AND WERE PLAYED JUST FOR FUN; OTHER MODELS DISPENSED TICKETS, WHICH WERE REDEEMABLE FOR CASH OR PRIZES.

BECAUSE THE GAMES DEPENDED LARGELY ON CHANCE, THEY WERE WIDELY EQUATED WITH SLOT MACHINES. CIVIC GROUPS AND LEADING MAGAZINES ATTACKED PINBALL.

PINBALL WAS BANNED IN MANY STATES. IN NEW YORK, THE CITY OUTLAWED THE GAMES IN 1942 AND MAYOR FIORELLO LAGUARDIA PERSONALLY TOOK PART IN SMASHING THEM.

IN 1947, IN HOPES OF GETTING AROUND ANTI-GAMBLING LAWS, A NEW FEATURE WAS ADDED THAT INCREASED THE SKILL FACTOR IN PINBALL -- THE FLIPPER.

BUT SOME MODELS' PAYOUTS OF FREE GAMES -- OFTEN REDEEMED FOR CASH BY STORE OWNERS -- REMAINED UNACCEPTABLE IN MANY AREAS.

EVEN MACHINES THAT OFFERED NO PAYOUTS WERE CONSIDERED QUESTIONABLE, SINCE SOME PLAYERS WAGERED ON THEIR GAMES.

WE CAN'T HAVE KIDS GAMBLING ON GAMES -- IT'S IMMORAL!

HA! THAT'S $5 YOU OWE ME!

THE INCREASINGLY NOISY, GARISH DESIGN OF THE GAMES -- WHICH HELPED ATTRACT KIDS -- ALSO FOSTERED ADULT DISAPPROVAL.

DING DING DING DING!

WHRRR!

THURK THE WARRIOR

PREHISTORIC CHALLENGE

BIMP KA-CHUNK-A-CHUN

KLANG!

THE OLD STIGMA LINGERED IN THE MINDS OF MANY. NOT UNTIL THE '70s WERE PINBALL MACHINES MADE LEGAL AGAIN IN NEW YORK AND LOS ANGELES.

JUKEBOXES, TOO, HAD SHADY BEGINNINGS, AS THEY FIRST BECAME POPULAR IN SMALL PROHIBITION-ERA SPEAKEASIES THAT COULDN'T AFFORD LIVE MUSICIANS.

THE MANUFACTURERS FIRST CALLED THEM "AUTOMATIC PHONOGRAPHS," BUT "JUKEBOX" STUCK -- TO THEIR DISMAY.

"JUKE" WAS BLACK SLANG FOR WICKEDNESS. A "JUKE JOINT" WAS A BROTHEL, OFTEN WITH DRINKS AND MUSIC DOWNSTAIRS.

AT THE END OF PROHIBITION, THERE WERE ABOUT 25,000 MACHINES IN THE COUNTRY. THEY NOW SPREAD RAPIDLY INTO RESTAURANTS, SODA SHOPS, BOWLING ALLEYS, AND MORE.

DESIGNS BECAME INCREASINGLY ELABORATE AS MANUFACTURERS COMPETED FOR PLACEMENT AND CUSTOMER ATTENTION.

BY 1940, THERE WERE ABOUT 400,000 JUKEBOXES IN ACTION.

IN THE '40s AND '50s, AS TEENS CULTURE GREW, JUKEBOXES WERE A VITAL OUTLET FOR MUSIC THAT WAS SHUNNED BY MAINSTREAM RADIO -- R&B AND ROCK AND ROLL.

SODA FOUNTAINS WITH JUKEBOXES BECAME TEENAGE HANGOUTS -- AND WHO KNEW WHAT TROUBLE THIS FRENZIED MUSIC MIGHT INSPIRE?

MANY ADULTS WERE SCANDALIZED. IN 1955, SOMERVILLE, MASSACHUSETTS, BANNED ROCK RECORDS FROM LOCAL JUKEBOXES AS A "CRIME PREVENTION" MEASURE.

MINORS ARE FORBIDDEN BY LAW TO OPERATE THE MACHINE

ELSEWHERE, KIDS WEREN'T ALLOWED TO PLAY JUKEBOXES AT ALL.

BUT BY THE LATE '50s, RADIO COULD NO LONGER IGNORE TEENS, WHO NOW ACCOUNTED FOR 70% OF RECORD SALES. ROCK WAS ON THE AIRWAVES, TRANSISTOR RADIOS PROLIFERATED -- AND JUKEBOXES WENT INTO DECLINE.

IN THE '70s, A NEW BREED OF COIN-DEVOURING AMUSEMENTS WAS BORN -- THE VIDEO GAME. PONG SWEPT THE NATION IN 1973.

FAR OUT!

BWEENK! BOINK! BWEENK!

HOME SYSTEMS WERE SOON DEVELOPED-- FIRST FOR TV, LATER FOR COMPUTERS. SEARS SOLD 150,000 HOME PONG GAMES FOR CHRISTMAS IN '75.

YAAAAH!

BWEENK! BOINK! BWEENK!

IN 1976, DEATHRACE, IN WHICH PLAYERS SCORE POINTS FOR RUNNING DOWN PEDESTRIANS, DREW THE IRE OF PARENTS.

COOL!

KRASH!

DEATHRACE

OF COURSE, THERE ARE MANY INNOCUOUS GAMES, TOO, SUCH AS PAC-MAN.

PUCK MA

PUCK MAN

(IT WAS ORIGINALLY TO BE CALLED PUCK MAN -- UNTIL SOMEONE REALIZED HOW EASILY VANDALS COULD ALTER THE P...)

AS GAME GRAPHICS GREW INCREASINGLY SOPHISTICATED, GAME VIOLENCE GREW INCREASINGLY GRAPHIC. IN 1993, THE SENATE HELD HEARINGS ON THE SUBJECT.

SHOCKING!

OUTRAGEOUS!

WAIT YOUR TURN!

COMMITTEE HEARING ROOM

THE VIDEO GAME INDUSTRY AGREED TO POLICE ITSELF BY ESTABLISHING A RATINGS SYSTEM -- UNDER WHICH THE CARNAGE HAS INCREASED.

KEWL!

IN 1996, NINTENDO SOLD ITS ONE-BILLIONTH GAME CARTRIDGE. THOUGH PLATFORMS COME AND GO, IT SEEMS SOME FORM OF QUESTIONABLE RECREATION WILL ALWAYS BE WITH US.

GET USED TO IT.

INTERNET BLOODBATH

DIDJA EVER WONDER WHAT THAT STRANGE LITTLE SYMBOL ON SOME COMICS COVERS IS? WELL, IT GOES BACK TO A TIME WHEN A LOT OF PEOPLE WERE ASKING...

COMIC BOOKS THREAT OR MENACE?

COMIC BOOKS WERE BORN IN THE MID-'30s-- FIRST, AS REPRINTS OF NEWSPAPER STRIPS.

HEY, LOOK!

THE DEBUT OF SUPERMAN IN 1938 INSPIRED A WAVE OF SUPERHEROES, AND COMICS SALES SOARED.

IT'S A BIRD!

IT'S A PLANE!

IT'S OUR SALES FIGURES!

THE NEW MEDIUM WAS BEING NOTICED-- BUT NOT ALWAYS FAVORABLY.

GOOD LORD! CHOKE!

IN 1940 AN EDITORIAL IN THE CHICAGO NEWS CALLED COMICS "PULP-PAPER NIGHTMARES" FULL OF SEX AND VIOLENCE.

SAY, I MAY HAVE TO GO BUY ME SOME OF THESE COMIC BOOKS!

IN RESPONSE TO SUCH ATTACKS, SEVERAL PUBLISHERS LAUNCHED "UPLIFTING" FACT-BASED ADVENTURES, BIOGRAPHIES, AND THE LIKE. THE GENRE FLOURISHED BRIEFLY.

MANY ADULTS, ESPECIALLY BORED G.I.s, WERE NOW READING COMICS. BUT BY THE END OF THE WAR, SUPERHERO SALES WERE SLUMPING. PERHAPS SOMETHING NEW WAS NEEDED TO APPEAL TO THE OLDER AUDIENCE.

SOON CRIME AND ROMANCE COMICS BECAME THE NEXT BIG THING.

HEY KID-- GEDDAWAY FROM DERE!

LURID CRIME

RACY ROMANCE

MURDER CARTOONS

KIDS WERE STILL VORACIOUS COMICS READERS. IN 1947 AN ARTICLE IN THE NEW REPUBLIC COMPARED CHILDREN'S "COMIC BOOK HABIT" TO DRUG ADDICTION.

GOTTA GET MORE!

BUT PROBABLY THE BIGGEST THING TO HIT THE MARKET IN 1947 WASN'T A COMIC BOOK AT ALL -- IT WAS A MAN NAMED DR. FREDERIC WERTHAM.

WERTHAM WAS A NEW YORK CITY DEPARTMENT OF HOSPITALS PSYCHIATRIST. HE WORKED WITH TROUBLED ADOLESCENTS, AND THEIR READING HABITS WORRIED HIM.

YOU STUPID BROAD! I OUGHTTA--

HONK HONK

SHUT UP, YA BUM!

KRASH

MAYHEM TALES

Comics

DARLING CRIMEO

IRONICALLY, HIS FIRST PUBLIC STATEMENT ABOUT COMICS CAME WHEN HE WAS TESTIFYING AGAINST CENSORSHIP. HE CLAIMED COMICS WERE FAR MORE HARMFUL THAN THE NUDIST MAGS THAT WERE ON TRIAL.

...BUT THESE ARE WORSE!

GASP

LURID CRIME

BASED ON HIS OWN PATIENTS, WERTHAM CONCLUDED THAT COMICS CAUSED JUVENILE DELINQUENCY. HE BEGAN AN ANTI-COMICS CRUSADE, SAYING THEY WERE...

...DEFINITELY AND COMPLETELY HARMFUL.

SLOBBER FUNNY BUNNY

COP SMASHERS

WERTHAM ESTIMATED THAT A TYPICAL 16-YEAR-OLD COMICS READER HAD VIEWED 18,000 PICTORIAL ACTS OF VIOLENCE.

CRIME

FEW ADULTS DEFENDED THE GARISH MEDIUM.

MOM-- NOOOO!

CITIES ACROSS THE COUNTRY BEGAN BANNING "HARMFUL" COMICS. IN SOME PLACES COMICS WERE BURNED.

IN 1948 SOME PUBLISHERS RESPONDED BY ADOPTING A SELF-IMPOSED CODE OF STANDARDS.

BUT THIS CODE HAD LITTLE EFFECT ON THE CONTENTS OF THE COMICS. WERTHAM DECLARED THAT SOME OF THE WORST OFFENDERS LABELED THEMSELVES "WHOLESOME."

EVEN AS PUBLIC PRESSURE AGAINST COMICS WAS RISING, A NEW GENRE WAS CATCHING ON...

THE PREMIER HORROR PUBLISHER WAS E.C. COMICS, OWNED BY WILLIAM GAINES.

HIS FATHER MAX HAD BEEN IN THE COMICS BIZ FROM THE BEGINNING AND FOUNDED EDUCATIONAL COMICS IN 1945.

WHEN MAX DIED IN 1947, BILL CHANGED THE NAME TO ENTERTAINING COMICS.

IN 1950 THE SENATE'S KEFAUVER COMMITTEE STUDIED THE POSSIBLE LINK BETWEEN COMICS AND CRIME. GAINES WAS CALLED TO TESTIFY ABOUT HORROR COMICS.

DO YOU THINK THAT'S IN GOOD TASTE?

YES--FOR THE COVER OF A HORROR COMIC.

EXPERTS TESTIFIED...

JUVENILE CRIME HAS ACTUALLY DECLINED IN RECENT YEARS.

THE COMMITTEE DECIDED COMICS WEREN'T SO HARMFUL AFTER ALL.

BUT FREDERIC WERTHAM HADN'T CHANGED HIS MIND. HE WENT TO WORK ON A BOOK THAT HE HOPED WOULD AROUSE THE PUBLIC.

KLIKETTY-KLIK-KLIK-KLAK.

THE RESULT, SEDUCTION OF THE INNOCENT, ATTACKED COMICS IN GENERAL AND CRIME COMICS IN PARTICULAR. PUBLISHED IN 1954, IT MADE QUITE A SPLASH WITH PARENTS--

--ESPECIALLY SOME OF THE IMAGES IT REPRINTED.

WERTHAM SAID COMICS FOSTERED UNHEALTHY IDEAS ABOUT SEX AND WERE PREOCCUPIED WITH BREASTS-- WHAT HE'D HEARD TERMED "HEADLIGHTS."

IN FACT, HE CLAIMED, IF YOU LOOKED CLOSELY YOU COULD FIND SEXUAL IMAGERY HIDDEN IN COMICS ART.

...? IT'S GOTTA BE HERE SOMEWHERE!

WERTHAM ALSO SAID HIS YOUNG PATIENTS HAD TOLD HIM THEY'D LEARNED HOW TO COMMIT CRIMES FROM COMICS.

WERTHAM INCLUDED IN HIS DEFINITION OF "CRIME" COMICS SUCH INNOCUOUS HEROES AS BATMAN AND ROBIN...

...WHO WERE, HE CONTENDED, OBVIOUSLY GAY.

THE SENATE HELD MORE HEARINGS, AND THIS TIME WERTHAM TESTIFIED. ONE SENATOR CONCLUDED THAT COMICS ARE...

...PACKED WITH EVERY FORM OF VICE, SADISM, AND VIOLENCE CONCEIVABLE.

THE SENATE URGED PUBLISHERS TO CLEAN UP THEIR ACT, AND MANY STATES WERE CONSIDERING RESTRICTING COMICS SALES. THE PUBLISHERS DECIDED TO WRITE A NEW CODE AND MAKE IT STICK.

CONFORMING COMICS NOW CARRIED A SEAL OF APPROVAL, AND WARY DISTRIBUTORS WOULDN'T TAKE NON-APPROVED COMICS-- BUT THIS WAS ALL "VOLUNTARY," THUS DODGING QUESTIONS OF FREEDOM OF THE PRESS AND CENSORSHIP.

THE CODE ELIMINATED ALL COMICS "UNSUITABLE" FOR YOUNG KIDS--MUCH LIKE BANNING ALL BUT G-RATED MOVIES.

IT SPECIFICALLY FORBADE "DISRESPECT FOR ESTABLISHED AUTHORITY" AND GLORIFICATION OF CRIMINALS--ALONG WITH VAMPIRES, ZOMBIES, WEREWOLVES, "EXCESSIVE" VIOLENCE, AND TITLES USING THE WORDS HORROR OR TERROR.

WERTHAM HIMSELF WOULD HAVE ALLOWED BROADER MATERIAL FOR OLDER READERS. HE CALLED THE NEW SYSTEM HYPOCRITICAL AND SAID THAT IN CODE-APPROVED COMICS...

...MURDER LOOKED MORE LIKE A GAME.

COMICS WERE FORCED TO BECOME WHAT MANY STILL THINK OF THEM AS -- A "KIDDIE" MEDIUM. SALES FELL AND PUBLISHERS WENT UNDER, AS MANY FORMER READERS TURNED TO A NEW PASTIME.

RAT-A-TAT-TAT!

PUBLISHERS RETREATED TO SAFER GROUND--SUPERHEROES AND HUMOR.

HEY, KIDS! COMICS

BY 1970 THE CONTROVERSY WAS LARGELY FORGOTTEN, AND A FEW COMICS THAT FAILED TO WIN CODE APPROVAL WERE SOLD WITHOUT INCIDENT.

AT THE SAME TIME, UNDERGROUND COMICS — FULL OF SEX, DRUGS, AND DISRESPECT FOR AUTHORITY — TRIED ALTERNATIVE DISTRIBUTION.

DESPITE "ADULTS ONLY" LABELS, SEVERAL WERE BUSTED FOR OBSCENITY.

COMIC BOOK STORES WERE CROPPING UP ALONG WITH NEW DISTRIBUTORS LESS CONCERNED ABOUT THE CODE. NEW PUBLISHERS, SELLING ONLY TO COMICS SHOPS, FOUND THEY DIDN'T NEED THE SEAL.

THANKS TO THE SHOPS, PUBLISHERS COULD OFFER A WIDE VARIETY OF PRODUCTS, ATTRACTING OLDER READERS--AND HORRIFYING SOME PARENTS WHO STILL THOUGHT OF COMICS AS "KID STUFF."

SEVERAL COMICS SHOPS HAVE BEEN BUSTED ON OBSCENITY CHARGES, AND SOME HAVE BEEN FORCED OUT OF BUSINESS--TOUCHING OFF ANOTHER DEBATE WITHIN THE INDUSTRY ABOUT SELF-REGULATION.

IT'S YOUR FAULT!

PUBLISHER
SHOP OWNER
CARTOONIST

TODAY AMERICAN COMICS REMAIN IN A PRECARIOUS POSITION--LOOKED DOWN ON FOR BEING TOO JUVENILE, YET ATTACKED EACH TIME THEY TRY TO GROW UP.

SCHIZO COMICS

IN MANY COUNTRIES, JUST AS THERE ARE BOOKS AND MOVIES FOR DIFFERENT AGES, THERE IS A WIDE ARRAY OF COMICS--AND MILLIONS OF ADULTS ARE AVID READERS. BUT IN AMERICA...

ME READ COMIC BOOKS? DON'T INSULT MY INTELLIGENCE!

WHO JUST FOUND OUT HIS GIRLFRIEND IS REALLY A--

FACTOID BOOKS

TRADING CARDS WERE INVENTED IN THE 1880's TO HELP SELL OTHER MERCHANDISE BUT HAVE LONG SINCE BECOME AN END IN THEMSELVES. STILL SOLD IN RANDOM ASSORTMENTS IN SEALED PACKS, THEY CHALLENGE KIDS TO...

MOST OF US ASSOCIATE THEM WITH BUBBLE GUM, BUT TRADING CARDS FIRST APPEARED IN CIGARETTE PACKS--PARTLY TO ATTRACT CUSTOMERS, PARTLY TO STIFFEN THE FLIMSY PACKS.

PICK-A-Card
COLLECT THE SET!
70,000 CARDS TO COLLECT

I'LL TAKE A PACK O' WIFFYS!

THE CIGARETTE IN WHOSE PACK one finds a PICTURE OF A GEL!
WIFFY
CHAW BACCY

OF COURSE, MANY SMOKERS GAVE THE CARDS TO THEIR CHILDREN. KIDS SOON BEGAN TRADING WITH FRIENDS, TRYING TO COLLECT COMPLETE SETS.

OVER THE NEXT FEW DECADES, TOBACCO CARDS FEATURED SUCH SUBJECTS AS INTERNATIONAL NAVAL FLAGS...

...BASEBALL PLAYERS...

GEE, POP, HURRY UP AN' SMOKE THOSE SO'S YOU CAN GET SOME MORE!

GREAT! I GOT THE SET!

I'M GONNA START SMOKING SO'S I CAN GET ME OWN!

YEAH! ME TOO!

KOF KOF KOFF KOF KOF KOF KOF KOF KOFF KOF

...AND "SPORTING GIRLS".

I THINK I'LL KEEP THIS ONE FOR MYSELF.

ABOUT 1910, BASEBALL GREAT HONUS WAGNER OBJECTED TO THE UNAUTHORIZED USE OF HIS LIKENESS ON A CIGARETTE CARD, SAYING HE OPPOSED TOBACCO USE (THOUGH PERHAPS HE OBJECTED MORE TO NOT BEING PAID).

THE CARD WAS WITHDRAWN, AND ONLY ABOUT 50 ARE NOW KNOWN TO EXIST. ONE MINT-CONDITION SPECIMEN WAS RECENTLY SOLD FOR $640,500!

I'LL GIVE YA TY COBB FOR WAGNER.

WELL--OK... I'LL PROBILY REGRET THIS LATER.

Baseball STATS

PITTSBURG

AROUND THIS TIME, MORE CARDS WERE BEING AIMED DIRECTLY AT KIDS, AS CANDY COMPANIES BEGAN INCLUDING THEM IN SWEETS SUCH AS CRACKER JACK.

EW! GROSS!

BUBBLE GUM BECAME POPULAR ABOUT 1930, AND MAKERS SOON BEGAN PACKAGING BASEBALL CARDS WITH THE GUM.

IN 1934, THE GOUDEY GUM COMPANY FOUND A NEW WAY TO BOOST SALES—ISSUING ONLY 239 OF A 240-CARD SET. DESPERATE KIDS KEPT BUYING...

GOTTA FIND NAP LAJOIE!

GOUDEY BUBBLE GUM BASEBALL CARD

SMALL-TIME GAMBLING HAS LONG FLOURISHED AMONG KIDS TRYING TO IMPROVE THEIR COLLECTIONS. SOME DEVISED GAMES USING THE STATS LISTED ON THE CARDS.

HA! JOHNNY BENCH BEATS BILL FREEHAN!

CARD-FLIPPING WAS ALSO POPULAR. LIKE DEDICATED CRAPS SHOOTERS, KIDS SPENT HOURS HONING THEIR TECHNIQUE. THE WINNER TOOK BOTH CARDS—THE LOSER KEPT ON PRACTICING.

FACE DOWN! I WIN!

WHILE BASEBALL PREDOMINATED, MANY OTHER TYPES OF CARDS HAVE BEEN PRODUCED. A GRUESOME 1938 SET BORE THE SLOGAN "TO KNOW THE HORRORS OF WAR IS TO WANT PEACE!"

WOW! INNOCENT CIVILIANS GETTING BOMBED!

EXPLODING TRAINS! COOL!

PILES OF BURNING CORPSES! NEAT!

MACHINE-GUNNED NUNS...

...AND DOGS EATING THE DEAD!

WOW!

PLUS ÇA CHANGE....

IN 1962, TOPPS RELEASED THE LURID MARS ATTACKS SERIES. OUTRAGED PARENTS FORCED TOPPS TO WITHDRAW THE CARDS.

BURNING FLESH

19

RECENTLY, GUM HAS LARGELY BEEN ELIMINATED FROM CARD PACKS. TO INCITE BUYERS, MANY COMPANIES NOW FOLLOW GOUDEY'S '34 EXAMPLE AND INCLUDE LIMITED-EDITION "CHASE" CARDS IN THEIR SETS.

GOTTA FIND THAT HOLO-CARD!

ACTION HERO

GAME PLAYING AND COLLECTIBILITY HAVE BEEN COMBINED IN THE RECENT "MAGIC: THE GATHERING" SERIES. DESPITE SOME FUNDAMENTALISTS' FEARS THAT THE GAME INVOLVES DEVIL WORSHIP, MILLIONS HAVE BEEN SOLD.

IT'S NOT SATANISM—ITS JUST CAPITALISM!

YOG SOTTHOTH!

FACTOID BOOKS 100% TRUE

CALL IT SUCROSE, GLUCOSE, FRUCTOSE, OR JUST SUGAR -- MOST KIDS SEEM TO CRAVE SWEETS, AND ADULTS TEND TO VIEW THEM AS A GUILTY PLEASURE. HUMANS MAY SIMPLY BE BORN WITH A... **SWEET TOOTH**

SOME RESEARCHERS BELIEVE OUR TASTE FOR SWEETS WAS AN EVOLUTIONARY TOOL -- STEERING EARLY HUMANS AWAY FROM HARMFUL PLANTS AND TOWARDS HIGH-CALORIE FOODS TO FUEL THEIR STRENUOUS LIVES.

YAH!

SUGAR CANE WAS CULTIVATED IN ASIA MORE THAN 2,000 YEARS AGO, AND SUGAR WAS FIRST REFINED FROM IT AROUND 500 A.D. SUGAR GRADUALLY REACHED EUROPE AS A LUXURY ITEM.

COLUMBUS CARRIED CANE TO THE NEW WORLD WHERE IT FLOURISHED. SLAVE PLANTATIONS THROUGHOUT THE CARIBBEAN SUPPLIED EUROPE FOR CENTURIES.

THE PROCESS OF REFINING SUGAR BEETS WAS DEVELOPED IN GERMANY IN THE LATE 1700s. WHEN IMPORTED SUGAR WAS CUT OFF DURING THE NAPOLEONIC WARS, EUROPE'S BEET INDUSTRY GREW QUICKLY.

KNOWING PEOPLE'S TASTE FOR SWEETS, THE BURGEONING PROCESSED FOOD INDUSTRY BEGAN ADDING SUGAR TO EVERYTHING FROM BREAKFAST CEREAL TO SOFT DRINKS IN THE LATE 1800s.

YUM!

VICTORIANOS

TODAY, 3/4 OF THE SUGAR WE EAT IS ALREADY IN THE FOOD WHEN WE BUY IT -- COMPARED WITH JUST 1/3 IN 1909. NOT SURPRISINGLY, INDIVIDUAL CONSUMPTION HAS SOARED 73% SINCE THEN.

SOUNDS DELISH!

GLUCOSE, DEXTROSE, HIGH-FRUCTOSE CORN SYRUP, MALTOSE

FROZEN PIZZA

SOME BLAME HIGH SUGAR CONSUMPTION FOR VARIOUS CHILDHOOD BEHAVIORAL PROBLEMS, THOUGH THE TOPIC REMAINS CONTROVERSIAL. OTHERS BELIEVE SUGAR HAS ADDICTIVE QUALITIES.

ZOOM

THE AVERAGE AMERICAN CONSUMES ABOUT 3 POUNDS OF VARIOUS FORMS OF SUGAR EVERY WEEK -- FOUR TIMES THE USDA'S RECOMMENDED LIMIT.

CHOMP *CHOMP* *CHOMP* *CHOMP*

FACTOID BOOKS

COPYRIGHT INFORMATION

Village of the Damned copyright © 1999 Dave Stern and art by Ivan Brunetti

Phenix City copyright © 1999 Steve Vance and Bob Fingerman

Fantasy Island copyright © 1999 Dave Stern and Rick Geary

Las Vegas copyright © 1999 Steve Vance and Deryl Skelton

The Deuce copyright © 1999 Dave Stern and Alan Kupperberg

Rated XXX copyright © 1999 Dave Stern and Alwyn Talbot

The First Drug copyright © 1999 Steve Vance and Dan Spiegle

Battle of the Booze copyright © 1999 Steve Vance and Tom Sutton

Carry Nation copyright © 1999 Steve Vance and Lennie Mace

Noble Disaster copyright © 1999 Steve Vance and Hilary Barta

Izzy & Moe copyright © 1999 Steve Vance and Armando Gil

White Lightning copyright © 1999 Steve Vance and Hunt Emerson

What's in the Bottles? copyright © 1999 Steve Vance and Joe Staton

Friends of Bill W. copyright © 1999 Steve Vance and Dan Burr

So You Wanna Know About Alcohol? copyright © 1999 Steve Vance

The Stoned Age copyright © 1999 Steve Vance and Wm. Marshall Rogers

Cocaine: The Curse of the Incas copyright © 1999 Steve Vance and Galen Showman

The Poppy's Strange Fruit copyright © 1999 Steve Vance and Gregory Benton

The Opium Wars copyright © 1999 Steve Vance and Alec Stevens

The Age of Absinthe copyright © 1999 Steve Vance and Kieron Dwyer

Hemp Through History copyright © 1999 Steve Vance and Ovidiu Nedelcu

Reefer Madness copyright © 1999 Steve Vance and Salgood Sam

Peyote: Sacred Cactus of the Southwest copyright © 1999 Steve Vance and John Estes

Albert Hoffman copyright © 1999 Steve Vance and James Romberger

Timothy Leary, Psychedelic Guru copyright © 1999 Steve Vance and James Romberger

America's Hidden Plague copyright © 1999 Steve Vance and Glenn Barr

Caffeine Fiends copyright © 1999 Steve Vance and Bahadir Boysal

Vice Styles of the Rich and Famous copyright © 1999 Steve Vance and John Cebollero

The Roots of Tobacco copyright © 1999 Steve Vance and Donald David

Seeds of a Nation copyright © 1999 Steve Vance and Steve Mannion

Buck Duke, Cigarette King copyright © 1999 Steve Vance and Charles Adlard

Gunsmoke copyright © 1999 Steve Vance and Russ Heath

Lucy Gaston vs. The Coffin Nail copyright © 1999 Steve Vance and Ted Slampyak

Smoke and Mirrors copyright © 1999 Steve Vance and Terry LaBan

Warning! Cigarette Companies May Be Hazardous to Your Health! copyright © 1999 Steve Vance and Seth Fisher

Marlboro World copyright © 1999 Steve Vance and Gray Morrow

Prostitutes of the Gods copyright © 1999 Steve Vance and Rina Piccolo

The Golden Age of Prostitution copyright © 1999 Steve Vance and Jennifer Graves

Harlots and Holy Men copyright © 1999 Steve Vance and Joe Staton

Mystery John copyright © 1999 Steve Vance and B.K. Taylor

Whores of War copyright © 1999 Steve Vance and Sam Glanzman

The Victorians' Secret copyright © 1999 Steve Vance and Michael Collins

Hollywood's Madams copyright © 1999 Steve Vance and Steve Smith

The Happy Hooker copyright © 1999 Dave Stern and Glen Hanson

The Mustang Ranch copyright © 1999 Steve Vance and Alan Kupperberg

Sex Slaves copyright © 1999 Steve Vance and Colleen Doran

The Pimp copyright © 1999 Steve Vance and Denys Cowan

Mayflower Madam copyright © 1999 Steve Vance and Christian Alamy

The Evolution of Porn copyright © 1999 Steve Vance and Wm. Marshall Rogers

Anthony Comstock copyright © 1999 Steve Vance and Karl Heitmueller, Jr.

Live Nude Girls copyright © 1999 Steve Vance and David Monahan

Master of the Pornoverse copyright © 1999 Steve Vance and John Cebollero

King of Porn copyright © 1999 Dave Stern and Bob Fingerman

Sexual Revolutionary copyright © 1999 Dave Stern and Russ Heath

Patriot of Porn copyright © 1999 Dave Stern and Mark Poutenis

The Sultan of Sleaze copyright © 1999 Dave Stern and Danny Hellman

Aphrodisiacs copyright © 1999 Steve Vance and Floyd Hughes

Basic Instinct copyright © 1999 Dave Stern and Stephen Sadowski

The Devil's Invention copyright © 1999 Dave Stern and Randy DuBurke

The Winning Ticket copyright © 1999 Dave Stern and Tayyar Ozkan

Tumblin' Vice copyright © 1999 Dave Stern and Michael Collins

The Godfather of Gambling copyright © 1999 Dave Stern and Brad Teare

History-Making Bets copyright © 1999 Dave Stern and Gordon Purcell

The Anti-Gamblers copyright © 1999 Dave Stern and Vincent Deporter

Bright Lights, Big Bucks copyright © 1999 Dave Stern and Robert Snyder

The Dream Factory copyright © 1999 Dave Stern and Stephen DeStefano

The New Buffalo copyright © 1999 Dave Stern and Salgood Sam

Virtual Vegas copyright © 1999 Dave Stern and John Heebink

Breeding Ground of Vice copyright © 1999 Steve Vance and Roger Langridge

Comic Books — Threat or Menace? copyright © 1999 Steve Vance and Sergio Aragonés

Pick a Card copyright © 1999 Steve Vance and Hunt Emerson

Sweet Tooth copyright © 1999 Steve Vance and Nick Bertozzi

BIOGRAPHIES

WRITERS

STEVE VANCE
Steve writes, draws, and hatches crackpot schemes for global domination in the comfort of his secret underground base somewhere in Southern California. He has also written stories for *The Big Book of Hoaxes* and *The Big Book of Bad* for Paradox Press. (He also drew page 44.)

DAVE STERN
Dave was a rotten kid who gleefully swindled his high school buddies in their weekly penny-ante poker games. Working on this book brought back some fond memories for him. He's written others, including the forthcoming *Your Secrets Are My Business*.

ARTISTS

CHARLES ADLARD
"Don't listen to those men in the long coats — I didn't draw *The X-Files*... ever...no, no really...I didn't. But I do draw *Shadowman*! Oh yes! Oh yes!" (Page 83)

CHRISTIAN ALAMY
Christian's extraordinary ability to draw slower than any other human being is the result of a failed genetics experiment led by the French government in 1968. He is currently hiding out in Brooklyn. (Page 120)

SERGIO ARAGONÉS
Sergio is the creator of the award-winning comic *Groo*. His comics and illustrations have appeared in *MAD*, and most recently in *Sergio Aragonés' Louder Than Words* from Dark Horse Comics and in *Fanboy*, written by Mark Evanier, from DC Comics. (Page 179)

GLENN BARR
Glenn's projects have included the graphic novels and comics *Cliff's Wild Life, Technocracy Blues, Mars on Earth*, as well as *Brooklyn Dreams* for Paradox Press. His animation work includes *The Ren & Stimpy Show* and *Baby Huey*. (Page 72)

HILARY BARTA
Eats food, breathes air, and draws comics. (Page 33)

GREGORY BENTON
Gregory's cartooning wonderment has appeared in *Details, High Times,* and in his own comic book *Hummingbird*. Gregory is a high-falootin', rootin'-tootin', free-bootin' son of a gun. In case you had any doubts. (Page 52)

NICK BERTOZZI
Nick is very adept at drawing nipple rings and inebriated barflies. Find out for yourself in the self-published *Incredible Drinkin' Buddies* and the brand-spankin' new *Tranquilizer*. (Page 186)

BAHADIR BOYSAL
Bahadir lives in Turkey, where his art and comic strips appear regularly in the weekly *Leman* and the monthly *Lemanyak*. (Page 74)

IVAN BRUNETTI
Ivan is still working on his comic magazine of "zany, madcap, degenerate filth," *Schizo* (Fantagraphics), and contemplating suicide. He is an inspiration to us all. (Page 6)

DAN BURR
Recent work can be found in *The Big Book of Losers, The Big Book of Thugs, The Big Book of Freaks,* and in *The Spirit: New Adventures*. Further excavation may uncover the graphic novel *Kings in Disguise*. (Page 42)

JOHN CEBOLLERO
John recently discovered his long-lost skate key in an enormous glob of wax that was excavated from his ear. He is now in search of little Timmy Monahan, who put it there in the first place. When he finds him, he will kill him. (Pages 75 and 128)

MICHAEL COLLINS
Mike took up comics after realizing that, as a flabby white guy from Britain, he would never achieve his ambitions: to become president of the U.S.A. and/or one of Diana Ross's Supremes. (Pages 107 and 153)

DENYS COWAN
A twenty-year comics veteran, Denys illustrated the award-winning *Question* series and the acclaimed Batman adventure *Blind Justice* with Batman screenwriter Sam Hamm. He was also a founding member of the groundbreaking Milestone Media comics imprint. (Page 118)

DONALD DAVID
While working on pages for this book, Donald was abducted by drunken, cigar-smoking whores. They offered to take him to their Pleasure Palace, but Donald had to refuse because he had a Paradox Press assignment to finish. Now, that's dedication! (Page 78)

VINCENT DEPORTER
Vince draws cartoons in Belgium, France, and the U.S. including "Fourmidables," in the magazine *Spirou*, and "Roméo," which has appeared in *Maxi* for over 12 years. He has recently done Superman illustrations for DC's licensing department. (Page 159)

STEPHEN DeSTEFANO
Stephen has been a professional cartoonist for over 15 years. He has spent years mastering the art of the shrug, and often teaches it to old Chinese men in Washington Square Park in exchange for free tai chi classes. He was born in Queens, New York. (Page 168)

COLLEEN DORAN
Colleen is the writer, artist, and creator of the series *A Distant Soil*. She worked on *Sandman* and drew the graphic novel *Wonder Woman: The Once and Future Story* for DC. (Page 115)

RANDY DuBURKE
Randy's work for DC Comics includes covers for *Animal Man, Darkstars, Ms. Tree,* and *The Shadow*. He drew the story "Big Shot" for the DC/Vertigo anthology *Gangland*, as well as *Hunter's Heart*, a Paradox Graphic Mystery. (Page 145)

KIERON DWYER
Crankypants rules! (Page 60)

HUNT EMERSON
Hunt Emerson lurks 100 feet in the air, in sight of the New Hindu Temple on Soho Road. At night, the dome is lit from below in blue light. (Pages 39 and 184)

JOHN ESTES
John has painted *Tales to Astonish* for Marvel, numerous trading cards, and the *Batman/Deadman* hardcover graphic novel for DC. (Page 66)

BOB FINGERMAN
When Bob isn't drawing weird stuff for Paradox, he's illustrating his comic *Minimum Wage* from Fantagraphics. Which you should buy and read. Right now. Or Bob will come to your house, sit on your lap and say, "Love me, love me, love me!" until you do. (Pages 7 and 131)

SETH FISHER
...a.k.a. Fishmonger, owes his mother for his crazy obsession with art. See his art in *Heavy Metal* and other fine publications. (Page 94)

RICK GEARY
Rick is an occasional contributor to *MAD*. His last graphic novel was *The Borden Tragedy* and his latest is *The Fatal Bullet*, a study of the assassination of President James A. Garfield, both published by NBM. He also publishes a line of unusual postcards. (Page 10)

ARMANDO GIL
Armando is known for his inking work on *Ka-Zar, The Micronauts, The 'Nam,* and *Master of Kung Fu*. He is an equally gifted penciller as seen here and in issues of *Conan*, the *Jurassic Park* comic, and others. (Page 37)

SAM GLANZMAN
A veteran combat comics artist, Sam's credits include *The Iron Corporal, Jungle Tales of Tarzan, Combat,* and *Green Berets* for various publishers, and for DC, such classics as "The Haunted Tank" and "U.S.S. Stevens." (Page 105)

JENNIFER GRAVES
Thanks to the efforts of kind folks like Andy Helfer, she don't have to rob banks no more. (Page 101)

GLEN HANSON
Glen is an award-winning designer, illustrator, writer, and art director. His work has appeared in publications as diverse as *Entertainment Weekly, Time Out, The New York Times,* and DC Comics and The Cartoon Network's *The Flintstones and The Jetsons* comics. (Page 112)

RUSS HEATH
Russ's career includes work for Harvey Kurtzman's *MAD, Blazing Combat, National Lampoon,* and long stints on *Sgt. Rock* and other DC war comics. Recent work: *The Punisher* and *Legends of the Dark Knight.* (Pages 87 and 134)

JOHN HEEBINK
John Heebink writes and draws "Wrathbone and Bitchula" for *Action Planet Comics,* draws *Space Chicks and Businessmen* and storyboards for TV commercials. (Page 172)

KARL HEITMUELLER, JR.
Karl has done tons of artwork for Warner Bros. Records, where he is currently employed. Seven years of his comic strip *The Retail Adventures of Kalli & Rex* were collected into a book you can't get. (Page 124)

DANNY HELLMAN
...With a clumsy yank the blindfold was gone. I could see the girl again. She had made a costume change — she was now wearing crisp surgical scrubs. "Don't look so worried, sweetie," she said, twirling a scalpel in her hand. "What do you need a brain stem for, anyway?" (Page 138)

FLOYD HUGHES
Floyd lives in Red Hook, Brooklyn with his wife Mayleen and two children. (Page 140)

ALAN KUPPERBERG
Since 1971, New Yorker Alan Kupperberg has drawn *Justice League, Firestorm, Warlord,* et cetera for DC Comics, and *Spider-Man, Thor, The Avengers, Captain America,* and others for Marvel. (Pages 19 and 113)

TERRY LaBAN
Terry wrote and drew the series *Unsupervised Existence* and *Cud* for Fantagraphics Books, *Cud Comics* for Dark Horse, and *Eno and Plum* for Oni Press. He's also written numerous books for DC/Vertigo. He lives in Chicago and never leaves the house. (Page 90)

ROGER LANGRIDGE
Roger used to draw *Zoot!* for Fantagraphics until he found out that his manager, Brian Epstein, was taking all the money. Roger is survived by his widow, Yoko Ono. (Page 174)

LENNIE MACE
"Don't call me a cartoonist. Don't call me an illustrator or an artist, either. But whatever you do, don't, repeat, *don't* call me 'that ballpoint pen guy.'" (Page 30)

STEVE MANNION
Steve Mannion has gazed into the Abyss and seen the Abyss staring back. According to Steve, the Abyss says, "Hello." (Page 80)

DAVID MONAHAN
David is a student at the Joe Kubert School in Dover, New Jersey. This is his first published comics work. (Page 127)

GRAY MORROW
Gray has drawn the comic strips *Flash Gordon, Friday Foster, Buck Rogers,* and currently does *Tarzan.* He drew stories for *Creepy* and *Eerie,* has done work for Marvel and DC, as well as hundreds of book covers and magazine illustrations. (Page 98)

OVIDIU NEDELCU
Ovidiu was born in Romania and lived in California for most of his life. He loves painting and b-ball. He's a Christian and a follower of God. He looks forward to a future in comics and illustration. (Page 62)

TAYYAR OZKAN
Tayyar's collection *Caveman: Evolution Heck* recently came out from NBM. He also drew *Bushwacked, Pet,* and *Cave Bang* for Eros. His *Caveman* comic, started in 1998, is published regularly. (Page 149)

RINA PICCOLO
Rina is the author of three cartoon collections, including *Rina's Book of Sex Cartoons.* Her work has appeared in *Glamour Magazine, Mademoiselle, National Lampoon* and many others. (Page 100)

MARK POUTENIS
His girlfriend's mother *still* doesn't know what he does for a living.
>"You're a cartoonist?"
>"Something like that...."
>"Funny animals and the like?"
>"Something like that...."

(Page 136)

GORDON PURCELL
Gordon is known for his work on *Star Trek, Silver Sable, The X-Files, Lost in Space,* and *Xena.* He lives in Minnesota with Debra and son Jack. His personal vice involves a ferret, a pair of pants, and a little gentle dance (Don't judge). (Page 157)

WM. MARSHALL ROGERS
—was born at the beginning of the half-century and is still alive. (Pages 46 and 121)

JAMES ROMBERGER
James drew *Vertigo Vérité: Seven Miles a Second* (published by DC) as well as short stories in the *Weird War Tales, Gangland,* and *Heartthrobs* anthologies. His art has appeared in numerous gallery shows. He lives in Manhattan's Lower East Side. (Pages 68 and 69)

STEVEN SADOWSKI
...lives in Vancouver, British Columbia. He really hates writing bios and wonders who he'll be between on this page. He's done some *Starman* comics for DC and loves getting mail! He also wants to say, "Hi, Mom!" (Page 142)

SALGOOD SAM
By day an extra in a film by Fritz Lang, Salgood skulks home from the set each night and, following the orders of an enchanted salamander living in his large intestine, he draws. (Pages 63 and 170)

GALEN SHOWMAN
Galen likes to draw. He has done album covers for The Wipers, illustrated for various magazines, and co-created and illustrated *The Lost* and *Renfield* for Caliber Comics. (Page 47)

DERYL SKELTON
Deryl has done work for such diverse clients as Donald Trump (his painting hangs over Ivana's fireplace and over the Donald's bed in his Trump Tower digs), Archie Comics, DC Comics, and the Fitzgerald Hotel and Casino in Las Vegas, where he created the Mr. O'Lucky casino mascot. (Page 14)

TED SLAMPYAK
Ted created, wrote, and drew *Jazz Age Chronicles* for Caliber Press, pencilled *Neil Gaiman's Mr. Hero* for Big Entertainment, and *Roadways* for Cult Press. He lives in Bristol, Pennsylvania with poet/writer Rachel Astarte Piccione. (Page 88)

STEVE SMITH
Steve has been using the alphabet for many years. Other examples of his penmanship and pictures may be found in *Negative Burn, Aesop's Desecrated Fables,* and along the 101 freeway. (Page 110)

ROBERT SNYDER
Robert was an editorial cartoonist at *The Baltimore Sun.* He routinely drew corrupt police officers with pig snouts, and stupid politicians with their pants around their ankles. He got canned. (Page 164)

DAN SPIEGLE
Dan drew the *Hopalong Cassidy* strip for six years, and comics including *Lost in Space, Maverick,* and *Sea Hunt,* for Gold Key, *Blackhawk* for DC, *Crossfire* for Eclipse, and *Pocahontas* for Disney. He also drew the *Terry and the Pirates* comic strip for a year and a half. (Page 24)

JOE STATON
Joe has worked for Marvel on *The Incredible Hulk,* and for DC illustrating *Superman, Batman, Plastic Man, Green Lantern,* and many others. Joe illustrated *Family Man,* a graphic novel in the Paradox Mystery line written by Jerome Charyn. (Pages 40 and 103)

ALEC STEVENS
Alec is an illustrator whose credits include *The New York Times Book Review, The New Yorker, New Jersey Monthly,* and Tower Records' *Pulse.* (Page 57)

TOM SUTTON
Sutton should get more money than the other artists. He uses three times as much ink. Is India Ink made from real Indians? It's getting darker. (Page 26)

ALWYN TALBOT
Alwyn has a B.A. in illustration. His work has appeared in *Vorgarth, Negative Burn,* and *Kimota.* (Page 22)

B.K TAYLOR
B.K. was a staff writer on ABC's *Home Improvement* and Nickelodeon's *Eureeka's Castle.* His art and comics have appeared in *MAD, National Lampoon, Sesame Street Magazine,* and many others. (Page 104)

BRAD TEARE
Brad is the author of the graphic novel *Cypher.* He has also done illustrations for such publications as *Fortune* and *The New York Times.* He lives in Utah. (Page 155)

BIBLIOGRAPHY

SIN CITIES

Amsterdam: The Rough Guide. London: Penguin, 1997.

Bagli, Charles V. and Randy Kennedy. "Disney Wished Upon Times Square and Rescued a Stalled Dream." *The New York Times,* April 5, 1998.

Baker, Christopher P. *Cuba Handbook.* Chico, CA: Publishers Group West, 1997.

Barry, Dan. "New Year's Eve Ball will Drop in the Midst of a Metamorphosis, But Old Haunts and Ways Linger." *The New York Times,* December 31, 1997.

Blum, Ken. *Broadway: An Encyclopaedic Guide to the History, People, and Places of Times Square.* New York: Facts on File, 1991.

"Capture of Phenix City." *Newsweek,* August 2, 1954.

Castleman, Deke. *Las Vegas.* Oakland, CA: Compass American Guides, Inc., 1991.

Clark, Douglass. "Phenix Hoodlums." Letter to the ed.. *The Saturday Evening Post,* January 8, 1955.

Cotterell, Geoffrey. *Amsterdam: The Life of a City.* Boston: Little, Brown and Co., 1972.

"The `Do Your Thing' Capital." *Newsweek,* August 10, 1970.

Fodor's Las Vegas '98. New York: Fodor's Travel Publications, Inc., 1998.

Frommer's Amsterdam. New York: Macmillan, 1997.

Hess, Alan. *Viva Las Vegas.* San Francisco: Chronicle Books, 1993.

Hillyer, Katharine and Katharine Best. "The Angry Women of Phenix City." *McCall's,* September, 1955.

Insight Guides: Cuba. London: APA Publications: 1998.

Kennedy, Randy. "Luncheonette's Grill Turns Off for Good." *The New York Times,* October 20, 1997.

Kleinfeld, N.R. "It's Not Easy to Push Sex Into the Shadows." *The New York Times,* March 1, 1998.

LaGanga, Maria L. "Las Vegas Tries to Build Out of Its Slump." *The Los Angeles Times,* July 27, 1998.

Lonely Planet: Cuba. Australia: Lonely Planet, 1997.

Messick, Hank and Burt Goldblatt. *The Only Game in Town: An Illustrated History of Gambling.* New York: Thomas Y. Crowell Company, 1976.

Morais, Richard C. "A Letter from the Tippelzone." *Forbes,* June 17, 1996.

"The Odds Were Right." *Time,* June 28, 1954.

Patterson, John M. and Furman Bisher. "I'll Get the Gangs That Killed My Father!" *Saturday Evening Post,* November 27, 1954.

Portrait of Cuba. Atlanta: Turner Publishing, 1991.

Reid, Ed and Ovid Demaris. *The Green Felt Jungle.* New York: Trident Press, 1963.

"Scattering the Pigeons." *Newsweek,* August 16, 1971.

Shepard, Richard F. "Peep Shows have New Nude Look." *The New York Times,* March 23, 1968

Sheppard, Nathaniel Jr. "Hodas Is Cleared in Two Bombings." *The New York Times,* December 22, 1973.

Singer, Isaac Bashevis. *The Wicked City.* New York: Farrar, Straus, and Giroux, 1972.

The Los Angeles Times, 954.

ALCOHOL

"40% of Violent Crime Linked to Alcohol." *The Los Angeles Times,* April 6, 1998.

"Alcohol and Drug Consumption." *Britannica CD.* Version 97. Encyclopaedia Britannica, Inc., 1997.

Alcoholics Anonymous. (website). http://www.alcoholics-anonymous.org

Asbury, Herbert. "The Noble Experiment of Izzy and Moe." from *The Aspirin Age.* Isabel Leighton, ed. New York: Simon & Schuster, 1949.

Beason, Stan. "White Lightnin' — Caroline Style." *Caroline Edition Magazine* (website) http://www.bealenet.com/~studio7/moonshin.html

Behr, Edward. *Prohibition: Thirteen Years That Changed America.* New York: Arcade Publishing, 1996.

"Carry A. Nation." *City of Medicine Lodge, Kansas Community Network* (website) http://history.cc.ukans.edu/kansas/medicine/carry.html

"Closing In on Addiction." *Scientific American.* (website) http://www.sciam.com/explorations/112497addiction/

Coffey, Thomas M. *The Long Thirst.* New York: W. W. Norton & Company, Inc., 1975.

Doyle, Rodger. "Deaths Due to Alcohol." *Scientific American,* December, 1996.

Duffy, Patrick Gavin and James A. Beard. *The Standard Bartender's Guide.* New York: Permabooks, 1955.

Editors of American Heritage. *The American Heritage History of the 1920s & 1930s.* Ralph K. Andrist, ed. in charge, Edmund Stillman, narrative, with two chapters by Marshall Davidson. Nancy Kelly, pictorial commentary. New York: American Heritage/Bonanza Books, 1987.

Editors of Time-Life Books. *This Fabulous Century: 1920-1930.* New York: Time-Life Books, 1969.

"Expert Witnesses." *The American Experience/Crime and Punishment* (website) http://www.pbs.org/wgbh/pages/amex/crime/ra/evil.html

Furnas, J.C. *Great Times.* New York: G.P. Putnam's Sons, 1974.

"God's Strongmen: Carry Nation." *Discovery Channel Online* (website) http://eagle.online.discovery.com/DCO/doc/1012/world/history/strongmen/christians1.2.2.html

"History of Alcohol." *DrinkDrunk.* (website) http://www.drinkdrunk.org.au/core/history.htm

The Host's Handbook. New York: National Distillers Products Corporation, 1940.

Kellner, Esther. *Moonshine: Its History and Folklore.* Indianapolis: Bobbs-Merrill, 1971.

Maugh II, Thomas H. "Controlling the Habit." *The Los Angeles Times,* August 6, 1998.

Microsoft Encarta 98 Encyclopedia. Microsoft Corporation, 1993-1997.

"Moonshiners." Writ. Tom Verde. *Marketplace.* Radio prog. Produced by Marketplace Productions. University of Southern California. March 30, 1998.

Quillin, Martha. "Moonshine: An Art, a Crime and a Living History." *The News & Observer,* November 30, 1997.

Samuels, David. "Saying Yes to Drugs." *The New Yorker,* March 23, 1998.

Winkler, John K. "Izzy and Moe Stop the Show." *Collier's,* February 6, 1926.

TOBACCO

Barth, Ilene. *The Smoking Life.* Columbus, MS: The Genesis Press, 1997.

"CDC's TIPS: Tobacco Information & Prevention Sourcepage." *Center for Disease Control.* (website). www.cdc.gov/tobacco/

DeFord, Susan. "Tobacco: The Noxious Weed That Built a Nation." *Washington Post,* May 14, 1997.

Fahs, John. *Cigarette Confidential.* New York: Berkley Publishing Group, 1996.

"Few at Lucy Gaston Rites," *The New York Times,* August 23, 1924.

"Finds 'Kick' in Cigarette," *The New York Times,* January 25, 1922.

Goodrum Charles, and Helen Dalrymple. *Advertising in America.* New York: Harry N. Abrams, Inc., 1990.

Hilts, Philip J. *Smokescreen.* Addison-Wesley Publishing Co., 1996.

Holme, Bryan. *Advertising: Reflections of a Century.* New York: Viking Press, 1982.

Klein, Richard. *Cigarettes Are Sublime.* Durham, NC: Duke University Press, 1993.

Kluger, Richard. *Ashes to Ashes.* New York: Alfred A. Knopf, 1996.

Lamb, David. "Vietnam: A Smoker's Paradise." *The Los Angeles Times,* April 18, 1998.

Loewy, Raymond. *Industrial Design.* Woodstock, NY: The Overlook Press, 1979.

"Lucy Page Gaston Hurt." *The New York Times,* January 21, 1924.

"Lucy Page Gaston, Reformer, is Dead," *The New York Times,* August 21, 1924.

Sobel, Robert. *They Satisfy.* Garden City, NY: Anchor Press/Doubleday, 1978.

Taylor, Peter. *The Smoke Ring.* New York: Pantheon Books, 1984.

"Wayback Machine — Lucy Page Gaston." *Discovery Channel Online.* (website) www.discovery.com/area/wayback/wayback970623/wayback1.html

Weinstein, Henry "R.J. Reynolds Targeted Kids, Records Show." *The Los Angeles Times,* January 15, 1998.

DRUGS

Aaronson, Bernard and Humphry Osmond. *Psychedelics.* New York: Anchor Books, 1970.

"Absinthe." (website) http://www.transend.com.tw/~callisto/absinthe.html

"American Indian Soldiers Can Use Peyote." *Salt Lake Tribune,* April 16, 1997 (website) http://www.sltrib.com/97/apre/041697/nation_w/11439.htm

"Amphetamines." *The Hierarchy of Consumption.* (website) http://www.intranet.ca/~ott8459585/

"Basic Information about Absinthe." *Absinthe — The Green Fairy.* (website) http://www.geocities.com/BourbonStreet/1966/index.html

Beaubien, Greg. "Lethal and Legal." *Detroit News,* August 12, 1996 (website) http://detnews.com/1996/menu/stories/59923.htm

Brecher, Edward M. and the Editors of *Consumer Reports.* "Chapter 8: The Harrison Narcotic Act." The Consumer's Union Report on Licit and Illicit Drugs. *Schaffer Library of Drug Policy.* 1972. (website) http://www.druglibrary.org/schaffer//library/studies/cu/cu8.html

"A Brief History of Drugs." *Finnish Cannabis Association* (website) http://www.lycaeum.org/~sky/data/drughist.html

Cerf, Christopher and Victor Navasky eds. *The Experts Speak: The Definitive Compendium of Authoritative Misinformation.* New York: Pantheon Books, 1984.

"Cocaine." *The Hierarchy of Consumption.* (website) http://www.intranet.ca/~ott8459585/

Coffee Universe. (website). http://www.coffeeuniverse.com/

Coffee World: The Ultimate Guide to Coffee (website). http://www.btinternet.com/~roastandpost/findex.html

Cordes, Helen. "Generation Wired." *The Nation,* April 27, 1998.

TheDrink (website) http://cbcc.bcwan.net/~pedurwin.drink.htm

"The Drug Law Timeline." *Schaffer Library of Drug Policy.* (website) http://www.druglibrary.org/schaffer/history/drug_law_timeline.htm

Flippo, Hyde. "Peter Lorre — An Online Supplement to The German Way." *The German-Hollywood Connection* (website) http://www.german-way.com/german/lorre.html

Gilmore, Mikal. "Timothy Leary 1920-1996." *Rolling Stone,* July 11-25, 1996. Reprinted on Timothy Leary. (website) http://www.leary.com/archives/text/Articles/Rolling/part1.html

"Heroin Chic." *Indiana Prevention Resource Center @ Indiana University* (website) http://www.drugs.indiana.edu/prevention/heroin.html

Higham, Charles, and Roy Moseley. *Cary Grant: The Lonely Heart.* San Diego and New York: Harcourt Brace Jovanovich, 1989.

"The History of Coffee." *The Coffee Pot.* (website) http://www.geocities.com/~9145/coffee/coffee_history.html

Hoffman, Dr. Albert. "LSD: My Problem Child — An Excerpt from the Memoirs of the Man Who Invented Acid (and Reinvented Reality)." *High Times,* June, 1980.

Horowitz, Michael. "Interview with Albert Hoffman." *High Times,* March, 1976.

"Important Events Concerning Timothy Leary." compiled by Colin Pringle. (website) http://www.halcyon.com/colinp/leary-2.htm

"Interview with Albert Hoffman." *Omni Magazine,* 1981.

Katz, Ephraim. *The Film Encyclopedia.* New York: Harper & Row Perennial Library, 1990.

Keel, Robert O. "Narcotics." *Sociology 180: Alcohol, Drugs, and Society Lecture Notes* (website) http://www.umsl.edu/~rkeel/180/narcotic.html

Kennedy, Joseph. *Coca Exotica: The Illustrated History of Cocaine.* New York: Cornwall Books, 1985.

La Fee Verte Absinthe Gallery. (website) http://www.aluna.com/chapelperilous/absinthe/absinthe.html

La Motte, Ellen N. "The Opium Monopoly," Chapter XV - History of the Opium Trade in China. *Schaffer Library of Drug Policy.* (website) http://www.druglibrary.org/schaffer/History/om/om15.htm

"Lessons From the Vietnam Heroin Experience." *Internet Mental Health* (website) http://www.mentalhealth.com/mag1/p5h-sb03.html

Martin, Ralph G. *Henry and Clare.* New York: G.P. Putnam's Sons, 1991.

McCann, Graham. *Cary Grant: A Class Apart.* New York: Columbia University Press, 1996.

Microsoft Encarta 98 Encyclopedia. Microsoft Corporation, 1993-1997.

Morley, Jefferson. "Clare Boothe Luce's Acid Test." *Washington Post,* October 22, 1997.

Nazi Cult Beliefs. (website) http://marlowe.whimsey.com/~rshand/streams/masons/nazi.html

"Opium in China." *Schaffer Library of Drug Policy.* (website) http://www.druglibrary.org/schaffer/heroin/opichin1.htm

"Opium Through History." *Frontline.* (website) http://www.pbs.org/wgbh/pages/frontline/shows/heroin/etc/history.html

"The Original Coca-Cola Formula." *The Soda Fountain.* (website) http://www.sodafountain.com/softdrnk/cokercp.htm

Nahas, Gabriel G., M.D., Ph.D. *Cocaine: The Great White Plague.* Middlebury, VT: Paul S. Eriksson, Publisher, 1989.

"The Native American Church." *San Pedro Fanatic Visionary Cactus Guide.* (website) http://www.lycaeum.org/~iamklaus/native.htm

"Plants of Power." *BBC World Service Education.* presented by Nick Rankin. (website) http://ftp.bbc.co.uk/worldservice/education/plants

"Prescription Drug Abuse." *The Hatherleigh Company, Ltd.* (website) http://www.hatherleigh.com/Pdabuse.htm

"Prescription Drug Abuse Rivals Illicit Drug Abuse." *National Drug Strategy Network.* (website) http://www.ndsn.org/OCT96/PRESCRIP.html

Schlosser, Eric. "Reefer Madness" and "Marijuana and the Law." *Atlantic Monthly,* August and September, 1994.

Shalizi, Cosma Rohilla. "Sigmund Freud." *Notebooks* (website) http://www.physics.wisc.edu/~shalizi/notebooks/freud.html

Shipman, David. *Judy Garland.* New York: Hyperion, 1993.

"A Short History of Amphetamines." *Schaffer Library of Drug Policy.* (website) http://druglibrary.org/schaffer/cocaine/amphhis.htm

Siegel, Ronald K., Ph.D. *Intoxication.* New York: E. P. Dutton, 1989.

Stafford, Peter. *Psychedelics Encyclopedia.* Berkeley, CA: And/Or Press, 1977.

"Stimulants: Cocaine HCL." *Platte County Sheriff's Department.* (website) http://www.dps.state.mo.us/sheriff/platte/drugs/cocaine.htm

The Tea Council Limited. "The History of Tea." *The Tea Council Limited.* (website). http://www.teacouncil.co.uk/Teahist.html

"The Timothy Leary Biography." *Timothy Leary.* (website) http://www.leary.com/biography/index.html

"Where East Meets West." *The World Ahead Magazine.* (website) http://www.worldahead.org/wam/9707/w9707f2.html

Whitebread, Charles. "The History of the Non-Medical Use of Drugs in the United States." USC Law School, Speech to the California Judges Association 1995 Annual Conference. *Schaffer Library of Drug Policy.* (website) http://www.druglibrary.org/schaffer/history/whiteb1.htm

SEX AND MORE SEX

Atkins, Robert. "A Brief and Idiosyncratic History of Censorship." *FileRoom.* (website) http://fileroom.aaup.uic.edu/FileRoom/publication/ALT/atkinshistory.html

Barrows, Sydney Biddle and William Novak. *Mayflower Madam.* New York: Arbor House, 1986.

Bassermann, Lujo. *The Oldest Profession.* New York: Dorset Press, 1993.

Bennett, Vanora. "Sense of Adventure Betrays Many." *The Los Angeles Times,* December 6, 1997.

"Black Rhino and Trade." *American University Trade and Environment Database.* (website) http://gurukul.ucc.american.edu/TED/rhinoblk.htm

Bullough, Vern and Bonnie. *Women and Prostitution.* Buffalo, NY: Prometheus Books, 1987.

"Burlesque Show." *Britannica CD.* Version 97. Encyclopaedia Britannica, Inc., 1997.

"Campaign Against the Return of Military Prostitution." (website) http://www.subicnet.com/preda/navyback.html

"Carol Doda and The Topless Era." *North Beach Magazine.* (website) http://www.sfnorthbeach.com/g34.html

Clayton, Marc. "Prostitution 'Circuit' Takes Girls Across North America." *Christian Science Monitor,* August 23, 1996. (website) http://www.csmonitor.com/mixed_media/specials/children/part2a.html

Connell, Kim. "Drugs: New Danger for Party-goers." *Oakland Post,* November 19, 1997. (website) http://www.oakland.edu/post/fall97/971119/n2.htm

Corn-Revere, Robert. "New Age Comstockery: Exxon vs. the Internet," *Policy Analysis* No. 232, June 28, 1995. (website) http://www.swiss.ai.mit.edu/6805/legislation/cato-comstockery.html

"Escape From Sexual Exploitation, Myth Versus Reality." *The Paul & Lisa Program, Inc.* (website) http://www.paulandlisa.org/escapemyth.html

"Facts About Prostitution." *Promise: For Women Escaping Prostitution.* (website) http://www.sirius.com/~promise/facts.html

Flynt, Larry. *An Unseemly Man.* Dove: Los Angeles, 1996.

Fowler, Will. *Reporters.* Malibu, CA: Roundtable Publishing, 1991.

Global Survival Network. (website). http://www.globalsurvival.net

"God's Strongmen: Anthony Comstock." *Discovery Channel Online* (website) http://eagle.online.discovery.com/DCO/doc/1012/world/history/strongmen

Goldstein, Al. "The Dawn of Screw." *Nerve Magazine,* 1997.

Goodman, Mark and Lyndon Stambler. "Strictly Maternal." *People Weekly,* August 2, 1993.

Grenier, Meredith. "Love Tips from the Mayflower Madam." *Santa Monica Outlook,* February 10, 1997.

Heidenry, John. *What Wild Ecstasy: The Rise and Fall of the Sexual Revolution.* New York: Simon & Schuster, 1997.

Hollander, Xaviera. *The Happy Hooker.* New York: Dell, 1972.

Hughes, Donna M. "Sex Tours Via the Internet." *Feminista!* (website) http://www.feminista.com/v1n7/hughes.html

"I'm a Little Short of Cash Today,' He Told Me." *Covenant House.* (website) http://www.covenanthouse.org/sis/sis_arc96/sis_arc96_11.htm

Kaylin, L. "A Quickie with Al Goldstein." *Gentleman's Quarterly,* August, 1997.

Keerdoja, E. and P. Clausen. "Happy Hooker Looks Happily Retired." *Newsweek,* November 10, 1980.

Kendrick, Walter. *The Secret Museum: Pornography in Modern Culture.* Berkeley, CA: University of California Press, 1996.

Lamb, David. "Re-Education Camps Target Prostitution" *The Los Angeles Times,* January 9, 1998.

"The Legal Situation in Nevada." *The World Sex Guide.* (website) http://www.smutland.com/guests/prostitution/nv_legal.html

McDonnell, Etain, Karuna Buakumsri, and Pattara Danutra. "Prostitutes in Japan." Reprinted from *Bangkok Post,* August 15, 1993. (website) ftp://ftp.alternatives.com/library/womabuse/womw0021.txt

Morgan, Ted. "United States Versus..." *The New York Times Magazine,* March 6, 1977.

"Mustang Ranch IRS Problems." *Urban Legends.* (website) http://www.urbanlegends.com/sex/mustang_ranch_irs_problem.html

The Mustang Ranch Online. (website) http://www.mustangranchonline.com/

National Opinion Research Center General Social Survey. (website) http://www.icpsr.umich.edu/gss/

Once Upon A Time. Feature film. Atta Loma Productions, 1997.

Plimpton, George. "Checking In with Hugh Hefner." *Esquire,* January, 1992.

Pope, Victoria. "Trafficking in Women." *U.S. News & World Report,* April 7, 1997.

"Porn Figure Sturman Dies in Prison at 73." (Associated Press) *Las Vegas Review-Journal,* October 29, 1997.

Rasmussen, Cecilia. "History of Hollywood Madams Is Long, Lurid." *The Los Angeles Times,* November 30, 1997.

Rose, Al. *Storyville, New Orleans.* Tuscaloosa, AL: University of Alabama Press, 1974.

Roshan, Maer. "The XXX Files." *New York,* February 10, 1997.

"Royal Scandals." *Discovery Channel Online.* (website) www.discovery.com/area/history/royal/part2.html

Ryan, Cy. "Commissioner on Brothel Payroll." *Las Vegas Sun,* September 3, 1996. (website) http://www.lasvegassun.com/sunbin/stories/archives/1996/sep/03/505048036.html

Sager, Mike. "The Devil and John Holmes." *Rolling Stone,* June 15, 1989.

Schlosser, Eric. "The Bill Gates of Porn." *U.S. News & World Report,* February 10, 1997.

Sonner, Scott. "Two Sides Differ on Key Figure in Mustang Ranch Tax Inquiry." *The Oregonian,* August 9, 1998.

Specter, Michael. "Contraband Women." *The New York Times,* January 11, 1998.

"Statistical Information." *Free Speech Coalition.* (website) http://www.freespeechcoalition.com/industry/truth/stats.html

Sturdevant, Saundra and Brenda Stoltzfus. *Let the Good Times Roll: Prostitution and the U.S. Military in Asia.* New York: The New Press, 1992.

Tannahill, Reay. *Sex in History.* New York: Stein and Day, 1980.

"Transition." *Newsweek,* March 28, 1988.

"What Is the History of Legal Prostitution in Nevada?" *Georgia Power's Bordello Connection.* (website) http://www.gppays.com/index.html

Zacks, Richard. *History Laid Bare.* New York: HarperPerennial, 1995.

GAMBLING

"The Action Goes On." *Sports Illustrated,* March 16, 1998.

Bernes, Dave. "Minister Crusades into Vegas." *Las Vegas Review-Journal,* September 29, 1997.

Bowden, Charles. "Crapshoot Nation." *Gentleman's Quarterly,* April, 1998.

Chappell, Kevin. "Black Indians Hit the Jackpot in Casino Business." *Ebony,* June, 1995.

Christ, Steven. Special Reporting by Dan Yaeger. "All Bets are Off." *Sports Illustrated,* January 26, 1998.

"Culture Clashes: High Stakes." *Scholastic Update* (Teacher's Edition), February 10, 1995.

Dahl, Dick. "The Gamble That Paid Off." *ABA Journal,* May, 1995.

Fabian, Ann. *Card Sharps, Dream Books, & Bucket Shops.* New York: Cornell University Press, 1990.

Findlay, John M. *People Of Chance: Gambling in American Society from Jamestown to Las Vegas.* New York: Oxford University Press, 1986.

Fleming, Alice. *Something for Nothing.* New York: Delacorte, 1978.

The Gamblers. The Old West. Alexandria, VA: Time-Life Books, 1978.

Grant, Michael. *Emperor in Revolt: Nero.* New York: American Heritage Press, 1970.

Gwynne, S.C. "How Casinos Hook You." *Time,* November 17, 1997.

Longstreet, Stephen. *Win or Lose: A Social History of Gambling in America.* Indianapolis: Bobbs-Merrill, 1977.

McGraw, Dan. "All Bets Are Off for Offshore Bookmakers." *U.S. News & World Report,* March 16, 1998.

Messick, Hank and Burt Goldblatt. *The Only Game in Town: An Illustrated History of Gambling.* New York: Thomas Y. Crowell Company, 1976.

"Online Betting: A Big Gamble." *Kiplinger's Personal Finance Magazine.* April, 1998.

Pileggi, Nicholas. *Casino.* New York: Simon & Schuster, 1995.

Pollak, Kenan. "A Tribe That's Raking It In." *U.S. News & World Report,* January 15, 1996.

Pulley, Brett. "Study Finds Legality Spreads the Compulsion to Gamble." *The New York Times,* December 7, 1997.

Quittner, Joshua. "Betting on Virtual Vegas." *Time,* June 12, 1995.

"Rothstein a Power in Gambling World." *The New York Times,* November 7, 1928.

"Rothstein's Slayer Known, Says Banton." *The New York Times,* November 10, 1928.

Sifakis, Carl. *The Encyclopedia of Gambling.* New York: Facts on File, 1990.

Specter, Michael. "Russia Has the Fever as Rigged Lotteries Flourish." *The New York Times,* July 8, 1997.

Sterngold, James. "It's Easier to Beat Las Vegas than New York." *The New York Times,* March 9, 1997.

Weber, Thomas E. "On-Line Tribe Uses Loophole to Put Gaming on Web." *The Wall Street Journal,* February 4, 1998.

A World of Luck. Library of Curious and Unusual Facts. Alexandria, VA: Time-Life Books, 1991.

THE DEVIL'S WORKSHOP

Benton, Mike. *Crime Comics.* Dallas, TX: Taylor Publishing, 1993.

Colmer, Michael. *Pinball.* New York: New American Library, 1976.

Editors of *Consumer Guide: Baseball Cards.* New York: Beekman House, 1982.

Estren, Mark James. *A History of Underground Comics.* San Francisco, CA: Straight Arrow Books, 1974.

Daniels, Les. *Comix: A History of Comic Books in America.* New York: Bonanza Books, 1971.

Gelman, Woody, and Len Brown (publishers). *The Great Old Bubble Gum Cards.* New York: Prime Press, 1977.

Goulart, Ron. *Great History of Comic Books.* Chicago, IL: Contemporary Books, 1986.

Greene, Alan, M.D. "The Relationship Between Sugar and Behavior in Children." *Pediatric News,* March 3, 1996. Dr. Greene's House Calls. (website) http://www.drgreene.com/960303a.html

Hickok, Ralph. *Hickok's Sports History: Billiards.* (website) http://www.ultranet.com/~rhickok/billiard.shtml

Jensen, Russ. *Pinball History.* (website) http://members.aol.com/rusjensen/

Kent, Steven, Jer Horwitz, and Joe Fielder. *VideoGameSpot's History of Video Games.* (website) http://www.videogames.com/features/universal/hov/index.html

Kinsbourne, Marcel, M.D. "Sugar and the Hyperactive Child." *New England Journal of Medicine,* February 3, 1994.

Lupoff, Dick, and Don Thompson eds. *All in Color for a Dime.* Iola, WI: Krause Publications, 1997.

Lynch, Vincent, and Bill Henkin. *Jukebox: The Golden Age.* Berkeley, CA: Lancaster-Miller, 1981.

Mars Attacks. (website). http://www.marsattacksfan.com/homepage.htm

Martello, Thomas. "Jersey Company Offers Rare Honus Wagner Card in Promotional Sweepstakes." (Associated Press) *Detroit News,* February 15, 1997.

Monitor Sugar Company. *The History of Sugar.* (website) http://www.monitorsugar.com/htmtext/HISTORY.htm

National Amusement Park Historical Association. *History of Amusement Parks.* (website) http://www.napha.org/history.html

Pearce, Christopher. *Vintage Jukeboxes.* Secaucus, NJ: Chartwell Books, 1988.

Putnam, Judy and Shirley Gerrior. "Americans Consuming More Grains and Vegetables, Less Saturated Fats." *USDA FoodReview,* September, 1997.

Shamos, Mike. *A Brief History of the Noble Game of Billiards.* (website) http://www.bca-pool.com/history/hist.htm

Wizards of the Coast. (website) http://www.wizards.com/

THE LIBRARY OF BIG BOOKS:

THE BIG BOOK OF BAD

IT'S ALL GOOD!

THE BIG BOOK OF HOAXES

TRUE TALES OF THE GREATEST LIES EVER TOLD!

BIG LIES THE WHOLE WORLD BELIEVED!

THE BIG BOOK OF LITTLE CRIMINALS

63 TRUE TALES OF THE WORLD'S MOST INCOMPETENT JAILBIRDS!

LITTLE MEN. BIG SCHEMES. TOUGH LUCK.

THE BIG BOOK OF THE UNEXPLAINED

ALLEGEDLY TRUE TALES OF PARANORMAL PHENOMENA!

BY DOUG MOENCH and over 40 of the world's top comics artists!

STRANGE PHENOMENA REVEALED!

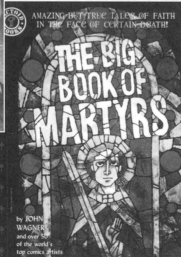

THE BIG BOOK OF MARTYRS

AMAZING BUT TRUE TALES OF FAITH IN THE FACE OF CERTAIN DEATH!

by JOHN WAGNER and over 50 of the world's top comics artists

TRUE TALES OF THE ULTIMATE SACRIFICE!

THE BIG BOOK OF THUGS

TOUGH-AS-NAILS TRUE TALES OF THE WORLD'S BADDEST MOBS, GANGS, AND NE'ER-DO-WELLS!

BY JOEL ROSE and 57 of the WORLD'S TOP Comic Artists

YOU WANT TOUGH? WE GOT TOUGH!